Age of Asango

Book II

Matt Russell

Dragon Tooth Press LLC.
PO Box 1353
Claremont, CA
91711
www.DragonToothPress.com
ISBN – 978-1-7328192-3-8

For my all five of my children.
Lilly, for filling my life with light,
Mattie, for making me laugh in the throes of massive sleep deprivation,
Jerry, for being willing to hang out with your nerdy dad,
Cirrus, because we all need a talker like you in our lives to smooth over the frustrations,
And for Soular, for being cleaner than any of us.

Chapter 1:
A Return to the Temple

The education of the shamalak boy was challenging at times, and yet I never felt out of patience. He was very clever, if not quite brilliant, but what allowed him to progress through the rigorous education I laid out for him was a pure love of knowledge and the heart to work through difficulty. No matter how hard I bore down on him, he never grew bitter or complained. Always he pushed himself to be better, and always he became better.

---*Taken from the Memoir of Master Bendick of the Lucinian Order*

Darius stared down the grassy hill in wonder at Kota's quick, elegant movements. The young swordsman danced around his tattooed opponent, whipping his training sword in a liquid series of clanking parries. Kota wielded the weapon as if it were utterly weightless. The brave little shamalak boy who had saved his life four and a half years ago had become a tall, broad-shouldered mass of corded muscle. He was wearing pants, but no shirt and Darius could see sweat dripping down his golden brown skin, all over his face, and around the sparse hair that grew from his thick pectoral muscles.

It took Darius a moment to recognize Kota's sparring partner. It was Glavius Denthar, whom Gretis had been training when Kota first came to the temple. The Onkai was grinning as if the two of them were playing a game. To him, perhaps it *was* a game. As Darius and some of the other legends of the past generation had aged out of their prime, Glavius had assumed the mantle of the finest swordsman in the order. Otho's letters had trailed on more than once of how the 'young bull' could trounce anyone in a duel. He was not trouncing Kota though. He was moving in and delivering quick successions of strikes, all of which Kota strained fiercely to parry. Glavius would then back off, giving the shamalak time to rest.

"Kota's footwork is beyond superb," Darius said as he watched the shamalak dodge back from a lateral slash. "You must be working him very hard."

"Harder than I ever worked any of you," Gretis said. She was standing next to him, her arms folded across her chest. She wore an ash colored tunic and matching loose pants with at least one blade he could see strapped to her belt. There was a focused grin on her face as her dark eyes shifted here and there to follow Kota's movements. Gretis had scarcely seemed to age at all in the years since they had last seen each other. Her skin was still smooth and flawless, and her build was as athletic as ever.

"I imagine from the way he is moving that you have begun to imbue him with the mysterious power of Sansrit Philosophy."

"Actually no," she said, moving a little closer to Darius and lowering her voice. "That is pure muscle and skill. I have not unlocked a shred of the power that lies within that boy."

The power that lies within... Darius blinked at the young inhuman fighter, considering how little he knew of the secrets of Lady Gretis's abilities. Kota seemed to finally notice that there was an unexpected guest. He darted back from Glavius and lowered his sword, signaling a pause in the match. Then he looked at Darius with a grin that seemed to come from the depths of his heart and shouted: "DARIUS!" He waved an open hand. There was no longer any trace of accent in his voice.

"Hello, my friend," Darius shouted, his arm rising to return the wave. He found it surprising how much he had looked forward to this reunion. After such a long time away, Darius had come *here* before returning to the central temple.

"Greetings, Legate Darius!" Glavius shouted, giving a respectful bow. Darius had known the young man only a little during his time in the central temple, but he had appreciated Glavius's friendly cockiness back then. He found himself grinning at the fact that some of that same bravado echoed in the young captain's voice now.

"Good to see you, captain," he called back.

Kota moved to set down his training sword on a nearby tree stump, but Gretis shouted in a hard voice: "I do not believe I gave you permission to break training."

"Sorry, ma'am," Kota said, the bright, friendly smile never leaving his face as he raised his blunted weapon back up and returned his attention to Glavius.

"How does his academic education progress?" Darius said as the two opponents resumed their dance of steel.

"Quite well, I am told. I give Kota an hour to read every day, and he never fails to use the time. He likes learning history, but Master Bendick is particularly impressed with his aptitude for mathematics. Overall, Kota is one of the finest academics in the school." She turned her head toward Darius. "How have *you* been, my former pupil? Tell me of your life at the southern temple."

"The southern temple," Darius said in a slow whisper. He had suspected for a long time that his appointment as head of the Onkai's southern headquarters had come at Gretis's urging. It was a clear stepping stone toward one day becoming bishop, which both excited and frightened him. "The temple is much smaller than here, and quite a bit more rustic. The men are extremely disciplined, which makes my job easy." He watched Kota counter one of Glavius's onslaughts with a beautifully executed upward slash that the Onkai managed to only narrowly dodge.

"Kota has missed you. His face lights up every time we receive one of your letters."

Darius stared at his shamalak friend, and an old fear returned to his mind. "How much longer before you make him truly dangerous?"

"Not long," Gretis said with a sigh. "His training is progressing far faster than I expected. In truth, he's the most talented swordsman I have *ever* seen." She chuckled. "He has no idea how good he is. He only ever spars against individuals far stronger than himself."

Darius swallowed. Gretis had been tutoring the finest swordsmen in the Onkai order for nearly twenty years. Such praise from her was not to be taken lightly. The thought that Kota could become a monster—a killer even more dangerous than her notorious son, Soulic—was terrifying. In a somber tone, he said: "I hope you know what you're doing."

"So do I," she whispered back, and there was a cadence of quiet fear in her voice. Before Darius could say anything Gretis shouted: "Kota, you may break for the afternoon!"

Kota looked up at her and called back: "Thank you!" and as he did, Glavius dashed at him in a blur of speed. He tackled Kota, and the two of them rolled around in the grass for a few seconds until Glavius rose back up with his victim in a headlock.

As Kota bucked and thrashed against the hold, Glavius looked up to Darius and said with a hearty laugh: "I'm sorry, sir. I've done the best I could with him, but this shamalak just can't seem to learn anything." Kota's hand snaked up to Glavius's throat, but the Onkai caught it by the wrist. Darius noted that Kota was laughing as well, even as Glavius dropped him to the ground and twisted his arm up behind his back. "I think it's his inferior intellect. Every time I try to teach him a new move, he grows confused and then sees a grasshopper or something and runs off to eat it. It's really very hopeless and—AHH!" Glavius yanked his hand away, and Kota rose up. His claws were extended and, from the way Glavius was gripping his wrist, it was apparent how the shamalak had used them.

Kota spun and delivered a jabbing punch to Glavius's cheekbone. It was a blow that might have left a nasty bruise on a normal man but would serve as little more than an irritation to a fully tattooed Onkai. Still, it granted Kota the chance to dart away, which he did. Glavius recovered quickly and ran after him, shouting: "Nice one, but it ain't that easy!" The two of them fell into a brief chase before Glavius managed to tackle Kota again.

Darius chuckled: "I see he's been making friends."

"Of course he has," Gretis sighed. "It's impossible for anyone with a half decent heart not to like Kota once they get to know him."

The two combatants wrestled around on the ground for a moment, and then Glavius rose and helped Kota up. The two of them picked up their training swords and carried them back to Gretis's house and then came bounding back up the grassy hill together. Glavius spoke first, pressing his right fist into his left palm and bowing as he said in a sharp voice: "Legate."

"Captain," Darius said with a nod. He *might* consider taking the young captain back south with him.

"I'll see you at the temple, sir," Glavius said as he lifted his gaze. He turned and broke into a jog in the direction of the town.

"It is good to see you again," the shamalak said in a surprisingly deep voice. He held out a golden brown hand, claws retracted. *He had grown so tall!*

"Good to see you, old friend," Darius said. He clutched Kota's hand and stared at the silver eyes. There still seemed the be the same kindness and honesty in them that Darius had grown so fond of years ago. "I am due for a meeting with Bishop Otho, but shall we go for a quick trip to the tavern? I would be happy to buy you a drink."

Kota tensed a little and looked at Gretis. She chuckled and said: "I am afraid students of the Sansrit path are forbidden to consume alcohol."

"I suppose that is sensible," Darius said. He had witnessed Gretis's truly lethal strength and speed more than once. It would be unwise for one with such power to become inebriated. Darius had heard that Starborn by and large refrained from alcohol for such reasons. He smiled and said: "Just a bit of food then."

Gretis tossed a silver coin very suddenly to Kota, and his hand whipped out with lightning speed and snatched it from the air. "My treat," she said.

"I thank you," Darius said with a nod.

Gretis smiled at him and then turned and sauntered toward her home, and he and Kota began to walk toward Temple Town. After they had gone only a short way, Kota said: "Lady Gretis tells me you are going to be the next bishop."

"Does she?" Darius said with a sharp laugh. "How incredibly forward of her."

Kota turned to him, frowning. "You have reservations. I thought you might."

"Really?" Darius said, surprised.

"Maybe I don't know what I'm talking about," Kota said, swallowing. "I'm sorry. It isn't my place to speak of such things."

"Speak your mind, please." He felt curious as to what insights his shamalak friend might have.

"If you wish," Kota said, his voice becoming low and serious. "You are thirty-three, correct?"

"Yes."

"And you received your tattoos at the age of fifteen. That means you will reach the point of recession in two years."

Darius turned and gazed at the young man. Kota was correct of course. The magic energies trapped in his tattoos would begin to wane soon. In less than two years, he would be forced to make a choice: renew his runes and commit another twenty years of his life to the order *or retire*. This had been at the center of his thoughts for quite some time.

"You believe I want to leave the Onkai Order?"

Kota frowned. "Again, I do not think it is my place—"

"Come off it. We are old friends."

Kota nodded as if to himself, then said: "You strike me as the kind of man who wants to be a father. You remind me of *my father* very much."

Darius felt a little surge in his stomach. Kota had guessed precisely at what had been troubling him. "Yes. If I become bishop, I cannot marry."

"You could eventually," Kota said with the slightest of shrugs. "Lady Gretis told me once that she is certain Otho will ask her to marry him when he retires." He leaned in a little closer and whispered in a playful voice: "She confessed she is not sure what she will say."

"Hah!" Darius laughed. The thought of the great Otho and Lady Gretis living together as husband and wife in some quiet home struck him somehow as horribly funny.

"I think you would be a very good father, Darius," Kota said.

"Thank you," Darius said, his face swelling into a smile. He could not think of a higher compliment. "What about you? Do you intend to return to your people and take a wife?"

"I don't know," Kota said with a grunting laugh. "Sansrit Philosophy does not require celibacy. I could... In my heart, I wish to have a family."

Darius felt his own heart ache just a little at these words. He could become the leader of the Onkai Order— have power and respect throughout the human world and go down in history as a renowned figure, or he could live for his own happiness. This thought lingered as they came to the edge of Temple Town.

"Hey, Kota!" a child of perhaps seven years in simple rough-spun clothes shouted as they stepped onto the main street. The boy threw a carved wooden ball through the air at

Kota, and his left hand snapped out and caught it. He tossed it back, and the boy tried to intercept it with outstretched hands but dropped it on the ground.

"Keep practicing," Kota said.

Darius grinned. He watched the way the town's people seemed to regard the shamalak in their presence. By and large, they did not seem frightened or revolted as they had years ago. Only a few of them even bothered to glance at him.

Kota moved through the crowd, seeming relaxed and at home. He led Darius to a large wooden stand behind which stood an old woman with straw-like gray hair. She was hunched over a wood-burning oven trying to stoke the fire with a thick wooden stick.

"Hello, Agatha," Kota said. "May I please help you?"

The old woman turned around, her wizened eyes lighting up. "Oh, Kota, you are so sweet," she said, tilting her head to the side and giving him a warm smile. "Oh, you have a guest." She looked up at Darius and said: "Hello, Onkai warrior."

"Hello," Darius said, nodding in respect to the elder.

The old woman strained to give a little curtsy, then turned back to Kota. "The oven is being *difficult* again." She looked up at Darius and said: "Sometimes Kota helps me with things. He is such a kind young man."

Darius thought he could almost see the shamalak's bronze skin flush. "It's no problem," Kota said, and he dropped under the counter and crawled on hands and feet to the stove. Then he took the stick from Agatha and manipulated the smoldering logs out from under the oven and began to fish out a sizable collection of ash and debris from inside the bottom chamber. Eventually, he took hold of a tattered brush and proceeded to clean with it. When Kota finally finished, he maneuvered the still slightly burning chunks of wood back in and blew on them until they were piping hot.

"All better," he said, crawling quickly back out from under the counter and rising. He brushed the soot from his hands on the bottom of his shirt and then fished into a pocket and came back with the silver coin Gretis had given him. "Two pies please."

"Oh no, Kota, let me treat you and your friend today," the old woman said, reaching out and closing his fingers around the coin.

"All right," Kota said with a smile. When Agatha turned to retrieve a fresh pair of pies still smoking from the oven, he smoothly slipped the silver coin into the little box that rested at the edge of her counter. The woman turned back around with two masses of bread clutched in mittens that smelled of meat and spiced gravy, and Kota's right hand reached out, hooked claws fully extended. He took a pie with his talons, skillfully keeping the steaming food away from his skin. Darius reached out, his own hand sheathed in the safety of a leather glove and took his pie. It smelled utterly delicious. In the southern temple, he had been forced to survive on the meager, tasteless rations the monks provided.

"Don't eat it for a few minutes," the old woman said, looking into Darius's eyes. "Let it cool until you can just touch it with your tongue without flinching. The flavor is best that way."

"I will. Thank you, my lady."

The old woman blushed just a little and said: "It is always an honor to serve an Onkai."

They left Agatha's stand, and when they were far enough away that she would not hear, Darius said: "I see you have made still more friends while I was away."

"In my tribe, it is a great honor to be of service to the elders. I suppose I am still driven to be a good shamalak." He cast a quick glance back at the old woman and said: "Agatha doesn't have anyone to take care of her. Her husband and sons died in the last demon war. I don't like that she has to wake up and bake every day just to keep herself fed and sheltered. She's a very kind lady—one of the first in this town to treat me like a person."

Darius pursed his lips. Elderly humans who had little or no money and no family to take care of them did not fare well in the empire. The Vestilite Order would at least give them bread, but such people were not likely to live out their final years in any kind of comfort or dignity.

"She is lucky to have a friend like you." He took an experimental bite of the pie. It was still a bit hot but tasted as delicious as it smelled.

Kota began to carefully consume his own pastry. They stood on the side of the street and ate together for a few moments without speaking, and then they both pulled handkerchiefs from their pockets and wiped their faces clean. When they were finished, Darius moved toward the temple and Kota followed.

As they came then to the grand entrance, the two soldiers standing guard immediately saluted, one of them shouting: "Greetings, Legate Darius."

Darius gave a quick nod and then turned to Kota. "This is where we part, but maybe we can do a little sparring this evening."

Kota grinned. "It would be an honor." He pressed his fist into his palm and bowed.

Darius watched his young friend go and then walked into the temple. As soon as he entered, he saw Otho standing in the middle of the hallway, his wizened eyes immediately locking on Darius's. Unlike Lady Gretis, the old bishop had most certainly aged. His beard had gone mostly gray, and some of the man's surpassing muscle mass had begun to lose its definition. He looked tired and nervous.

"Darius, I had heard you were seen at the edge of town," Otho said with a gruff smile. "You made excellent time getting here."

"Sir," Darius said, saluting.

"Yes-yes," Otho said with a tense nod. "I'm very glad to see you. Please come into my office." He gave a sharp gesture down the hall.

"Of course," Darius said. He was surprised to see the usually boisterous man so flustered. He followed Otho at a brisk pace through the halls of his old home.

"How have you been?" Otho grunted as they passed into his office.

"Quite well, sir. What's going on?"

Otho walked around his desk and dropped into his chair, causing it to creak a great deal. "*This* is going on," he said, tossing a rolled piece of paper that looked to have been sealed with the wax mark of a spear-tip, the insignia of the Nemesai. Darius opened the scroll and read:

> *Bishop Otho Vegen,*
>
> *I have been considerably disappointed that you have refused my requests to commit men to the apprehension of the vile heretic, Cassian Asango. Per my previous letters, he continues circulating literature throughout our empire that denounces our holy church. As I am sure you know by now, he has assembled an extremely poor translation of the Holy Enumis and has begun distributing to the common folk, as if they had the education and capacity to understand scripture! He seeks to 'empower' these ignorant fools to construct their own interpretations of the Gods' words. Men like you and I, who fought in the demon war, know what the arrogance of man can unleash upon this world.*
>
> *Further, Asango is using passages from his own translation to argue that the actions of my holy order are illegal! Any educated man with half a brain can decipher that the heretic's 'essays,' as he calls them, imply that the people have the right to rise up against our church's holy hand of justice! There can be no greater sin under the eyes of the gods! This kind of dangerous writing will plunge our great world into chaos and bring the*

wrath of the Gods down upon us all! He must be stopped!

I am convening a conclave of the heads of our church to settle the matter officially. On the eighth day of the month of Thorus, you will be present in our holy city of Anthos or forfeit your vote on the matter.

--Bishop Cromlic

"Gods!" Darius exhaled when he finished reading.

"Yes-s-s," Otho said. "He threatened to do this in his last letter. Cromlic's been sending me requests all summer for troops. The man doesn't think he can take the Starborn down with less than three hundred of my finest men—especially not with that dragon Cassian has." Otho's voice sounded furious.

"I'm sorry, sir," Darius said. "What are you going to do?"

"I'm going to present myself to the damned conclave and cast my vote. I am sure you will be pleased to know I will be voting *against* arresting Asango. That doesn't mean it won't happen. *Gods!*" He gazed up at the ceiling and shook his head. "This is a disaster. The church arresting a Starborn! It has *never* happened before." He looked at Darius and said: "I actually *like* the boy. He's done more for this order than any of his siblings. Hell, he replenished our supply of dragon's tears, which hadn't been done in forty years. When I have an especially dangerous mission to send my men on I, go to *Cassian* for help, and more than a handful of times it has been because of him that my men have come back alive—that includes *you*, of course, Darius." Otho slammed his fist down on his desk and hissed: "Why the hell does the boy have to be so damned reckless?"

"Cassian is Promethiock's chosen one. How can the church even consider taking action against him?"

"Promethiock is something of a gray area in religion," Otho muttered, gazing down at the scratches on his old wooden desk. "Cromlic is making the argument that the dragon is essentially a criminal, theologically speaking. It is an argument that has been made before." The bishop rolled his eyes. "As you might imagine, the boy's writings have long upset the Diaphan priests, as he speaks against giving money to the *greedy* preaching arm of the church." Otho gave Darius a sour look and said: "Translating the Enumis though... it's causing all kinds of uproar. In truth, I don't know how any of the other bishops will vote at this point."

"What a mess," Darius whispered.

"Yes, I suppose that is an appropriate enough word," Otho said. "The Onkai exist to keep humans safe from demons; not to hunt our fellow man, let alone *living miracles*!" He rose from his chair and looked Darius in the eyes. "Anyhow, the reason I summoned you is that I wish you to act as Bishop while I am gone."

"I—I am honored," Darius said, gazing down.

"You don't look honored," Otho muttering, giving him an appraising look. "That's probably a good part of the reason you're the best choice." Otho walked around his desk and put his hand on Darius's shoulder. "I don't want to hand my life's work over to a man who is foaming at the mouth for power. I want to give it to a *good* man. Do your duty and do it well, soldier."

"I will, sir," Darius said, his throat dry.

"Good. I might as well set off this afternoon. My captains should be able to fill you in on everything you need to know. The academy more or less runs itself, though I like to go down and tell the students war stories every so often. It keeps them inspired," he chuckled, "or maybe it lets me feel *inspiring*." He gripped Darius's shoulder and said: "I trust you, my friend. I will see you in about five weeks with either good or terribly bad news."

CHAPTER 2: THE BALL GUEST

I will not pretend that I see it as my holy duty to defeat Cassian. In truth, I respect many of his ideals, but he believes he can burn away centuries of tradition and force the empire to change nearly everything about itself. Cassian is my brother, and I love him, but I will kill him before I let him take the throne. He knows I can do it. I have trained half my life for our battle, and unlike Cromlic, I can see through all of his tricks.

--Dimitris Singet,
Starborn of the nineteenth generation

Thalice gazed out from under the shimmering veil that concealed her elven face, her eyes taking in the wondrous spectacle of humanity before her. Castle Asango had been decorated on every wall with beautiful red and gold linens that hung down the height of the walls and swayed in the soft coastal winds. She could hear the wild music of a human orchestra inside, playing flowing rhythms for the mortal guests. The sun had begun to set into the ocean horizon, and already there were torches lit everywhere on great metal sconces. Tall guards stood at attention at every doorway, dressed in dark black armor that had Cassian's unmistakable insignia on it. *How she longed to speak with him.*

Thalice could feel Cassian of course, as she always felt him. He undoubtedly sensed her presence as well, and he would come to greet her soon. For the moment, she stood observing the humans as they passed by her. Thalice had been afraid of these people once, long ago, before her dear one had changed her life. Now, strangely, she loved them. They were beautiful to her in all their flaws, the way they were beautiful to Cassian. For years, she had longed to move amongst his kind and learn more of their fascinating ways.

"Good evening, miss," a male voice said from the darkness behind her. Thalice did not turn. *No one was supposed to be able to notice her.* Her cloak was enchanted to ward off the attention of mortals. Slowly, so that she did not disturb the folds of her cloak, she moved her hand to the hilt of her short sword.

"That is quite a lovely garment," said the voice.

Thalice turned, readying herself to fight. She sensed no dangerous swell of energy, but the enemies of elves could be very subtle. What she saw surprised her: it was an elderly mortal man. He had long white hair oiled and combed back against his scalp and a neatly trimmed white beard. He stared at her with curious blue eyes that somehow bespoke of war and death and yet still seemed friendly.

"Who—" she started to whisper, controlling the vibration of her voice so that only this man could hear her, but then her mind made the connection to an image she had seen in her dear one's memory years ago. It was Cassian's favorite tutor, though the face was different, the wrinkles heavier, the hair whiter and thinner.

"My name is Somar Dojinko," said the old man with a friendly smile. "And I must say it is my very dear pleasure to meet you, young lady. Lord Cassian certainly attracts the attention of the most magnificent sort."

"How can you see me?" said Thalice.

Dojinko's grin broadened, and he displayed surprisingly white teeth for such an aged mortal. "I am afraid I have built up quite a resistance to mental magic," he said, tapping his temple and winking at her. "Please do not consider me a threat. Lord Cassian told me you would be coming. He is quite excited to see you again."

Thalice smiled under her hood and let go of her sword handle. "You are his friend and confidante," she said. "I have felt impressions of you in Cassian's dreams, I think. Tell me, does he speak of me?"

"Lord Cassian keeps much of himself locked away, as a Denigoth nobleman is expected to do," said Somar. "He speaks little of *anything* in his heart, but I could see in his eyes when he told me of the elf he met years ago that you are someone of *profound* importance to him."

Thalice took a step toward this aged man and drew back her hood, allowing him to see her face. The two of them shared a bond, it seemed. *They both loved Cassian.* The humans around her might notice her now, but she could have only hidden her presence for so long anyhow. It ultimately mattered little. She had accepted the risks of interacting with the mortal world in order to share this night with her dear one.

"Would you escort me in, general?" Thalice said, offering her arm. The title came to her very suddenly, though it seemed not from her own mind. Cassian was near—she could feel him—and stray thoughts and impressions were beginning to flow between the two of them.

"It would be my deepest honor," said Somar. He locked elbows with her and slowly began to walk her in through the wooden doorway.

"Will you help me understand how to conduct myself?" she whispered into his ear. "I have never been to a human ball before."

"Once you fully remove that cloak, I think, everyone will see an elf girl, and all will be in awe. I doubt you will have to do much of *anything* to impress these people after that."

They walked in through the enormous doors. The grand hall within was illuminated by the warm glow of dozens upon dozens of wall sconces and candle-lit-chandeliers. The several hundred people inside were dressed in finely tailored wool and vibrantly colored silks, and most seemed delighted to be in each other's company. Thalice hugged Somar's arm just a little tighter as she stepped into this crowd of humans.

Her eyes fixed on Cassian very suddenly as he approached her. His wonderfully imperfect human face had grown more distinctive since she had last gazed upon it, and his hair had darkened to a deep auburn. He was taller and looked more like a man than a boy, though even back when she first met him, his green eyes had seemed ancient. He wore a simple high collared tunic accented with a square medallion hanging from a gold chain embossed with the Asango crest of a stallion's head. A rich crimson cloak was fastened at his neck with a simple round button of carved onyx. He looked almost astonishingly regal.

"My lady," he said as he approached her, a brilliant smile on his face. He came very close and then dropped into a smooth bow. "It pleases me beyond measure to see you." He made a gesture, and one of his servants dashed to Thalice's side and held out his hands. With a dizzying wave of nerves, she removed the enchanted garment, revealing her blue silken dress to the room, along with the fact that she was an elf among them. "You look beautiful," Cassian whispered.

Thalice felt herself blush, which was not something of which elves were ordinarily capable. Nearly all eyes in the ball turned to her, and a disturbing silence fell over Cassian's great hall. Even the musicians ceased playing. Cassian flashed her a smirk. She could feel his amusement, and it relaxed her. As she stood facing him, the sound of whispers began in every direction.

"Thank you for coming," he said as if all the gaping eyes upon both of them did not matter in the slightest. Somehow, looking into his dark green eyes, becoming enveloped by his confidence, they did not bother her either.

"Of course I came," Thalice whispered. She would have traversed any distance for him.

He reached out and took her hand in his, and then he turned suddenly and faced the mass of people who stared at them both. "My friends," he said, his voice flowing with immense volume from every direction through an unbridled display of magical capacity, "this is Thalice of the noble house of Corostine. She is my *honored* guest, and I have invited her here to experience the hospitality that we humans have to offer." He cocked his head slightly in the direction of the musicians, making eye contact with one of them. Within a few seconds, they resumed the tune they had been playing, and the party began again.

Cassian turned his attention to her once more and held out his hand. "Would you do me the honor of a dance?" Thalice felt her heart flutter. *This was wrong of course.* Elf girls did not dance with human males, and certainly not in a human party where mortals were imbibing alcohol. "You will be all right," Cassian whispered in her ear, and she knew instantly he had been reading her every thought. This was utterly disarming and intimate at the same time.

"Of course I will, if you wish it," she said. She took her dear one's hand, and the two of them walked to the center of the stone floor.

Cassian glanced at the musicians, and they brought their slow-moving piece to an end and began a faster-flowing symphony. "Forgive me, my dearest Thalice, but we must put on something of a show," he whispered in her ear. Before she could answer these words, Cassian dropped into a smooth bow and then shot back up. His hands clasped with hers, and the instant they did, her mind was filled with many hours of careful dance instruction. Cassian had practiced for months for this single evening under the guidance of private tutors, sometimes even slipping into their minds and retrieving muscle memory, all of which he telepathically conferred upon her in the span of a brief second. Thalice felt her body begin to move. It knew exactly what to do. Her arms and legs mirrored Cassian's with perfect synchronicity. She became swept up in the fast movements of the dance, and happiness overcame her.

This was how the young human had ruined her! She understood it more clearly than ever as she gazed into his deep green eyes and swung her body with his. Mortals, with their incredibly finite time, tasted of life with such fiery emotion, and her Cassian was a blazing sun.

Thalice then felt the awe of the humans all around her. They were staring in wonder at the Starborn and the elf. Amidst the effortless movements her body made, she spoke telepathically: <You are *using* me to amaze these people—to add to your own legend.>

<Yes, I am,> he answered back without a trace of shame. <Do you wish to stop?>

<No!> her mind almost screamed the word, but she buried her next thought: *I would do anything for you, my love.*

Their bodies began to move faster and faster, and then Thalice felt the subtle flow of Cassian's magic course through her. It mingled with the energies of her elfish flesh, guiding them in ways she had never imagined. Suddenly the two of them were lifted up into the air. As they heard the shrieks below, their two bodies continued to move in rhythmic strides, no longer using the floor as a base from which to push but spinning and swaying with complete freedom.

<Only with you could I ever dance like this,> she heard him whisper in her mind.

<Only with *you* would I ever do *anything* of this kind,> she answered back.

Cassian willed his musicians to continue playing despite the growing shock and confusion from the crowd below. He had such magnificent powers of concentration. Their two bodies swayed and spun together in the air for several minutes, floating up to the beautifully carved dome ceiling of his hall where they danced upside down upon the surface for a few amazing seconds, and then they lowered back to the floor. When the music finally ceased, and the two of them separated and bowed to one another, the great hall erupted into thunderous applause.

<Let us go out to the terrace before they swarm us,> Cassian said, gazing into her eyes as they both rose.

<Of course,> Thalice answered, and she held out her hand. Cassian took it and led her to a flight of carved stone stairs. Large, armed guards flanked the two of them from behind.

"Here we are," Cassian said as he led her through a set of wide doors onto an enormous stone-tiled balcony that overlooked the lush landscape below. "I eat my breakfast here most days," he said, speaking with a soft affection in his voice. Behind him, she saw the guards form a wall in front of the doorway, their hands holding steadily on their sword-hilts. *They were alone.*

Within a few seconds of the doors shutting Thalice felt the presence of a creature of enormous power, and she turned her head to see the breathtaking form of a young dragon flapping its great, bat-like wings in the dim starlight. This was Titus, Cassian's gift from the great Promethiock. It was her dear one's companion and his servant, his ally and his child all in one. The creature dropped from the air onto the terrace floor in a tumult of pounding, scaly feet and claws clacking against stone. On four legs, its back was shorter than that of a horse, yet its long, flexible neck allowed the head to lift high above the two of them. The dragon plodded across the floor to where they stood, blazing yellow eyes fixed on Thalice.

She might have felt frightened, except that she knew this creature was nearly as profoundly connected to Cassian as she. It was telepathic and, though little more than an infant by the standards of its own ancient race, intelligent. As it moved its scaly head level with hers, she reached out and put a hand on its nose. The scales were so rough they might have cut her hand if the dragon moved too suddenly, but it seemed to understand this about itself, and it wished her no harm.

"He has wanted to meet you for a long time," Cassian whispered. Then, with a soft chuckle, he said: "I refer to Titus as a *he* all the time, but that is not quite accurate." He scratched the end of the scaly beak-like nose and said: "Dragons do not have *genders* as we do. They reproduce from themselves alone. Still, it feels... *inappropriate* to refer to my incredible companion as *it.*"

"If the creature can give birth to a child one day, would it not be more logical to refer to it as a *she*?" Thalice said with a smirk.

Cassian returned her smile and said: "I suppose the argument could be made. I am learning to ride *her*." He stepped around the creature and rand his hand over the folded, bat-like wing on its right side. "It takes a great deal of concentration from us both. Titus's wings do not exactly carry that heavy body purely through physics. There is a great deal of *magic* involved, but it is primal stuff. Unlike me, this wonderful creature was *born* to fly."

Thalice reached to Cassian's mind for more explanation, and he allowed it without hesitation. She stepped inside his memories and experienced the way he could will his body through the air. It took enormous concentration and was quite draining to the aura inside him. The other Starborn believed Cassian's obsession with levitation was only another part of the flashy manner with which he wielded his magic. To Cassian though, it was a means through which to develop concentration and control. Ever since his power had awakened, he had strived to master it as no Starborn ever had, and his dragon provided a new means through which to develop that strength. He would make himself weightless on its back, and the two of them would traverse enormous distances together in the air.

"Run along now," Cassian whispered to Titus. "We wish to be alone." The dragon gave a strange grunt at this that sounded a bit like metal scraping against stone, and then turned and bounded toward the edge of the terrace and leaped over the side. Its enormous wings spread immediately and carried its great mass into an astonishingly smooth glide.

The moon shone down into Cassian's eyes as he turned to Thalice then. "So often I wonder what has happened to you," he said. "I can always feel you. I know when you are happy or sad, but I cannot speak to you. It is maddening at times. Can you see me? Do you try?"

"I have tried so many times," Thalice said, gazing at him. "There are countless things I would like to know about you. I also want to talk to you about—" she paused, wondering if she were being too forward. She gazed at her dear one and sensed his affection for her, and she knew she could speak to him about anything. Now just as before, there were no barriers. "I never stop worrying about the enemies that conspire to kill you."

"Would you like to meet a few of them?" Cassian said with a soft chuckle. He gestured to the guards who blocked the doorway to the terrace. "Every one of those men has tried to assassinate me."

Thalice stared at the armed guards, some of them hulking masses of muscle, and some of them small and lithe. "You broke their minds," she whispered.

"Yes," said Cassian with a casual shrug. "I developed a technique to shatter the mind of a man and then reshape and reassemble the pieces as I see fit. It is incredibly tedious work, but it allowed me to make good use of my supposed killers rather than simply end their lives. They are loyal to me now to the point of death."

"And you see no problem in removing an individual's free will?"

Her dear one raised an eyebrow. "I know things are much different in the elven world than with my crude and lowly race. You do not often have the kind of criminals that we do." He pointed to the guards and said: "Each of those men agreed to murder a teenage boy for money. Their *free will* is a danger to society, and I am quite happy to remove it from them, yes. As I said, I did not kill them, nor am I making them suffer. They are calm, useful, and no longer a threat."

Thalice rolled her eyes and said: "No more than you are, I suppose."

Cassian's grin widened. She knew well how he loved to be challenged by those he respected. He would debate with her for hours on end if that were what she wished, but it was not.

"I have heard you translated the Enumis," she said softly. "You did not tell me you were going to do that."

"I do not like to discuss such things when we visit," he said in a low voice. "My time with you is one of my only refuges from all of this."

"You cannot expect me not to care about such things. Now that the common man has access to the holy scriptures in a language he can understand, the church's authority will be diminished, which I am certain was your aim."

"Of course it was. I have made it extremely difficult for them to *lie.*"

His grin made her tremble with frustration. "There must be repercussions for this act. Tell me of the danger that surrounds you now."

Cassian grimaced a little, then muttered: "As you wish." He gazed up at the stars and whispered: "I expect a rather dramatic rise in the Nemesai Order's efforts to rid the world of me. They already have fierce allies among the landowning nobles in the eastern farmlands because of all the things I have written denouncing slavery." There was an angry glint in his eyes as he spoke.

"And the Emperor?"

"He continues to watch, not taking a side."

"If your actions have finally provoked the church heads too far, you could be executed." she said, her voice trembling a little.

"All mortals die," he whispered. He was maddeningly calm.

Thalice bit her lip, hesitating. She had meant to say what she was about to in a more composed manner, but it seemed she could not compose herself around Cassian, and the words tumbled out: "What if you could escape being mortal?" She took his hand in her own. "It has only been done thrice since the dawn of time, but there is a way to bond the life-force of a mortal to that of an immortal. Your life could be joined to mine, and you could live as long as I, transfixed in the perfect prime of your youth." She swallowed, then whispered: "I would do this for you, because...I love you that much."

Cassian gazed at her for a long moment in silence, holding her hand. She could sense his imagination running through the possibilities of an immortal life with her, but it was weighed against a furious resolve. Then his thoughts focused into a single decision, and he said: "I am sorry, my darling." His face was grim. "If I did what you ask, I could not take the throne, for I would no longer be human." He gazed down at the stone tile beneath his feet. "This is how I must live my life. I swore an oath on my mother's grave, and I must keep it."

Tears flowed down Thalice's cheeks. "Please," she whispered.

The calm smile returned to Cassian's face. "Existence would be so beautiful with you," he whispered. "If my life had not taken the course that it did, I would have accepted your offer in a heartbeat. Still, for the rest of my brief time, I shall have this moment with you when you offered me eternity and told me you loved me." His smile intensified. "It will be my secret comfort through all the hardships to come." He stood and gently cupped her face in his hands. "And please know that I love *you* more than I think I shall ever be able to love anyone else." He pulled her into a sudden, deep kiss.

Thalice could not tell how long it was until their lips parted. Never in her existence had she experienced such emotion. She only knew that a feeling of pure joy pervaded every fiber of her being, but that ecstasy was almost immediately tainted as she opened her eyes and gazed upon her one true love, who she knew was doomed to die.

Thalice moved against Cassian, resting the side of her face against his shoulder. There was nothing left to say. He had rejected her offer, as she had perhaps known deep down that he would. Still, it hurt. She would have to leave him now to return to the quiet pleasures of her elven existence and hold a secret locked away within her heart that no other elf would understand. Thalice was not a contented immortal creature of nature. She was hopelessly and painfully in love with a mortal who believed he could overcome the world.

CHAPTER 3:
THE RED BLANKET

My brother loved to antagonize the Nemesai. The entire empire knew that he had defeated Cromlic, and that the Bishop was too afraid to go after him again on his own. Cassian's followers are quick to tout this defiance as moral character. They conveniently forget the small folk who now suffer the wrath of the Nemesai after Cassian pushed too far.

-- Telemachus Vale,
Starborn of the Nineteenth Generation

Livia cast a quick, nervous glance up at the red blanket that hung out of the second story window over the market square, and her heart gave a little flutter. She knew what it meant and immediately dropped her gaze to scan for Nemesai soldiers. The marketplace was bustling with midday activity. People were moving about, talking loudly to one another, and conducting the normal array of daily business. There was not a single Nemesai to be seen anywhere, but that did not mean that none were watching. Some in the order were sorcerers who bore no tattoos, and who could blend in and surreptitiously observe the thoughts of others. Still, the presence of the blanket sent a little thrill through her. It signaled that someone had managed to get hold of more of the writings of the infamous Cassian Asango.

"Livia!" Iona's voice came as an excited cry from the left. She turned her head and watched her sister come bounding up. Iona was clutching her rough spun sack, and it was filled with several little bulges. "They have pheasants!" she exclaimed as she darted between pedestrians. Her face was flush beneath her thick brown hair. "I'll make these tonight! You and I can have our own!"

Livia frowned and raised her left hand, palm open, and pointed to its center with her right index finger. This was one of many gestures in the silent language that she, Iona, and Hervin had developed. Iona immediately tensed and said: "Seven coppers, but...how often do they have pheasant?"

Livia rolled her eyes and opened the bag Iona clutched. There were four birds, each scarcely larger than a street rat. *Iona was as bad with money as Hervin*. It had probably been a mistake to allow the girl access to the family's strongbox, but then Livia could not be responsible for everything. She took in a slow breath, letting her annoyance pass away. Then she smiled at Iona and gave a little shrug. Pheasant indeed was delicious, at least when Iona cooked it.

"I should get this home," Iona said, still beaming. "Do you have anything else to do?" Livia gave a nod, and Iona said: "Alright. I'll see you later." She turned and flounced down the street. Livia noted that several young men stared surreptitiously at her sister as she went. Iona had become quite pretty in a vibrant and wild sort of way. Her ever-present glow perhaps added to this in many subtle ways. The time might come soon when men of a particular kind tried to buy her from Hervin, as many had attempted to purchase Livia over the years.

Livia shook these thoughts off. She was in the marketplace to purchase supplies for the kiln, and ink and paper for Hervin's store. She strode past the vendors, keeping her eyes away from the blanket above. Instead, Livia let them fix on the paper seller's tent down the way. It was one of the nicer tents in the square, and one of the few that employed an armed guard at all times. She gazed at the tall, heavyset man standing at the entryway. Livia had never seen him before, which meant he probably wouldn't know about her—*the town mute*. His right hand rested on the hilt of a curved sword in a scabbard on his belt. The man had dozens of tattoos on his hulking bear arms—not mystic tattoos like those of the Nemesai or Onkai—but crude, black depictions of snakes and eels curling around. As Livia approached, he looked her up and down slowly, and his thick lips curled into a smile that seemed hungry.

"You wish to buy paper, little slave?" he asked. Livia nodded. "Do you have money?" She pulled her coin pouch from her pocket and shook it, letting the man hear the clink. His hand shot out with surprising speed and gripped her wrist. Livia tensed, but she knew what was coming next and let it happen. She could do nothing about it, for she a slave.

The man took her purse, releasing her wrist so he could pour the coins from her pouch into his hand. He inspected them for a moment, and then slid them back in. As he extended the purse back to her, he said: "Alright, you can go in." Livia took her money back and started to walk past, but the guard hunched down so that their faces were level and said: "Who's your master, sweetheart? You're the prettiest slave I've ever seen. Do you think if I gave him a few desseks, he would let me—"

"Attillus!" a voice rang out in an angry shout from inside. A tiny man in fine white silks whom Livia knew well came stalking out with a scowl on his face. "This is Livia! She is one of my regular customers. Stop harassing her!" Septicus, the city's main paper supplier, leaped up and slapped the far larger man across the face. The massive brute drew back in shock, and Livia saw rage flash in his eyes, but Septicus was utterly unafraid. He glared up at the giant and said: "Apologize to this girl. *NOW*!"

The large man's lips curled up, and he took in a seething breath, then hissed through his teeth: "I apologize."

"We will speak about this *later*," Septicus snarled. He turned to Livia, and his creased face became serene and jovial so quickly it was almost comical. "Please come in, my dear."

She followed Septicus into the tent. As the flap closed behind them, he said: "I apologize for Attillus out there. Former soldiers sometimes take a bit of breaking in before they are fit for society."

Livia gave him a nod. She understood the need for a guard. Septicus was a small man who dealt in a fairly valuable and extremely easy to steal commodity.

She looked around the tent. Inside there were several tables with blank sheets of fresh parchment that appeared wonderfully supple. Livia had a strong preference for papyrus, which she knew Septicus kept in the wooden chests in the back of the tent. Papyrus was not as durable or long-lasting as parchment, but the latter paper had to be drawn on with ink, whereas gritty papyrus could take marks from charcoal and thus could be erased several times with a stone and a bit of hard rubbing. This made it vastly superior for accounting records, and also for Livia's own unique needs. Still, parchment written in ink was best for contracts and bills of sale over large quantities of goods as they were tricky to alter.

"You want to see the papyrus first, I assume," Septicus said.

Livia smiled and gave him a nod. Septicus brought her over to one of the large chests. As soon as he opened it, the crisp, leafy scent of the material tickled her nose and filled her with delight. *She loved paper.* This was an attitude that she and Septicus shared and was likely why he treated her with such friendliness despite her social status. She gazed down at the hundreds of brownish yellow sheets stacked neatly upon one another, not yet fastened to wood to make scrolls. To Livia, the simple papyrus was power—the power to communicate.

"Since it's *you*, my dear, I will go to two sheets a copper," Septicus said, eyeing her.

She turned and looked into his dark green eyes. The man did his best to remain calm and impassive, as most did who had had experience dealing with her. They had some idea of her powers of perception, but she doubted if any of them suspected how far that ability went. It was growing stronger all the time. As she stared at Septicus, she saw a touch of deceit mixed with his fondness for her, and a nervous calculation behind his words. There were other paper sellers in the city, and they received their shipments from the same traders. If he was apprehensive about the price, then that meant that it was not his best offer. She gazed a second longer and knew with certainty that the cost of paper had gone down.

Livia tilted her head a little and held up four fingers. Before Septicus uttered a word, she knew that four sheets a copper was too much. She judged from the level of tension that appeared in his eyes that this was either close to or exactly the price he had paid for the paper.

Septicus coughed and said: "Now, my dear—"

Livia shook her head and spread her hands out, palms down, indicating that she had given up on that idea. She held up three fingers. Instant relief flashed in Septicus's eyes, but not complete relief. He was hesitating. Livia shook her three fingers firmly in front of him and cast a hard stare. Septicus knew her well enough to understand that she had set her mind on this price and would not change it. It was fair, and her business was important enough to him that he would not wish to lose it.

With a sigh and a defeated slumping of shoulders, the small man muttered: "How many sheets do you want?" Livia held up three fingers and then made a fist. "Thirty it is," Septicus said with a nod. He walked over to a table where there was a clay bowl of water where he dipped his hands and then dried them with a small cloth. The man was quite religious about the way he handled his merchandise, which Livia respected. With clean hands, Septicus walked over and carefully began counting out thirty sheets, and Livia counted out ten coppers from her pouch. She placed the coins on Septicus's table, and he nodded at them and placed the sheets down, doing his best to make sure they were in a neat stack, and then he gently rolled them up. The little man then pulled one of the lengths of twine from his pocket that he always seemed to have ready and tied the bundle up and handed it to Livia. As he did, he said: "As usual, I ask you don't tell anyone the price I gave you."

She pursed her lips into a slight smile and pointed to them, raising her eyebrows as if to say: *I cannot speak. Remember?*

"Have a fine day, my dear," the man said with a nod.

Livia nodded and turned around and passed back out through the tent's entry. The large, tattooed man's eyes fixed on her immediately. She felt them travel unabashedly up and down her body, lingering in places they should not. She suppressed the urge to slap him and broke into a brisk walk, but she slowed her pace after a dozen steps, not wanting to let the man think he had flustered her too much.

It irritated Livia to acknowledge that she had grown used to this kind of treatment from certain types of men. She knew this sort of attention was a dangerous thing for a slave to receive. Livia was not quite a person under the eyes of the law, but only a piece of chattel. To accost a slave was little more a crime than accosting another man's pig. This was the social system that the great Cassian Asango was supposedly going to change. As Livia thought on this, her eyes flicked back up to the red blanket in the window.

It was always a risk to associate with the *'Cassianites,'* as the more aggressive of the infamous Starborn's followers had recently named themselves. Their group in the city was made up mostly of slaves who had little supervision as well as the city's free but destitute citizens, though rumor had it that, in other places in the empire, wealthy merchants and businessmen were actively participating. Livia had heard whispers of slave-masters being attacked, and slaves set free, and even of Nemesai being beaten in the streets by attackers in cloth masks. Such things terrified and excited her. It was thrilling to dare to believe that the empire could be a different place.

She opened the wooden door of the tall building. This time the Cassianites were meeting in an inn known as *The Rabbit's Foot.* It was an old and dilapidated structure that had been part of the city for as long as Livia could remember, somehow taking in just enough money to stay open without ever earning funds sufficient to cover most basic repairs. When Livia entered, she saw a very tired looking old man sitting behind a desk. He glanced at her and squinted for a moment, then said: "Would you like a room, my dear?" Livia shook her head. The man only squinted harder, and she felt a tinge of frustration. Communicating with someone with poor eyesight was exceedingly difficult for her. After a moment, the old man said: "Just visiting someone then?" Livia moved very close and gave an exaggerated nod. The old man shrugged and said: "There seems to be a lot of that today." His eyes went down to a piece of wood in his hand, and he returned to whittling with a small rusted knife.

Livia took a nervous breath as stepped onto an unnervingly creaky stairway. She had to remind herself as she tiptoed up the steps that she was a comparably light girl, and that if the rotting wood were going to give way, it would not likely do so under her feet. She made it up the steps and stared at a short hallway with four doors. Only one of them would have been facing out where the blanket had been hung, and thus she knew right where to go. She walked along a creaking hallway to a grimy wooden door and knocked three times in quick succession, then paused for a few seconds and knocked a fourth time as other slaves had told her she should do. There was a scampering of feet behind the door, and then a young, male voice said aloud: "What's the password?"

Livia rolled her eyes. No one had told her anything about a password, but she recognized the voice behind the door. It was Davin Mesk, a slave from the incredibly wealthy Prethian estate. Davin, she knew, had the position of secretary to the home, which evidently took up very little of his time as she often saw him sitting about the town engaged in conversation with anyone who would listen to him. He was one of the lucky slaves whose owners were so wealthy that they could afford to keep a servant for nearly every task in their home. Why he was a Cassianite when he had things so much more comfortable than other slaves was a bit confusing, but then Livia knew him to be the kind of person who loved to be excited about something and loved even more to hear himself talk.

She gave the knock again, and Davin's voice came back more irritated: "What's the password." Livia shrugged and gave the knock a third time, but she only got to the second rap before the door creaked open and Davin peered at her through the crack. "Oh, Livia!" he said, his eyes widening with excitement. He took a step back and swung the door open, a wide grin coming across his face. Davin was a short, thin boy a year or so older than Livia herself. As he looked at her, she saw the usual nervous attraction in his eyes. Davin was not quite in love with her, but he had been harboring a crush for years. "I didn't know you were interested in *the cause*," he said with a laugh. "At least, I didn't think you would know about the sign. *Of course* you're interested in the cause!" He cast a sudden, nervous glance over her shoulder as if remembering that what they were doing was dangerous, and then he said in a whisper: "*Come in.*"

Livia tentatively stepped into the room, which was little more than four walls, a chair, and an extremely old looking cot upon which sat a second slave from the Prethian home, a much larger young man the town knew merely as Hoss. Hoss had his hand just under the blanket, and he looked to be loosely gripping something there. Immediately she saw the nerves in his eyes and guessed he had a weapon. *Was it sword?* Could this pair actually be so foolish? A slave caught with soldier's armaments could have his hands chopped off.

"I know you can read," Davin said, walking over to a small sack that rested behind the bed. "You'll like this." He reached inside and drew out a small, neatly folded pamphlet that was made of a much finer paper than the stuff she was holding under her arm. Livia walked over and took it from Davin's hands. The substance was so smooth and pliant, like nothing she had ever seen. It had beautiful printing on the front that read: *'A Call for Freedom.'*

"Oh, you like the paper," Davin said. He leaned in and said in a hushed voice: "Rumor has it our Starborn leader has gotten hold of some machinery from the dwarves. Supposedly, it makes paper out of *wood* of all things! It's good stuff though, isn't it?" He ran his finger up and down the surface of the pamphlet. Then he looked into her eyes and said: "Anyway, Asango talks a lot about what he calls the *coming age of reason.* It's amazing stuff! I can't really follow *all* the language in it, but there is quite a bit about the *inherent natural rights* of all human beings." He gave her a twitching smile and hesitated before saying: "I... I would love to discuss it with you when you've read it. I mean—I could talk, and you could write—like we used to do sometimes." He reached up and scratched the back of his head, and his eyes moved all over the room except where hers were.

Livia gave him an awkward smile and then lifted her coin purse out of her pocket and held it up, giving Davin a questioning look. The young man raised his hands and said: "Oh no, I wouldn't dream of taking money from another slave. Don't worry about it. Lord Asango's people distribute these for free, and they even give us a little money to help us deal with some of the...*difficulties* of distribution."

Livia smiled at him again in thanks and tucked the small pamphlet into the middle of her roll of papyrus sheets. She turned and started for the door, but before she opened it, she cast another look at Hoss. He remained stern. His hand had not moved from its concealed place under the blanket. She waved a quick goodbye and stepped out, hurrying quickly down the hall and back down the stairs and out of the building. There was a wonderful thrill at having dared to acquire the dangerous piece of literature.

Livia wanted more than anything to believe that the radical Cassian Asango could rise to the throne. Most merchants in the city, from what she overheard here and there, were sure that the other Starborn contender, Dimitris, would defeat the "mad" young Cassian. Livia worried that she was indulging in foolish hope. She reminded herself that even if Cassian succeeded in becoming crown prince, it might be ten or even twenty years before he actually took power. Asango was close to the same age as herself, which logically meant by the cycle of the star that Emperor Tacitus would be around seventy. This was certainly an old age, but Starborn lived longer than most people. It was not unheard of for their lives to reach a century or more in length. Still, the thought of an end to slavery happening at any point in her lifetime was terribly exciting.

Livia was running all of this through her mind as she made her way back into the central marketplace when there was a sudden tingle in her body. It was subtle at first, but it grew over several heartbeats into a sensation of searing pain. She gasped and looked down. There was no point on her body at which the horrible feeling seemed to begin, and she checked desperately to see if she had stepped on something. The pain expanded. It tore through her muscles, and suddenly Livia lost control of her arms and legs. She dropped to the city street, her roll of paper falling out of her arms and crumpling under her elbow. Before she knew what was happening, her body began to slide along the street as if being dragged, though no one was touching her. In nearly the blink of an eye, her body had slid into the alley between the inn and the building next to it, and there she came to a sharp halt at the feet of a tall man in a heavy cloak. He had a thick brown beard and eyes that stared with savage, predatory anger.

The man did not speak, but stepped over her, and she was able to look up enough to see that he cast a look around. Evidently, what had just happened had transpired quickly enough that no one noticed, for when he turned back, his eyes were calmer and more confident than they had been. He moved to her and lifted his left hand and whispered: "*Eskathia, Des Moroko.*" Livia felt her body rise up from the ground to a standing position, only she kept rising so that her feet dangled above the ground. More pain ripped through her, and she tried reflexively to thrash against it but found she could not move.

"You *stupid* little slave," the man said in a low voice, his features curling into a sneer. He started walking, and Livia felt herself being whisked backward in pace with him. Her body floated in agony to the end of the inn and then swung sharply to the right. The man followed her behind the building where the two of them were alone in a little fenced off area at the inn's back. As soon as the man's eyes fixed on Livia, she sailed into the back wall of the Rabbit's Foot where she slammed so hard her vision nearly went black. She would have fallen forward if some invisible power were not holding her firmly in place.

"Pretty thing, aren't you?" the sorcerer said in an icy voice. He took a step toward Livia, and the pain in her body redoubled. She was terrified as she had never been. The man seemed to sense this, and he hissed: "Yes-s-s-s, you should be afraid, you little *rat*." He pulled the neck of his cloak open and let Livia see the spear tip insignia on his leather armor. The man was a Nemesai sorcerer, which was the most terrifying thing she could imagine. Her body trembled in as much as it could move, and her eyes began to gush with tears. He cast her a cruel smile and said: "Your life is over, you stupid, *stupid* little slave." The invisible force around her tightened, making it difficult to breathe. He leaned into her ear and whispered: "You're the one who cannot speak, aren't you? *Livia*? That's all right. Before I arrest those two idiots you just met with, I would like to know how much you know about Asango's distribution network." He leaned in closer and hissed: "I'm going to take a look inside your mind. It *will* hurt!"

He reached up and put a rough, calloused hand on Livia's forehead. Within a few short seconds, she felt a strange sensation in her skull. Her vision blurred, and she became entirely focused on an alien presence prying its way into her thoughts. She could feel it, like a ravenous beast clawing at her consciousness, and without thinking, she tensed and drew back from it, closing herself off. It was something like rolling up into a ball, but inside of her own mind.

"WHAT?!" the Nemesai hissed. He leaned in and snarled into her ear: "How the hell did *you* learn occlusion?" Livia opened her eyes, trying to look at the man, but her vision was still hazy. He gritted his teeth and said: "You think you can block *me,* you little *Slave*? I've been doing this for twenty years!" He pressed his hand harder into her head, and she felt the beast once again inside her mind. It slashed and tore wildly at her mind, transmitting an unbelievable level of pain. Livia began to panic. The sorcerer's attacks were boring into her, tunneling closer and closer to the most private and sacred places. In a wave of terror, Livia lashed out at the intrusion with the same part of her mind that she had drawn up around her thoughts. She thrashed blindly, not even beginning to understand what she was doing.

"HAHHHHHHH!" the Nemesai screamed. He drew back from Livia, suddenly clutching at his own face. She felt the invisible magic around her body weaken and dissipate, and she dropped back to her feet. The sorcerer continued to clutch at his face, shrieking. Livia blinked, focusing her eyes on him as he thrashed around. He managed to let out several guttural whimpers of pure agony before his body slackened. His arms fell to his sides, his jaw dropped open, and then he was still. Still shaking with terror, Livia peered into his eyes. They had rolled back into his head. He was breathing, but only in a slow, high-pitched rasp.

It took her a moment to think even at all. She had no idea what she had done to this man. She took a quick, terrified look around, expecting more Nemesai to come running to attack her, but after a very long moment of waiting, nothing happened save for the man's continued rasps.

After another moment, Livia found the courage to take several shaking steps back to the alley. No one was there. Off in the distance, she could still see her roll of papyrus sheets half crumpled where the sorcerer had attacked her. She glanced back at him. His eyes remained listless, their lids twitching.

Livia was too frightened to think. After another moment of hesitation, she was somehow able to make the decision to leave the alley. She moved toward the street, still expecting at any moment that Nemesai men would descend on her. Ever so slowly and nervously, Livia reached down with hands that could barely work and gathered up her paper. Then she rose and looked around the street. People were going about their business as usual. *Nothing seemed amiss.*

Panicked beyond reason, Livia turned and started walking toward her home. She could not think of anything else in the world to do.

CHAPTER 4:
THE PATH TO INSANITY

The Sansrit path is perhaps the oldest form of harnessing preternatural power known to mortals, yet its champions have never risen to the height of kings as those born with sorcery have. For thousands of years, its followers have been content to live quiet, often secluded lives, acting only from shadows and with great restraint. We know virtually nothing about their disciples save that if enough of them ever wished to pose a threat to this world, they most certainly could.

---Dracus Mobius,
Starborn of the eleventh generation,
first bishop of the Onkai Order

Kota listened to the wind blow against the tree branches above him as he sat upon the small blanket Gretis had knitted for him. He let his thoughts fade distantly away from his consciousness as she had taught him. Kota became a still and silent part of nature, entirely at peace. He breathed in slowly through his nose and let the many scents of the forest tickle his senses. His eyes were shut, and there was a distant awareness that the sun had set and the air around him was growing cold, but this did not bother him. Kota had learned to control his heartbeat and make his body warm even in snow. This was the beginning of Sansrit Philosophy: a quiet mind, free of the weight of thought and emotion, focused on the body and the world around it. He had spent entire days in this state at Gretis's instruction.

He detected intrusion.

Kota had only a fraction of a second's warning before the sword came at him. Gretis was impossibly silent, but he could still hear the faint beat of her heart. His hand moved without hesitation to the handle of the training sword sitting across his lap. The sound of his master's blade cutting through air told him that the attack was coming from behind, and he whirled around, whipping his sword up horizontally to block either a downward or possibly lateral swing from where he guessed her to be. Kota felt the two metal blades clack against each other and he smiled just a little.

"Impressive," said a voice that did not belong to Gretis.

Kota shot up and turned. Standing before him was a man perhaps ten years older than himself, with thick dark hair and olive skin like Lady Gretis. He was not quite as tall as Kota, though he had a lean, athletic build and stood with dangerous confidence. The man was clad in deep brown leather armor, and he had a long, silver sword in his hand. There was a smile on his face, though it did not seem to be a friendly smile.

"Who are you?" Kota said.

"All you really need to know is that I am an enemy," he said. Without another word, he swung his sword at Kota's throat. On instinct, Kota raised his own weapon to parry the blow, but the power behind the attack was far more than he anticipated, and his own sword was ripped out of his hands. It whipped through the air, striking a tree and then falling to the ground. Before Kota could take a step toward it, the tip of the man's silver blade was at his throat.

"Hmm," the attacker muttered. "No real power yet." He sighed and lowered his sword and walked over to Kota's weapon. He picked it up and, to Kota's surprise, tossed the thing back handle first. As Kota's fingers closed around the hilt, the man said: "Let's try again."

"Who are you?" Kota said again, his throat dry.

"If you let yourself be distracted by such things, you'll end up CUT!" the man said, shouting the last word as he swung for

Kota's face. Again, Kota blocked the blow, and he was surprised to find that this time the strength behind it was far closer to his own. He dodged back from the parry, dropping into the Nuthrak stance instinctively, fixing his eyes on his opponent. Whoever this man was, he could kill Kota with ease, but he was not doing so. Still, there was no friendliness in his dark eyes, and Kota had the sense that if he failed to defend himself well, this stranger would slice into his flesh without mercy.

A quick thrust came toward Kota's chest. He blocked to the right and dodged his body to the left. As soon as he caught his footing, he delivered a counter-thrust, swinging his sword laterally into the man's face. His opponent dodged away in a blur of speed, dancing back several feet and letting out a soft chuckle.

"Beautiful counter!" the man grunted. "I would have lost an eye if you were a bit faster, which begs the question—" he moved forward so fast that Kota barely had time to attempt to block. He was only vaguely able to follow what happened next, but it seemed that the tip of the man's weapon hooked under the guard of his own sword and snapped it out of his hands. A fraction of a section later, his opponent was holding both swords crisscrossed just in front of his neck like a giant pair of tailor's scissors. "Why hasn't she unlocked any of your power?" his attacker whispered.

"Get away from him!" Gretis's voice came in cold anger from the right. Kota shifted his eyes and saw her standing in quathic stance, blade in hand. She held a real sword with sharp gleaming edges.

"Oh relax," the man said. He moved the blades away from Kota's throat and dropped Kota's sword on the ground as he turned to face Gretis. "I don't have any interest in killing your student," he cast a sideways glance at Kota and added: "not yet anyhow."

"What are you doing here?" Gretis said, her voice still sharp. She did not lower her blade.

"I heard you had taken on a new apprentice. I thought I would come and say *hello.*" He stepped slowly toward Gretis, his weapon rising subtly in the air. Gretis remained still, watching him with narrowed eyes. "He's very good," the man said. "In terms of form, he's utterly perfect."

"Yes, he is a better student than you ever were. He works harder, and he never complains."

The man cast another quick glance back at Kota, his jaw clenching, and Kota stared back. He was reasonably sure this man was Soulic, Gretis's son and first apprentice. She had never spoken of him, but Kota had learned bits and pieces of the story from Darius and some of the other Onkai. From what he knew, Soulic was a deadly killer who possessed all the skill, strength, and power of his mother, and he was, at least to some degree, insane.

"Is he going to be strong?" Soulic said in a voice of controlled anger. "Stronger than I? I'm curious about that. They say shamalaks are the best trackers in the world. Perhaps you're training him to hunt me...to do the job you could not."

"Kota has nothing to do with you," Gretis said, and she took a step toward Soulic. "If I should want you dead, I shall kill you myself."

"There's the mother I know," he said, his mouth curling into an angry smile. He dashed at her very suddenly then. Their two swords clashed together in the air so hard that Kota could almost feel the impact in his bones. Mother and son danced around each other, darting and whipping their blades around with unbelievable speed. Kota stared stupidly as their weapons clashed two and even three times in the span of a second. Within that blurring chaos, each of them seemed to move with incredible precision. It was terrifying and yet strangely beautiful. Neither seemed to be able to gain the upper hand on the other.

After a minute or two of this fierce dance, Soulic leaped fifteen or so paces back and shouted: "Peace, mother." He lifted his sword and slid it into the scabbard in his belt, and then he looked to her as if silently asking if she would do the same. Gretis hesitated, then sheathed her weapon.

"Why are you here, Soulic?" Gretis said. "If it is only to look over Kota, then you have done so, and you can leave."

"Actually I came here to speak with you. Perhaps we might go somewhere and talk?"

Gretis let out a dark chuckle. "You *do* remember how close my home is to the Onkai Temple, don't you?"

"I'll take the risk. Let's go for a walk."

Gretis sighed and looked at Kota. "Try to go back to meditating if you can. I will speak to you later. Do *not* follow us."

"Y-yes, ma'am," Kota said.

Gretis moved slowly to her son, and they fell into step together, walking away from Kota. They strode for a time in silence, growing smaller and smaller off in the trees until Kota heard Gretis's voice softly in the distance say: "How have you been?"

"Quite well, mother," he said. "I have managed to accomplish quite a bit since we last saw one another."

Soulic's voice grew quieter in the distance, and Kota's heart began to thump with curiosity. For years, Gretis's failed apprentice had been a mystery to him. Soulic represented what could go wrong with Sansrit Mastery—whatever had happened to him might happen to Kota as well. Kota thought it his right to understand this malady. Thus, nervously, he chose to disobey Gretis for the first time and crept closer, so he could continue to listen to the conversation. He moved on the balls of his feet, keeping silent and staying behind brush and trees.

"Did you kill another officer?" Gretis said, her voice stern.

"No, I have been focused on other things for a time. Actually, I thought I might give you another chance to answer my question before I resumed my quest." His voice lost its playfulness as he said: "Who is my father?"

Gretis hesitated, then said in a soft voice: "I will not participate in your crude revenge game."

"I thought you might say that. That is why I procured *this*," Soulic said. Kota managed to sneak behind some thick bushes, and he peered through the leaves to see the young man unroll a large scroll in front of his mother. "These are the names of every general and commander serving in the time I would have been...*conceived*."

"Where did you get that?" Gretis said, her tone becoming slightly tense.

"I can get anything and go anywhere now," Soulic said with a chuckle. He reached inside the collar of his leather armor and drew out a golden amulet that hung from his neck. Kota peered at it. He could not tell for sure, but it seemed to look just like the *Elokien* Cassian had taken from the demon sorcerer nearly five years ago in the battle that had burned itself so profoundly into his memories.

"Where did you get *that*?" Gretis said, her voice even tenser. "The elves will kill anyone walking around with their enchanted items."

"The elves have no more chance of catching me than those Onkai imbeciles." Soulic cast a vicious smile at her and said: "As to where I got this, Denigoth has made *many* enemies in its conquests, and some of them are quite resourceful. I have made friends, mother. But that is hardly the point." He tucked the Elokien back into his armor and shook the scroll. "There are thirty-six names on this list. If you don't tell me who my father is, I am just going to work my way down it. More people will die than need to—not that the lives of these gods-damned murderers mean much. Still, I thought I would give you the chance to save me some trouble."

Gretis did not speak for a moment. They had both stopped walking, and she was staring at Soulic through narrow, angry eyes. "Your father died two years ago," she said finally.

Soulic's whole body seemed to convulse, and Kota heard him hiss: "Don't lie to me!"

"His name was Remus Kivild. I can see his name on your list there." She reached out and touched Soulic's scroll.

Soulic wrenched the paper back from her and snapped: "YOU'RE LYING!" He threw the scroll to the ground and took a step back, whipping his sword from its hilt. "Tell me the TRUTH!"

"I have told you the truth," Gretis said, her voice soft and calm. She made no move to draw her own weapon but stood perfectly still. "I am afraid you have gone to all that trouble for nothing."

"YOU BITCH!" he snapped, and he brought the tip of his sword up to her neck. Kota began to panic, but Gretis remained perfectly still as Soulic shouted: "You just picked a name of someone you knew was dead. You had this lie *ready for me!* You knew I would come here sooner or later." He leaned into her face and snarled: "Tell me the truth, or I'll kill your little shamalak appren—"

Gretis's sword came out so fast that Kota was not sure he saw any movement at all. It seemed to simply appear at the end of a swing, and the top half of Soulic's weapon went spinning through the air away from him. A fraction of a second later, Gretis's silver blade was at his throat.

"As I said, if I wish you dead, *I shall kill you,*" she said in a sharp, slow voice. Her son was glaring at her, clenching his jaw, not daring to move. "I have not done so yet because, so far as I know, you have never taken the life of an innocent. I have wanted to believe there was still something *good* in you, for all the evidence you've given me. However, if you so much as *touch* Kota again, I will cut your head from your body. Is that clear, *my son*?"

Soulic took several rasping, angry breaths, glaring at her, then he hissed: "Extremely, *Mother.*"

"Good. Now get the hell out of my sight." Gretis slid her weapon into its sheath and then turned back in Kota's direction. Soulic's face twitched with hatred as she walked away from him, and after a few heartbeats he turned and stomped off into the forest.

Kota kept perfectly still as Gretis passed by the bush in which he was hiding, yet without even looking in his direction, she said: "I believe I told you to meditate, Kota. You owe me fifty laps around the meadow this evening."

Kota swallowed and stood up. "Y-yes, ma'am," he said. He rose to his feet and moved to her side. "I am sorry. I should not have disobeyed you."

"No, you should not have," she said, her tone still cold.

They walked in tense silence back toward the place in the forest where Kota was supposed to have been waiting. He could hear Gretis's heart pounding like thunder in her chest all the way and felt a little nervous walking next to her. He had never seen her so upset.

When they reached his meditation blanket, she gazed down and said in a dry voice: "I am very sorry, Kota." He turned and looked at her. Her hazel eyes were filled with pain.

"I-It's alright," Kota said, forcing himself to smile at her. “Soulic didn't hurt me."

Gretis looked as though she were about to cry. "I should never have trained him," she whispered. Her gaze lifted to Kota. "Tell me please, Kota, do you harbor anger you have kept secret from me? Do you hate me for how hard I make you work? Do you hate the townspeople who still whisper behind your back?" Her eyes were wide. She looked almost frightened.

"I don't hate anyone," Kota said.

Gretis stared at him, her lips pressed together. He had never seen her look so worried. After a moment, she whispered: "You're a very fine young man, Kota. I want you to know that I..." she broke off, swallowing. Then she straightened and said in a more even tone: "Please resume your meditation."

Kota started to obey but then hesitated. There was a question he needed to ask. "Is that what you're afraid of? Will I become dangerous if there is anger in my heart when you—" he searched his mind. Gretis had explained so few of the secrets of Sansrit Philosophy to him. He borrowed Soulic's phrase: "When you *unlock my power*."

Gretis remained silent for a moment, her face expressionless. Then she said in a soft voice: "That is part of the danger, yes. Soulic...learned a secret about his birth I never meant him to know. It filled him with hatred for *his father*, and perhaps for me and even himself. He never told me he knew. He kept his hatred locked inside." Her tone became bitter as she added: "Such deep, unresolved feelings taint the spirit, and they can be incredibly dangerous to a student of the Sansrit."

Gretis took a sharp breath and then went on: "The time is coming very soon when you and I will bring out all that is inside you, Kota. Your mind and body are ready. What comes next however..." she hesitated, then whispered: "I told you long ago, the danger to your kind is far greater than to a human. You might do well to forget this path and return to your people. You would be the finest warrior in your tribe, and you are a talented scholar. I am certain you could become chief if you wished it."

Kota stared into Gretis's dark, mysterious eyes. Always she spoke cryptically of the worry she bore about what lay ahead in his training. He knew he could not turn away though. Not out of fear. He leaned down, for he towered over her now, and said: "What did you see when you took my hands in yours five years ago? Tell me."

Gretis blinked and then said in a quiet, distance voice: "I saw a warrior so much greater than myself that I doubted everything I was." She glanced down at the forest floor. "You will understand soon. I will take you far into the wilderness, and I will teach you everything. Until then, you must continue to do as I tell you."

"I—I will," he said.

CHAPTER 5:
A LONG FORGOTTEN EDICT

"I swear to all the gods I repent!"

Arkas smiled as the man before him shivered, his trembling limbs causing tiny clinks in the chains hanging from above. Arkas stared at him through the dim candlelight, managing his best semblance of a concerned expression. He was sitting in a comfortable chair, his arms folded before him, exuding an air of calm authority in the dingy Nemesai cell. Arkas had spent several days torturing the short little farmer. This man, named Elias, had been accused of worshiping the false gods of the east in secret rituals conducted in the forest. Arkas had telepathically determined within seconds that the simple farmer was entirely innocent of the charges—it was probably something an enemy said of him. That had made the case far more interesting. Forcing people to confess to sins they had not committed was a delightful game.

"I find your repentance insincere," Arkas whispered into Elias's ear. The poor fool was half starved and covered in sweat. He had been in the custody of the Nemesai order for more than a week, away from his wife and children, away from everything except fear and pain. "I am afraid we shall have quite a few more sessions."

"NO!" Elias screamed, sweat dripping down his face. "Please! I confess! I repent! I'll do whatever you want!"

"I know," Arkas said, unable to suppress a chuckle. The man was just like so many before. At first, he had proclaimed his innocence—*because he was innocent.* There was a delicious pleasure in taking that truth away from him. Arkas's telepathy told him that the poor fool was quite near to believing that he actually *had* committed the crimes of which he was accused. Within another session or two, he would accept absolutely anything Arkas told him as the truth. In the end, human beings were absurdly weak.

Arkas drew his left hand back—the hand that still had five fingers—and Elias let loose a terrified shriek. Arkas had honed a technique to setting every nerve in the human body into searing pain through carefully focused magic. Through a simple touch, he could imbue more suffering upon a person than most mortals could imagine, and the effect was instant.

"High Inquisitor!" a voice came from the door half a heartbeat before Arkas's hand could touch the sweating forehead of his prisoner.

"What do you want?" Arkas snarled back. "I am busy!" It irritated him to no end to be interrupted amidst an inquisition. Breaking '*sinners*' was one of the only pleasures left to him.

"Bishop Cromlic requests your presence immediately," the voice called through the bars of the cell door.

"Why?"

"I... I don't know sir, but several monks from the Lucinian order arrived perhaps fifteen minutes ago."

Arkas's spine arched, and he lifted his gaze from the trembling peasant. *A visit from Lucinians was not to be taken lightly.* "Is the bishop meeting with them now?"

"I believe they are waiting to be seen," the underling said.

Arkas gazed down at his prisoner and whispered: "We shall resume this *conversation* very soon, I assure you." This elicited a delightfully pathetic squeak from the man as he turned toward the door.

Arkas moved out into the hall amidst three Nemesai soldiers. They saluted him, lifting hands to tattooed foreheads. He nodded coldly. There were a handful of men in the order whom he liked—men who saw the world the way he did. Most Nemesai lied to themselves though, telling themselves day and night that the 'Gods' wanted them to torture sinners back into the light. *As if such a thing were possible.* If there were truly anything *good* in the world, it had nothing to do with the Nemesai.

Arkas strode down the dim corridor, hearing the moans of the prisoners locked away in their cells. He made his way up into the main hall of the central Nemesai temple. From the icy gloom in the massive vaulted room and the soft glow of wall torches here and there, he ascertained that evening had fallen. It seemed he had lost yet another entire day in the dungeons.

"Where is the bishop?" he said.

"In his study, sir."

Arkas nodded and ascended another flight of stairs to the upper level of the temple and crossed the inner terrace to the bishop's office. The door was open, and so Arkas stepped through it. He found Cromlic hunched over his desk, nervously drumming his fingers on the surface. The man looked utterly terrible, but then he often did these days.

"You have heard about our visitors, I presume," Cromlic said, his voice sharp and raspy. His yellowing eyes shifted to the left wall, the other side of which, Arkas guessed, the Lucinian monks were waiting. "I have attempted to read their minds, but it seems they are both extremely adept at occlusion."

That is why he wants me here, Arkas thought. The old fool's abilities were slipping. He cleared his throat and said: "I assume they are here about the vote."

"Well of course they are!" Cromlic snapped, slapping a veiny hand down on his desk.

Arkas stared at the wheezing old man, wondering if he were still afraid of him. "Was either of the men carrying a scroll?"

"What?" Cromlic muttered.

"A scroll," Arkas repeated. "I assume if Bishop Milos were sending you official word, it would be in the form of a scroll sealed with his insignia."

Cromlic blinked at this and stroked his ashen beard. "No," he said after a moment.

"Curious," Arkas said.

"Yes, it is," Cromlic exhaled. He glanced up at Arkas and said: "Go and fetch them. Bring them back here and then remain in the room."

Go and fetch them... Arkas had trained himself not to react to the bishop's condescending commands. He would kill the old bastard someday—perhaps someday very soon. For the time being though, he could only content his hatred by taking amusement at the holy man's slow descent into madness. It still haunted Cromlic constantly that he might slip and mention either of Cassian's parents and trigger the curse. Asango had not specified the rules entirely to the mental magic he had woven into the bishop's brain, leaving Cromlic to wonder if even referring to people with the same names could trigger a catastrophic aneurysm within his skull. His face went just a little pale whenever he heard 'Lilliana' or 'Uritheus' mentioned in any context. Cassian's assertion at the end of that horrible day had come to pass: the bishop had *"learned true fear,"* and it had made him a shadow of who he once was.

Arkas left the study and walked to the small room down the hall where he found two members of the Lucinian Order in brown robes sitting straight and upright in their chairs. They both turned their heads to face him as he entered. One was a man in his late twenties—handsome in an angular, severe sort of way. The other was quite ancient—perhaps as old as Cromlic himself, with a bald head and surprisingly alert blue eyes.

"Hello, brothers of the church," Arkas said. He gave a nod and said: "I am Arkas Adronicus, Starborn of the Nineteenth Generation." As he said this, he noticed the younger man—*just for a fraction of a second*—shift his gaze to Arkas's right hand. *'The Claw-Hand-Prince,'* many in the empire now called him. The bite Cassian's dragon had taken out of him had become the stuff of jokes and mocking songs. The young monk did not get to see the mauled appendage though. Arkas kept a leather glove on his right hand at all times. It was carefully stuffed in places to make his hand appear whole.

"My prince," the younger monk said, rising. "I am Sullivan Mensk."

"Prince Arkas," the elder said second, also rising. "My name is Cordus Silkim."

"Good to meet you both," Arkas said, "The bishop will see you now." He stepped away from the door, not holding it for the guests, and walked back to Cromlic's study. The two men entered a brief moment after he did, and both introduced themselves to Cromlic, who motioned them to sit before his desk. Arkas moved next to the bishop and remained standing. He fixed his eyes on the younger man as the conversation began.

"Good evening, gentlemen," Cromlic said. The elder opened his mouth to speak, but the bishop said: "I am afraid I have no time for proper pleasantries. Please be so kind as to come to the purpose of your visit immediately."

The two monks glanced at each other, and then the younger one, Sullivan, spoke: "We wish to share information with you about the heretic, Cassian Asango."

A little thrill passed through Arkas. The monk had referred to Cassian as '*the heretic.*' That was quite a good sign, and this was evidently not lost on Cromlic, for the old man leaned forward across his desk and said in an excited voice: "Then please share. Is your bishop going to vote for excommunication?"

"Well...no," the older monk said in a grim voice.

"WHAT?!" Cromlic shouted. "Why the hell not?"

<Calm down,> Arkas telepathically whispered in the bishop's mind. Cromlic turned and glared up at him, but Arkas stared back and continued: <You are projecting *weakness*. Compose yourself.>

The bishop drew in a slow breath, seeming to grudgingly accept the advice as the younger monk said: "My associate and I believe our master is...*misguided.*"

"But the two of you understand Asango should be declared an enemy of the church," Arkas said.

"Of course he should," Sullivan said, his tone full certitude. "Translating the Enumis—it was never meant to be done. Putting the holy scriptures into the hands of common imbeciles will have tremendous consequences to the future of theology."

"That is...why we are here," the elder monk said. "We want to see every one of those translated texts burned. They are far too dangerous—they could cause a split in the church."

"A split in the church?" Arkas said, raising an eyebrow. He guessed he knew what the man meant by this, but it was best to hear it outright.

"There already is division in the church," said Sullivan. "Asango gains new followers every day—men and women who believe that they are qualified to interpret the laws of our Holy Gods for themselves because they can read a few poorly translated words. Can you imagine how many idiotic interpretations of the Enumis we are soon to have? Every damned fool on the street will think himself expert enough to question the clergy."

"Yes, exactly!" Cromlic snapped, slamming his fist down. "Why can your bishop not see this?"

"He believes..." Sullivan answered, grimacing a little, "that *knowledge* will ultimately enlighten. Our bishop, unfortunately, agrees with Asango that the common man should learn to read, and that translating the holy book may lead to a revolution in literacy in the empire."

It probably will, Arkas thought, though he said nothing.

Cromlic muttered through his teeth: "If your order is set against mine, then what can you possibly offer me?"

The two men glanced nervously at one another again, and then the older one said: "First I must ask a question. Assuming you could never gain the blessing of the conclave of bishops, would you still arrest and kill Asango?"

Cromlic's face became sour. "I would kill the heretic this very instant if I could, but he is... *remarkably* formidable."

"We believe we have discovered a contingency," the elder monk said, his tone sounding troubled. "Should all else fail, we have perhaps found a way to defeat—*even kill*—Asango, no matter what his resources."

The younger monk drew a folded piece of parchment from under his sleeve and nervously unfurled it across the bishop's desk. Arkas hunched over and scanned the document. It was a tattered thing, the ink worn and barely legible, and *of course,* it was written in Dhavic. Fortunately, Arkas's years under the bishop's thumb had made him into a moderately adept scholar, and he worked the translation in his mind with only a little difficulty here and there. The scroll seemed to be a historical account—a series of edicts made by the first emperor of Denigoth. It discussed punishments for thieves, for murderers, for rapists, and then—Arkas let out a loud gasp. His heart leaping in his chest, he turned to Cromlic, who was staring back at him, a mirrored look of exhilaration on his face.

"We could kill him—without the Onkai or anyone else!" Arkas said.

"Would—would your father allow it?" Cromlic half wheezed.

"I think so—he has always said Asango must fight his own battles—yes—I think he would refrain from interfering."

Cromlic stared down at the scroll again, probably re-reading the beautiful passage near the middle. "I had no idea," he whispered.

"We believe the information was suppressed by the seventh emperor—for fear of the church at the time," the younger monk said.

Cromlic drew in a slow, trembling breath, and Arkas could almost see the wheels in his head turning. "For this to work, Cassian has to be in the capital." The bishop switched abruptly to telepathy as he added: <My spies tell me your father is about to order Asango into military service. It may be *years* before he sets foot in the royal palace.>

<We must proceed with our current plans. This is a last resort.>

<Yes. It would be preferable that Cassian meet death legally, or at the hands of Dimitris.>

Arkas nodded, though he recoiled inside. It was true that Cassian's death in any form would come as a great relief, but it was irritating to be reminded that even after his years of service to the Nemesai order, the bishop did not see him as the future emperor. *Always it was Dimitris...*

"How many others know of this?" Cromlic said, staring at the two monks.

"We kept it secret," the younger monk said with the hint of a cocky smile. "The more people know of the trap, the higher Asango's chances of side-stepping it."

"Agreed," Cromlic said, just before he telepathically whispered to Arkas: <Can you tell if that statement was truthful?>

Arkas was already scanning the men. As the bishop had said, they had both been trained thoroughly in occlusion. Their thoughts were obscured behind strong mental walls, yet emotion was leaking through. Arkas sensed what felt like sincerity. <I *think* they are telling the truth.>

<This is too important to leave to guessing. Find out for certain. Use the cells in the western wing. No one is there. I don't want anyone to overhear their screams.>

<We should wipe the memories of the men here of this visit. You should lockdown the temple immediately.>

<Agreed,> the bishop whispered back. He hesitated, then said: <When you are finished, set their bodies out on the road at least half a league away.> Cromlic's anxiety leaked through his psychic commands. <Make it look like they were attacked by bandits.>

<Understood> Arkas replied.

"I thank you for bringing this to my attention," Cromlic said to the two men, his voice icy. "You have given me a great deal to consider, and I must bid you goodnight. High Inquisitor Arkas will see you out."

"Oh," the younger monk said. He hesitated, then said: "We are in agreement, are we not—about the copies of the Enumis?"

"Of course we are," Cromlic said with a tense smile. "I promise you I will make it my life's mission to see every last shred of Asango's legacy burned away, once he lies dead at my feet."

"Ah...good," the young monk said.

"Gentlemen," Arkas said, gesturing for them to rise. "Before you go, I was wondering if I could ask for your opinion on a piece of archaic text I found tucked away in our west wing. Would you mind following me?"

"Of course," the elder monk said with a friendly smile.

Arkas returned his grin and stole a quick glance at his bishop. The old man was staring down at his desk looking almost horrified. *Was he really troubled by killing a few monks?* Arkas rolled his eyes at the doddering old fool and led the two men out into the hallway. His mind was already spinning through dozens of different scenarios. *How much did this actually change his plans?* Arkas was not sure. It was only a few months now until the Norn's prophecy would come to pass. If her prediction proved true, he would acquire a weapon that could kill his father—the man many believed to be the most powerful Starborn who ever lived. Surely, such a tool could kill Asango, as well as Dimitris and Cromlic, but there was no way to be certain. He did not know the nature of this *weapon*—perhaps it could only be used once, or it had other strange limitations. *No, it was best to keep as many avenues of attack open as possible toward Cassian.* One way or another, the son of a whore who had humiliated him in front of the whole empire, and whose pet had mutilated Arkas's hand, was going to die.

CHAPTER 6: CURSED

We think of Promethiock's gift as the greatest blessing humankind has ever received, and it is. Magic has allowed the fragile, mortal race of man to rise up and face all the enormous challenges of this world time and again. It can be used to heal and to repair and to build, but not all who have possessed the gift of sorcery have used their power for good. We who wield magic must always remember that it is a tremendously dangerous power that has brought down terrible consequences upon innocent people.

---Telemachus Vale,
Starborn of the nineteenth generation

Why had she not warned Dalvin and his partner about the Nemesai? Livia imagined the two Cassianites in chains. Were they being tortured even now as she sat there in her bed? Her stomach twisted painfully as she watched her little Iona sleep so peacefully under the folds of her rough spun blanket. Their two cots were little more than an arm's length apart in the tiny room they shared. Livia had spent the entire night clenched in terror next to Iona, her imagination inventing dozens of different scenarios for what had happened. She had no idea if the sorcerer had been working alone or with others. She did not know if he were alive or dead, or if he had communicated anything about her. Perhaps the man was still unconscious. Perhaps he had awoken only a short time ago. At any moment, Nemesai soldiers could come bursting into the Sondal home to capture her or kill her on the spot. This thought had been recurring over and over throughout the night, and every distant sound she had heard from the world outside her room had filled her with silent terror.

"Huh-h-h-h," Iona yawned as she sat up and stretched her arms. She was wearing the same tattered, over-sized tunic she wore most nights, and her wild brown hair was a mess all about her shoulders. When the young girl finished stretching, she turned her head and looked at Livia, muttering in a tired voice: "Good morning. Why are you up already?" She blinked a few times, and then her eyes focused, and she peered closer at Livia. "Hey!" she said, her eyebrows rising in an expression of surprise and worry, "are you alright?"

Livia swallowed, wincing slightly under Iona's gaze. She felt horribly tired. Her eyes hurt, and her skin was covered in oily sweat from hours upon hours of terror-induced alertness. Iona could detect the stress, and concern flashed in her kind, loving eyes.

"Did you not sleep?" Iona said.

Livia breathed very slowly as she met her surrogate sister's gaze. She had considered telling Iona the truth for a brief moment the night before, but that would put the sweet girl in even more danger than Livia had already done. Instead, she reached for her paper and charcoal pencil, which were on the small table between the two heads of their beds, and wrote with a creaking hand:

I have a terrible headache.

"Oh, I'm sorry," Iona said when she read the words. She reached out to touch Livia's head, but Livia could not quite help flinching sharply away from the sudden movement. This, of course, drew more concern from Iona. "Did something happen last night? I was worried about you when you stayed late at the shop."

Livia forced a smile and shook her head, clenching her toes within her socks as she did. Lying to Iona of all people felt terrible, but it was a lie of protection. She held up the paper with the sentence she had just written and tapped at it, emphasizing that a headache was all that was wrong.

Iona's dark eyebrows knitted together in consternation. "Did you even eat the pheasant I left out for you?" Livia managed another smile and a nod, though this was also a lie. Eating had been the last thing on her mind. She had stayed for hours in Hervin's shop under the pretense of doing a careful audit of the books, which she sometimes undertook. Livia had sat alone at the desk, debating taking the money the mysterious Lady Gretis had given her and attempting to flee the city. She had ultimately concluded that leaving immediately after the attack would draw heavy suspicion from the Nemesai Order, and a mute girl with a slave tattoo would be an incredibly easy thing to find in any of the cities to which she might run. She had no confidence in her ability to survive if she tried to vanish into the untamed forests of the empire either. Being alone in the wild would mean being defenseless against the crude sort of men who leered at her every time she stepped out into the streets.

After several nervous hours, Livia had also realized that the sorcerer might not wake up, which meant running away could cast suspicion on her where none would have otherwise arisen. That logic seemed incredibly flawed now. If naïve little Iona could see how flustered and disheveled she was, what chance did she stand?

"I... I'll make breakfast," Iona said. "I'll fetch you some water first though."

Livia ached with thirst. The city's aqueduct would have cool, crisp water this early in the morning. Perhaps because she could not think though, she shook her head and gestured to the kitchen, indicating that Iona should instead begin the day's cooking.

"Maybe a little later," her sister said. The young girl turned to the shelves where she kept her work clothing and quickly changed into her rough spun dress and apron and disappeared into the kitchen.

Livia gripped the sheets under her hands. *What was she going to do?* Was she putting the family in danger simply by being among them? These panicked thoughts ran uncontrolled as she heard Hervin thump out of his bedroom. Through her thin door, Livia listened to him speak to Iona in his kind, fatherly voice: "Good morning, my dear."

The Nemesai sometimes held masters responsible for the actions of their slaves! Livia's eyes moistened. With the right pretext, the holy men could force Hervin to confess to following the heretical ideals of Cassian Asango. Then they could confiscate his business and all of his savings and property, *including Iona*. The entire family could be doomed because of Livia's foolishness. She could not allow that to happen.

Stiffening, Livia picked up her paper and pencil from their resting place on her small table. There was only one thing to be done. With a shaking hand, she wrote

My Confession:

I, the slave named Livia, confess to conspiring against the church. I did this in secret, without the knowledge of my master or my slave sister, Iona. My master trusted me and gave me a great deal of freedom, and I used this to my advantage. I hid literature from him that denounced the authority of the Nemesai. No one influenced me to do this. I wanted a life where I was not a slave, and so I turned to the teachings of Cassian Asango. To this end, I attacked a member of the Nemesai order.

I am guilty, and I make no excuses. Please have mercy on me. I offer to serve the church for the rest of my life as penance.

--Livia Sondal

She swallowed, gazing at the paper. It would be her damnation if she ended up using it, but it might save everyone else. There came an odd sensation of calm at having written it. She could at least exercise *some* control over the situation, however small and pitiful it was.

Livia moved to the shelves and threw on a dress and then folded up her confession and slipped it neatly into her pocket. Her hand had just fallen on the bit of rope that served as the handle to her door when she heard a sharp knock come from the front of the house.

If Livia had a voice, she would have screamed. Instead, she took in a shrill breath and flattened against her wall, feeling a sickly tingle in her face as her blood drained away from it. In this stupor, she gazed around her small room, searching for a hiding place or a route of escape even though she knew none existed. Through the walls, Hervin's voice reverberated: "Yes? Who's there?" Livia began to breathe very fast. She was shaking so hard that she had to lean against the wall to keep from falling.

"Good morning, Hervin!" a voice Livia recognized said. It was Pontis, one of the city's shipmasters with whom Hervin had done a great deal of business over the years. As she heard his voice, she let out a deep sigh and stumbled over to her bed. Her head was spinning.

"What a nice surprise," Hervin's voice boomed with its usual friendliness. "What are you doing here? May I offer you breakfast?"

"Oh, I thank you, but no," Pontis said. "I did not come here to eat." There was a brief pause, and then the man said in a more serious voice: "From the look on your face, I don't think you've heard yet. There has been a bit of trouble."

"Oh?"

"Yes. The whole town is abuzz about it." There was a shuffling of feet and then a creaking which told Livia that the guest had taken a seat at the family table. "Last night, old Macgovin found an unconscious man behind his inn." At these words, Livia's fear renewed itself.

"Was he beaten or merely drunk?" Hervin said.

"Neither, it seems, but let me get to that. Macgovin tried to examine the man to see who he was. It turns out, he was a Nemesai – one of their high inquisitors no less from the markings on his armor."

"Good gods!" Hervin exclaimed.

"Indeed. Macgovin and a few of his servants brought the man to the Vestilite temple for healing. The priestesses worked over him for a long time, but they couldn't wake him up. It was very strange—at first, they thought it might have been some kind of poison. Whatever it was, he just lay there twitching. In the end, they suspected some kind of *dark magic*."

"Good gods!" Hervin said again.

"Yes-s-s," Pontis said.

"Hervin, who are you speaking with?" Lady Sondal's voice bellowed.

"Pontis is here. He's been telling me about a bit of trouble in the town."

"Trouble? What trouble?" There was a patting of heavy, naked feet on the floor. The cow was an especially clumsy creature in the morning. She bounded out and exclaimed: "Did something happen in the town?" The woman was always hungry for gossip. She had probably stumbled out in her nightgown.

"Oh, my lady, good morning," Pontis said.

"Good morning," she grunted. "What's going on in the town?"

Pontis retold the brief story nearly word for word as he had to Hervin, pausing at the appropriate places for dramatic effect. He was something of a gossip as well. This grated against Livia's mind. She was desperate to know if the tale went any further. Her very life depended on the fate of the Nemesai.

"Anyhow, the Vestilites eventually called in Septimius," Pontis finally added, and Livia tensed. Septimius was the city's new resident sorcerer, having assumed the informal position after Dathrose, the former arcane practitioner, had had his difficulties with the Nemesai on a day that had been burned into Livia's memory. She knew little of Septimius, but sorcerers could heal with magic, and that meant the Nemesai might already be back on his feet.

"Was Septimius able to help the poor man?" said Lady Sondal.

"Well, he managed to wake him up." Livia's heart thundered in her chest once more. "They got him talking, but...well...he couldn't remember anything—I mean *anything.* The poor soul didn't know his own name. From what I hear, he seemed more like a child than a man. He didn't understand he was a Nemesai, and barely seems to comprehend the world around him."

"What could do such a thing to a man?" Hervin exclaimed.

"What *indeed!*" Pontis said, his tone rising. "That's where things get interesting. The Nemesai was a sorcerer. Near as Septimius could tell, his mind had been ripped apart, memories and all. It isn't easy to do that to a sorcerer, let alone an elder one. Septimius thinks it must have been some kind of curse—a curse on a level he couldn't begin to perform."

Livia blinked. Her mind shifted from fear of punishment to the moment the Nemesai man had begun to burrow into her consciousness. She had felt something within her attack him. She had thought at the time she was doing it herself, but...*could it have been dark magic?* Livia had never known why she could not speak—why it caused her enormous pain to even try.

Could there be a living curse inside of her that was powerful enough to shatter the mind of a trained sorcerer?

"It must have been one of the followers of that wretched little Cassian Asango," the cow spat. Then she added in a suddenly frightened voice: "Or maybe the young devil himself! Could he be here? In our very city?"

"Not likely," said Pontis. "I had some sailors in from his port only last week. They told me Asango had been summoned North by General Romulus. He's at the other end of the empire."

"Well, one of his followers then," the cow said decisively. "Who else would dare to attack a Nemesai?"

Hervin sighed. "That would mean that the *Cassianites* have highly adept sorcerers in their ranks. Can you imagine?"

"That Asango boy is a *demon*!" the cow said, and Livia heard what sounded like a hand slapping down on the table. "When the Nemesai came for his parents, they should have killed him as well. Think of how dangerous he is now. He has a *dragon* at his command! Oh! Goodness! I need to calm down. Iona, fetch me a bit of wine."

"Yes, my lady," Iona said in her usual obedient voice.

"Anyhow," Pontis said, clearing his throat, "the reason I came here to tell you all of this is because you need to be ready. The Nemesai are going to want to know what happened to their sorcerer. There will likely be a great many *questions* asked, and the Nemesai are...*the Nemesai*."

"Well, I don't have anything to hide," Hervin said, though Livia heard the nerves in his voice. "I didn't even know the order had men in the city this time of year."

"Who truly knows how they operate?" Pontis grunted.

Livia felt a little wave of relief wash over her. If the man had not been found until evening, then it was unlikely that he had been working with partners. This meant she was *possibly* safe, at least in the short term.

"The Nemesai will catch whoever did this," the cow said. "All we can do is try to help the poor man." She raised her voice and said: "Iona, you will bake him a pie." There was a pause, and then she added: "And I think we should send Livia to the Vestilite temple. Perhaps the man is in need of stitches."

"If he were in need, they would have come and woken her," Hervin said. "I prefer to have Livia with me in the shop today, especially if there is a rogue sorcerer or two running around."

Livia's thoughts began to spin once more. There would be an investigation soon, *if one had not already started*. The Nemesai would almost certainly look into who was staying at the Rabbit's Foot Inn. Dalvin and Hoss would need to flee before that happened. She had to get word to them. There was also the matter of her having been seen entering the inn, but the innkeeper had not known her by sight, and he had remarked that many people had come and gone that day. For all she knew, a dozen or more people had come to read Asango's pamphlets after she had left, and the innkeeper had not seemed to see well either. If Dalvin and Hoss made it out of the city, Livia might never be connected to the crime—*unless the sorcerer regained his memory*... She shook her head, forcing down the fearful notion. Her confession was ready if that happened. For the moment, it was time to move past her fear and take what actions she could.

"Well, I must be going," Pontis said. Livia heard the sound of a chair being pushed back.

"I thank you for coming to tell me all of this," Hervin said.

"Yes, thank you very much," said the cow.

"I will see you later today, Hervin," Pontis said, and then the door closed.

"My goodness," the cow said. "To think, something like *that* happening in our city." There almost seemed a touch of glee in her dramatically frightened tone.

Livia breathed slowly, running through her decisions one more time in her mind. She could find Dalvin easily. He slumped around town every day. She could give him some of the money she had stashed away. Convincing him to flee might be difficult, but she could do it, and a significant portion of her problem could be solved by afternoon if all went well.

Amidst this plan, Livia could not help thinking of the matter of the "curse." *Was she really the victim of dark magic?* Why would anyone bother with a slave? This led once more to the long unanswered question of who her parents were. Hervin had bought her when she was four from a passing slaver who apparently had not offered any information about her past other than that he had picked her up from a caravan a few days before. Livia had no memory of that time at all or anything before it. For years, she had suspected that her parents were more than slaves. Livia knew she was smarter than any slave she had ever met. She had learned to read at the age of four with scarcely a shred of instruction, and by the time she was seven, she could do complex calculations in her head faster than Hervin could write them out. *More than any that though, there had been that strange moment years ago when she had seen visions of Cassian Asango...*

None of it had ever made sense. Livia was crippled in a different way than any human she had ever heard or read about. Could it all be the result of dark magic? Had some cruel sorcerer done this to her—stolen her life and her voice? This was a very old wound she had done her best to forget about, but this new evidence was ripping it wide open. *Who was she?* The most infuriating thought was that she might never know.

"Livia?" Iona said as she pushed the door open. She had a bowl of broth no doubt from the pheasant bones she had left simmering overnight with savory herbs and vegetables. It smelled wonderful. "Please eat. I'm worried about you."

Livia blinked at her kind-hearted little sister and then nodded. She walked over and took the warm bowl in her hands and gave a smile of thanks.

"Did you hear everything Pontis was talking about?" Iona said.

Livia nodded as she sat down on the bed and sipped a bit of soup from the poorly carved wooden spoon in her hand.

Iona's lips curled back, revealing her teeth as she muttered: "It's really scary."

Livia gave a silent laugh through her nostrils. Iona had no idea just how frightening the last few moments had been. The soup settled some of the churning in her stomach. Soon, she would need the strength it would give her.

"Should I tell Hervin you're too sick to come to work today?"

Livia shook her head sharply. Things needed to be done. No one would protect her but herself. That was the ultimate truth of her life.

CHAPTER 7: TROUBLE AT THE TAVERN

Kota leaned back against the curve in the thick branch behind him, enjoying the gentle summer breeze on his skin. He was in his favorite tree, relaxing and letting his legs dangle down. Gretis had worked him half to death in the morning, but this was his own time. He had a borrowed book from the Onkai library, an autobiography of the founder of the Onkai order, Dracus Mobius. Kota loved stories of the Starborn. They reminded him of Cassian and his great adventure years ago.

Distantly, he heard footsteps on the drying grass behind him. They were far too heavy to belong to Gretis. He cocked his head a little, not taking his eyes from the book. The visitor made a soft grunt as he walked, and Kota instantly registered the voice.

"You're back early," Kota said, finishing the paragraph he was reading.

"Should'a known you'd be in a damned tree," Glavius said.

Kota sighed and rested his leather-bound book in a split between branches and then turned and dropped backward out of the tree. He arched his back as he fell, flipping his body so that he landed in a smooth crouch on the grass beneath him. Then he spun around, expecting a quip from his friend, but was surprised to see a dark, troubled look on Glavius's tattooed face.

"What's wrong?" Kota said.

Glavius drew in a breath and said in a low voice: "I—I'm going to the tavern. Are you free?" Kota had never seen the cocky young man look so upset.

"O-of course," Kota said.

He turned toward Gretis's home. She had been inside all morning, but when he walked up, her voice came through the window before he could even ask: "You may go out for two hours with Glavius."

"Thank you!" Kota shouted. Gretis often let him break from his training to spend time with Glavius and other young Onkai. She seemed to place a great deal of importance on his friendships. He opened the door and snatched up his white tunic, which he slipped over his chest as he turned back to his comrade.

"Otho should be back by tonight," Glavius said as they started walking down the familiar path. "I wanted to beat him here so I could see how Darius is running the temple." He still sounded troubled but seemed to want to make small talk for the moment.

"And how is it?" Kota said.

Glavius shrugged. "From what I can tell so far, I'd say a bit more organized. Darius might be just a tad cleverer than Otho in certain areas. It'll be interesting to see what happens when he becomes bishop."

"It isn't certain that he will," Kota said, thinking back to the conversation he and Darius had had a few months ago.

"No one turns *that* job down," Glavius said. "It's an enormous honor. Even Starborn have given decades of their life to it. Besides, Darius is the best man for the job, and he knows it. He'll rise up and do his duty in the end." Glavius seemed to force a grin as he added: "And when he does, he'll promote me to legate, and I'll be put in charge of the southern temple, and you can come use that nose of yours to help me track demons."

"I think I could go along with that," Kota said. He found the prospect of a partnership with his best friend to be quite exciting.

They came to the town, which was bustling about as it usually did in the middle of the day. Together, they walked through the crowd and arrived at the Bear's Claw Tavern.

"You're damn well going to have a drink with me this time," Glavius grunted as they passed in through the swinging wooden doors.

"Gretis would knock the hell out of both of us."

"Yeah, she probably would, which makes it a little more exciting, doesn't it?" He walked up to the edge of the bar between two patrons and said: "Two mugs of the strongest stuff you got."

"Yes, sir," the tall, thin man behind the counter said.

"I really can't," Kota said.

"Eh, if you *really can't* then I'll just suck them both down, but why don't you just sit down and smell it for a few minutes and see if you're tempted."

Kota rolled his eyes as they walked over to an empty table near the entryway. He and Glavius took seats across from one another, and his friend leaned back in his chair and glanced around the large room. "Not too many stares in our direction. Down south people gawk at you if you're covered in runes, but up here, there's nothing remarkable about an Onkai and a shamalak having a drink together."

"I'm not having a drink," Kota reminded him.

The bartender brought two large, frothy mugs to them, and nearly as soon as Glavius's touched the table he snatched it up and began to gulp down the foul smelling brew. "Gods but I've missed this ale!" he said after a full swig. He took several more aggressive guzzles, and after a moment or so his body seemed to slacken a bit. When he was near to finishing the first mug, he let out a sigh and muttered: "One of my men lost his sword arm in a battle." Kota looked sharply into his friend's eyes, shocked by the abrupt statement. Glavius started on the second ale and went on, his eyes narrow, "Kobold took it right off in a surprise attack. Poor kid dropped to the ground screaming, blood spurting everywhere. Patroclus was his name. He was only seventeen." Glavius took down several hard gulps, and as he did his eyes glistened and grew a little redder. "Have you ever seen a kobold?"

"No," Kota said.

"They aren't servants of Daibok. Just kind of tribal demons I suppose... no wings... but they're fast as all hell. If I'd been any slower, Patroclus's head would have been taken off."

"But he's alive?" Kota said.

"Yeah," Glavius murmured, his expression grim and downcast. "The rest of us managed to kill the monster, and we tied off Patroclus's...*stump* and carried him back to the temple. He's alive, but he's *done* as an Onkai. I mean... he could have stayed if he wanted to and been assigned to some kind of...*administrative* work, but he didn't. Young Patroclus retired. It was his first mission!" Glavius blinked at the table. "At least he'll be comfortable. The order gives a healthy stipend to soldiers who get crippled in the field. Maybe he'll find a nice, pretty girl and..." Glavius wrapped his fingers softly on wood. "I keep asking myself if I should have had the men in a tighter formation. I didn't think there was any danger yet. None of us did. We were three Gods-damned minutes into the patrol. That's a kobold for you though. They're tricky." Glavius took another slow drink from his mug and whispered: "I keep seeing that bloody stump every time I close my eyes."

"I'm sorry," Kota whispered, not knowing what else to say.

"It's alright," Glavius said, sitting up straighter in his chair, a twitching smile playing across his face. "That's the nature of the job. It's the bravest, noblest work in the world! Still," he raised his eyes to Kota's, "we could damn well have used someone with ears like yours, and a nose that could pick up demon stench." He breathed in slowly, then said: "If I'm ever bishop, I'll bring in shamalaks. We need your people. I mean, it's not like we can use dogs most of the time."

Kota stared at his friend's slightly glazed eyes. Some of the books in the Onkai archives told tales of the early days in the order when it had been commonplace to use trained dogs to track demons. The problem that had been quickly discovered was that many demonic creatures emitted a miasma that would turn most animals vicious in an instant. The order had stopped using hounds when one had unexpectedly turned and attacked a renowned captain in the midst of a fight. He had been entirely unprepared for this, and it had cost him his life and turned the tide of the battle against the soldiers.

"I am sure many of my people would happily volunteer to help the Onkai."

Glavius shrugged as he took a long sip, and when the mug came away, he grunted: "The hell with *helping*. I'd give them tattoos."

Kota's eyes widened. "That would be sacrilege."

Glavius rolled his eyes. "Nonsense! We're a military organization. I understand the reasons Bishop Dracus built the order under the church, but all this other foolishness..." His eyes locked on Kota's and he said: "You'd make a better Onkai than almost any soldier in the order," he smirked and said: "not *me* of course, but just about anyone else. Hell, you ripped a demon's eyes out when you were eleven. You think that kind of courage is easy to find in the human race?"

"But we are lower creatures," Kota said, more as a test to see what Glavius would say than anything else. He was incredibly intrigued by what his friend was saying.

"That's horse shit!" Glavius said, slamming his second emptied mug down. "The Norn's never called your kind *lower creatures.*" He gave a dramatic shrug. "Who did? I asked the archivist that question a year ago. You know what he told me? Near as he can tell, the term originates from a nine-hundred-year-old treaty with the elves, and it refers to your people and a couple of others being lower than *them,* not us." Glavius seemed as though he was about to say more when his eyes suddenly shifted up past Kota's shoulder and widened with sudden, deathly serious shock. "What the hell?" he exclaimed.

Kota whipped his head around and saw a very, very large Onkai standing in the doorway glaring directly at him—*only the man was not an Onkai.* His armor was different—more sharply angled with spikes sticking out from the shoulder plates—and he had the inverted spear-tip down the center of his forehead that Kota had seen in drawings in several tomes from the archive. *The man was a Nemesai!* At his presence, all conversation in the tavern ceased. Kota heard hearts begin to pound all around him, and he smelled the stink of fear.

"Shamalak," the huge man shouted in deep, almost guttural voice, his bearded face seeming to stretch unnaturally with the word, "you are under arrest!" The words struck Kota like a knife in the stomach.

"What?!" Glavius shouted. Kota heard the quick, sharp scrape of a chair behind him that told him his friend had leaped to his feet. "What the hell is this?"

The Nemesai's dark eyes shifted past Kota, and he snarled: "Do not even *think* of interfering, Onkai. We are taking this *creature* by order of Bishop Cromlic."

"Like hell!" Glavius shot back. He drew his sword from his scabbard.

The muscles on the sides of the Nemesai's jaw pulsed with fury. "I very *strongly* suggest you put that sword away, boy!"

"Don't call me boy, you gangling oaf!" Glavius snapped. "I've killed *demons*! When does an inquisitor face anything that can actually fight back," his voice took on a dangerously mocking edge as he added: "Other than Cassian Asango?"

Veins stood up around the Nemesai man's eyes as he shouted: "Come in!" Behind him, perhaps fifteen men who also bore the markings of his order dashed in through the doorway. They filed into two groups at their apparent leader's sides, and each one of them raised a crossbow and aimed it at Kota and Glavius. The tall man cast a vicious smirk and said: "Put your sword away right now and *apologize* for your disrespect, Onkai, and I *may* forgive your impudence."

Kota turned to Glavius, his heart beating faster and faster. To his surprise, Glavius gave a laugh: "You forget where you are, you dumb bastard? Maybe you noticed the enormous Gods-damned temple up the road that has *Hundreds* of my brothers just inside. You kill an Onkai and every one of you will be a corpse on the ground inside of half an hour*!*"

The Nemesai leader began to tremble with anger. "By holy law, you have no right to interfere with—"

"Interfere with *what*?" Glavius snapped. "Kota's a shamalak! Your order exists to punish *human* sinners."

"That is not for you to decide. We *are* taking him."

"Then you're going to have to kill me," Glavius said, his eyes narrowing.

"No!" Kota said, he held up his hand to Glavius, looking into his friend's eyes. He had not realized Glavius was so loyal to him. "I'll go with them."

"The hell with that!" Glavius snapped. His left hand whipped out and gripped Kota's wrist and yanked him around the chairs while, at the same time, Glavius's right foot kicked the table up onto its side with the top facing the enemy. Kota heard a slew of arrows strike the tabletop as he was pulled behind it. Glavius cried out: "I'll kill the first ten of you that try coming back here if any of you wants to find out how a *real* soldier fights!"

Kota heard the sound of crossbows being nervously reloaded, but no immediate flurry of footsteps toward them as he might have expected. Glavius let out a fierce laugh and pulled a curved white horn from his belt that he blew as hard as he could. An enormous burst of rumbling sound blared through the tavern.

"Hey, jackass!" Glavius shouted, a vicious smile on his face, "I just summoned my brothers. How about I give *you* the chance to put your sword away and apologize?" He started to peek up over the tabletop, but Kota grabbed him by his shirt and pulled him down.

"They reloaded their crossbows," Kota whispered.

Glavius shrugged and blew his horn again, and Kota had to cover his ears to mute the terrible sound. "Relax, little brother," Glavius said, though he was trembling just a little even as he smiled.

The tavern was incredibly quiet for a moment. Most of the townspeople inside, Kota noted, had taken refuge behind tables as Glavius had. The poor souls were utterly terrified. The Nemesai seemed to be locked in hesitation. If they were communicating at all with each other, it was with looks or hand signals. Kota would have heard the slightest whisper. After a moment of this strange, tense silence, he caught the sound of many boots pattering over the street outside at the speed with which Onkai moved.

"In here!" Glavius shouted. "In the tavern!"

The footfalls grew louder and louder and then suddenly Kota heard Darius's voice boom: "What's going on here?"

The Nemesai leader's voice answered with a deep growl: "You are Acting Bishop Darius? One of your *men* interfered with a legal arrest."

"Arrest of whom?"

"A shamalak all of you refer to as *Kota*!" The man spat the name with disgust.

"What?" Darius said in a sharp voice. There was a pause, and then Darius said aloud: "Kota, are you in here?"

Glavius and Kota rose together, and he saw Darius standing with a small army at his back at the tavern entrance.

"Sir," Glavius shouted, "these men fired arrows at me."

Darius glared at the Nemesai leader. He was more than a head shorter than the giant of a man, but he seemed the fiercer of the two. "What the HELL do you think you're doing, Inquisitor?"

"I...am acting on the orders of my bishop," the Nemesai answered. His voice was still sharp, but it was more subdued than it had been. He pointed to Kota and said: "This shamalak is under arrest for heretical practices."

"He isn't *human.* You cannot arrest him."

"I can, actually. There is precedent for this, and if you interfere with me in any way whatsoever on the matter, you will be breaking theocratic law proclaimed by the Norn herself, Arkioth Novolo."

'No trespass,' Kota translated the Dhavic words without even thinking about them. He had read a great deal about the

law of non-trespass. Each God or Goddess had a specific domain, and the orders of the church were empowered to act within that domain. By decree of the Norn centuries ago, no order could interfere with the religious acts of another. Kota stared at Darius as this realization washed over him. Under theocratic law, his friend could do nothing to protect him.

Darius glared at the man for a moment. As he did, Glavius shouted: "Sir, these *Imbeciles* fired on me!"

Darius hesitated, his gloved hand tightening around the hilt of the sword at his belt. "They were...*technically* within their rights, Glavius," he said, the words coming out in a tone of bitter hatred.

"Yes," the Nemesai leader said, his face relaxing into a smile. "Order your man to stand aside, *acting bishop.* That shamalak is under arrest."

Darius clenched his jaw in suppressed fury, and said through his teeth: "Glavius, stand down."

"Sir!" Glavius shouted, kicking the table in front of him. "We can't let them do this." Darius said nothing, and after a few nervous breaths Glavius shouted: "Sir, *please*!"

"Come over here, Glavius," Darius said in a voice that trembled with frustration.

Glavius let out an unintelligible grunt and marched over next to Darius. When he was there, he said in a low, desperate voice: "You're not really going to let them take Kota, are you?"

Darius gave no answer but stared up at the Nemesai leader and said: "That *shamalak* has been more or less adopted by a Sansrit Master. I should advise you that she will *take issue* with this—unless you are here to attempt to arrest her as well."

"We are aware of your Lady Gretis, and we are looking into *her* as well, but we are not moving to arrest her at this time."

Glavius gave a sharp laugh. "You're all dead men! Your nearest temple is what, four days from here? You'll never get that far with Kota once Gretis hears what you've done. I doubt any of you will last 'till sundown, you stupid—"

Darius silenced Glavius with a hand across his chest. Looking the Nemesai in the eyes, he said: "I cannot guarantee your safety if you take that boy." His eyes narrowed as he added: "And I am not obliged to provide you with any protection if you do."

"Hmm," the Nemesai grunted, the smile never leaving his face. Kota had the sense the man had been expecting this. "You *are* obliged to protect me if I claim sanctuary in your temple, and I *do*. My instructions are to conduct the shamalak's interrogation within the refuge of your walls."

Glavius hissed, and Darius stepped forward, glaring into the taller man's eyes with such intensity that the inquisitor edged back. "You think I'm going to let you torture someone within the Onkai Temple?"

"I do," the Nemesai said, staring coldly back. "You will protect me as I torture him and, if I find it prudent, as I *kill* him."

Glavius lunged at the Nemesai leader, who leaped away just as one of the Onkai soldiers caught the back of Glavius's collar. Two more took hold of his arms, and one grabbed him by the waist. Struggling against all of them with surprising force, he snarled: "I'll cut your head off!" He made several more desperate thrashes, his face red with rage.

"You will reprimand that man!" the Nemesai leader said in a furious voice.

"Glavius, you are fined half a dessek," Darius said in a terse voice. This drew smirks from several of the Onkai and a scowl from the Nemesai leader. Darrius narrowed his eyes at the towering man and said: "I imagine you and your men were *hiding* somewhere nearby, waiting for Kota to step away from Lady Gretis. Perhaps you have a spy or two in our town." Darius gave a sharp look around, and Kota gazed about himself. Most of the people in the tavern were still tentatively standing behind their hiding places.

"This is a plan to get at Gretis, sir," Glavius said, still in the grip of his brothers. "They were afraid to go after her directly, so they're laying a trap."

"No, they aren't trying to get at *her,*" Darius said, still staring into the Nemesai leader's eyes, "but she's part of the plan—her relationship to Kota and her influence on Otho. This is all a fairly *naked* play to strong-arm our bishop into changing his vote regarding the arrest of Cassian Asango."

The Nemesai leader blinked and then gave a gruff laugh. "My order would never resort to such coercion. However, out of respect, I will not begin the boy's interrogation until Bishop Otho has returned and I have spoken with him."

"How gracious," Darius said through gritted teeth. He turned to Kota, hesitating for a brief moment, and then saying: "I'm sorry, Kota, but you will need to go with these men *for now.*"

"Good that you see reason," the Nemesai said.

Darius turned back to the tall man and said: "You think you can bully the whole world, don't you? It isn't going to work."

"Thank you for your opinion, *acting bishop,*" the Nemesai said with a chuckle. He moved across the room to Kota and reached inside a large clinking pouch on his belt where he fished out a pair of shackles. "Hold out your wrists, *Kota.*"

Kota stared up into the man's dark, cruel eyes and slowly lifted his arms.

CHAPTER 8: DIMITRIS

If only I could have stopped the war between my brothers, history might have taken a different course. Cassian and Dimitris were alike in so many ways, both immensely strong, both focused, and both utterly implacable in the pursuit of the throne. They could have been the greatest of friends, but instead they were opposing forces whose collision was always destined to be terrible.

---Telemachus Vale,
Starborn of the nineteenth generation

Cassian gazed ahead at the vast expanse of tents and campfires in the grass-covered valley as his tired horse trotted into the war camp. The sun was just beginning to set, and he could smell meat roasting and stew boiling all around him. He made a rapid estimate based on the number of cots to a tent and the number of tents from front to back and left to right that roughly eleven thousand soldiers and staff were present. It was a sizable force for policing a border, but not sufficient to invade another nation or defend Denigoth from anything more significant than marauders. Still, the ocean of armed men dressed in fresh uniforms and outfitted with the latest in steel weaponry, shields, and armor, conveyed a degree of prestige and importance that he did not overlook.

Neither Cassian nor his tutor knew the reason he had been summoned over two hundred miles northeast save that the emperor had ordered it. The two of them had made the trip without an entourage, both preferring the simplicity of riding horses and living off the land and the supplies that could be bought every so often along the way. Titus, Cassian's ever-present reptilian companion, had shadowed them, staying hidden during the day while they forged ahead and then flew silently to their camp in the night. This was for the best. Travelling openly with a dragon would cause all kinds of attention, and for Cassian, the trip had been a chance to spend a few more days with his tutor and friend. He had the sense that, whatever the purpose of this strange summons, it would ultimately lead to him parting with the old man.

"Hell of a welcoming party," said Somar, gazing around the camp from atop his stallion.

As their mounts brought them nearer, Cassian's head began to throb. It was unnerving to be in such close proximity to so many minds at once. Errant thoughts and images began to flow into him, and he forced himself to shut them out. "This is no simple show," he said. "These men are assembled for a reason."

"Of course they are," muttered Somar with that wonderful knowing chuckle that Cassian knew he would miss. The old man had asked that they refrain from discussing anything about the reason for the summons until now, perhaps in preparation for one final test. "Tell me, boy, why are we here?"

Cassian felt the other minds fade away and was grateful to Somar for engaging him in deduction. "We are less than ten miles from Goderland, which we have of course heard rumors is being attacked by bandits."

"How brilliant you are to make that connection," said Somar with a nod that was playfully condescending. "Now, *without* telepathy, tell me what you see when you look at these men."

Cassian gazed at the soldiers, trying to perceive them all as his tutor would see them. His eyes swept around the enormous camp, stopping here and there on what seemed significant. "That soldier there is practicing his thrusts," said Cassian, gazing at a young man only a few dozen yards from them. "He is young. He looks both focused and quite nervous."

"And what does that tell you?" said Somar.

"He is likely mentally rehearsing for a battle he expects to wage in the near future," Cassian said.

"And what does that suggest about this army?"

"They are here on a mission—probably to engage the enemy marauders."

"What does the number of men here suggest about these '*marauders?'*"

Cassian chuckled, enjoying Somar's deductive game. He wondered if his mind would continue to work this way once the two of them were parted. "In all likelihood, they are a small army rather than a disorganized band of outlaws. There is little of value in this section of the empire—just farms and livestock—which suggests they are stealing food and taking slaves."

"Reasonable enough," Somar muttered. "And why might *you* be here?"

"I am to participate in the battle. This is probably a test. The Emperor wishes to see if I have the stomach for battle, or perhaps I am to be apprenticed to the general."

"You *are* twenty now."

"Yes, the age our own the emperor first took to the battlefield. I may be put in charge of a small force to gauge my capacity for command."

"This would not surprise me."

The two of them shifted their gaze to a young man in brilliantly polished armor walking briskly in their direction. As he came closer, Cassian noted the neatly trimmed beard, the oiled, tied back hair, and the effortlessly staunch pose that all suggested this person was of noble birth. Almost without thinking about it, Cassian reached into the young man's mind. Immediately, he sensed a wall much like Somar's, yet not nearly so strong. With a little effort, he could take things from the noble soldier's mind—possibly even without him noticing. Cassian noted this for later possible use.

"My name is Corporal Tabien Maloric," the soldier said, his voice half friendly, half stern. "May I know your names, gentlemen?"

"This is Cassian Asango," said Somar.

The corporal nodded, looking pleased. "We were not expecting you for at least another day."

"I go where my emperor directs me, and I do not tarry," said Cassian.

The corporal nodded. "Excellent answer!"

Cassian ignored the silly compliment and said: "Where is General Romulus?" The name had leaped into his mind a split second before he uttered it. It was a name and title rolling around the thoughts of soldiers all over the camp—their commanding officer. Cassian had heard of Romulus, and not always in positive tones. The man was said to be a brutal, ruthless commander.

With a smile, the corporal said: "He is in his tent speaking to the other Starborn."

"The other—" Cassian started to say, but then he froze. His senses leaped out at the speed of thought, and an impression came back like lightning, rippling through every corner of his mind. He felt the person upon whom he had spent the last six years of his life focusing, measuring, and playing a never-ending battle of mental war.

"This is not a simple matter of having me fight in the army," said Cassian, his voice reflecting the unexpected mortal seriousness of the moment. "*Dimitris is here.*"

"What?" said Somar. He gazed around, looking tense and confused.

Cassian felt his rival's mind focus suddenly on his. "He has just realized I am here." Something almost like fear passed through Cassian for an instant. Dimitris was and had long been the most significant threat to him and was perhaps the one human other than the Emperor that might be able to kill him in single combat. He mastered these feelings immediately. If this was to be a competition, he would be the victor. Cassian believed this in the pit of his heart.

<My brother is trying to read me.> he telepathically transmitted to the old man.

In a soft whisper, Somar said: "Can he?"

<I do not believe so.>

"Can you read him?"

<Just a little.> Cassian shut his eyes to close himself off from his human senses and focused through his psychic lens. <He is somewhat afraid, but also eager.>

"Good! You can use that."

The corporal stared at the two of them, not understanding the nature of the conversation they were having in the least. After a moment, he spoke up: "I am sure the general will speak to you shortly. May I show you to your tent? One of the highest quality has been constructed for you with several beds in it. We anticipated you might come with servants and—"

"My companion is not a *servant*," Cassian said, the words snapping out almost by reflex. "This is Somar Dojinko. I am sure you have heard the name." Cassian felt some sense of satisfaction as a wave of awe overcame the corporal's mind.

"My apologies, sir," the youth stuttered. "We would be honored to construct a tent for the legendary General Dojinko."

"Please do not go to any such trouble on my account," the old man said with a chuckle. "I am an officer no longer—I have not been for many years."

Cassian heard Dimitris's voice whisper in his mind suddenly: <My brother, I am sitting down with our host. I would be honored if you would come and join us. I think it is time we finally met in the flesh.>

He mused at the relaxed confidence Dimitris was exuding. The telepathic voice was smooth and polished. He did not seem to know that Cassian could sense his fear, or perhaps did but wanted to show how insignificant it was. <Yes, I think it is time,> Cassian answered.

He turned to Somar. "I have been invited to sit with our host and my rival. You are free to join." He suppressed a smile, knowing the old man would not be able to resist this first confrontation any more than he could.

"I believe I will," Somar said, and the old man's tired body seemed to take on new life. Their shared love of challenge would surely be what he missed most.

Looking confused, the corporal spoke up: "I would be happy to escort you—"

"We require no escort, young man," Somar said as he strained to lower himself from his stallion. After Cassian had dismounted as well, the old man gestured to their horses and said in an abruptly authoritative voice: "Please bring our luggage to our tent and see to our animals."

"Yes, sir!" the corporal said, his body whipping into a salute.

After the corporal disappeared, Cassian said: "Do you miss being in command?"

"I am very fortunate to have found other pursuits since leaving."

Cassian chuckled softly at this non-answer. "Yes, I think things may be about to grow... *exciting*."

"Stay alert."

"Always."

The two of them walked together through the camp, Cassian's eyes shifting to the soldiers here and there, studying their weapons and armor. Denigoth had been moving away in the last decade from inducted militia into a professional military. These men—many of them close to Cassian's age—were not farmers and laborers called away for a brief battle but had chosen soldiering as their careers. Memories flowed from them here and there, flashing images of combat training that began around the age of twelve or thirteen and went on for years.

Cassian and Somar eventually came to a tent the size of a large house in the middle of the camp, the entryway of which was made of exquisite draperies of deep red embroidered with gold thread. Ten soldiers stood at attention, with five on each side of the threshold. The one closest to Cassian said: "You are Lord Asango, are you not?"

"I am."

"General Romulus is expecting you." He gestured to the entryway.

Cassian nodded to the soldier and stepped between the two clusters of men, Somar following closely behind. He entered the tent and gazed around at the golden and marble statues that adorned the first room. The floor was made up of ornate rugs. There were tables with solid gold water urns, and even enormous paintings somehow carefully hung from the tent's intricately complex skeleton of wooden poles. They were only in the first room of a dividing path of doorways.

"Romulus enjoys his comforts," Somar said in a cautiously soft voice.

Cassian smiled. He knew from the way the old man lived that Somar had little desire for such opulence. This entryway was meant to convey power and prestige, but to Cassian, it felt...*vulgar.*

"Lord Asango," a deep voice boomed from a room to the right. "Please do come in."

Cassian walked over the carpeted floor and came into a second room where he saw a large man with a neatly trimmed beard of bronze and silver sitting in a carved wooden chair. Cassian's eyes lingered on the man only long enough to give him a respectful nod, and then they locked on his one great rival. Rising from his seat at the enormous table in the room's center, Dimitris flashed him a smile and extended a gloved hand.

Dimitris was taller than Cassian, with a stronger and more athletic build. He was remarkably handsome with his manly chin and symmetrical features, his oiled, wavy black hair, and his deep blue eyes. Cassian could not help thinking that his brother looked far more like a great ruler than he did.

"Greetings, Cassian," said Dimitris as they clasped hands. "It is so good to meet you after all these years."

Cassian smiled back. *It was good.* He had been waiting for this moment for quite a long time.

"This is General Romulus," Dimitris said with a graceful gesture toward the enormous man.

Romulus rose, his rugged face contorting into a smile with which his fierce brown eyes did not wholly align. He held out a thick arm with a golden bracer at the wrist and said: "I have long wanted to meet the boy who faced Promethiock. My men have spoken of you as a *legend* for years."

Cassian smiled and extended his hand. He still disliked flattery – especially when that flattery was insincere. Romulus did not particularly like him. The general was not quite so talented at blocking telepathy as Somar, nor was he as subtle or charming. He had risen as high as he had in the empire for very different reasons, Cassian suspected.

"This is my tutor, Somar Dojinko," said Cassian to both men.

Dimitris flashed another charming smile and took Somar's hand and said: "It is a great honor to finally meet *you*, sir."

"The honor is mine in every way," said Somar.

"Please let me shake your hand as well," Romulus said, reaching across the table to Somar. The two men gripped each other's wrists as two fellow generals.

"Pleased to meet you, Romulus," said Somar. "I have heard much about you."

Romulus held his smile for a moment longer and then made an arching gesture with his hand toward everyone in the room and said: "Shall we be seated?"

Cassian and Somar took up chairs next to Dimitris across from Romulus. Once they were all in their places, the general gazed at Cassian and said: "I am quite pleased that you arrived so quickly. I might enjoy entertaining a pair of Starborn in my camp under other circumstances, but I am afraid there is some degree of urgency to why you two have been summoned."

"Yes, why are we here?" Cassian said.

Romulus answered in a grim voice: "The emperor wishes to test the two of you in battle."

"Test us how?" Dimitris said. His voice was neutral and composed.

Romulus leaned forward in his chair and knitted the thick fingers of his hands together as he said: "A force has been raiding to the north of this position. I am to assign *one* of you to command this legion to eradicate the threat."

"*One of us,*" Cassian said, turning to Dimitris.

They stared at each other as Romulus said: "Whichever one of you produces the superior battle plan."

"What happens to the loser?" Cassian said.

"He will be under the command of the winner," Romulus answered.

Somar took in a deep, sharp breath through his nose. Cassian knew why. This was not a simple test of leadership. He and Dimitris were being maneuvered into direct conflict with one another. Before eleven thousand witnesses, one of them was about to be forced to accept the superiority of the other. In Denigoth's current military-minded societal state, this contest would confer enormous weight upon the balance scale between them over who was the superior contender for the throne.

With raw telepathic force, Cassian ripped abruptly through Dimitris's psychic defenses, causing his rival to widen his eyes and draw back in shock. He was able to catch just enough from his brother's mind before the mental walls redoubled to sense that this was not some clandestine plan Dimitris had known about, which could only mean the Emperor himself was behind the matter.

"You have two days to formulate sound, tactical plans," Romulus said, interrupting the silent psychic battle the two of them were waging. "You will both submit your proposals to me morning after next. I will then decide the winner by midday."

"Understood," Cassian said in a calm voice, but he did not understand at all. *Why were the two of them being pitted against each other so early and so directly?* He had assumed their competition would last years - even decades - and without any manipulation from the Emperor. They were both only twenty, and in the span of two days, one of them would receive a proclamation of inferiority to the other from the most decorated military officer in the empire.

"Good that you understand," Romulus said with a fair degree of smugness in his tone. "I would enjoy sharing mid-day meal with two Starborn, but if you wish time to formulate your plans, I understand entirely."

Again, Cassian gazed at Dimitris. The situation was not ideal, and yet they both faced the same circumstances. In the end, it had always been a contest between the two of them, and, whatever form that contest took, Cassian knew he had to rise to it.

"I believe I will begin now," he said, rising from his chair.

"I as well," said Dimitris, rising in turn.

"That is probably best for both of you," said Romulus. He turned to Somar and said: "You must not interact with your pupil during this trial."

"Is that right?" said Somar in a dry voice.

"You are a legendary tactician, sir, as many know. Your input would constitute an unfair advantage in a competition between two contenders for the throne." His bushy red eyebrows knitted together, and he said: "Such interference in a matter of state would constitute treason by my reasoning and would call for your execution."

Cassian's felt his blood turn to acid in his veins. Romulus was enjoying threatening his former fellow general. *The bastard was drunk with power!* Romulus started to add something, but Somar abruptly spoke up, saying: "I understand completely, General Romulus. Actually, I would very much enjoy taking lunch with you while the two Starborn go about their imperial business."

"Excellent," said Romulus with a satisfied grin that made every muscle in Cassian's body coil. Still, he knew better than to openly challenge a general of the Imperium over such a matter. The perfectly relaxed smile on Somar's face helped to calm him.

The general turned to Dimitris and said: "I have learned that you employ Sardonis Alexi as your military tutor. I require him to step away from this as well. Would you be so kind as to send him to me?"

"Of course," said Dimitris.

"Good, I dismiss you both," said Romulus, still sounding pompous.

Cassian and Dimitris left the tent together, walking side by side. When they had passed a few dozen steps beyond the ears of the guards, Dimitris said in a low tone: "You see what all of this is, I am sure."

"Of course, but I do not know why. The emperor cannot possibly be *sick.* He will not need an heir for many years to come."

"Perhaps the Senate is putting pressure on him to name a crown prince."

Cassian sighed. "Do you think anyone in this world could exert pressure on Tacitus?"

Dimitris chuckled softly. "No, I suppose not. We do not then get to know why we are pushed to each other's throats." His voice took on a dark edge laced with mirth as he added: "But we *are* at each other's throats."

"Yes," said Cassian.

Dimitris hesitated, then said: "We might step off this path before one of us dies." The implied threat barely disguised yet given with remarkably little hostility. They both stopped walking and turned to face each other. As the soldiers went about their business around the two of them, Dimitris said: "I know what you want, Cassian."

"Do you?" Cassian said. "I suspect your next words will closely resemble the dozen or so offers Telemachus has made on your behalf in the last few years.

Dimitris flashed him a brilliant smile. "Can you imagine what you and I could accomplish together?"

"With you as emperor? Yes. Not a great deal. Certainly nowhere near enough."

"I am willing to limit the powers of the Nemesai, Cassian—limit them to such a degree that nothing like what happened to your parents will *ever* happen again."

Cassian let a dark chuckle escape his throat. "Really? Is that what you told Bishop Cromlic when you accepted all the special tutors he provided you, or when he himself instructed you in all those terrible forbidden spells his order has kept secret from the world?" Dimitris started to respond, but Cassian interrupted him: "I would wager Cromlic has spent several *million* desseks preparing you to kill me, brother. Where do you suppose all that money came from? His men tore it away from poor families whom they *deemed* guilty of sin. You knew that, and you accepted all of his gifts, so do not stand there and smile at me and pretend you and I share the same ideals."

The muscles around Dimitris's eyes contracted and he closed his lips and said telepathically: <I understand that to change the world, I first need to deal with it as it *is*, Cassian. You seem to understand this as well. I did not see you refusing to work with General Romulus just now. He has killed *far* more innocent people in the last decade than the Nemesai Order in the entirety of their history.>

Cassian bristled. <Yes, he is a bloodthirsty beast who needs to be dealt with, but Denigoth ultimately requires a military to exist. It does *not* require hypocritical *holy men* who tear people out of their homes for daring to *think* about the world in terms other than their religion, or because a man feels attraction to other men, or for any of the other petty justifications they have to torture and murder and steal.>

<Yet your hands are not clean, my brother. That is my point. We both stand within moral shades of gray, and yet we both want to move toward the light.> Dimitris drew in a slow breath, keeping his eyes fixed on Cassian's. <You are the one I respect most in the world other than Tacitus himself. You are my brother. I would work with you over Bishop Cromlic in an instant, if you would only take my hand.>

Cassian stared at his brother for a long time. In his heart he had always longed for this friendship. He had never sought it though, and there was good reason. <You would not though—not truly.>

<I would!>

<If, as Emperor, you were to place severe limitations on the activities of the Nemesai, they would declare you an enemy of the church as they have done me. The Diaphan priests are Cromlic's pets, and he would coerce them to speak against you, perhaps even to call on their parishioners to rise up, and then you would be forced to either tolerate revolt or send in the military against men of the church.>

<We could deal with—>

Cassian interrupted his brother: <Aside from *that,* if you were to attempt to end slavery, the nobility would turn against your rule. They would never give up their *property* and the absurd wealth brought in every year by slave labor. You would face revolt in your outer territories first, and it would grow like a cancer through the empire. Eventually, you would have to choose between bending to the terms of your own lords or, again, sending your armies. I know you, Dimitris. You would not place Denigoth in such a state of civil war out of friendship to *me.*>

<You have followers all over the empire, Cassian. Our people are becoming more and more ready for change. We could work together to sway public opinion even further from the old institutions.>

<You think you can out manipulate the *church*?> Cassian smirked. <All they have to do is say the word '*hell*,' and half the empire falls to its knees and does whatever they command.>

"And what would *you* do?" Dimitris said, resuming speaking with his human voice. He suddenly looked tense and desperate.

<What would I *do*?> said Cassian. <It is what I *am.* I am not afraid to stand up to them—*truly stand up.* I will *execute* Nemesai who attempt to torture and kill my citizens, because they are nothing but murderers. I will grant freedom of religion and protect that right with military force. I will flood the empire with copies of my translation of the Enumis and institute public education programs so that people can read it for themselves and see the hypocritical nonsense that is carried out under so-called *theocratic law.* I will laugh when I am proclaimed a damned soul, because the condemnations of Bishop Cromlic do not frighten me in the slightest.>

Cassian took a slow breath, calming himself. <It is not merely that the church is wrong. They are only able to do what they do because the people are kept ignorant and powerless by a grotesquely wealthy and powerful few.> He lifted his hands and gestured around. <All of this is built on the backs of slaves—on a system where ninety-five percent of the wealth and land belongs to a tiny handful of noble families, most of whom care more about the tapestries in their homes than the people they rule. With eyes wide open to every consequence, I intend to destroy that social order because it utterly disgusts me, and I will dedicate my life to building something better. I will overcome *everything* that stands between me and my vision, and if you do not step down, I will start by defeating you, my brother.>

The two of them stared at one another in silence for a long moment, Dimitris's brilliant eyes gazing with anger and shock at Cassian's words. Finally, he said: <Very well, Cassian Asango. Let us see which of us is the better tactician.>

CHAPTER 9: FAMILY

Iona gazed at Livia's sullen face, watching the beautiful girl fold the house linens over the dinner table. Her sister's movements were sharp and jerking, as if she were silently expressing hatred for the task. As Iona tried for perhaps the hundredth time to guess at what was wrong, Livia's eyes shifted abruptly to her, and she quickly returned her attention to chopping carrots. Laundry day was usually Iona's favorite time of the week because she and Livia spent so much time together, but her sister had been in a strange, nervous state for almost a week. She knew Livia was not sleeping most nights. The normally confident girl jumped every time someone came to the door, and she was irritable all the time, which was causing the tension to rise between her and the mistress of the home.

"More wine, Iona," Lady Sondal said, holding up her goblet from across the room. She was lying atop the new cushioned sofa Hervin had bought. It was only mid-day, and the woman had already consumed an entire urn and was well into her second.

"Yes, my lady," Iona said, the words coming reflex. She picked up the clay vessel from the table and darted over to her mistress's cup and poured. When she finished, she swished the urn around and said: "This is all we have left in the house."

The lady rolled her eyes and said: "Send that wretched *mute* out to fetch some more from my *dear husband's* shop."

At these words, Iona heard a sharp intake of air behind her. She turned to see Livia clutching at the sheet in her hands, and she whispered: "I—I'll tell her, mistress."

"Bah!" Lady Sondal grunted after a long sip of wine. "She can *hear* just fine." The woman raised her voice and said: "Livia! Go! I order you!"

Livia's shoulders contracted, and she stood frozen for a brief moment and then threw her laundry down onto the table and turned toward the door in a brisk walk. It opened just before she got there, and Hervin stepped in.

"Hello, everyone," he said, wearing his usual friendly smile. He gazed at Livia for a moment, raising an eyebrow. "Are you heading out?"

Iona spoke for Livia, as she often did, "Lady Sondal sent her to fetch an urn of wine, Master."

He turned to his wife. "Are you out *already*?"

"Of course I am!" his wife snapped. "How else am I supposed to relax when the Nemesai still haven't caught the rogue sorcerer?"

Hervin fidgeted, a look of frustration playing across his round face. He took a breath and then said: "My dear, I think we need to have another talk about the *cost* of all this wine. I must remind you it isn't made locally. It has to be shipped or carted all the way from—"

"Do not speak to me of *cost*!" the woman said in a loud voice with a dismissive sweep of her hand. "You feed these two *slaves* meat nearly every night. If you want to save desseks, perhaps you should stop treating them like they're your daughters! I am your *wife*, and when my father bestowed his noble-born daughter on you, it was with the understanding that you would see to her comfort."

The muscles in Hervin's neck tensed, but he managed to say: "Yes-s-s, well, perhaps we shall speak of this another time." He turned to Livia, who had remained near the door in silence. "Why don't you come back with me after we have our meal?" He glanced at Iona and asked: "Will it be ready soon?"

"Yes, master," Iona said. "The bread is ready now if you like." She gestured to the loaf that was cooling on the small table in front of her.

"It looks delicious," Hervin said, flashing a kindly smile of crooked teeth that almost seemed to melt the tension in the room.

Lady Sondal glared at Livia and said: "I don't want that ungrateful mute to have any. She's been a sullen little badger all morning. I think she should go hungry for a few days. That will perhaps teach her to appreciate what we give her."

Livia did not look up, but her smooth skin went a touch redder. She stood still, staring down at the floor, her shoulders rising and falling in a slow rhythm of barely controlled anger. The look in her eyes frightened Iona.

"Come now, my dear," Hervin said with a nervous laugh. "Livia works very hard. She needs to eat to help me at the shop and do everything else she does." He turned to Iona and said: "Set a nice plate for Livia please, dear."

"I said *NO*!" Lady Sondal bellowed in a deep-throated shout. "And I have changed my mind. Iona will go and fetch the wine." She eyed Livia with narrowed eyes and said: "I know if I let this little wretch out of my sight you will find a way to feed her, Hervin." The woman's pouty lips curled into a sneer as she added: "It is *my will* that she learn her *lesson*."

Livia continued to glare at the floor, the anger in her eyes growing more and more intense. Iona began to breathe very quickly. She could feel that something terrible was unfolding.

"Enough of this," said Hervin, his voice unusually assertive. He looked at Livia and said: "Go to the shop, take a handful of coppers and eat whatever you wish."

"NO, she will NOT!" Lady Sondal shouted. She rose abruptly from the sofa, spilling wine onto her robes and the floor. In a huff, she marched over to Hervin and said in a ferocious voice: "I have tolerated *enough* of your indulgence of that skinny little cripple!" She leaned in closer to his face, and he drew back a little. "Two slaves ran away this week from the Prethian estate! That has filled this little fool with ridiculous notions." Lady Sondal gestured to the table where a stack of folded linens rested. "Just look at her shoddy work! She thinks she is too *good* to fold our sheets! I can see it in her dull little *slave eyes."*

Livia's fists were clenched so hard the knuckles were turning white. Iona darted between her and the woman of the house and said: "I'll b-be happy to fetch your wine. Why d-don't you rest, and I'll make you some nice marzipa—"

"Don't try to interfere with this!" Lady Sondal hissed down as the back of her hand slammed into Iona's face. Pain whipped through her cheek, and there was a brief instant of blackness in her vision before she stumbled to the floor.

"Oh! You wretched BEAST!" Hervin shouted, glaring at his wife. Both Iona and Livia turned to look at him in complete shock. "Gods! What the hell did I do to deserve such a Spoiled, Vicious..." He stumbled on his words, the fury beginning to melt from his face. Hervin's mouth trembled for a moment, and then he said in a quieter voice: "I think this afternoon has gotten quite out of hand. Perhaps we should all just—"

"Did you call me a *beast*?" Lady Sondal said, speaking each word slowly. Her eyes were as wide with rage as Livia's had been, but they were far more terrifying. "You dirty little peasant. You call *me* a beast?"

Iona watched Hervin's face turn several shades paler. "My dear—"

"You—you pathetic little man!" the woman hissed. She leaned into him, and his eyes widened. "You spineless little ass. What did *you* do to deserve *me*? My grandfather was a senator!" She leaned in even closer, and Hervin took a step back. His wife made a sweeping gesture at Livia and Iona and said: "You think these slave girls are your daughters because your blood is as low and dirty as theirs."

"You...you need to calm down," Hervin said.

"Hah!" Lady Sondal cackled. "You think I'm going to listen to you after what you *Dared to* say to me?" The woman was taller and bulkier than he was, and that fact had never been more apparent. "Do *I* disgust *you*, peasant?" She raised her arm in the air, her palm open in an obvious threat to smack him.

"Tell me, you sniveling, lowborn creature. Tell me your *opinion,* you son of a *merchant*! You weak, ugly, pathetic little—"

Livia's fist struck Lady Sondal's nose out of nowhere, hitting hard enough to knock her head back. The woman's enormous form stumbled, and she had to jerk her leg back to catch herself. With a shriek, she raised her hands to her face. When they came back, they were dripping with blood.

Livia was glaring at her. Her lips were curled up, revealing her perfect white teeth as a hiss escaped through them.

"You little *bitch!*" Lady Sondal whispered, looking back and forth between Livia and the blood on her hands in an expression of disbelief. For a long moment, she stared at the blood in silence. Then her mouth slowly began to curl into a cruel smile. "*You little bitch,*" she repeated. "Do you know the penalty for a slave striking her owner?"

Livia drew in a sharp breath. Her eyes widened, and her beautiful face shifted suddenly into one of horror. She took a step backward and began to tremble.

"They're going to *kill* you!" Lady Sondal said, and her grin broadened. She turned toward the door and yanked it open and shouted: "GUARD! I NEED A GUARD! MY SLAVE HAS ATTACKED ME!" She went bounding out of the house, continuing to shout.

Livia put her hands to her mouth. Her skin had become a sickly pale. Tears began to roll down her face, and she hunched forward into a silent sob. Iona had never imagined her sister could look so frightened.

Hervin put his hand on Livia's shoulder and exhaled: "Don't worry! N-no one is going to kill you!" He fidgeted for a moment and said in a nervous voice: "W-wait here!" He turned and dashed into his room in the back of the house, and Iona heard a fierce rummaging from within.

Livia began to pace back and forth, more tears rolling out of her eyes. Iona rose and moved to her. The only thing she could think to do was throw her arms around her sister. She hugged Livia tightly, and after a few seconds, Livia hugged her in return, sniffling.

"SHE'S IN HERE!" Lady Sondal shouted. Two men in bronze helmets and breastplates with short swords at their waists marched into the room. At their arrival, Livia jerked away from Iona and flattened herself against the wall. She looked utterly terrified.

"Did you strike your owner, slave?" the closer of the two guards said in a sharp voice. He was a large man with a thick beard and gray eyes that threatened violence.

"Livia is not a slave!" Hervin shouted. He came running out of his room with a sheet of parchment in his hand. The little man moved between the men and Livia and repeated: "She is not a slave."

"WHAT?!" Lady Sondal shouted. She stomped past the soldiers. "She is most CERTAINLY a slave!"

"No, she is NOT!" Hervin shouted. He shook the parchment in his hand and said: "I freed her two weeks after I bought her and adopted her as my daughter." He shoved the parchment into the guard's hand and said: "You can clearly see the censor's insignia. This was done legally. I have several witnesses." He blinked then. Everyone in the room was staring at him in shock. He turned to Livia, his eyes wide with remorse as he said: "I—I'm so sorry. I should have told you—I was just so afraid of..." he cast a nervous glance back at his wife, "but I... I don't care anymore!" He turned to Iona and said: "I did it for you as well. Neither of you are slaves."

Lady Sondal bellowed: "You—I don't believe this—you *ADOPTED*—" she put her head between her hands and began to hiss through her nose.

Livia moved over to Hervin, still trembling and looking uncertain. He swallowed nervously and said: "I should have told you. I'm such a coward, but..." his eyes welled up, "I've *never* thought of you as a slave—you had to know that."

A pair of tears dripped from Livia's eyes. She drew in a deep breath and then moved to Hervin and pressed her face into his shoulder and slowly curled her arms around his neck. She made almost no sound, but Iona could tell she was crying from the way her shoulders bounced up and down.

The guard blinked several times at this display, and, though he looked very confused, he seemed to have been touched. After a few heartbeats, he rolled Hervin's parchment up and muttered: "Well, you should really get freedman tattoos for these girls. If you hadn't been here to show me this paper, we would have had to..." He swallowed, gazing at the still sobbing Livia, and then handed the parchment back. "I suggest you see to it immediately."

"Yes, I will," Hervin said with a nod.

Lady Sondal made a strange guttural sound from behind her hands.

The guard sighed, gazing around the room at everyone present. He drew in a breath and then exhaled: "Since this girl is your legal daughter, this is a *family matter*." He turned to leave.

Lady Sondal reached out and gripped the guard by the arm. "The girl struck me!" she snapped, pointing at Livia with her other hand. "That lowborn little piece of trash struck *ME!*"

The soldier gazed down at the hand on his arm in irritation and said: "Then her *father* can punish her as he sees fit." He reached up and brushed her hand away and added: "It's really none of our business." With that, the man turned and walked with the other guard out of the house.

After they left, Lady Sondal threw her hands up in the air and shouted: "I cannot BELIEVE you!" She glared at Livia, who continued to sob on Hervin's shoulder. "You think I will stand for this?! Do you think I will share my home with a former *slave*—call her my *daughter?!*"

Livia lifted her head slowly from Hervin's shoulder and turned to face the lady. There was no longer any fear in her eyes at all. Her mouth held the faintest trace of a smile.

Lady Sondal gritted her teeth. "Look at *you,* you filthy little tart! I bet you're already making plans. Now you have the freedom to flaunt your lowborn prettiness about town. Why don't you go run along and do the only thing you were ever meant to do? I wager you could be the richest whore in the city until your looks disappear in a few years."

To Iona's surprise, Livia's smile only broadened, and she laughed silently.

This enraged Lady Sondal. Her eyes shifted to Hervin, and she said: "I want this little slut out of my house! NOW!" Hervin drew in a breath, looking very uneasy. Lady Sondal took a step toward him and hissed: "Throw her OUT! I demand it!"

"I..." Hervin muttered. He moved his hand to Livia's shoulder and said: "She's my daughter." Livia's mouth trembled, and a fresh set of tears leaked down her cheeks.

"Your *daughter*?" Lady Sondal whispered. She gritted her teeth and said: "Are you *actually* choosing that little slave over *me*—your *noble born* wife?! You—you would not *dare!* Tell me it is not true. Tell me you have not lost your *mind*!"

Hervin stuttered: "I...I..." he gazed into the eyes of his wife and then looked down and whispered: "I cannot do what you ask."

Lady Sondal's thick hands clenched into fists. "You *will* throw her out, or I will *leave you*!"

Hervin continued to gaze at the floor. Livia, however, met Lady Sondal's glare with still dripping eyes and pointed sharply to the door with a hateful smile.

The enormous woman looked at her and then at Hervin. She began to breathe very hard and snarled: "I mean it! I will leave! I will go back to my father's estate!"

Livia pulled a piece of paper from her pocket and set it down on the table near her and began to write as still more tears flowed from her eyes. When she finished, she turned to Iona and held up the message. It read:

Tell this disgusting cow I will pack her
bags for her as a final service.

Iona's mind was still spinning with what had just happened. When she saw the words, all she could mutter was: "L-Livia offers to pack your b-bags."

Lady Sondal's face turned a frightening red, and she exhaled the words: "She... she *offers*..."

Livia spun with a smirk and walked to the linen closet and drew out a large rough spun sack and then whisked into Lady Sondal's room. The sound of drawers being opened echoed through the house.

"D-Don't you touch my things!" the woman of the house snarled. She ran to the broom closet and snatched out the wicker rug-beater she had used many, many times over the years to punish Livia and marched toward the doorway, grunting: "You little bitch! I'm going to—"

Livia shot out of the room, her hands going to the rug beater. She and Lady Sondal engaged in an extremely brief struggling match that resulted in Livia yanking the thing away. The large woman staggered back, huffing. Livia glared at her, gazed down at the rug beater, and then gazed back, her eyes narrowing.

Lady Sondal grunted: "Don't you DARE! Don't you even THINK about it, you little piece of trash!"

Livia raised the rug beater over her head and ran at her former owner.

"OHHHH!" the great woman shrieked. She ran for the front door, moving faster than Iona had ever seen her move. Livia followed her up to the doorway and then halted, staring out as her former mistress continued to run shrieking in the streets. Livia walked back to the sack she had stuffed and carried it to the door, where she flung it out. She then walked back past Hervin, who stood utterly bewildered, and gave him a swift kiss on the cheek. Then she moved to the linen closet, took out another sack, and returned to Lady Sondal's room again.

Iona stared as her older sister carried bag after bag to the door and tossed them out. After the fifth trip, Livia looked at

Iona and seemed to read the worry from her eyes. She pulled out her paper and pencil and wrote:

She's just sitting out there on the street.
We should call a horse and cart for her
when I'm finished.

After reading the words, Iona found herself moving to the doorway. She walked out and saw, past a pile of spilling over sacks, the woman of her house sitting on the ground looking down at the stones and dirt beneath her. Her face was red and sullen, and she looked utterly miserable. Iona moved to her side and knelt down and whispered: "Are you alright, my lady?"

Lady Sondal let out a dark laugh. "I'm not *your lady*, Iona."

"But are you alright?"

The woman grimaced. In a low rasp, she said: "My life is such a pathetic joke." A pair of tears rolled down her face, smearing her thick makeup. "I didn't think I could sink any lower. Betrayed by my *peasant* husband—not that he *ever* loved me!" She cried into her hands for a moment, letting out loud sobs for all the passersby on the street to hear. Through her fingers, the she moaned: "It isn't fair! I was the fattest, ugliest daughter of a noble lord. That's how I ended up married to a lowly man like Hervin. No one of any worth would have me." After a moment more of sobs, she lifted her face and stared at Iona. "Can you imagine anything so pathetic? Being chased out of my house by my own slave? It's all a cruel joke. What have I ever done to deserve any of it?"

Iona heard the sound of another sack hitting the street, and she turned to see Livia standing in the doorway. Her older sister looked at her for a brief moment and then rolled her eyes and moved back into the house.

"You can probably come back inside in a little while," Iona whispered. "I'll make your bed for you and bring you more wine if you wish."

Lady Sondal frowned. "No, child, I will not live with that man and that..." She drew in a slow breath, as if bracing herself, then said: "I am done here. My father will take me back. I will make him."

Iona swallowed. "I... I'm sorry you're so unhappy."

The woman turned and looked sharply into Iona's eyes. "Do you think I need your pity?" She stood up then, stiffening. "Tell that pathetic little man that I require a hundred desseks to cover my travel expenses to return to my family." She turned and glared at the Sondal home and said: "I leave you all now to your miserable, peasant lives."

"I—I'll tell him," Iona said. She walked into the home and told Hervin that his wife required money to return to her home. This drew another smile from Livia, who moved to the house strongbox, opened it, and immediately began counting money. Hervin stared after her for a moment and then walked clumsily to his armchair, slumping down into it. Iona moved to him and said: "Are you alright?"

"I..." he said, blinking. "I suppose I don't know."

She bit her lip, unsure what to say. Finally, she whispered: "Did you ever love her?"

Hervin laughed as if to himself. "I suppose I don't know that either." He frowned, muttering: "She was just sort of thrust upon me. My father told me the day I turned eighteen that he had negotiated a wonderful match for our family. By sundown, I was married. He wanted... noble blood in our line I suppose, but we were never able to have any..." Hervin shrugged. "Still, I've always tried to be a good husband to her."

"Do you want her to stay?"

He gazed down at the floor, hesitating before murmuring: "I *should*..." For a long moment he did not speak, and then he whispered: "I think she will be happier back with her father."

Iona gazed down. It seemed there was nothing to be done. After a moment, she leaned in close to Hervin and whispered: "Thank you for freeing me. You're the kindest man I've ever met, and it's an honor to be adopted as your daughter, and...I love you."

He looked up at her with wet eyes, a wonderful smile on his face, and said: "Thank you, my dear."

CHAPTER 10:
RULES OF THE TREATY

I am sure there will be debates for hundreds of years on our conclave's decision not to excommunicate the Starborn, Cassian Asango. Bishop Cromlic argued that the blessing of Promethiock should not spare the boy from the judgment of the Gods, for not even the Great Dragon himself could escape their justice. We of the Lucinian order debated this issue long ourselves and ultimately determined that Promethiock was imprisoned, but he could not be destroyed, even by deities. Among all the celestial beings, he is the closest to us and was our champion. If not for him, our race would have died away many centuries ago. Thus we chose to respect the blessing of Promethiock, and to await the unfolding of his Chosen One's destiny.

---Bishop Elethius of the Lucinian Order

Kota stood in the center of his cell as the Nemesai leader stared at him. The man's name was Sebastos, and he had the rank of high inquisitor. He had had Kota stripped of his shirt, an act that was likely meant to make him feel frightened and helpless. Gretis had made him meditate wearing only a loincloth while he sat in snow though and being shirtless was hardly a bother compared to that. The cruel eyes of his jailor were another matter. Kota was afraid, but Gretis had been training him for years because she believed him to be a great warrior. He would not shame her by showing cowardice.

Time was growing confusing. Kota thought he had spent at least a night in this place, though day and night were challenging to differentiate, given the lack of light. The Nemesai had kept him alone, declaring that any visitation would interfere with the holy inquisitional process. Kota had heard Otho through the walls grudgingly agree to this with the words: *"While I consider your proposal."* There had been a great deal of shouting before that, which rumbled through the stone and steel, and much of it had been from Gretis. She had screamed that the second anyone laid a finger on Kota, she would know, and she would castrate and kill every Nemesai in the church. It had taken Otho at least half an hour to convince her not to merely force her way into the cell. Through all of this, Kota had been kept secluded. The high inquisitor was his first visitor.

"I understand you have, *remarkably,* been taught how to read," Sebastos said. His tone seemed to indicate a disgusted sort of amusement.

"That is correct," Kota said.

The Nemesai cast him a dangerous smile. "I see courage in your eyes. We *like it* when we get ahold of one with courage. Pride is the most satisfying sin in all the world to destroy." His gaze traveled up and down Kota's body, and he whispered: "How many years did it take you to develop this marvelous physique?" The tall man leaned in toward the bars and hissed: "It will take *seconds* to destroy all that work. My men like to slice and cut pieces away from truly defiant sinners. You might do well to lower your gaze and show penance before you actually begin to irritate me."

"Penance for what?" Kota said, continuing to stare at the inquisitor.

Sebastos's eyes seemed to grow more dangerous, and he whispered: "For partaking in the heretical teachings of that *whore Sansrit Master.*"

At these words, Kota's claws began to extend from his fingertips. They longed to slash at anyone who dared to speak so of Gretis, but some part of his mind knew better than to show anger. The Nemesai was trying to provoke him, and his only way to keep his wits was to remain calm. He closed his fists and let his claws poke into his palm and said evenly: "The only thing Lady Gretis has ever taught me is how to fight and how to quiet my mind."

"*Quiet your mind*," the Nemesai repeated, the amusement returning to his voice. "And what does that entail?"

"Sitting down, shutting my eyes, and letting my thoughts fade away. I meditated all night in this cell." Kota gestured with shackled hands to the small pile of hay that the Nemesai had graciously provided for him to use as a bed.

"Mentally shutting out the gods I wager," the man said with a tone of satisfaction.

"There is no law in the Holy Enumis against meditation."

Sebastos let out a dark chuckle, and he said in a gruff, sarcastic tone: "*You* have read the Holy Enumis?"

"Every word," Kota said. "I was extremely careful to study all the laws laid down by the Norn and the original five bishops, as well as the first Starborn. I have been a guest and student of a religious order for the past five years after all. It was important to me to respect their customs."

"You can read Dhavic?" the Nemesai muttered, his eyes showing disbelief.

"I can, yes, but I read most from the newly translated Enumis. Bishop Otho purchased several copies and made them available in the temple library. "

"He did, did he?" Sebastos's eyes narrowed. "It seems the heresy of Asango reaches further than we had realized." He leaned in still closer to the bars. "You *knew him,* didn't you—Cassian Asango?"

"I did."

"No doubt he was fascinated by your people's lack of belief in the Gods. You do not believe in them, do you?"

"I do believe in them," Kota said, "but they have never made a requirement of my people that we worship them. The

Norn has never spoken a single declaration regarding the shamalak to my knowledge, which causes me confusion upon what grounds you have you arrested me?"

Sebastos rolled his eyes. "Do you believe I would explain myself to a lower creature?" He held up a whip with eight leather wires and said: "You're barely more than a wild animal, and you're *lying to me!* That woman has taught you her Sansrit heresy and you, being the hideous product of humans *mating* with wild dogs, are demonstrating a dog-like loyalty to her. This is your last chance to lower those beastly eyes and start confessing before I scour your face with this." He snapped the whip sharply against the bars, causing them to make a high-pitched whine.

Kota shut his eyes and drew in a slow breath, calming himself as Gretis had taught him. Then he gazed again at the High Inquisitor. "I am *not* the product of humans laying with dogs. I *am* a shamalak though, and so I have excellent hearing. For example, while I was meditating last night, I heard Otho shout at you that I had better not have a single mark on me. I heard you wait for him to leave, and then you quietly muttered something about cutting his face. Then, a few moments ago, I heard you say to someone that you couldn't touch me, but you thought you could still scare me into confessing something because I am a weak-minded lower creature. I am sorry, but whatever I am, there is nothing to confess."

Sebastos's lips curled into a sneer of pure hatred. He began to actually tremble with anger. After a few sharp breaths, the man reached down into a pocket and drew out a large, iron key and opened the cell door. Kota's heart quickened as the Nemesai stormed in and took him by the back of the neck with a vice-like grip. *He had pushed the man too far.*

"Not another word, you little vermin!" Sebastos snarled into Kota's ear. "Now *walk*! We are going to talk to the great *Bishop Otho* right now!"

Kota was forced to make quick, tiny steps with the heavy chains on his ankles. The much taller man pushed him quickly down the dark hallway, and more than once he started to lose his footing, but the long-fingered hand around his neck kept him from falling and thrust him on. They crossed out into the dungeon's antechamber where the other Nemesai were standing around conversing with one another. They looked up as Sebastos thrust Kota forward and growled: "I have decided that Otho's time has drawn to a close. We are going to see him now."

The tattooed men immediately fell into ranks in front of and behind their commander. They moved in a tight formation up the stairway that led into the rest of the temple. Kota had to hop up each step as the hand gripped him from behind.

When they came to the top, they emerged into a large hallway where several Onkai men were moving about. Sebastos shouted at them: "Soldiers, go and fetch your Bishop. Tell them the High Inquisitor demands his presence, or the shamalak's throat will be slit." He whipped a dagger from somewhere behind and held it in front of Kota's neck.

This elicited fear in some of the Onkai's faces and anger in others, but one of them said in a terse voice: "We will go and find him." They scattered.

"Remain quiet," Sebastos whispered, and he moved the blade a little closer. The man's hot breath blew on the fur of his ear. Kota stood still, his muscles coiling so that he might fight in whatever capacity he could if the opportunity came.

There was a pounding of footsteps rumbling down the hall, and, after a moment, Otho, Gretis, and Darius came marching at the head of perhaps sixty Onkai soldiers. When Gretis saw Sebastos holding a blade to Kota's throat, she quickened her pace, moving ahead of the others. She drew her sword in a flash from a scabbard at her belt and screamed: "You SON OF A BITCH!" There was murder in her eyes.

"Get back, wench!" Sebastos shouted, and one of his soldiers aimed a crossbow at Gretis. She continued forward, accelerating, and the High Inquisitor grunted: "Kill her!"

"NO!" Otho shouted, his eyes wide.

An arrow flew at Gretis's chest, but her left hand whipped up with utterly unbelievable speed and caught it mid shaft, stopping it dead in the air. She tossed the thing away and moved even faster, becoming a blur as she drew back her weapon.

"GODS!" Sebastos shrieked in terror, wincing backward and pulling Kota with him.

"*STOOOOOOP*!" a voice shouted from down the hall, and it boomed like thunder from all around, rumbling the very floor beneath them the way Cassian's had years ago in the forgotten city. Gretis's eyes widened, and she froze midway through a swing that would have taken Sebastos's arm off at the shoulder—*just to the left of where Kota's face was.*

"*Gretis!*" Otho cried, catching up to her in a wheeze. He put his enormous gloved hands on her shoulders, and they both turned to look down the hall to the left at something Kota could not see.

"Everyone stop," the voice came again, and it still reverberated unnaturally as it had before, yet it did not seem quite so panicked. After a moment, an incredibly handsome young man of perhaps twenty years in a rich silken white tunic and flowing black cape came bounding into the room. He was gasping for air, his face damp and flush, as if he had been running for a long time. When he made it into the center of the fairly perplexed crowd, he panted: "Oh thank the Gods! No one's dead yet." He locked eyes with Gretis and managed to exhale: "Please put the sword away, my lady. There won't be any need for violence." A smile of perfect white teeth flashed across his smooth features.

"Who are you?" Otho said.

The newcomer straightened up, drew in a deep breath, and exhaled: "Telemachus Vale, Starborn of the Nineteenth Generation." His eyes shifted again to Gretis, and he held up a hand, saying: "Please, I beg that you put the sword away. This is all about to be under control. You have my word." Very slowly, Gretis lowered her weapon and returned it to its scabbard. "Thank you," Telemachus said with another gleaming smile. "Gods, if I'd gotten here a second later..." He hunched forward for a moment, then panted: "My apologies to everyone. I sit behind a desk for most of every day and," he gazed up at the army of Onkai and added: "unlike you incredibly brave men, I'm not used to this much excitement."

"What is the meaning of this?" Sebastos managed to shout. The hand that held the knife to Kota's throat was trembling.

Telemachus turned to the Nemesai and said: "Let's not have a blade at anyone's throat." His right hand flicked up.

"Wha—" Sebastos grunted as the dagger wrenched suddenly free from his hand and whisked through the air to Telemachus, who caught it in a smooth, effortless catch.

As if by reflex, a few of the Nemesai soldiers raised their crossbows, but the Starborn glanced at them and shouted: "Ho! None of that!" and with an upward sweep of his free hand, the crossbows all lurched free of the men's grips and slammed into the ceiling above, splintering to pieces. Telemachus' extended fingers twitched to the right, and the chunks of wood and metal slid across the stone and congealed into a small cluster, which then dropped to the floor.

Sebastos made an unintelligible grunt somewhere between shock and anger, and he raised his right arm to lock it around Kota's throat, but Kota easily wriggled free and hopped away. Gretis moved in a blur between him and the Nemesai and half drew her sword. Sebastos flinched back and glared at both of them, and then at Telemachus. "You cannot do this!" he snarled. "Not even a Starborn has the authority—"

"Authority!" Telemachus shouted back, and his grin grew a shade fiercer. "That is actually *exactly* what I came here to discuss." He straightened up a little more and huffed: "On what grounds have you assumed the authority to arrest a shamalak?"

"I..." Sebastos stammered, hesitating, and then he said: "I am high inquisitor. I need not explain my actions to anyone but my Bishop."

"Oh no matter, I'll just look inside your head," Telemachus said in a soft mutter. His eyes narrowed, and he leaned a little forward, peering at the Nemesai. Sebastos's eyes widened, and his face grew panicked. "Yes-s-s, just as I thought," Telemachus whispered. "You're using the Vendrith Accords as your pretext." He lifted his head and moved it in a slow swivel, addressing everyone as he said: "As some of you may know, the Vendrith Accords are a roughly nine-hundred-year-old set of agreements the human church reached with the elves over, among other things, religious authority. One particular line more or less translates to: *'Humans may govern themselves in all matters of religion, but the theocratic governance of other sentient creatures falls under the authority of the elven people.'* This is, of course, the reason why the human church has never tried to indoctrinate people like Kota here." He gestured to Kota.

"That is correct," Sebastos said through gritted teeth. "However, there is a clause below what you just translated that states that we, the Nemesai, have the right to intercede if a member of another race is practicing heresy amidst human beings."

"You forget the rest of that line," Telemachus said with defiant chuckle "that the *right to intercede* shall only occur when no member of the elven court is available to arbitrate."

Sebastos gave a sneering laugh. "The elves have not seen fit to have anything to do with human affairs in nearly eight centuries."

"Not until now," Telemachus said with a calm smile. He gestured to his left, and a hood drew back from a thin, cloaked figure. Kota blinked as he saw the movement of shimmering bronze fabric, and he had the sense that this figure had been there all along, but he had not noticed it, or *could not* notice it. He watched in wonder as an impossibly smooth, flawless female face appeared with intricately braided golden hair, long ears that were pointed like his own yet without fur, and eyes that glowed a burning turquoise. This elven girl looked at him for an instant, casting a little wink. She was breathtakingly beautiful, appearing to be perhaps a year older than Kota himself, though what the signs of age meant in an elf was difficult to guess. There were gasps all around the room. Kota thought he had never seen so many gaping eyes in all his life.

"This is Lady Thalice of the House of Corostine," Telemachus said.

There was a moment of awed silence, and then Otho said in a humble voice: "My lady," and he lowered his head. Immediately, the Onkai around him followed his example and gave little bows to the girl. Kota pivoted on his chained feet and made a bow as well, and, somewhat to his surprise, so did Gretis. Only the Nemesai remained upright. They all seemed to be stupefied.

"I thank you for your kind respects, most noble Onkai," Thalice said, her voice humming with a wonderful, inhuman cadence that tickled Kota's ears. She walked over to him, casting a smile. "Hold still please." She made a very sudden movement, her left hand knifing as it came down in a slash at the chains that bound his hands. Just before her thin fingers touched the metal, they flashed an almost blinding yellow. The chain snapped, and two halves of a link fell to the floor, sliced through the middle in a clean, perfect cut. "I should never like to see one of your kind in chains," she whispered.

Thalice whirled then and faced the Nemesai. "High Inquisitor, I believe it is my right under our treaty to arbitrate this matter."

Sebastos fidgeted, then said in a tone of forced calm: "Yes, of course it is, my lady."

Thalice nodded to him and then turned back to Kota, Gretis, and Otho. "It may surprise many of you to know that my people are well aware of Sansrit Philosophy and have been for thousands of years." Her glowing eyes shifted to Gretis. "There are those among us who know *all* of its secrets." The elf smiled and slowly gazed around the room as she went on: "Many centuries ago, humans who studied the arts of the Sansrit Path were welcomed into our cities. We found a kind of kinship with them that we had never known with any other creatures." Thalice's exquisite smile broadened as she said: "You see, in all the world, Sansrit Masters are the most like what *we* are."

There was muttering all around, and Kota's ears took in every whisper.

"The blade-witch is like an *elf*?"

"What does that mean?"

"Can you believe there is a real elf in the temple?!"

Thalice put small hand on Kota's shoulder and said aloud: "I give the Nemesai Order full assurance that Sansrit Philosophy makes no affront to the Gods, but in fact, it makes full acknowledgment of their existence within its doctrines. Therefore, I exercise my right to give summary judgment: Kota of the shamalak people is guilty of no heresy and must, therefore, be immediately freed." She bent down and made a little sweep of her finger. There was another flash of yellow accompanying the sound of splitting of metal, and the two halves of the chains binding Kota's feet parted.

Otho breathed a deep sigh of relief, and he walked over to Kota and rested a thick hand on his shoulder, though it was to Thalice that he spoke: "I thank you from the bottom of my mortal heart, my dear."

"As do I," Gretis said in a tone filled with respect.

Kota stepped toward her and said: "I owe you the most thanks." He turned to Telemachus and said: "To you as well, Telemachus Vale."

The Starborn walked over and clapped Kota on the elbow. "It is no trouble. You are a friend, even if you do not realize it. Thalice and I have both already met you through Cassian's memories."

"The brave little shamalak," Thalice said. She craned her neck to look up into his eyes. "You have grown quite large."

Otho turned to the still speechless Sebastos and said in a deep, fierce voice: "I believe that concludes your business with us, and I think now you can get the *hell* out of my temple."

The high inquisitor glared at Otho, then at Kota, and then finally his eyes fell on Telemachus. "You have chosen to stand with your brother Cassian, Telemachus Vale. That will be *remembered* in days to come."

"Gods above," Telemachus said, rolling his eyes. "I am standing on the side of *peace*. Can you truly not see that? How many enemies do you intend to make on this trip? Perhaps you will threaten our elven guest next?"

Otho glared at Sebastos and said: "Oh-h-h-h, if he tries that, I'll have a very nice excuse."

Glavius appeared from the crowd of soldiers and moved to Otho's side and whispered: "Please allow me, sir." His eyes fixed on the high inquisitor, and he said: "This ugly bastard's just too damned tall. I think he'd be so much easier to look at if I shortened him up by say...a head." Otho gave a little chuckle and patted Glavius on the back.

Darius's right hand moved to the hilt of his weapon, and he said: "Sir, these men have no more official business here, and there is no impending threat. Technically, they no longer have grounds to claim sanctuary."

Otho smiled as he stared into Sebastos's eyes. "My men do not seem to like you, High Inquisitor," he said. "I think you should leave and tell Cromlic that his plan has failed." The Bishop's thick eyebrows knitted together, and he moved his own hand to the hilt of his sword. The instant he did, the sound of metal scraping against metal hissed through the hall as every Onkai present drew his weapon. "Why don't I give you to the count of *ten*?"

"This will *not be forgotten*!" Sebastos hissed through his teeth as he took a few nervous steps backward. Kota heard the violent pulse of the man's heart and caught the stink of his fear in the air. The High Inquisitor turned and walked at a *very* brisk pace down the hall to the right, his men moving in a tight formation behind him.

"Take care!" Glavius shouted after them. "The road is a dangerous place at night. I hope nothing should befall you all."

They all watched the Nemesai group disappear, and then Telemachus said: "Perhaps we might go and talk somewhere, Bishop Otho."

Otho nodded and said: "Yes, come this way." He made a sweeping gesture through the crowd of Onkai soldiers still standing about. The men parted immediately, and he and Darius walked side by side through them.

Kota was not sure as to whether he was meant to be part of this talk, but the elven girl moved to his side and gracefully slid her arm into his, whispering with a breathtaking smile: "Shall we?" Kota swallowed and fell into step with her, the newly split chains on his ankles clinking softly along the floor. Gretis and the Starborn moved together behind them.

The group made their way through several intersections of stone hall to a small room with a large wooden desk. Otho entered first and dropped into a thick wooden chair and then gestured for the rest of them to take the chairs across from him. There were four, which suited the group perfectly. Darius closed the door behind them, and everyone sat down, Kota finding a place between Gretis and the beautiful elf girl. As he sat down next to her, she casually ran her index finger over the shackle on his left wrist, and again there was a tiny but brilliant yellow flash as the metal split apart.

"I cannot thank you enough for helping us," Otho said to the two guests to the temple.

"Yes, how did you even know to come?" Gretis said.

"My brother has many spies who report on the Nemesai Order, but now that he has gone to fight for the empire, he assigned most of them to report to me," Telemachus said. "I suppose that is fortunate. If Cassian had learned of this, he might have flown here on his dragon and *handled* the matter quite differently than I did."

"I might have liked to see that," Otho muttered with an amused chuckle.

"So would Bishop Cromlic, I think," Telemachus said, his voice becoming troubled.

Darius nodded. "Yes, I do believe Asango attacking a High Inquisitor—within the Onkai Temple no less—would have worked quite well to Cromlic's advantage."

Telemachus nodded. "Cromlic has almost certainly become aware that Cassian has informants watching his every move. This ploy was likely designed either to force the Onkai into supporting my brother's arrest or to provoke him into doing something foolish. It was a clever enough tactic, but of course, Cromlic did not expect us to be able to enlist Thalice here to speak on Kota's behalf."

Gretis reached up and rested a hand on Kota's shoulder and said: "You are quite lucky, Kota. Few people in the world have such powerful friends."

Kota felt a little flustered at these words, but Telemachus quickly cut in: "Few people are *unlucky* enough to become caught in the center of a war between the Nemesai and a Starborn. His troubles may not end here."

"Hah!" Otho grunted, his gaze fixing on Thalice. "Kota has the word of an actual *elf* on his side. Short of being declared the *Messiah*, I doubt there could be greater protection from the Nemesai."

"Officially yes," Telemachus said in a grave voice. "Unofficially, the bishop is free to use *unofficial agents*." The Starborn's gaze fixed on Kota's, and he said with a grim sigh: "We have just embarrassed the Nemesai Order, and you are the very centerpiece of the affront. Cromlic is still seething over the humiliating defeat Cassian dealt him years ago." Telemachus breathed in slowly, hesitating, and then said: "We should assume the Bishop will kill you if he can. He has been trying to poison my brother or arrange an *accident* for him for years. Cassian has been able to thwart their attempts because he is one of the most powerful telepaths in the world, but you possess no such advantage." Telemachus' gaze swept the room, and he added: "None of you do." A troubled silence passed over the small office.

"Fortunately, I have a way to protect you," Thalice said in her wonderful elven voice. She rose from her chair and faced Kota, and said: "Student of the Sansrit Path, I extend to you an invitation to the Talsian Grove." Her burning turquoise eyes shifted to Gretis, and she said: "The invitation is granted to both of you. You may come and live in my house while Kota's training is completed."

"Gods!" Darius whispered. The look on his face seemed to mirror what Kota was feeling. So far as the historical texts in the Onkai's archives told, no mortal had been invited to live among the elven people in hundreds of years. Kota could not speak.

Otho stared at him with an astonished expression and whispered: "I dare say no human assassin could touch you there."

Gretis cast the elf girl a kind smile and drew in a very slow breath through her nose. There was a distant, wondrous look in her eyes, as if she were letting her imagination run free. After a moment though, her expression lost some of its luminescence, and she said in a soft whisper: "No. You honor us both beyond measure with your most gracious offer, but we cannot accept. The time has come for me to draw my pupil's power out." Her gaze shifted to Kota. "That will be dangerous, even to creatures such as elves. I must take him deep into the wilderness, far from anyone whom he might hurt." Gretis moved her hand to Kota's wrist and squeezed as she looked into his eyes. "I feel there is no more time. We shall go this very night."

Kota drew in a deep breath.

"I understand," Thalice said with a soft nod.

Telemachus cleared his throat and then looked at Gretis, saying in a troubled voice: "When you were about to take the inquisitor's arm off, I felt what was coursing through you. I had no idea Sansrit Masters wielded such power."

"That is why I must take Kota far away," Gretis said.

There was a moment of silence as the Starborn stared at the two of them. Kota had the sense that he was being telepathically probed, and it was more than a little unnerving. Finally, Telemachus straightened and extended his hand. "It was a pleasure to finally meet you, *Kota of the Nakawa Tribe*." He spoke the words just the way Cassian had years ago, and for an instant, Kota's mind leaped back to that fateful meeting. Telemachus' voice pervaded that flash of memory, though the young man's mouth did not move: <I worry a great deal for you, my friend.>

The Starborn turned and said his goodbyes to everyone else then, explaining that he had urgent business. Though Otho pleaded for Thalice to stay for a meal with him, she politely excused herself as well and departed with Telemachus, stopping only briefly to remove the rest of Kota's shackles with her strange power. After that, Gretis told Kota to go to the kitchens to get some food before going to her home to pack his things. She stayed behind to speak to Otho alone for a few moments. As Kota left the room and made his way through the temple, he considered all that had happened. He walked slowly, his senses dulled by the weight of introspection. He was terribly excited and terribly afraid of what was about to come.

perhaps two hundred able-bodied men and get them into place, they should be able to pick off Tarnath's men at their leisure after the initial attack. I would position them about a quarter mile back from the entrance, so they do not give away the trap. Once the avalanche takes place, there will be no rush. Depending on whether Tarnath is killed in the rock fall and how much panic is generated, this may be enough to elicit surrender. If not, our main force will be positioned at the opposite opening. The enemy will be running desperately away from arrows sent from unseen places above for nearly two miles. They will be exhausted and terrified, and I estimate we can obtain a quick surrender when they see an organized force ready to cut them down."

"Fascinating," said Romulus. His eyes shifted to Cassian's. "We won't be accepting anyone's *surrender* though. These men invaded Denigoth, and every one of them must be put to death."

Cassian swallowed, saying nothing to this. The thought of pointless slaughter repulsed him, but now was not the time to make that point.

Romulus continued: "I do question what you will do about the scouts this Tarnath will inevitably send ahead."

"I already know who they are," Cassian said. "I took the liberty of invading their minds. They will ride ahead, see our forces in position, and ride back telling Tarnath exactly what I wish them to say."

Romulus stroked his chin. "This all very well might work."

"It *will* work, and I estimate that our side will suffer extremely minimal casualties if we take any at all. I will be flying above on Titus, my dragon, overseeing every aspect of the battle and issuing commands telepathically."

"You can fly around on that creature's back?" said Tarnath, gazing at Cassian with undisguised awe.

"I can."

Romulus took a very slow and loud breath through his nose, looking intently down at the map. "There won't always be a clever *trick* like this available to you in battle," he muttered. "Still, this is *extremely* impressive." After another moment, his head cocked up, and he said: "I have made my decision. Come."

Cassian followed Romulus out of the tent where the small contingent of guards immediately stood to attention and saluted. Romulus nodded vaguely at them and then turned his attention to Dimitris, who was seated about fifty paces away at a tree-stump table across from Somar of all people, playing a game of cornerstone. When Dimitris saw Romulus, he stood, and Cassian sensed a wave of nerves from his fellow Starborn.

Romulus walked up to Dimitris. "My boy," the general said in a smooth and friendly voice, "the plans you provided were adequate, yet this young man's were far better." He gestured to Cassian. "I believe Lord Asango here can carry out the operation with scarcely a man lost on our side. That is why I must grant *him* command of this force. You are to submit to his orders in this venture, Dimitris Anondine."

Cassian felt the shock and anger in his brother almost immediately. The two of them locked eyes, and Cassian knew that Dimitris was not at all ready to accept this outcome. The calm, friendly game of cornerstone was just a display for the men to see. His brother had been more obsessed with this victory than Cassian had realized.

"What is this *plan*, if I may ask?" Dimitris said, straining very hard and failing to sound composed and gracious.

"It is not your place to ask," Romulus said, his voice suddenly cruel, and more than loud enough for many of the soldiers about to hear. "You have lost. At least have the dignity not to simper like a child over it."

Cassian's gaze shifted to the general. These words were designed to stoke the flames that were obviously burning in Dimitris—*to humiliate him*. Cassian wondered why, and so too did Somar, judging from the way the old man was eyeing Romulus. There was little time to consider this suspicion though, for at that moment Dimitris was a far more important concern.

"You are both inducted into the imperial army from this moment forward," said Romulus. "Lord Asango, you may now give your friend here any orders you wish, and he *will* submit to every one of them."

Dimitris's eyes narrowed at the General, and then they flashed to Cassian's. "Did you *bribe* him? Did you manage to invade his mind? I know how skilled you are at telepathy." His voice was filled with undisguised venom.

"Be careful how you speak to your superior officer, *boy*," said Romulus sharply. "You can be whipped just like any other soldier."

Dimitris glared in shock at these words. Cassian noticed then that perhaps twenty soldiers had gathered around this spectacle and were listening intently, and more were flocking over. Dimitris was discerning this as well from the way his eyes shifted around, and it was feeding his anxiety.

Cassian took several quiet steps toward Somar and whispered to the old man: "He's provoking him on purpose."

"Yes-s-s," Somar whispered back. "Look at Romulus's eyes."

Cassian gazed at the general, seeing him the way Somar had taught him to observe men. There was calculation in Romulus's eyes, and also traces of exhilaration, as if everything were going according to plan.

"Take control if you can," Somar whispered, "before it is too late."

Cassian said aloud: "Dimitris—"

"Hold, Commander Asango," Romulus said, raising a hand to silence Cassian. "Dimitris Anondine, you *will* submit to Asango's authority, and you demonstrate that by bowing your head at your superior officer's feet, *NOW*!"

"That is beneath his dignity, sir," Cassian said sharply.

"His *behavior* here is beneath his dignity," Romulus said. "I expected more composure from a Starborn, but your friend here is disgracing himself with this *tantrum*. I will not have it!"

More men had gathered now. At least a hundred soldiers were forming a loose circle around this confrontation. Most of them were staring wide-eyed, but a few were whispering to one another and quietly chuckling at Dimitris.

"You will KNEEL!" Romulus said, his voice booming.

"What are you doing?!" Cassian shouted, glaring at Romulus. The general did not even bother to look at him, but Dimitris did for a brief instant, and it seemed that somehow Cassian's attempt to defend him had only provoked him further.

"You are going to have to fight your brother," Somar said, hunching over a little and whispering from behind a hand scratching at his nose. "This was all planned—setting one of you against the other. I can't tell why."

Cassian felt Dimitris's anger harden into violent intent. He could not concede now. He could not kneel in front of all the men around him after being so brutally spoken down to by Romulus. If he did, word of the humiliation would spread throughout the empire.

"This is a disgusting joke," said Dimitris. He glared at Romulus. "I do *not* accept your orders, nor do I accept your judgment. I am Starborn! It is my sacred right to challenge Asango at any time in our contest." Dimitris locked eyes with Cassian, and he said in a cold voice: "We have both long known it would come to this, my brother. I always thought you would be the instigator, but I challenge *you* to a duel to the death!"

Before Cassian even knew what he was saying, a single word snapped from his throat, as if by reflex: "Accepted!" He could scarcely believe this was happening, yet now that Dimitris had made the challenge, *there was no turning back.*

The two gazed at each other for a moment in near perfect silence, which was remarkable given the number of men now surrounding the two of them. Cassian sensed the pangs of regret in Dimitris that their destinies had led to this, and he felt a mirrored pain within himself that was more profound than he might have anticipated. In another existence, the two of them would have been the dearest of friends. Cassian would have happily conceded the throne and spent his life helping Dimitris rule and inventing and theorizing with Telemachus, and the world might well have been all the better for their partnership. But that was a different world, and a different Cassian whose parents had not been taken from him and executed.

"Do you wish time to pray?" said Dimitris, his voice almost trembling.

"No," said Cassian. "I make you the same offer though."

Dimitris took a long, seething breath, and as he did Cassian's eyes shifted to Romulus. Though he could penetrate very little through the carefully trained psychic defenses of the general at that moment, he sensed excitement *and satisfaction.*

"No, let us decide this right now, my brother," said Dimitris, his voice dry and harsh.

"Agreed," said Cassian. The word tore at his heart, but he ignored the pain.

Dimitris gestured to an open grassy field at the east end of the camp. "There is as good a place as any, I suppose."

Cassian turned to Romulus. "Pull your men back at least three hundred paces from us and tell them to be ready to run if our battle grows out of control."

"Understood," said the General with a nod, barely able to contain his grin. Cassian hated Romulus more than any other creature in existence at that moment.

"Shall we proceed?" Dimitris said.

Cassian answered telepathically first: <Do not do this, brother. You will die.>

<I have trained to kill you for years, *brother,*> Dimitris answered, radiating confidence.

There was truly no turning back. Without further word, Cassian began walking toward the center of the field. He felt Dimitris following close behind, with well over three hundred men looking. More were taking notice every moment. In the close confines of the camp, word that two Starborn were about to battle to the death was spreading like wildfire. Soldiers were running from tent to tent, screaming the news. By the time they both walked to the center of the field, Cassian guessed, there would be well over a thousand observers, and by the time *one of them was dead*, the whole camp would be watching.

Cassian shut all of this out as he came to the center of the grass. Anything less than his complete focus would yield Dimitris victory. This knowledge allowed him to let go of his compassion. Instead, he surrendered himself to the section of his mind that had carried him through every assassination attempt since he was eleven years old. This part of him had always been able to transcend fear. It was ruthless, calculating, and operated on the unshakable belief that it could overcome absolutely anything. Through this lens, he assessed his brother. Dimitris possessed understanding of terrible ancient battle magic and arcane secrets that far exceeded Cassian's knowledge. None of that was to be feared though. It was a puzzle to be solved.

"I give you one final chance to concede, Cassian," said Dimitris. His voice was hard, but it betrayed hints of fear. He could not hide the rapid beat of his heart or the trembling of his hands. Cassian's own heart was pounding hard in his chest, but not like Dimitris's.

"You are not ready to die, brother," Cassian said, his words coming out cold and harsh. "It terrifies you. I have no wish to kill you, but if you attack me, your life will end right here, at twenty years old, on a patch of unimportant grass."

"You cannot defeat me in single combat," Dimitris said with a vicious laugh.

"I can, and you know it."

Dimitris stared at Cassian, and then at the now hundreds upon hundreds of soldiers that had gathered around them both. His face grew pale, and he spoke in a soft, distant voice: "There is no turning back for either of us. This was always our destiny."

"Can you not see we are being manipulated into it?"

"Of course I can," he said, gazing down. "But what can either of us do? This is our Emperor's will." His raised his eyes in a glare. "Ready yourself, Asango."

Cassian stared back, though he no longer gazed upon his brother. Dimitris had become a threat to his life, and there was no place for sympathy in the equation of survival. "I am ready."

Dimitris raised his hand and whispered something inaudible, and Cassian sensed the particles in the air accelerate around his own body. A split second later, he was enveloped in an ocean of flame. Cassian's magic formed a protective cocoon instantly, holding back the inferno around him with an impermeable golden layer that extended a short distance from his body at all points. The tactical part of his mind instantly deciphered Dimitris's intentions: He was putting him on the defensive—trying to overwhelm. The logical response was clear. Cassian reached out through the flames with his magic and found Dimitris, who had moved away and was already concocting an even greater attack. He raised his right hand and hissed: "Reskiat," and an explosion of lightning shot from the tips of his fingers, leaping through the fire and finding its unseen target on the other side.

Cassian sensed Dimitris strain as he dropped his attack, forced instead to summon his own barrier to defend himself. In that instant, Cassian focused his will, sending a concussive blast of raw magic outward in every direction. The flames puffed away into nothingness, and as they did, he saw Dimitris holding out his right hand and chanting.

For a precious few seconds Cassian was utterly transfixed. Dimitris was using one of the legendary blood moon spells. It was completely unlike anything Cassian had ever studied. A great swell of mystical energy swirled in a cloud of dark smoke where Dimitris gestured. It shaped itself into what looked like an enormous wolf of black flame with blood red eyes. The thing glared at Cassian, bearing translucent gray teeth within its wisping mouth. Beautiful and terrible, the spell was *conscious*, he sensed, given life and the necessary degree of intelligence to carry out a single goal: *kill its target.*

Cassian's eyes shifted back to Dimitris, and he instantly grasped the tactical advantage of this conjuration. The creature could attack independently of Dimitris, thereby putting Cassian on the defensive while leaving Dimitris free to formulate offensive magic. For a brief instant, Cassian thought of summoning Titus. His dragon could likely destroy the beastly spell with ease, but then that would be a form of cheating. The creature was of Dimitris's magic, which meant Cassian could only answer it with his own power.

The wolf leaped at Cassian, whisking through the air as if its shadowy form were entirely untroubled by gravity or friction. It was on him almost instantly, burning claws slashing against Cassian's shield of magic. He allowed this to happen, knowing that it would drain valuable power but needing the chance to evaluate the creature. There were hissing black sparks as energy grated against energy, and Cassian noticed immediately that there was no physical force to the blows. He understood. Spears and arrows would pass through the conjuration, for it had no real form. The image of the wolf was meant to terrify, but it was really only a controlled cloud of magic. All the true power was focused in the teeth and claws.

Dimitris attacked again suddenly, sending a vortex of emerald flame at least eight paces in diameter directly at Cassian. This spell was a far simpler construction than the creature and much more immediately destructive, and it was heading at Cassian faster than he could dodge.

Locking his focus on the spiraling flames, Cassian focused his mind and wrestled enough control of Dimitris's spell that he was able to turn its path and send it whisking into the snarling black wolf. The creature made a terrible scream as the blast struck. Evidently, it could feel some degree of pain, yet it did not die. The attack only immobilized the thing for a moment, sending it in a shrieking backward tumble.

Dimitris stared aghast, and a great swell of fear leaked from the barrier around his mind. He was shocked that Cassian had able to take control of the spell. Seeing this opening, Cassian charged forward, willing his body to lift off the ground and soar, blood hot in his veins. He knew he was going to win. Dimitris might have access to terrible ancient spells, but Cassian possessed superior control over magic.

Looking half terrified, Dimitris cried out "Hazak!" The air around his hand began to hum and hiss with electrical energy. Cassian sensed this and reacted. Lightning attacks were impossible to dodge and incredibly efficient at depleting mystic shields if the defender was unprepared. Still soaring forward, Cassian cried: "Vesthrok Dokshai!" calling on the spell he had used to enter Promethiock's prison years ago. Some part of his mind had already noted that he was ever so slightly faster than Dimitris at manipulating magic, and this was about to save his life. Just before the eruption of crackling lightning burst from his brother's hand, a great sphere of invisible filaments formed around Cassian's body. The two spells collided in such a brilliant flash that Cassian was forced to shut his eyes. He stopped his telekinetic charge and dropped to his feet then, too disoriented to continue.

"Krethrack Noss!" Dimitris cried, and a swell of translucent purple energy rushed from his hand—a river of destructive power Cassian did not recognize, jolting at sharp angles. At the same time, Cassian sensed the wolf attacking him from behind. He was about to be overwhelmed.

NO! Cassian thought, determination blazing through every fiber of his soul. He raised his right hand toward his brother, not casting spell, but sending raw magic down into the ground between them. Through sheer will, he summoned up a wall of dirt and stone thick enough to absorb Dimitris's spell. As an explosion of earth occurred, Cassian whirled to face the creature. Its jaws were flying at him. He focused more of his power and ripped into the intricate magic that held the beast together. With a terrible scream, the wolf tore apart and vanished into nothingness.

Cassian turned back and stared through the cloud of dust, seeing his brother standing across the newly formed crater between them. The mental barriers between the two of them had worn away in the expenditure of magic, and their minds were naked to one another. Cassian saw that Dimitris had been holding back, just as he had. Neither of them had ever killed anyone, and no matter how fierce the contest between them, they still saw each other as brothers.

<We can end this in a draw,> Cassian said telepathically. <I'll shake your hand in front of everyone.>

Dimitris's eyes narrowed, and Cassian felt him hesitate, but only for a brief second. <I would still be forced to serve under *your* command,> he answered in disgust. Cassian could feel the resignation in his brother's mind, as well as the sudden swelling of his still astonishingly vast magical power. <I wish it could be another way, but one of us has to die, Cassian. I am sorry, but it will be you.>

Dimitris began to whisper words Cassian could not hear, for the wind picked up around the two of them. Then there came a terrible crackling sound as Dimitris pulled dozens of spectral entities from other dimensions—places Cassian had never even known existed in the cosmos. His power gathered and combined in ways that seemed impossible. The construct of magic that formed was an enormous lateral vortex of swirling light that shimmered in a myriad of shifting colors. At first, it was a blur, but the energy crystalized and took shape into sharp angles, ever-shifting, ever-spinning in an almost hypnotizing three-dimensional pattern.

Cassian gaped. He had never seen spell-work so intricate or so terribly potent. The construct emitted a terrible shrieking sound that was almost deafening, and as it swirled, the intensity of its power caused rocks and debris to float up into the air. Cassian knew there could only be one possibility: this was the legendary *Drathnakal,* or, as it had become known by later generations, *Saikon's End*. According to legend, it had been invented by the first Starborn over a period of several years in an attempt to shatter the impenetrable cosmic stone that made up Promethiock's prison. Centuries later, Dracus Mobius, Starborn of the seventh generation, had used it to kill Saikon, the first known Demon King. It was said to be the most powerful destructive spell ever conceived by man—a force so dangerous that it had been kept secret for generations, *yet Dimitris had acquired and mastered it.*

Sweat dripped down Cassian's face. So close to the spell, there was no chance he could dodge. He knew as well that no magical defense he could throw up would protect him. The Drathnakal had been used to kill dragons and obliterate castle walls. *Still, it had never been used against another Starborn.*

Cassian had imagined a moment like this many times. He had known Dimitris would have access to the most potent schools of magic in the world, and he had anticipated that his survival might one day rest upon a single theory: *the greater the power in a spell, the greater its complexity and ultimately the delicacy of its construction.* In the case of the Drathnakal, Dimitris had needed to summon forty-six spectral entities from the cosmic ether to control and direct the tremendous energy, and thus his mind was divided to forty-six ever-shifting points.

Cassian spoke no words and cast no spell of his own. *His mind was his weapon.* He focused his will and thrust his hand out with two fingers extended, willing every shred of his mental and magical strength into a blazing white beam of raw magic that he fired directly into the center of the Drathnakal.

The thin stream of white energy ripped through all of the intricate threads that held his opponent's spell together. The Drathnakal immediately began to break apart, crackling and bursting out of Dimitris's control. Two things happened at once then: Cassian's attack struck Dimitris in the chest, and the forbidden construct of magic exploded out in every direction.

Cassian was hurled backward. His aura reacted automatically with what little power it had left, forming a barrier around his flesh that just barely kept the bones in his body from shattering. He sailed fifteen paces through the air and then went skidding on his back along the dirt and grass.

When the violence of the explosion finally stopped, Cassian's body screamed of injury. He did not care about the pain though. Cassian forced himself to rise, for he could feel his brother behind the cloud of dust and smoke the spell had wrought from the ground, *and he knew what he had done.*

"Brother!" Cassian screamed. He ran forward, tears already welling in his eyes. He could feel cold death seeping through Dimitris's young body faster than any healing spell could repair, and he knew even before he found the bloody mess of flesh lying on the grass some thirty paces back from the explosion that he had killed his brother.

Cassian heard cheers erupt all around him as he knelt down and clutched Dimitris's limp body in his arms. He felt his brother die there and then, all the great beauty of his life fading to nothing... because Cassian Asango had killed him.

"*Oh, Gods!*" Cassian whispered. He stared down at the now still, disfigured face. It was the most horrible moment of his life.

CHAPTER 12: THE WEIGHT OF SIN

Somar sat quietly across the table from Cassian as the sunlight grew dim in the windows. The boy had not spoken in hours. After defeating Dimitris, he had simply walked to his tent and sat down on his cot exactly where he was. Somar had sat with him in silence for most of the day, knowing that Cassian needed him. The first kill was a terrible thing for anyone to endure, but even more so for those who possessed the depth of mind that his beloved pupil did.

"This is what the emperor wished," Cassian said abruptly in a dry whisper, staring down at the table.

"Yes, it was," Somar said.

"The matter could have been decided without death. Dimitris was brilliant. Even if he did not become emperor, he could have made enormous contributions to this world."

"Yes, he could have."

Cassian's eyes shifted up and met Somar's. They were fierce. "Why did I have to kill him?"

"I do not know. It is possible that the church had some hand in this. Perhaps they presumed their golden Starborn would win and rid them of you. Still, it is unlikely they were the sole puppeteers. The way Romulus was speaking to Dimitris... he would not dare such a thing unless instructed to do so by the emperor himself."

"Agreed," said Cassian his voice sharp. "But again, why?" He rolled his eyes. "I felt the Emperor watching our battle. Tacitus observes me all the time, but I know *nothing* of his mind."

"You will, I think. There is very little question now who will be named as crown prince and heir." This assumption flowed from Somar's longstanding acceptance that Arkas, the Emperor's own son, was not a true contender. The question as to why this was had never been answered, but Somar had blindly believed it for so long that it now felt like a given.

Cassian made a dark smile, but almost instantly his eyes moistened. A pair of tears dripped down his face. "I killed my brother, just like Keska said I would."

"*He* challenged *you*."

Cassian shot up from the cot. "Yes! And I *took his life*!" He took several slow, seething breaths, and then said through clenched teeth: "It was a horrible death. I felt his terror as he went." Cassian sank back to the cot, more tears rolling down his face, though his expression was hard.

"You will bear this for the rest of your life, Cassian," Somar said, and he moved to his pupil's cot and sat next to him. "Many a soldier has felt what you are feeling, including me. I will not lie to you. The guilt will be horrible. You shall relive the moment hundreds of times in your mind. It will be a long, long time before you will feel anything resembling happiness again, but you must live with the consequences of your actions. You owe that much to the empire now—you owe it even to Dimitris." He put a hand on Cassian's shoulder. "Take this time to grieve, because you need to, but understand that there is no escaping what happened today, and so you must be strong."

To Somar's surprise, this elicited wheezing laughter from the Cassian. Even as tears dripped down the young man's face, he shook his head with a troubled smile.

"What?" said Somar.

"Funny that you should use those exact words," the boy whispered. He gazed down at his legs and said: "Did I ever tell you about the day my mother died, old man?"

"We have never spoken of it except when we first met."

Cassian let out a long sigh, a mixture of intense emotions playing across his features. "I was eleven. I did not know that I was a Starborn yet, but my mother and I both possessed exceptionally strong talent in magic. It was a bond we shared.

My father did not possess the sorcerer's gift, but he did have a fine title in the empire and a great deal of land, so I inherited much from both of them." Cassian chuckled: "Parents with magical bloodlines sometimes have to produce twenty children before conceiving a single sorcerer, but my mother gave birth to a Starborn on her first go."

The boy swallowed, gazing up at the ceiling of the tent. "She was such an amazing woman. She spoke nine languages and possessed an almost preternatural capacity for mathematics, science, and history. We were telepathically linked even when I was a young child, and much of that information glided from her mind to mine, as did the essence of her beautiful heart. I loved her more than anything in the world."

Cassian's eyes filled with hatred as he said: "They *took* her and my father in the middle of the night. Twenty-three men came. Four of them were sorcerers, six of them had tattoos, and the rest were militiamen from the next village over. Our guards just let them in. *No one stands in the way of the church.* I felt them rip her from her bed, and I tried very clumsily to attack them. One of the sorcerers hurled me back into a wall and knocked me unconscious with a bit of magic I could now counter with a thought.

"When I woke up, they were already long gone. My telepathic connection to my mother reestablished itself as soon as my eyes opened though and... I felt them... *torturing her.* They were trying to force her to write a confession and repent. My father... he was a kind man, but not a brave one. He confessed quickly to all manner of *humanist* sin, such as failing to pray to *Mother Esuna* for a good harvest and instead having his farmers rely on crop rotation and irrigation techniques. They rewarded him with a quick slice to the throat. My mother though... she knew those horrible bastards were going to kill her no matter what. She held out for *days,* giving them nothing. It pained her to know that I was watching all of it, and she tried to push me away, but even then, my telepathy surpassed hers. I stayed connected to her every minute of the three days they had her, right up until the moment that they gave her one final chance to confess and then cut her head from her body. I felt her die then."

Cassian paused, and a fresh set of tears dripped down his face. His voice was surprisingly even when he resumed: "In the last instant before her life was stolen, she whispered to me: '*You must be strong, Cassian.*' I was not strong though. Her death ripped a hole in me larger than anything I had ever imagined. I was overcome with sorrow to such an extent that I believed going on to be impossible." He rolled his eyes at Somar and said: "At eleven years old, I decided to kill myself. I snuck away from the castle that night and went up into the mountains to the north. I hiked up for hours in the darkness to a peak I knew...to throw myself off, so I could join my parents."

Cassian gazed down at the table then and a long moment of silence passed. Eventually, Somar said: "What stopped you?"

"Nothing. I jumped." Cassian shut his eyes as if sinking into the memory. "I leaped outward and felt the wind and gravity take me. Immediately, I saw jagged rock rushing up. It was at that moment, when I looked death in the face and felt terror rip through every cell in my body, that my world changed. All the barriers in my mind shattered. I felt myself fill up with more magic than I had ever known, and suddenly I could sense the world around me—*the Universe*—in ways I had never dreamed. All of it happened in a fraction of a second, but in that instant, I understood exactly what I was. I heard my mother's words in my mind once again: *You must be strong, Cassian,* and I willed myself to cease falling and came to a stop in the air. I think that was the greatest moment of clarity in my life. I knew I was a Starborn, and I knew what that meant. I could become emperor if I dedicated myself completely to the goal." Cassian blinked. "That was when I decided the purpose of the rest of my life."

He smiled. "I am the youngest Starborn ever to reach the ascension to my powers, though in doing so I dragged Dimitris,

Telemachus, Keska, and even that little wretch Arkas into ascension a few seconds later. None of us were ready for the profound connection we experienced in that moment, but it came nonetheless, and they all felt my pain, my anger, and my determination smash through ancient and sacred barriers that had never before been broken for ones so young as we." Cassian swallowed dryly, then added: "That is why they are all afraid of me."

Somar reflected on this and said nothing but continued to gaze at his pupil. The boy seemed not to be finished speaking, and Somar was contented to let him say whatever else he wished.

"At first I only wanted to stop the Nemesai," Cassian eventually resumed. "My plan was simple: become emperor and outlaw religious persecution. As I grew older though, and my telepathic mind began to reach all over the world, I started to see *other* things that were as ugly and unjust as what had happened to my family. The church is only allowed to do what it does because the masses are too weak, too poverty-stricken, and too uneducated to challenge what is being done to them. The vast majority of humans on this planet live their entire lives under the oppression of a cruel and greedy aristocratic class. Their existences are used up in labor so that a handful of wealthy, intermarried families can bathe in luxury and power and live well above the very laws they use to strangle their *subjects*." He gritted his teeth. "I realized it was all part of the same disease. The way this empire governs is wrong—all of it! My parents dared to explore humanism, and the church broke into my house, took my mother from her bed, tortured her for days and then cut her head off and it was *LEGAL*!" As he screamed the final word the table in front of him snapped in half.

Cassian took several slow, cautious breaths, stilling himself. Then he said: "I knew I would have to play the game though. It was the only way I could possibly achieve my goals within my lifetime. It would be absurd for some angry young man to try to overthrow the largest government in the world, but a boy who had a one-in-five chance of achieving close to absolute authority in that government might actually succeed." Cassian swallowed. "But I also knew... or came to learn, that Dimitris would never let me have the throne without a fight."

"It was always going to come to a battle between the two of you," Somar said in as soft a voice as he could manage, "and you must not ever forget that it was *he* who challenged you."

"It was the most terrible thing I have ever done, and I was manipulated into it—*both of us were*." He gazed down, his green eyes alive with anger, yet he breathed quite softly, and his body had ceased to tremble. Somar could almost see him hardening his heart, as he had seen men do many times after they took life. "You warned me it would be like this—that the empire is run by ruthless, cunning men. General Romulus was *grinning* as we walked off to kill each other." Cassian's eyes lifted and met Somar's in an iron stare. "I have stepped into the pit of snakes, and now they have begun to slither around me. They have not realized yet that I am the snake with the biggest teeth."

CHAPTER 13: THE FORETOLD WEAPON

Arkas gazed nervously as the burning sun began to disappear behind the rooftops of the backwater city. He had been sitting on the stone bench in front of the sundial for hours, just as instructed. There were only a few moments left for the Norn's prophecy to be fulfilled. He squirmed under the tension, thumping the heels of his fine boots into dirt and crabgrass. This was the correct date and the correct time, and he had had to construct a careful excuse about family business to his *master,* Bishop Cromlic, to leave the capital. Yet as he gazed around with not only his eyes but his Starborn senses, he detected nothing out of the ordinary, which was troubling.

So many thoughts were racing through his mind. *Cassian had killed Dimitris...* On one hand, Dimitris had been an obstacle in Arkas's path to the throne, yet on the other, it was not Dimitris who had been prophesized to kill Arkas. *Cassian Asango will challenge you to a duel. You will lose.* The words had echoed in his mind for years, and every time Cassian overcame death, that prophecy seemed more inevitable. Still, the Norn had promised him a weapon that could kill his father. Surely it would have to be something of truly awesome power to overcome the great Emperor Tacitus. It was going to *fall into his lap,* or so she had said. Arkas's eyes shifted about, scanning the streets and the sky and fixing often on the crudely carved stone sundial. The thing was speckled with bits of moss and bird droppings—hardly the backdrop he might imagine for receiving a weapon of prophecy.

He watched a few peasants walking about, plodding along in their simple lives. Most of the city's people had returned to their homes for the evening, and the few still out had no idea they were standing in the presence of a living miracle, or the importance of what was about to happen. *Or would it happen?* Could the Norn have lied? She was a notoriously cunning and deceptive creature, but the Enumis stated many times that she was incapable of actually lying. But then... *where had those words in the holy book come from?* Most had been spoken by the Norn herself.

Arkas choked on his doubt. *There was so little time left!* He gazed out at the beams of sunlight filtering through the alleys of the ugly buildings and watched with mounting panic as they grew dimmer and dimmer. His eyes shifted up to the harvest moon. It was already visible in the sky, and even the faintest trickles of the stars were beginning to appear.

A cold terror crept through his flesh as the sun finally set. Arkas jerked his head and began to gaze around again. *Why was it not appearing?!* Years of his life had centered around this single moment. He had taken steps against his own father and enslaved himself to the cruel leader of the Nemesai because of the Norn's promise. Yet the sky was turning to black, and he felt not even a trickle of power around him save from the energy pulsing in the tattoos of the men he had hiding in nearby alleys. He gazed back at one of them, Dunlin, a hulking murderer he had rescued from his father's gallows. The man met his eyes from under the hood that concealed his heavily marked face. Dunlin knew nothing. *Of course he knew nothing!* Arkas felt confusion in the brute man, and it mingled with his own. He felt furious. *This had all been a cruel joke!*

"OH!" a female voice shrieked, and Arkas turned around just in time to see a girl stumble backward. She fell across his lap, and his right arm moved reflexively to catch her. She turned to him, a pretty young thing with wild brown hair. "I'm so sorry!" she exclaimed. As she spoke the words, his eyes shifted to the tattoo running down her cheek. It was the mark of a slave, but it had two curving lateral lines across the neck denoting that she had been legally freed.

Arkas clutched the girl's shoulder, excitement rippling through him. "It's you!" he hissed.

Her young face grimaced and turned to glance at the hand that clutched her. She looked back at Arkas and said: "D-do I know you, sir?"

He made a quick scan of the girl's mind. If she was the weapon, she did not seem to know *anything* about it. Her head was filled with simple thoughts about preparing food and folding clothing, and of a childish kind of peasant love for her *family*. As he read all of this, her name appeared in his mind: *Iona Sondal.* "What's going on?" he said. He tightened his grip on the girl. "Are you hiding it from me somehow? I warn you, do *not* try to deceive me!"

This Iona's eyes widened, and she cried: "I—I don't know what you are talking about, sir! Please, there must be some kind of misunderstanding!"

Bewildered, Arkas began to focus all of his magical senses upon the trembling girl, but just as he did, a thin hand closed on the wrist that gripped her and gave a sharp yank. He had not expected this, and it was enough to pry his grip loose. Iona wriggled off of his lap, and he turned and glared up at a second girl with the markings of a former slave, this one tall and blond and utterly beautiful. Her blue eyes stared fiercely at him. By reflex, he reached out to her mind to ascertain if she knew some secret about Iona, but his psychic tendrils encountered a shockingly powerful mental wall—one so strong it almost reminded him of Cassian's.

The blond girl's face filled with fear at his mental touch. She drew back, looking as though she were going to scream, yet no sound came out. Iona scurried to her and looked nervously back at Arkas, whimpering: "P-please don't hurt us!"

She would not get away! Arkas rose and waved his right hand. There was a shuffling of feet from behind. Dunlin and his other man came bounding up. Iona gave a little shriek as Dunlin's tattooed hand took hold of her wrist. He twisted her arm up behind her back and then brought a knife up to her throat with his free hand and hissed: "Don't move—don't make a sound." Iona whimpered but did not speak.

Arkas's other man, Stavros, a cruel but incredibly efficient mercenary he had acquired in the North, drew a dagger and pointed it at the blond girl, who had gone very pale, and said: "Do I cut her throat?"

Arkas gazed around. The city street was relatively empty, but a few townspeople had stopped to gape at what was happening, and one man was running away, probably to call the city guards. Arkas lifted his left hand in the direction of the fleeing peasant and said: "*Aradrak*!"

Instantly Arkas's magic flared from his palm and formed into a blazing green orb of death. The ball whipped through the air and struck the man in the side. His body changed direction abruptly and slammed into the back wall of a building. He bounced and fell limp to the street.

Iona gave a little shriek, but Dunlin jerked her body and hissed: "Quiet!" She fell silent.

Arkas turned his gaze to the trembling blond girl, though he spoke to his underling: "Stavros, I need you to cover our escape. I wish to leave *quietly*."

"Understood," Stavros said in an icy voice. He pulled a concealed sword from under his heavy cloak and dashed toward the remaining two witnesses. Arkas shifted his gaze to Iona and gestured to the silent girl. "Is she your sister?" he said.

"Y-yes, sir," Iona squeaked.

Arkas hesitated, considering, then whispered: "It has to be you. I have no use for her."

He raised his hand in the direction of the blond girl and said: "Seithiak Neresketh." Two spectrals moved through him, combining discrete pockets of his energy into a small, swirling cloud of inky black energy. It would rupture the girl's heart within her chest. There would be no clear proof that she had been killed by sorcery – certainly no evidence that it had been done by a Starborn.

"NOO!" Iona screamed. Dunlin let go of her arm behind her back and cupped a hand over her mouth and moved the blade a little closer to her neck, snarling: "*Not another sound*!"

Arkas did not hesitate. He willed the construct of deathly magic at the blond girl. Surprisingly, she let out no scream but only shut her eyes and cringed, her hands going up in a desperate gesture of self-protection. Then something happened that Arkas did not expect: the spell shattered in the air, bursting into thousands of tiny translucent fragments that dissipated into nothingness.

"WHAT?!" he snarled.

The blond girl flinched, but then opened her eyes and looked at him. There was confusion in her face.

"What's going on, boss?" Dunlin said, his voice tense.

"I—I don't know," Arkas rasped. He glared at the blond girl, his eyes falling again on her slave mark. *Who the hell was she*? He lifted his right hand, this time not even bothering to form a spell. He willed raw magic out through his fingers to crush her throat. His power moved at the speed of thought to her flesh, yet the instant it touched her it recoiled back, returning with such force that he felt several bones in his hand snap. He wrenched back his limb with a scream of agony.

The blond girl blinked and ran a finger over the place on her neck where his magic had touched her. She still looked confused, but some of the terror left her eyes. Blood was rushing to Arkas's shattered hand, and he was unable to hold back a whimper from the pain. *What was happening?* How could this former slave stand against him? In a panic, he gathered his will to attack her again, but to his terror, his own energy failed to obey his command. Instead, it began to turn on him!

"GHHH!" he screamed as a sensation of searing pain erupted through his body. His own magic burned and ripped at his muscles and his nerves. "STOP IT!" The agony only grew, and he realized in a flash of terror that his own Starborn power was going to kill him.

Dunlin moved very suddenly. He threw Iona to the ground and slammed the metallic handle of his dagger into the side of the blond girl's skull. Arkas saw her eyes roll back as she fell unconscious to the ground, and the terrible onslaught of his magic ceased. He collapsed to his knees, gasping.

"D-do I kill her?!" Dunlin hissed back over his shoulder. He stood over the unconscious girl, his fingers trembling around the handle of his weapon.

"N-no," Arkas managed to wheeze. He gazed at the slumped form as a sickening realization crept into his mind. "J-just leave her."

The man hesitated. "H-how did she do that to you? Are you sure *she* isn't the weapon?"

"S-she isn't," Arkas rasped as he rose to his feet. He knew *exactly* what she was. He took a nervous step back from her, feeling his whole body—his *entire soul* shiver with fear. He had not wanted to believe that she existed, but there she was, *just a few paces away.* The Norn had known that this girl would be here when she set him on this path, and if Dunlin had not acted when he did, Arkas would have died. He drew still further away. Much as he burned to end the wretch's life for the pain she had caused him, there was no telling what would happen if they killed her.

"Leave the little bitch," he said, shaking off his fear. The link had been broken. He turned to Iona, who was once again trembling on the ground. She had not tried to run, having stayed for the sake of her sister. *Loyalty was such a ridiculous trait!* He knelt over her and moved the hand that was not broken to his mouth and pulled his half stuffed glove off with his teeth, revealing his gnarled mess of a right appendage to the air. Iona shrieked as he moved it to her forehead. He needed to see in that moment that the world was within his grasp—that she was the weapon he had spent years anticipating.

The girl hyperventilated as his magic permeated her skin. It seeped around into her blood and bones and into the soft, shifting organs. There was nothing at first except the infinitesimal energies of living flesh, but then he caught a sense of something. It was not in one single point but was a kind of field that burned very quietly all throughout her body. It was unworldly—utterly unlike anything Arkas had ever felt. It was not magic. It was something . . . the only word that came to mind was that it was *purer* than magic. Whatever it was, its power was incalculable. *This was indeed the weapon that could kill his father!*

Arkas made one more sweeping scan of Iona's mind. He could detect no mental connection to the vast energies within her. The power did not react to her thoughts or emotions. Indeed, she had no idea of its existence. Incredibly, this former *slave* was the unwitting vessel to what might be the greatest force in the entire world, and she was *his!*

Arkas stood and let out a laugh of pure delight. Then he gestured at the girl with his left hand and whispered: "Estrakia Nesveth." A spell formed instantly and whisked into her. He felt it pull just enough blood from her brain to render her unconscious. She fell limp, but he willed his magic into a large, gentle hand around her so that she did not hit her head. *This girl was the most precious thing in the world!*

"Get the horses," Arkas whispered to Dunlin. He turned then and gazed back at Stavros. The man had dragged the bodies of the witnesses into an alley and thrown some loose fence planks over them. He was pacing about now, making sure that no more unfortunate souls happened to wander onto the strange scene.

As Dunlin disappeared around the corner to retrieve the steeds, Arkas took one more look at the blond girl. The Norn's trap had nearly succeeded, but luck had been on his side. Was that not proof that he was meant to prevail? Was it not proof that he alone was meant to rule Denigoth?

CHAPTER 14: THE SPIRIT WORLD

Kota knelt silently in front of the small domed hut he and Gretis had constructed together from long tree branches and the tanned skins of cows. They had traveled for three days away from the Onkai temple, deep into the mountains and wilderness where the terrain had never truly been mapped by man. Gretis had ridden a horse and brought a second steed to carry supplies, but Kota had asked to travel on foot, and she had allowed it. The days on the road had been a time of quiet introspection, but that was over now.

A cold wind was blowing softly against his skin, though he hardly noticed it. His eyes were fixed on the orange glow within the hut. Gretis was stoking the fire and pouring her concoctions into it. In only a few moments, the ceremony would begin. Kota's blood was pumping hot in his veins. He was utterly terrified and utterly thrilled.

Gretis crawled out through the small opening very slowly, her hands crunching dead leaves on the ground beneath her. For once, her long hair was not tied back but fell in a wavy mane down her shoulders. She was clothed in a simple brown tunic and leather pants. All of her silver jewelry was gone, and her face was entirely unpainted. She had a wild look about her that he had never seen before.

"Are you nervous?" she said in a gentle voice.

"Yes," Kota whispered.

"That is good. There is no room for arrogance on the journey we are about to take."

"It will be a journey then?" Kota said, frowning a little. As usual, she had told him nothing. Three days of camp and travel and not a single secret of what was to come had spilled from her lips.

Gretis cast him a gentle smile and said: "It will be the truth."

"Always riddles," Kota muttered, his body giving a little shiver.

"That is the way it has always been done," she said with a soft laugh. "But I think tonight I must go beyond that just a bit." Her voice lost some of its humor as she said: "Before we go in there together, I must finally tell you about Soulic."

Kota felt his eyes widen. Gretis had never spoken of her son, even after the encounter in the forest. Kota gazed at the blade witch, years of cumulative curiosity welling up in his mind, and he almost smiled. The distraction from his fear was a welcome one.

Gretis sat down on the leaves, crossing her legs. She was not bothered by the cold or the dirt of the forest but was at peace with these things, much like a shamalak. "I must tell you a bit about my life before I began my study of Sansrit." Her lips curled into a wry smile as she said: "If you can possibly believe it, I was a princess once."

Kota felt his eyes widen once again. He stared at Lady Gretis, and she made a small giggle.

"I was a soft and spoiled girl. I suppose I was something of a beauty as well. Many princes and kings sought my hand, but my father was not quick to give me away." Gretis took in a slow breath, and her eyes lowered. "We do not have time for many details. My kingdom was very small and..." her throat seemed to tighten as she whispered: "the *Denigoth Empire* consumed small kingdoms quite aggressively back then. An army appeared at our borders, and in the span of less than a month, my home was destroyed, my parents and my brothers put to death, and I... *became a prize* to one of the men who had overseen it all."

Kota sat in silence, too shocked to speak.

Gretis was quiet for a moment, staring down into the leaves in front of her. Then she lifted her gaze and said: "In a short time I was pregnant... *with Soulic.* I believed then that I would live out the rest of my life as a slave and so would my child. All hope had escaped my heart." Gretis looked up at the stars. "My father had befriended an old Sansrit Master many years before. I was told he was present at my birth, but I had no memories of him. His name was Aldar, and he was a very old, very wise, and very kind man. When he learned what had happened to my family and my kingdom, he came. Aldar found me and managed to free me from my captors. He took me away and cared for me—helped me through my pregnancy. Over that time, he looked inside of my spirit as I did yours when we met. Aldar told me that I had the strength to become a great Sansrit Master, and he offered me a new life and a new purpose. He warned me though that I could not walk down that path with hatred in my heart." Gretis gave a dark laugh and picked up a dead leaf from the ground and peered at it. "Perhaps you cannot imagine the conundrum this was for me. Aldar would grant me the power to avenge my honor and the lives of my family upon that cruel commander and his men, but I had to forswear all vengeance to acquire the strength." She lifted her eyes to Kota's and said in a very serious voice: "A Sansrit Master wields terrible power, and that power comes from the deepest recesses of the spirit. If that part of you is tainted with hate, it can become an all-consuming curse."

"You managed to let go," Kota whispered.

"I did, though I cannot describe how difficult a thing that was. There are no laws in the Denigoth Empire against what that man did to me and to my family. To forswear my vengeance was to allow him to grow old in the comfort and wealth that was built upon the deaths of my parents and brothers and sisters." Gretis shut her eyes and whispered: "It was the most difficult trial of my life—more so even than the training itself."

She did not speak for a moment but remained still. Her fingers closed around the leaf she had been holding, crushing it as a whisper escaped her lips: "Soulic was not able to banish his hatred as I did. I might have helped him with it, but I did not understand its nature."

"Why did he hate?" Kota said.

A bitter smiled crossed Gretis's face. "He managed to get hold of a journal I kept—one that I thought was quite secret from him. I had told him a lie that his father was a young soldier who died in battle. I thought this best." She clenched her jaw and said: "perhaps the deception added a sense of betrayal to his anger. Whatever the case, he did *not* forswear vengeance. He planned to murder the man who violated his mother." She blinked and whispered: "I suppose in a way it was a noble sentiment—a simple love for me." Gretis cocked an eyebrow up at Kota and said: "Would you not want to avenge your mother?"

"I... I might," he admitted. Kota thought briefly of the mother he had left so long ago and found himself wondering if he was now as close to the human sitting before him as he had been to her.

Gretis straightened up, the emotion in her face fading to a sober and serious expression. "The path I am about to lead you down is not like that of the Onkai. Their power is external. It simply makes them physically stronger. The energy you shall know will come from deep within your heart, and once it is drawn out, you will have no ability to suppress it." Her eyes hardened, and she said: "*My son* is ruled by his anger. He cannot be reasoned with. I do not know if anything but death will ever free him, and so it will be with you, Kota, if you hold hatred, or jealousy, or any other dark emotion in your heart. So I ask you once again, and you must answer me truthfully, for there will be no going back once we begin: Do you hate the Nemesai who took you prisoner? Do you hate me for making you train twelve and thirteen hours in a day? Do you hate *anyone*?"

Kota hesitated for a moment as he considered all Gretis had told him, and then he felt a calm smile come over his face. "I thank you for trusting me with this truth, and I understand," he said. He reached out and took her hand, and his voice cracked just a touch as he said: "I could never hate you, Mother of Wisdom. I hold you in the deepest place in my heart. It is for you that I can be strong."

A pair of tears dropped out of Gretis's eyes, rolling quickly down her smooth face. She started to speak but then choked back, and she simply clutched Kota's fingers. Eventually, she gave him a very warm smile and said: "Then let us begin."

Gretis crawled into the hut and Kota followed. The small, round room they had constructed glowed from the light of the red fire embers in its center. The thick scent of burning wood and oil struck Kota hard as he sat down at the burning pit. He stared at his teacher as she knelt before the flames and reached into an animal skin rucksack. Gretis drew out a large clay jar and removed the thick cork at its top, revealing a black powder that had the faintest bluish glow to it. He watched her take a large pinch of the substance and sprinkled it over the embers, and immediately a thick white smoke hissed up.

"Do not be afraid to breathe this," she said in a soft voice.

Kota took an uneasy whiff of the white smoke through his nose and was surprised to find that it did not sting his nostrils the way normal smoke might. It felt clean and smooth, and he was able to draw it deep into his lungs.

"Yes," Gretis whispered as she drew another clay jar from her bag. "Close your eyes and breathe as I taught you."

Kota obeyed, placing his hands in his lap automatically in his normal meditative pose. He inhaled more of the strange white smoke, and then he heard the sound of the second jar being opened, and shortly after there was a second hiss from the fire pit. A new scent made itself known in the air, thick and chalky so that he could taste it on his tongue. It reminded him of roses and lilac. Kota concentrated on his breathing. He felt his heart begin to slow and the muscles in his body began to release all the little bits of tension coiled within them.

The sense of warmth and relaxation that always washed over Kota when he meditated came, but it was stronger than usual. His body pulsed with a delightful sensation of serenity. It was like being in the deepest and most relaxed sleep imaginable, only he was awake and alert. His ears twitched gently at the sound of Gretis putting more of her concoctions into the fire, and then more hisses of smoke permeated the air with new, strange scents.

The image of a warm and wonderful field of yellow light appeared in Kota's mind. It enveloped his form, and it pulsed and shifted with his slow breathing and the soft and distant beat of his heart. He felt Gretis take his hands in hers, and when she did, he perceived a second light, this one a shade of soft blue that mixed with his own. By some unknowable instinct, Kota sensed this was her—a part of her spirit that was touching a part of his. They were together. Whether he had been meditating for only a few moments or for many hours, he could not begin to guess. All he knew was that his consciousness was expanding in ways he had never imagined, and Gretis was there to guide him.

There came a tugging sensation, as if Gretis's spirit were pulling against his, and then they were both soaring together. Kota did not see anything at first but only felt a sense of gliding movement. Slowly though, he began to see brilliant streaks of light all around the two of them, like hundreds upon hundreds of tiny stars of every color shooting past. And then they stopped, the sense of movement ceasing as abruptly as if they had slammed into a wall, yet he had felt no collision. There was a cool breeze on his skin and the sensation of soft, wet grass beneath his feet. The lights faded, and Kota saw that he was standing in the midst of a vast forest of rolling hills and trees that stretched high into a moonless, starless night sky.

Feeling disoriented yet strangely at peace, Kota gazed down at the claws on his toes. The grass beneath them shimmered softly, moving between opacity and translucence so that he could intermittently see through it into a blackness that matched the sky above.

"Where am I?" he said, and his voice echoed in liquid reverberation from a thousand different directions.

"You may think of this place as the spirit world," Gretis's voice answered in the same splashing echo. She appeared before him in a soft flash that began to fade immediately, but he saw her smile, and it gave him a small sense of reassurance amidst the impossibility of what he was seeing. "I have brought you as far as I can. You must go the rest of the way yourself."

The forest around him continued to shift slowly back and forth from being real and visceral to a shimmering mirage. Kota felt his feet sink into the grass. It gave in unexpected ways under him as if made of dough, and as he shifted his weight, he saw little ripples flow out.

"What am I doing here?" he said, gazing around at the ever-shifting, ever disappearing forest, trying to hold fast to any sense of reality.

"You must find your own answer to that question," she said in a whisper that hissed from all around. "I can give you no help now."

At that moment, Kota heard the sound of a deep, wet sniff that shifted into a loud exhalation of air that shook his very bones. It was the noises of a beast sniffing out its prey, but the pitch and volume told of a creature more massive than any Kota had ever encountered. He turned and gaped as a tremendous black silhouette moved behind the trees. It was larger than anything in the world—a mass of terrifying muscle that stood as tall as the Onkai temple. The creature was moving on four legs, and the pounding of its great paws sent shockwaves through the grass like waves in the ocean. The ground lifted Kota up and dropped him back down so that he had to dig the claws on his toes into it to keep from being thrown.

He stared as this impossible creature moved from behind the trees and began to slowly walk toward him, feeling too awestruck to run. *How could anyone escape from something so massive and powerful?* Time seemed to slow as the monster drew nearer, and some part of Kota's mind began to note details of its form. It had thick, powerful limbs covered with an orange-bronze fur that billowed in the intangible wind. The tremendous head came into view, revealing a black nose like that of a forest cat, and black lips that curled up around thick fangs that Kota knew could rend his body to gnarled meat with an effortless bite. The creature's features were somewhere between those of a wolf and a lion, yet its eyes did not seem entirely beast-like. They were silver, just like Kota's own, and he could somehow sense that there was a degree of intelligence behind them.

The beast moved within fifty paces or so, then stopped and stared at Kota. He involuntarily gasped and took a step back, and the creature followed him with its eyes, not moving. Kota's mind struggled to make sense of what he was seeing. Gretis had called this place the spirit world. What did that make this creature? He stared at it, taking in the teeth and the fur and...*the claws.* Kota found himself gazing down at his fingers. Some instinct from deep inside boiled up, and he extended his own claws. The instant they snapped out, a low growl came from the beast's throat that shook the world. When the sound died away, there was perfect silence in the forest save for the creature's soft breathing, and the thump of its great heart. Kota listened to that heartbeat and felt it at the same time, *for it exactly mirrored his own.*

He swallowed as he stared into the silver eyes, and an epiphany too great to believe washed over him. Five years ago, he had left his tribe to venture out into the wilderness and perceive his spirit, and now, in the depths of his heart, Kota knew he was finally gazing upon it. This was the most profound moment of his life. This creature was distinct from his conscious mind, and yet part of him. It was his courage and his strength, and so much more. He could feel its power—raw and primal and enormous. That power lay inside of him. It had always been there, waiting to be called upon.

The beast roared, and the wind of its breath pushed his hair back. It bared its teeth and crouched, readying to charge. Kota knew he should be terrified, but as he gazed at the snarling monster, a thrill came over him. *This was the truth of his existence!* If this creature were a part of him, then he would face it. Somehow, he knew this was what he had to do.

As the beast bounded forward, Kota ran directly at it, his claws tearing into the ethereal grass beneath his feet. His spirit was on him in two great strides, its enormous mouth open and low to the ground. Kota leaped toward the jaws, unafraid. His clawed hands closed around two massive fangs in the air, and there was an explosion of energy. Brilliant blue light tore and crackled through him like lightning. Kota knew this was his spirit's power, and he embraced it. He felt strength beyond anything he had imagined filling up inside him. The forest vanished away then. *He no longer had need of it.*

Kota's conscious mind went hurtling back the way it had come. Again, he passed through the ocean of burning stars, but much faster than before. He willed himself out of the spirit world and back into his physical body, the full might of the beast moving with him in a flash of violent and beautiful power.

Suddenly he was in a domed hut standing on his two feet, letting out a roar so thunderous that the animal skin structure around him trembled. Every muscle in his body was flexing. His claws were out, and they were larger than they had ever been.

Kota heard a gasp, and he looked down and saw a human woman staring up at him with a frightened expression. He thought he knew her, but he could not remember. She stood up slowly and looked into his eyes and said: "Kota!"

The name registered in some distant part of his mind, but he paid it no attention. This human was of little interest. The power coursing through him ached to be used. He turned and gazed at the thin layer of animal skin that stood between himself and the rest of the world. The thought came to him that he should pass through it, and instantly his legs snapped him forward. His body tore through the tent and hurtled twenty or thirty paces in the span of a second before his feet came to a rough skid through the leaves. He laughed aloud at his own wonderful speed.

"Kota!" the woman shouted from behind him. He turned to face her. There seemed to be power from her that was something like his own. She took a step forward and said: "Can you understand me?"

He tried to make sense of the words but could not. The human frowned at him and then her body whipped over the leaves in his direction. She moved with speed like his, and as he saw this, he gave a laugh and whirled away from her. *This was a game of chase!* His legs launched him forward into a cluster of trees. It was terribly dark, but his body knew how to navigate, and he darted and leaped through the brush. The air whipped at his face, and the trees passed behind him in quick blurs left and right. At one point, he perceived a low branch in his path a little thicker than his head, but his hand moved of its own accord and batted the thing. There was a snapping sound and a spray of splinters, but no pain at all.

Kota accelerated his movements, giggling at the thought of the woman trailing somewhere behind him. *He was faster than she was!* As he shot further and further ahead, his eyes suddenly fixed on the soft orange glow of a fire off in the distance. Curious, he whipped toward it, his legs kicking up dirt and leaves in a wild pace.

A few heartbeats later Kota came to a skidding halt on a rough patch of dirt just before the fire. He gazed around and saw that he was in a clearing. Two large humans were sitting by this fire next to a pair of horses. They were looking at him with wide, frightened eyes.

"W-what in the hell?" one man said, rising to his feet. He was a heavyset human with a thick brown beard. "W-what are you?"

"Look at its eyes!" the other man shouted, rising as well. He had a thick tuft of closely cropped blond hair, and he wore something at his belt that Kota vaguely recognized as a sword. "He's some kind of demon!" this man hissed, and he drew his weapon out, shouting with a furious glare: "Get the hell out of here!" And then he swung his sword.

Kota watched the blade come. The swing seemed ridiculously slow and clumsy. He easily leaned back and let the weapon swipe pass harmlessly through the air, and he let out a chuckle. The man grunted and swung again, this time at Kota's ribs. Still laughing, Kota whipped his stomach back, and once more the sword struck nothing but air.

"He's so fast!" the blond man shrieked, and he lunged forward in a desperate slash. It amused Kota to leap upward over the blade, and he commanded his legs to launch him. A split second later his feet were above his attacker's head, but he seemed to have misjudged his power, for his body continued to rise for several heartbeats longer.

"OH GODS!" he heard a shriek from below and looked down at the man, who was quite a way down. The human stumbled back as Kota's body finally began its descent. The cool air rushed up for a few heartbeats, and then his feet met the grass, his legs absorbing the impact in graceful silence as he dropped into a crouch. It was then that he sensed the crossbow.

Kota could feel the other human—the one with the beard—behind him, trembling with the weapon in his hands. Kota shut his eyes and let a strange new perception overtake his mind. He *felt* the tension in the bowstring—felt the muscles in the man's arms as he tried to aim, and then there was the snap of the trigger. Most fascinating of all was the bolt as it shot. Kota felt it flying forward and perceived the way its tip sliced through the cool night air. Without opening his eyes, he spun around and caught the thing with his right hand by the shaft. *This was wonderful!* He gazed at the bolt for a moment and then tossed it back to the man. The human looked at him with an expression of terror, but Kota pointed to the arrow and then patted himself on the chest several times. *He wanted to keep playing this game.*

"Kota!" the woman's voice came once more from behind in a furious shout. He turned and saw her. She had a sword in her hand. Kota took a few steps back from her in surprise, and as he did, he passed behind one of the horses that had been tied to a tree branch. The horse bucked immediately, and both of its great legs shot out.

Kota knew he could move easily out of the way, but it occurred to him that being kicked by a horse might be amusing so he turned to face it. The two hooves rammed into his chest. Kota felt the power in his body crackle in resistance to the blow, and he remained still as the horse's body jerked forward from the force reflected back at it.

"That horse just kicked me!" Kota said with a loud laugh, and then he remembered that he could speak. He looked at Gretis, who was scowling at him, and he began to make sense of where he was and what he had just done. Swallowing, Kota turned to the two men. Their faces were white with fear.

He swallowed and said: "I—I'm sorry!" Then a wave of dizziness came. Kota blinked, trying to focus on Gretis, but her image blurred. He felt his legs buckle beneath him, and then his vision went black.

CHAPTER 15: RECRUITMENT

Somar stumbled out through the red cloth that made up the door to his and Cassian's tent. The boy had disappeared at some point in the very wee hours of the morning, which was quite troubling given the mental state he been in the night before. The two of them were surrounded by soldiers who were commanded by one of the most ruthless generals in Denigoth's history, and Cassian's sense of propriety and restraint could be...*unpredictable*.

"Excuse me, have you seen Lord Asango?" Somar said to a group of six soldiers who were walking in a line in front of his tent. They all stopped and turned to him.

"Oh yes, he's causing quite a ruckus," said a tall soldier with thick black stubble on his face. "He's walkin' around the camp with his dragon asking the men strange questions and writin' on a stack of papers with magic. Damndest thing I ever seen! He just looks at the page and letters appear."

A shorter, rounder soldier said excitedly: "Yeah, and General Romulus summoned him just a little while ago, but when the messenger came and told him, Asango just looked at the man and said 'No.' We're all kind of wonderin' what's going to happen next. Nobody says *no* to Romulus, but then Asango is a Starborn, and—"

"Where is he?" Somar said sharply.

"A few rows of tents that way," said the tall soldier, pointing to the east.

"Thank you," Somar said, and he broke into the closest thing to a run his aged body could manage, stumbling around soldiers and camp equipment. He went through three rows of tents before he spotted Cassian speaking to a handful soldiers not much older than himself. Titus was seated a few feet behind him gazing around and, from the look of things, making the soldiers around him extremely nervous. Half out of breath, Somar sprinted toward the gathering.

"At what age did you enlist?" said Cassian.

One of the young soldiers started to answer, but Somar called out: "Lord Asango, might I have a word?"

Cassian cocked his head toward Somar, then turned back to the soldiers and said: "Stay here, please. I will be back in a moment." He walked to Somar and said: "Yes?"

"May I ask what you were doing just now?"

"Recruitment," the boy said in a matter-of-fact tone.

"Recruitment for what exactly, may I ask?"

"My personal guard."

Just then, a group of three soldiers approached, with one man walking in front and the other two flanking him. The leader said in an official, yet at the same time nervous voice: "Lord Asango, General Romulus has instructed me to remind you that you have been inducted into his army, and that military law requires you appear before him when summoned." A rumbling growl escaped Titus at these words, and the soldier visibly winced.

"Hmm," Cassian grunted. He lifted the stack of papers in his left hand, upon which Somar noticed many names had been written, and pulled a blank sheet from the back and narrowed his eyes at it. Beautifully written black letters began to appear on the page, here and there tiny puffs of smoke emitting from them as they took shape, as if Cassian were burning them into the sheet. The words were written in Dhavic, but Somar mentally translated them to <Cease annoying me immediately, Romulus. I can kill you from anywhere in this camp.>

Somar suppressed a gasp as his pupil handed the paper to the soldier and said: "Give him this.". The man stared at the page with a look of incomprehension. *At least he had bothered to write it in the scholar's language.* After a moment, the soldier muttered: "Yes, sir."

When the men had gone, Somar said in a quiet hiss: "What the hell are you doing?"

"I told you, I am recruiting my personal guard."

Somar could have slapped Cassian at that moment. Instead, he said: "You are committing insubordination to a General of the Imperial Army. If you do not back down immediately—and I'm not even sure you *can* at this point—Romulus is going to—"

"Going to what?" Cassian said with a shrug. "What in the world do you think that *General* is going to do to me?"

"Well, you are openly disobeying direct orders from a superior officer, and in fact, you just threatened him with murder *In Writing*! By all rights, he could have you killed."

"You think he would dare touch me now?" Cassian said, his eyes cold. "I am going to be the next emperor."

"You have not been named crown prince yet."

"No, but it is extremely evident that I will be now," Cassian said, shrugging. "That is power, and I am choosing to use it."

Somar kept his voice quiet as he said: "Dammit, Cassian, I know you are upset, but this is beyond reckless, even for you!"

"On the contrary, this is all calculated," said Cassian. He leaned in closer and whispered: "What Romulus can and cannot do to me now is extremely ambiguous. Undoubtedly, Emperor Tacitus commanded him to provoke a fight between Dimitris and me." The boy's face twitched in a barely detectable expression of anger as he referred to the duel. "I do not know why, and I do not believe Romulus does either, which means he has no idea how important I am to his emperor. He will not dare attempt to kill me."

Somar narrowed his eyes. "And based on what happened with the Nemesai a few years ago, you're not exactly easy to arrest, are you? You're defying him openly—putting him in a position where he either has to kill you or leave you alone. Why?"

Cassian tilted his head so that his eyes were perfectly level with Somar's. "What do you think I would be forced to do under the command of that disgusting man?"

Somar took a slow breath, understanding immediately what Cassian was doing. Romulus was a brutal commander known to butcher entire villages who did not surrender to him at the first prompting, including women and children. Under Romulus's command, the boy would likely be ordered to commit mass murder. This was something Somar had been considering for some time, though he and Cassian had never discussed the matter.

"Fine," Somar said, "I understand your reasons, but you're playing an incredibly dangerous game. This is not what I taught you."

"I learned a great deal from you, old man," Cassian said, "but I am *not* you, and I am *not* playing." He turned his head in the direction of Romulus's tent. It was only a few hundred paces away. "I find I dislike killing, and I will not be anyone's butcher. If I must fight in the military, it will be on my own terms."

"And you believe that Romulus will just hand over whatever men you write on a list after you just embarrassed him in front of his own camp and threatened to murder him?"

"That and the supplies I need, yes," Cassian said. "Actually, I would appreciate it if you would look over my requisition orders before I submit them. This will be my first time managing an army after all."

Somar let out a very long sigh and gazed up at the clouds. He had long since lost the energy to try to talk the boy out of his brazen actions. After watching Cassian directly threaten Bishop Cromlic in front of the whole world and tell the great dragon to do his worst, was any of this behavior surprising?

"I will look over whatever you have," Somar muttered, shaking his head and trying to let go of the tremendous anxiety of being this boy's friend, which was something of an ongoing problem. "You damn well better write a letter to the Emperor explaining yourself though."

"Tacitus is acutely aware of everything I am doing." Cassian tapped his right temple, which Somar knew represented telepathy.

"And he approves of your actions?"

"He is content to silently observe how I handle Romulus. It is another way he is measuring me, I suppose."

"The Emperor certainly gives you a great deal of leeway, doesn't he?"

"He does not give me anything. I take it." Cassian sighed: "I think it amuses him."

"I see," Somar muttered. His eyes shifted to the boy's list that, upon further inspection, had more information than only names. There was age, approximate height, number of battles participated in, combat specialties, and then a series of numbers with other symbols that Somar did not recognize at all. Gritting his teeth, he muttered: "I do not wish to detain you then, except to say that I should like to know more about this personal guard of yours when you have the time."

"The whole continent will know soon, I promise you," said Cassian.

Somar accepted this answer with a nod and turned back in the direction of his tent. His mind swam with everything that had happened in the last cycle of the sun. Cassian had been thrust into all the chaotic depths of military life, and soon would follow into the ever more treacherous waters of politics. The boy was no defenseless little fish though, but a clever and powerful serpent. That was what Somar had wanted, and yet it troubled him to see it realized. The bright-eyed young man with all of his absurd ambition and sense of wonder about the world seemed gone now. Somar was rapidly becoming a very old man, and he considered his life to have been a remarkable one, but he supposed he had never been—nor would ever be again—as happy and fulfilled as he had in those years with his surrogate son, with their debates on so many different things, their games of cornerstone, and all their discussions of philosophy, literature, and history. This chapter was closing, and it filled him with an unexpected pain as he shuffled between the soldiers.

"Hello, old man," a feminine voice with a strange and wonderful cadence whispered in his ear.

Somar turned in shock to see the beautiful face of Thalice, Cassian's elven consort, staring at him under the hood of her familiar silvery green cloak. He let out an involuntary gasp as he saw her, but a feeling of relaxation washed over as the elf's turquoise eyes sparkled up at him as she said: "I see you are going for a stroll. May I walk with you?"

He felt his mouth curve into grin. Truly, it warmed his heart to see this magnificent creature. Her radiant smile was such a gift after the death and bleakness of recent events. "I think I should love nothing more in the world at this moment, my dear," he said. He offered her his arm, but she shrank back.

"We must not touch," Thalice whispered. She peeled back the fold of her cloak to reveal a glowing blue crystal the size of an apple hanging from a thin chain around her neck. "The enchantment that keeps me hidden from him takes enormous power, and yet it is incredibly fragile. If it were to fail, fifteen thousand soldiers would suddenly become aware that a female elf is in their presence." She gave a soft, silvery laugh.

"I see," he said. He considered Thalice's words as they fell into step with one another through the soldier's camp, noting she had said *'hidden from him.'*

"I needed to come," she whispered as if to explain the impossibility of her presence. "The Norn told me that my dear one would take a life for the first time. I had to be near him."

"Must you hide? It would do the boy enormous good to see you now."

"No, I do not think it would. I know my Cassian very well. He would not wish me to see him just now. It would distract him and add to the shame he already feels for killing his brother."

"Then why did you come?"

"Because I love him."

Somar gazed around. Soldiers were walking around both of them, talking to one another. He had no understanding of elven mysticism, but he had the impression that whatever spell kept her concealed also somehow kept the men around them from noticing that he was speaking to her.

"Well, in any case, it warms my heart to see you, my dear. I am honored that one such as you should know one so lowly as myself."

"You are quite free and shameless with your self-deprecation, but we both know there is nothing truly humble about you, Somar Dojinko."

He laughed. Thalice reminded him very much of Cassian at that moment. She seemed strong and direct like he was, and yet there was also a gentle grace that was unlike anything Cassian possessed. Somar cleared his throat and said: "Do we humans seem silly to you, with all our little facades?"

The elf gave a small shake of her head. "I might have thought so once, if not for Cassian. After what he and I shared though, I feel I understand mortals more profoundly than any of my kind ever has. Your facades, your humor, and so many other things are beautiful to me." She gazed down at her feet. "So filled with emotion you all are from the moment you are born until your deaths." Somar noted the slightest shift in her voice as she spoke the final word.

"It terrifies you that Cassian will die," he said.

Her impossibly perfect face showed traces of pain. "That is one of the reasons why elves do not mingle with humans. It is alien to us to form a bond with another that will not continue through the centuries as we will."

Somar blinked. "Death itself is alien to you." He gazed at her, in all her youthful beauty that he knew would not wither in a thousand years. "Tell me, if you would, what happens to elves when they become ancient? Surely the world would be overrun with your kind if none of you ever cease to exist."

There was a silent mental thrill at asking about one of the great mysteries of the immortal people, and it was good to focus on something other than Cassian at the moment.

"Many different things may happen," Thalice said in a quiet voice from under the folds of her hood. "The simplest answer is that we change. For myself, I chose rebirth in my last life."

"Your last life?" Somar raised an eyebrow.

"Does that seem strange?" the elf laughed. "My previous incarnation lived to be over eighteen hundred years old. That was enough for her. Even an elf's mind has limits on how long it can savor life before all taste is finally lost. She needed to be born again, and so she cast off her physical form and relinquished her energy into the world, knowing it would be transmuted into new elven life."

"What of her memories?"

"They are deep within me. I could call them all up if I truly wished, but then that would overwhelm this young mind I now have, and the Thalice you and Cassian know would become only a tiny fragment of this consciousness. My former incarnation would not want that, and neither do I of course. Someday, she and I will become one, but not yet."

"What a wonder it must be to live as an elf," said Somar.

"What a wonder it must be to be *him*," she said, and she gestured back toward Cassian. Somar gazed behind and saw his former pupil standing on top of a table giving a speech to perhaps thirty men. "He is building his army," Thalice whispered. "I know everything he plans to do."

Somar turned to her and saw two crystalline tears drip down her smooth face. They shone brilliantly in the morning glare, catching and refracting the light into tiny rainbows. "I do not know much of my former life, but I know that in over eighteen centuries, I never loved anything so much as I love Cassian." She bit her bottom lip for an instant. "He has infected me with human emotion, and I cannot discuss these feelings with my people because they would not begin to understand." Thalice caught one of her tears on her finger and gazed at it.

"Cassian will destroy and remake the world, as he has destroyed and remade me. That is what he is." She gazed into Somar's eyes and murmured: "We must let him go now, you and I."

He took a slow breath, returning to the pain of saying goodbye to the boy. "I am glad you are here with me to see him off."

"As I am glad to have you, dear old man."

They both gazed again at Cassian, watching him make his emphatic gestures to the growing crowd and seeing their excited reactions. The girl was right of course. It was time to let Cassian go now. Their paths would cross again before Somar's body withered away, he was sure of that.

"Tell me, my dear, would you ride out into the forest with an old human and have tea before you return to your people?"

Thalice gave him a delighted grin, displaying a row of gleaming teeth. "I should like nothing more in all the world at this moment." They began walking together toward the eastern exit of the camp where the horses were kept, away from all the men, and away from Cassian.

CHAPTER 16: RESOLVE

Hervin kept crying. Livia watched as he read her account of Iona's abduction for the fourth or fifth time. It stung to see him in pain, but even as Livia stared at him, her mind wandered to the things she had not written down. Without thinking, she ran her fingers over the place on her neck where the horrible young sorcerer's magic had touched her. She was certain it had been magic, for it had felt just like when the Nemesai sorcerer had attacked her, only this time... something seemed to have been *awakened* inside her.

"There wasn't any blood on the ground when you woke up?" Hervin whispered, his face pale.

She shook her head.

"Why would this man think our Iona is a weapon?"

Livia grimaced. The loss of Iona hurt so much... she had perhaps not fully understood how much the silly girl meant to her until now—*her best friend in the world.*

"She must still be alive," Hervin whispered. "Don't you think?" He stared at her, his face desperate.

Livia still had her charcoal pencil in her hand from writing the account. She reached forward to a clean sheet of papyrus on the table, her hand shaking a little as she wrote:

I think so.

She paused for a moment, then added:

I remember the one who took her. I will draw his face. Then you have to go to the city guard and tell them you witnessed everything.

"What?" he grunted, staring at the words. "Why?"

Livia frowned at Hervin, and after a moment realization dawned on the man. He nodded. *Of course, Livia could not be the sole witness*. No one would take the word of a former slave seriously. It sickened her to admit to herself that likely no one would care much that a house slave—freed or not—had been abducted. If Iona had been the daughter of a lord, the whole countryside would be out hunting for her, but they would be lucky if the guards even bothered to question anyone. Livia forced back tears and willed herself to focus. She had to try, after all.

"Y-yes, please draw the picture," Hervin whispered. He fidgeted in his seat for a moment, then stood abruptly and said: "I—I think I should take the horses and search the local roads. I'll try east first, then—"

Livia put a hand on his arm and shook her head. The leader had been a sorcerer, and from what Livia could recall from their encounter before she had been knocked unconscious, he was a very powerful one. There were the other two men as well—enormous brutes with apotheosis tattoos like Nemesai. They would be three or four times stronger than normal men, and much faster, and their eyes had been so utterly merciless... No, Hervin was no match for such a group, and she did not need to explain this to him. The look she gave him melted his resolve almost immediately, and he sank back into his chair and whispered: "What should I do then?"

Livia swallowed dryly, and then took charge. She moved her charcoal pencil to her paper once more and wrote:

You must reread the account over and over until every detail is burned into your mind. I was there, but you are the witness. I will draw the face, and then we will go.

"Y-yes," Hervin said, and he picked up the note she had given him. His hands trembled as he began to read and whisper the words.

Livia went to the room she shared with Iona and retrieved a large sheet of papyrus from the tray under her bed. She brought it to the table in the dining area and laid it perfectly flat, smoothing the edges. For a dozen heartbeats, Livia stared at the page and reached back to those horrible few moments before the world had gone black. It terrified her to picture the young man who had attacked her, but she forced herself not to recoil from his image. His pale face took shape in her mind, and his dark hair. There had been something around his neck—a silver chain—Livia's stomach twisted as she thought it might be the necklace of a Nemesai High Inquisitor, but then she shook her head. He was far too young to possess such a rank. The details were enough though, and so Livia pressed the charcoal tip of her pencil to the center of the page very gently and began to sketch.

The face took shape slowly, starting with the nose. Livia could feel tears leaking out of her eyes as her hand worked, but she dabbed them away with her sleeve. Her sketch, she knew almost immediately, was going to be perfect. She used shading to create the depth and what some of the books she had read on geometry called "the third dimension." At times as her fingers moved, the process became almost automatic, and her mind wandered again to when the magic had touched her.

What in the world had happened? It had started as a rumble in her chest when the young man had hurled his spell at her. Livia remembered shutting her eyes, and then there was a... *reaction*. The thrum inside her grew, and the conjuration had shattered in the air. That had been nothing though compared to the instant a piece of the young man's invisible magic had touched her skin. Then she had felt it. His power had been flowing all around, attacking and killing, but when it met her flesh it recoiled back so hard and fast that the bones in his hand had snapped. Livia had willed his own magic to attack him, or that had been how it seemed. There was little sense to any of it, except that connecting to the power had felt so very... *natural*... and even... *familiar*.

Livia's hand continued to sketch as her mind sifted through the ever-growing chaos of her thoughts. For the second time in a handful of weeks, she gave serious contemplation to who she was—who she had been before a slave mark had been placed on her cheek. As soon as that thought came, it was drowned out by one far more urgent: that horrid young man could be torturing Iona at that very moment, or worse... Livia could think of no way to decipher either of these conundrums. Her innocent little sister could be half a day's ride in any direction now.

Her stomach was twisting as she finished the final details of Iona's abductor onto the page and then pulled her hand away and gazed at her work. It was good—all the details someone would need to identify the young man were there.

Livia quickly drew out her writing paper and wrote:

Hervin, you must take this to all the city exits right now and ask if anyone has seen this person in the last few hours.

As soon as she finished the last word, Livia picked up both pieces of paper and ran them to Hervin, nearly shoving them into his hands. He looked up at her, confused, and then he gaped at the image she had drawn, his eyes eventually shifting to her note. After a few seconds, the small man looked up at her and said: "Y-yes, right now." He clutched the papers to his chest and dashed for the front door and fumbled with the latch. He was breathing quickly as he darted out the doorway.

Livia glanced down at her written account of the incident, which Hervin had dropped onto the floor in his haste. Her mind flashed back through the words she had scribbled, and she wondered: *Who would take them seriously?* Who would care? The Vestilite sisters loved Iona, but Livia knew that they could do virtually nothing to help. Even if Hervin managed to figure out the direction Iona's captors had taken her, no army would be sent—certainly not a force strong enough to counter a powerful sorcerer and cutthroat soldiers with apotheosis tattoos.

Still, *she had somehow managed to counter that powerful sorcerer*. Livia's thoughts returned once again to the strange battle she had waged with him. She continued to feel a shadow of... *something* within herself. What was it? If she could overcome the young man's magic again, perhaps a pair of tattooed soldiers was not insurmountable Livia stared again down at the discarded page, her stomach swirling with nerves as a thought entered her mind. *She had magic!* She was sure she did, but not the way others had it. Still, it was a part of her somehow. That was why she had seen the vision of Cassian Asango years ago with every other sorcerer in the world.

Feeling a flutter of nerves, Livia raised her hand in the direction of the page. She had no training in magic of course, but she concentrated on the tingling sensation—the aspect of herself that had awoken when the young man had attacked her—and tried to will it out toward the paper.

The power seemed to respond, for she felt the tingle suddenly shift from every part of her body to her palm and fingers, yet as it did, an unbelievable pain erupted in the front of her skull. It broke Livia's concentration, and she stumbled to her knees, feeling sickeningly dizzy. The room suddenly seemed to be spinning. Her heart had taken to pounding in her chest, and sweat was dripping off her forehead. She swallowed, leaning forward on her hands. The pain was horrible, and yet... she had felt it many, many times before. It was like the sting she felt when trying to form words with her mouth. Livia had attempted for years to overcome it when she was a child, but every time her lips and tongue worked to produce a single syllable, searing agony had ripped through her. It had happened over and over until she had given up, *but she would not give up now!*

Livia rose to her feet. Tears of anger dripped down her face as she raised her hand again. *To hell with the curse!* Iona's life mattered more, and if she could save her sweet little sister from that monstrous young man, then she did not care if it killed her. As before, Livia focused her will, this time readying herself for impending agony. It came once more—a sensation like rusted nails being pounded into her forehead—but she kept pushing, focusing through it on the paper.

Livia felt something like an invisible rope leap out from her palm into the air. The pain grew worse. Her vision started to blacken as tears beaded involuntarily from her eyes, but she blinked them away and forced herself to keep going. Her power seemed to extend through the air and moved to the paper and then coalesced around the page, and then—*Gods but she had never felt agony like this!* It was like trying to grip something with a hand that had no skin. Finally, it became too much, and Livia fell to her knees once again and began to shake on the floor, but then something so shocking happened that she jumped: the muscles in her throat engaged in a way they never had before, and she heard herself rasp out a scream.

Livia sat up panting, the pain slowly receding from her head. Never in her life had she heard her own voice... she did not even know she *had* a voice. Her throat ached a little from the exertion, but that did not matter. *She could speak!*

Slowly, nervously, Livia drew in a breath of air and tried to cry out again—*to make any sound*—but nothing came out, and to her sickening disappointment, a fraction of the tormenting sensation returned to her skull. It seemed almost to be warning her to stop what she was doing.

Livia wiped some of the sweat from her face and was shocked to see blood come away on her hand. She dabbed the bottom of her nose with her finger and quickly determined it to be the source.

Livia shook her head, new tears welling up in her eyes. *What the hell did any of this mean?* She turned in frustration and looked at the page on the ground, only... *where was it?*

There was no sign of the paper anywhere. She stood and swept the room with her eyes until they fell on a crumpled mass in the far left corner. Livia dashed over to it and knelt down. The papyrus had been bent folded and crushed into itself so tightly that when she picked it up it felt solid. Nervously, with hands still wet with blood, she unfolded the mass and saw an incredibly mangled version of the note she had written.

A silent laugh escaped her lips. *She had power!* Livia barely understood what it was or how to control it, but it was there! That meant that getting Iona back might be possible. As she pondered the implications of this, a bit of blood trickled into her mouth and she winced. Her mind began to race. *What was it that held her back?* Was the force of pain part of her magic, or separate from it? Whom could she ask? There was Septimius, the current village sorcerer, but did Livia dare go near him? She had nearly killed the young man seemingly just by coming into contact with his magic. What if it happened again to Septimius? Would she be able to stop it?

The door burst in behind her, and Hervin's voice came in huff: "Someone saw him riding North!" Livia turned and saw him clutching the drawing she had made, and when he looked at her, he let out a gasp. "My gods, what happened?!"

Livia gazed down at herself. Blood had seeped down the front of her dress and formed an enormous crimson stain. Hervin dashed toward her, but she held up a hand to stop him. Shaking slightly, she walked to the table and picked up her pencil. It slipped a little in her wet fingers as she scribbled:

I fell. Don't worry. I'm fine.

Livia was not sure why the lie came out, except a very deep instinct told her not to reveal any of what had just happened. Hervin seemed to accept the explanation, for he shook his head and said: "Someone saw the young man hitching up a cart while a pair of men loaded something into the back that—" he drew in a nervous breath, "might have been Iona."

Livia nodded and wrote:

We're leaving tonight. We'll search the road and all the inns going north. Get the sword your father gave you and put on warm clothing.

"Y-yes," Hervin muttered as he read the words, and he dashed back into his bedroom.

Livia went to her room and immediately opened the small compartment she had made in the wall below her bed, gnashing her teeth as she reached inside it. The money Lady Gretis had given her was still there. Livia had avoided taking it out or even thinking about it for years. When she had been a slave—or thought she had been—all those desseks represented the terrifying possibility of leaving Hervin and the only home she had ever known, miserable as it was in some ways. Now, the money had a far more important use. Livia could hire soldiers to help rescue her sister, or perhaps even pay a ransom. She would gladly give every coin to get Iona back.

Livia set the sack of desseks down on her cot and slipped out of her blood-soaked clothing. She did not bother cleaning herself much before throwing on another of her rough spun dresses. Her hands moved feverishly as she put on her warmest coat and slipped on the fine boots Hervin had bought her after his wife had left and he no longer feared to do such things. Finally, Livia slipped the clinking bag into her coat pocket and dashed out of her room to find her surrogate father, almost comically dressed in an inside-out tunic with his undergarments spilling out of his pants.

"S-should we talk to the city guard before we go?" he said.

Livia shook her head. It might take hours to get anyone to believe the two of them, and so much time had already been lost. She did not bother explaining any of this to him, but pointed at the door and gave a sharp, decisive nod.

"A-alright," Hervin said, drawing in a quaking breath. The two of them dashed out the front door and ran to the stable behind the house. Livia's heart was racing. She had no idea if this was a sound plan at all. The road north split in dozens of places. Iona could be anywhere. *Still, she had to try!* As Livia opened the stable door and drew out the horses, she prayed that she would be able to use the power she had when the time came, and that it would be enough...

CHAPTER 17: ANIMUS AWAKENED

"How do you feel?" Gretis asked.

Kota blinked, trying to clear away the fog in his mind. He was lying on top of several of the cow skins they had used to make the hut the day before. The sun was creeping high above the treetops, which meant he had slept—or been unconscious—through half the day. He sat up slowly and looked at his teacher. She was sitting on top of a tree stump, a steaming clay mug in her hand. The woman seemed uncharacteristically relaxed and happy.

"What happened?" Kota rasped. His neck felt stiff, and so he tilted his head from side to side and cracked the joints.

"You lost consciousness," Gretis said with a shrug, her voice strangely tranquil. "That usually happens shortly after awakening one's power. It happened to me and also to Soulic. You have been asleep for two full days." She gestured to the right and said: "I made you eggs and salt pork. It's a bit cold by now, but I am sure you are too hungry to mind."

Kota eyed the plate of food and his stomach contracted painfully in his ribs. Truly, he had never been so hungry in all his life. He moved over and began to wolf it down, using his claws to scoop up it up instead of the clumsy wooden fork on the blanket.

"Goodness," Gretis said with a chuckle.

He turned and eyed her, as he took his first desperate gulp. "Why are you so happy?" he grunted.

"Because you did not kill those people," she said, tilting her head back and casting a grin of pure happiness into the sky. "Oh Kota, I have been afraid every day and night for nearly five years of what would happen. When I saw you at that campfire, I felt such terror, but you—" she giggled, "you were trying to *play* with those men." Gretis bellowed out a loud, full-throated laugh. "They were utterly terrified, poor souls, but I managed to get the story out of them of what happened." She cast him a wry grin and said: "You actually tossed the man's arrow back to him!"

Kota swallowed down another great gulp of food and let out a small chuckle himself. He only recalled his encounter with the two men in flashes, but catching an arrow between his thumb and finger had managed to stand out in his mind. He relived the memory as he finished the last of his food and was surprised to find that he was still quite hungry.

"Here," Gretis said, tossing him an apple from in her bag. Kota caught the piece of fruit in the air and brought it to his teeth without hesitation, tearing viciously into it. "The hunger too is quite normal," she sighed. "It will pass when your body becomes accustomed to its new power."

As Kota swallowed, he tried to search inside himself for the 'power' of which she was speaking. Almost immediately, he felt its warm pulse within him, raw and immense. "Is it a part of me now?" he whispered.

"It was always a part of you, but more so now than ever before." Gretis moved to him and lowered onto her haunches. "For the moment, you should conceive of it as an entirely new set of muscles in your body. It will take time and training for your mind to develop control over the power and, much like a muscle, it can be cultivated and made stronger. Your potential, Kota, is..." she shook her head, then placed a hand on his shoulder and said: "Gods but I am delighted to find that the beast is guided by your kind heart. I should never have doubted it." She leaned in, a motherly smile playing across her smooth face as she asked: "Are you still hungry?"

Kota felt the tightness throughout his body. It seemed as though his insides had been emptied out completely. Still, he had an instinctive resistance to overeating. For centuries upon centuries, his people had survived by their quickness and agility. That legacy was as much a part of him as anything, and it revolted at the thought of overfilling his gut.

"I am fine," he whispered.

"As you wish, young warrior," she said. "Let me know when you feel ready. Now the next level of your training can begin."

Kota watched the Blade Witch rise to a standing position, and the new part of him that he had brought back from the spirit world followed her movements. It sent an image into his mind wholly separate from his vision. He *felt* her rise—felt the tension in her legs and the disbursement of weight between her two feet. He perceived every tiny movement that occurred within her from the muscles contracting under her skin to the beat of her heart. All of it was laid bare by a strange and somewhat frightening new awareness.

"Are you alright?" Gretis said, and he saw a pristine image within his mind of the shifting bones and sinew of her mouth as she spoke.

"I... It's showing me things... strange details about the way you move," he said.

"Already!" she exclaimed, and her eyes went wide. "By the gods! You are a true prodigy!" She eyed him and took in a deep breath, and he felt her lungs expand within her chest and the flutter of her heart.

Kota dropped his forehead into his hands. "It is making me dizzy," he whispered.

"You will grow used to it, I promise you," Gretis said, her voice warm and reassuring. "You are developing an entirely new array of senses, though the speed at which they are coming..." she shook her head and he felt what he could only describe as shockwaves from the movement. "Kota, you have no idea how talented you are. It took me nearly a *year* to develop what has come to you in the first few days."

"Can I make it stop?" he said, glancing up.

"I am afraid not, young warrior," she said, a conciliatory smile on her face. "Your animus is seeking a connection with your conscious mind. You must embrace it."

"My animus?" Kota said.

"Your *spirit* if you wish," Gretis said with a low sigh. "It has many names. In Dhavic, it is called the *dok-hrul.* However you wish to term it, your animus has its own awareness of the world, and you should by no means seek to discard that. It will become *extremely* valuable to you. Observe." Gretis reached down and picked up a piece of gray stone the size of a cantaloupe from the ground. She gave Kota a little wink and then, moving with a sudden burst of preternatural speed, she threw the rock directly at his chest.

The projectile came in faster than an arrow from a bow, and Kota might not have even had time to flinch, but his *animus* reacted. It lifted his hand instantly. He felt the stone collide so hard with his palm that it cracked and there was a spray of dust, yet there was no explosion of pain. The new power surged within his flesh, rendering it tougher than steel so that the impact felt something like a wad of paper crumpling against his skin.

"Wha—" Kota grunted, gawking at his outstretched limb.

"You see?" Gretis said in a smooth voice.

"I... I didn't choose to move my arm!" Kota said. He turned the cracking mass in his hand. His claws had sunk into it, piercing in as though the rock were a piece of fruit.

"Your animus decided to move your limb for you. It can react far more quickly than you can."

"It can control me?" Kota whispered. He drew his claws back into his fingertips and gaped at the deep triangular indentations they left in the stone.

"The force inside you can make tiny decisions on its own, separate from your conscious will, and it will automatically act to protect you from harm. That is *one* of the reasons Sansrit Masters are immensely difficult to kill in battle."

Kota dropped the rock to the ground and attempted to process what he had just seen and felt. He tried to relive the catch in his mind, but it had simply happened too fast. After a moment, he gazed up at Gretis and spoke the only thought that came to him: "You said in Dhavic, this is called the *dok-hrul.* In every text I have ever read, the soul is referred to as the *honnis.*"

The right side of Gretis's mouth curled up into a smirk, and she said: "Yes-s-s. I used a *different* word—one that does not appear in the Holy Enumis anywhere. What does that suggest to you, Kota?"

Kota considered the matter, and then answered: "Perhaps that the honnis and dok-hrul are different things?"

"Precisely," Gretis whispered. She brought her hands together and said: "Kota, you have ascended to a new level of being—one that most are unable to reach. I can tell you a story to help you make sense of it, but you must agree to keep this knowledge secret."

Kota swallowed. He would keep any secrets Gretis passed to him even unto death. "I give you my word," he said.

"I trust you, Kota," she said. The Blade Witch moved closer to him and sat down on the leaves, folding her legs. She reached out and took his hands in hers and said: "Tell me, young warrior, what legends does your tribe tell of how the shamalak came to walk this world?"

Kota gave an embarrassed laugh. "I suppose most humans would think our legends silly. My tribe has several stories about the origin of the shamalak, and they tend to contradict one another here and there. The common thread between them though is that we were once a race of great beasts, but long ago the great spirits from the cosmos, or *Gods* perhaps, stripped us of most of our strength and cursed us to walk on two legs and suffer the weaknesses of man."

"Hmm," Gretis grunted. "That is similar enough to the stories I heard when I visited a shamalak tribe in the north.

You may be quite surprised to learn that it is actually not far from what the Sansrit teach."

Kota gazed into Gretis's eyes in wonder. "What *do* the Sansrit teach?"

Her fingers grew slightly tighter around Kota's hands. "What I am about to tell you would be called blasphemy by any church official in the world." Her voice lowered as she added: "The first thing you must understand about Sansrit doctrine is that it purports the gods to which we humans pray did not create the world. It was here long before they arrived, and it had *life*."

Kota took in a slow breath through his nose, considering the implications of these words. The gods had *come* to the world, implying that they had originated somewhere else. This was indeed blasphemy.

Gretis went on: "Before the deities came and imposed their order, this world was completely wild and free of society, morality, and even what we now think of as intelligent thought. Still, there was a kind of order to all of it—even unity. Nothing in it had quite evolved to possess a soul, but all living things had an animus, from the plants in the forests to the fish that swam in the great oceans." Gretis tilted her head, looking thoughtful, then added: "Think of it as the oldest magic in the universe—the energy of *life itself*. All things that possessed its spark were then and are now connected." She cast him a glowing smile. "In time you will learn to feel this connection. I will teach you."

"I would be honored," Kota whispered. He was slowly wrapping his mind around what she was telling him.

Gretis straightened a bit. "For today's lesson though, I should remain focused on my original point. You see, the great storm of life in this world did not go unnoticed. The dark forces of the cosmos were attracted to it, and they came here to pervert and twist it into their own image. They were powerful but intangible, and so they resorted to infecting some of the creatures that roamed the land. That is when our world saw its first incarnation of what we now call *'demons.'* They were fierce, primal predators – monsters of tremendous size and power. These creatures had no higher intelligence, but only an instinct to kill or infect everything in their path."

"What stopped them?" Kota said. "Was it the gods?"

"Not the gods," Gretis said with a soft chuckle. "Not at first anyhow. Life defended *itself!* As I said, all living things are unified, and that unity gave rise to a collective spirit. In Sansrit Philosophy, this is called the *Ankus*, but you may conceive of it for the moment as the heart of our world. Somehow, it was able to pour great swells of its power into a race of beasts that had not been touched by the darkness. These creatures took on strength to match the primal demons, and they became driven by a deep instinct to defend the rest of nature. For countless millennia, they did their great duty."

Gretis eyed him and said: "Is this making sense to you?"

"I suppose it is," Kota said hesitantly. He was imagining great beasts roaming the world and doing battle with primal demons. "I am not sure what to make of this story yet."

"Well, I shall not attempt to explain what happened next. I have no better explanation than what is written in the Holy Enumis. Whether the gods willed consciousness as we know it into this world, or whether it came into being naturally, I cannot say. Whatever the case, intelligent life arrived, and brought with it something that no creature had ever possessed before: *the soul.* It was distinctive and separate from the animus. It did not come from the heart of the world, nor did it go there after death. With the advent of the soul came the arrival of the gods. These deities more or less obliterated the primal demons with their great power to make way for intelligent life to flourish. They also decreed that the ancient beasts that had fought the demons had no place in the new order."

Gretis ran her thumbs gently over Kota's fingers and said: "And now we circle back to the legends your people tell of how the shamalak race came to be. You see, the gods robbed the creatures of their physical form. However, they could not destroy the great power in the beasts' spirits any more than they could destroy the intangible demonic essence in this world. The lingering animuses roamed the lands without form until, after time unknown, they found a tribe of humans who lived in peaceful harmony with the natural world. Somehow, the ancient spirits were able to form a pact with this tribe, and they poured themselves into its men and women. The infusion changed the people, giving them claws and fangs and other features much like the beasts had had, as well as incredibly acute senses."

Kota pulled his hands away from Gretis's and extended his claws, gazing at them. "You are telling me that my people came from an ancient race of creatures the world created to defend itself?"

"I am telling you a *story*," she said. "I do not know how much of it is true, if any. It fits with many things I know. You will come to see as I see—perhaps far *better* than I have ever seen—and then you make up your own mind what to believe. I will only be able to guide you so far before you exceed me."

"How could I ever exceed you?" Kota said.

Gretis let out a soft chuckle and once again took Kota's hands in her own. "You are special, Kota, even among the shamalak. The power that was poured into your people has been diluted and spread thin over the centuries, but you—" she squeezed his fingers, "your animus—what did it look like?"

Kota's mind flashed to the impossible mountain of deadly power that had made the spirit world tremble before its feet. "It was..." He hesitated to put the creature's form into words.

"It was tremendous, was it not—larger than any creature you have ever seen?"

"Much larger," Kota whispered.

She let go of his hand and placed her palms on his shoulders. "I shall tell you the rest of this story another time, and a bit about a prophecy as well. For today, just know that—"

she gave a soft and beautiful laugh, "you are everything I ever dared to hope you would be, and so much more."

Gretis stood then and walked over to the side of the hut. Kota watched her draw out a large roll of cloth, his eyes briefly traveling to the gaping hole he had made in the structure the night before. Gretis unrolled the fabric on the forest floor, and the two training swords clattered out. She picked one up by the handle and tossed it to Kota. His new sense attuned to the motion instantly and he stood, extending his arm and angling his hand so that the hilt of the weapon fell precisely into his grip. As his fingers closed around it, he felt his new strength crackle inside him, as if excited.

"Shall we see what you can do, young warrior?" Gretis said, extending her blade and dropping into her favorite stance.

The sword felt as light as a feather in Kota's hand. He gazed at Gretis. She was the greatest warrior he had ever known. The thought of truly doing battle with her sent a thrill through his blood. He felt himself smile as he dropped into his own stance.

The two of them rushed at one another and steel collided with steel with such force that Kota felt a shockwave of air sting his face. More than ever before, he felt alive.

CHAPTER 18: CONFRONTATION IN THE WAR CAMP

A cool evening breeze whisked over Cassian's skin as he strode toward General Romulus's tent. His lists had been carefully organized and were now ready to present. He clutched them delicately as he gazed at the thirty men that had more or less created a human wall in front of Romulus's door. They were staring nervously back at him. The whole camp knew by now that he and the General were at extremely dangerous odds with one another, and most suspected a confrontation.

"I would like to see Romulus," said Cassian. He spoke loudly and with a tone of complete authority. As he met the eyes of the men, he was surprised at the lack of nerves in his stomach. Dimitris's death was still incredibly close to his soul, and his anger over it squelched all hesitation at what he was about to do.

A soldier with a brass helmet and chest armor approached, his face pale. "Romulus has given orders that you are not to be admitted, Lord Asango. He says that he has sent to the Imperium for orders on how to deal with your—" the man's voice went dry with nerves, "insubordination."

"Hah!" Cassian laughed. He could feel the eyes of dozens of men on him. Their minds were singularly focused on the threat he represented. That made things immensely easy. Taking advantage of their unified attention, he cast the tendrils of his psychic mind outward, finding clear and open paths to every victim. Not one in the crowd possessed even a fraction of the mental resistance that Cassian had honed his skills against in Somar.

"Let him in," he made them all think they heard Romulus's voice shout from inside the tent. "I will see Lord Asango."

There was a tremendous swell of relief as the wall of soldiers parted, happy to accommodate the terrifying Starborn rather than engage him. Cassian walked through them and parted the hanging bearskins that functioned as Romulus's front door. As he did, he quietly whispered an incantation, summoning a handful of spectrals into a spell that formed instantly around the tent.

"Hello, Romulus," Cassian said aloud as he entered.

"W-What is this?!" the General cried, and he bounded out from one of the great structure's inner rooms with a group of ten aged men at his back with long beards, each dressed in fine, silvery robes. "Guards!" Romulus cried aloud.

"They cannot hear you," Cassian said, stepping into the center of the room. "No one outside this tent can hear anything within."

One of the old men looked around and then shut his eyes. Cassian felt him reach out with a sorcerer's aura. "The boy has cast a powerful spell around us," he said.

"Obviously," Cassian sighed.

Romulus glared at him. "Do you have *any idea* what you are doing?"

Cassian stared at the General. *How well he understood things now.* The meager psychic walls around Romulus's mind were leaking out waves of anxiety. The authority the man thought he had was being threatened, and he was desperate to reestablish it.

"I know *exactly* what I am doing." Cassian took a step forward.

"Hold, boy!" the old man who had spoken before said, and he extended his hand, palm toward Cassian.

Romulus's face twitched. "You would do well to watch yourself. These men are all *Deklons*."

Cassian knew the term. 'Deklons' were the highest order of battle sorcerers in the Denigoth military. They were notorious as vicious murderers who worked together to construct spells that could wipe out half a village in an instant. The name of their caste was spoken of in terror all over the known world.

"Hello," said Cassian, looking the one who seemed to be the leader in the eyes.

"Be warned," the old sorcerer said, "we are entirely dedicated to keeping order in the imperial army, even against a Starborn. Do *not* make further threats against this general."

Romulus stared at Cassian for a moment, trying to gauge his reaction as Somar might. Then he forced a smile and said: "I hope you can now see the gravity of the behavior you have displayed today." His face became friendly—almost consolatory. "My dear young lord, I understand that Dimitris was likely the first person you have ever killed and that he was your good friend. Nearly every soldier in this camp knows the horrible pain of the first kill. What you have done today is understandable, even forgivable—"

"Save whatever foolish speech you have concocted," Cassian said.

Romulus's skin visibly reddened once more. "I am a *General* in the Empire! You—"

"BE QUIET!" Cassian snapped, amplifying and projecting the vibrations in the air of his voice to every corner of the tent. Romulus visibly flinched.

The leader of the Deklons stepped forward and said in a voice that trembled with rage: "This is your very *last chance,* boy—"

"All of you can be silent as well," said Cassian, turning and meeting the eyes of each sorcerer. "I know all about your caste, and it has been responsible for many of the most horrific acts of human slaughter ever carried out in the name of this Denigoth." He took a step toward them and said: "You disgust me, but you do not frighten me."

The leader narrowed his eyes and growled: "Your arrogant lack of respect for the brave men of this empire—"

"Have you murdered cowering children, *brave man*?" Cassian said, his voice sharp. He gestured at Romulus without looking at the general and said: "He has. Romulus demanded grain to feed his army from the great city of Sotomus, but the peasants hid some of their reserves away to keep their families from starving." Cassian turned and glared at the General. "You used Deklons to wipe them all out, did you not?"

Romulus hissed through clenched teeth: "I have always acted within the policy of this empire."

"Yes, I understand all about the grotesquely broad *policies* in place, and the ways men like you *interpret* them," Cassian said.

The Deklon leader cleared his throat loudly and snapped: "You have no place to question the actions of this army. Starborn or not, you are an inexperienced youth who has never borne the harsh responsibility of military conquest as we, the Noble and Elite soldiers of this empire have. Frankly, I find your contempt to be as childish as it is seditious."

"Do you?" Cassian said, raising an eyebrow. "Have you ever forced a sobbing peasant into your bed, my *noble and elite* fellow?"

The Deklon narrowed his eyes, saying nothing, *which was quite telling.*

Cassian turned back to Romulus. "Now, I have papers I would like you to—" he stopped speaking and turned to the Deklon leader. The old man's eyes were fixed on him with a look of intense concentration. *Was he actually trying to pry his way into the mind of a Starborn?* Cassian sensed telepathic strength roughly on par with Bishop Cromlic's. The assault might have actually worked on him a few years before, but now it was an absurd blunder. In trying to attack, the man had opened the doorway to his own mind. Cassian retaliated, sending the full force of his psychic strength back upon his opponent.

"GAHH!" the Deklon shrieked, and he fell to his knees clutching at his skull as it exploded with the pain transmitted into it.

As the man thrashed on the floor, Cassian stared at the rest of the Deklons, as if to dare them to fight. Every one of them stood frozen. *This was ugly business.* Cassian detested using his gifts to bully others, but he was standing face to face with some of the cruelest and most dangerous men in the world, and appeals to reason or morality were useless. Only two things moved them: their lust for wealth and power, and their fear. Cassian refused to indulge the former in any way, which left him singularly with the latter. He watched without pity as the Deklon leader let out one final shriek and then lost consciousness, going limp on the carpeted floor.

"Good, now I have a few papers that require your signature," said Cassian, walking past the remaining battle sorcerers and holding out his neat stack of sheets to Romulus. The General was still staring at his unconscious comrade, and his face was at least one shade whiter than it had been a few seconds ago. "You will reassign the three hundred and fifty soldiers I have picked to my sovereign command. This is represented in the first three pages. I also have a list of supplies I require, which you will order to be handed over to me at the time and in the manner of my choosing."

Romulus blinked and took the papers, gazing at them for a moment as if not understanding what they were. Then he looked up and said in a dry-throated voice: "I am not signing these."

"You will sign them and anything else I place in front of you," said Cassian. His tone was calm. He felt entirely in control, and he knew he was projecting this feeling.

Romulus swallowed, then hissed: "Do you have—"

"*Any idea what I am doing*?" Cassian said. "I am going to be the next *Emperor.* Within a year or two I will almost certainly be named crown prince, and by that time I will have achieved more military victories than you have acquired in your entire career. What do you think I will do to you then if you give me the slightest *hint* of trouble now?" He stepped forward until he and Romulus were only an arm's length apart, and he watched the much larger man shrink. "You have a decision to make. You can give me what I want, or you can make an enemy of me." Cassian's anger blazed within him, and he let it flow out in invisible tendrils of magical energy all around the room. Tables, chairs, and bookshelves began to snap apart into tiny pieces that flew about the room. "Make your choice *NOW!*"

Romulus looked down at the papers he now held in a trembling hand. "I... I will sign your documents."

"Thank you, General," said Cassian. There was no smugness in his tone. This entire encounter sickened him.

Romulus glanced nervously at the shattered table behind him and then muttered: "I will take them to my office and sign them. I... I will return in a moment." He disappeared behind a wall of cloth.

Cassian turned and glanced at the Deklons. Several of them were bent over and attending to their unconscious brother. One with a beard of gray-speckled-black looked up at him and said in a deep, throaty voice: "The path you are choosing is an extremely dangerous one, even for a Starborn."

"I agree," said Cassian. He looked down at the unconscious man. "Your companion will rise within a few moments. When he does, tell him I respect his loyalty, but if he attempts to stand against me again, he will die." Cassian paused, then said: "I suggest you and your fellow Deklons consider your options very carefully. I might have use for... *some* of you, but I think that most of your caste should quietly retire before I am named crown prince. I have no tolerance for the kind of tactics you employ, and standing against me would likewise be an *extremely dangerous path* to choose."

The old sorcerer only stared bewildered at Cassian as Romulus returned with signed documents in his hand.

"Thank you, General," said Cassian.

"You are... welcome, Lord Asango," said Romulus. His eyes were downcast as he spoke.

"Romulus," Cassian said, and the General looked up at him. "Answer me truthfully, or I will sense it: do you know why Dimitris had to die?"

The man hesitated, then exhaled: "No. I was told only to do everything in my power to instigate a fight between you two."

Cassian allowed these words to wash over him for a few seconds and then let the mystery pass. He handed a second copy of the list of names to Romulus and said: "Have these men assembled at dawn in the northern end of camp." He did not wait for a response but turned and walked out of the tent and back amongst the still on-edge soldiers who had heard none of what had happened. Cassian paid them no mind. He crossed the camp to his tent where he found Somar sitting in an armchair, the old man's bags neatly packed on either side of him, a roll of brown parchment in his hand.

His tutor stared at him for several seconds, then said: "So he gave you everything you wanted."

A small grin touched Cassian's face at his dear friend's powers of perception. "I am going to miss you a great deal, old man."

Somar ran his fingers over the parchment he held. "I was going to slip away." He let out a laugh, as if at himself. "I wrote you a letter."

"You mean you would actually pass up a chance to hear your own voice?"

"Yes, quite unlike me, isn't it?" The old man tucked the document into his pocket, and Cassian felt some small tinge of regret as he realized he might never know what his friend had written to him. "I let myself become convinced that the most important thing was to let you go as cleanly as possible."

"Was that Thalice's idea?"

Cassian had the satisfaction of seeing Somar's eyes go wide for once. Then the old man muttered: "That sweet girl *attempted* to conceal herself because she thought it would pain you to know she had been watching you."

"It did—*enormously*," said Cassian. "It just was not enough to stop me."

Somar breathed in slowly through his nostrils, seeming to consider these words. Then he rose and looked Cassian in the eyes. "I need to tell you this face to face, and if you have developed any respect for me in our years together, then I damned well call on it all right now, and I ask that you listen to every word I say, because there is no one else to tell you these things."

Cassian gave a nod and eyed his teacher.

"I see you becoming a vicious beast," Somar said without reserve. "You must have been quite forceful to back down *Romulus the Terrible* just now. I am proud of you for this, because to rise as far as you desire in this empire, one has to have extremely sharp teeth and not be squeamish about using them. But when you find this part of yourself and begin to truly exercise it, it is incredibly easy to become a cruel man. You are going to go into battle, and that will change you, as killing Dimitris has already changed you."

Cassian stared into the old man's eyes as he spoke. He had never seen them so intense.

"It takes tremendous strength of character for a man to retain all of his compassion and his integrity and his ideals in the face of war. Hardening your heart is not courage; it is cowardice. Do not forget that, lest you will become just like those deplorable oppressors you hate from the deepest parts of your soul."

The words stung, reigniting the pain of Dimitris's death, and Cassian became aware of how numb he had been for the last day. The surge of emotion was enough to produce a pair of tears. He blinked them away and took a very slow breath, meeting Somar's eyes for a long moment, and then he said: "Thank you, old man. There *is* no one else to tell me these things."

Cassian drew out a scroll he had sealed in wax the day before they set out and handed it to his former teacher.

"What's this," Somar said, peering down.

As the old man unraveled the paper, Cassian said: "I have named you steward of all my lands and business ventures while I am at war." He smiled at Somar and said: "Go and live as a coastal lord. It is not a bad life."

"I... I did not expect this," the old man said, shaking his head.

"I am certain you had your suspicions," Cassian sighed. He reached up and gripped his friend's arm. "I trust you more than any other to run my fief the way it should be run." With a smirk, he added: "And anyhow, it is the safest place in the world for you at the moment. Bishop Cromlic swore an oath never to return there or do you harm, and there is an extremely skilled contingent of soldiers there to keep you safe from all his attempts to sidestep that oath."

Cassian was satisfied to see the old man's expression fidget just a little into one of excitement. "I thank you, Lord Asango," he finally said.

"It has been an honor, sir," Cassian said as he held out his hand. His former teacher gripped it tightly and gave it a deep-felt shake. *No further words were necessary between them.* They drew apart, and the old man bent down and lifted his bags and left the tent in silence, and Cassian walked over to his bed and sat down, already mentally composing his first speech to his new army.

CHAPTER 19: A SLAVE ONCE MORE

Arkas stared down at the teenage slave girl as his sleeping spell slowly dissipated inside her. He had wrapped Iona in blankets with great care and had ridden in the back of the cart with her long through the night while his servant, Dunlin, drove the horses. The morning sunlight was beginning to radiate through the trees to the east. Akas eagerly watched as his captive's eyes fluttered open. Her breathing shifted, and then she let out a sudden gasp and shot up.

"Hello," he said in a gentle voice.

Iona looked at him and began to breathe very quickly. She turned her head from side to side, gaping at the forest brush that slowly passed them by as the wagon rode onward. Arkas could sense her terror. It was almost animalistic.

"Try to remain calm," he said in a soothing tone, the way he did when he was toying with one of his victims in the Nemesai dungeons.

The girl let out a gasp and stumbled forward on the floor of the cart. Arkas gazed into the chaos of her mind. She had discovered that her wrists had been tied behind her back. He watched as a pair of tears formed in her amber eyes and rolled down her cheeks.

"Who are you?!" Iona managed to sob.

"You don't need to know my name." Arkas knelt down over her in the cart. He had rummaged through her mind for the past few hours as she slept, taking in memories of the weak little man, Hervin, the cruel obese woman, Lady Sondal, and... *Livia*. "I am far more dangerous than your mistress ever was. If you defy me or try to run, I'll take a limb off." He made a lazy gesture at the cart wall just to the left of Iona's head and sent a burst of invisible power through his fingertips. The wood exploded in a loud and violent spray of splinters, and she screamed in terror and shrank down.

Arkas suppressed a grin. The girl had more power in her than any Starborn who ever lived, *but she did not know that.* He had studied her sleeping mind in depth and ascertained that she was not a stupid creature but was almost ridiculously humble and unselfish. Even now, he could sense her sifting through the memories of her capture and then jumping to an illogical concern.

"D-did you kill Livia?"

Arkas could not help but chuckle. "*That* is what you want to know most right now? Not if I'm going to cut you into bits or do any number of unspeakable things to you?"

"Is she alive?" Iona squeaked, more tears rolling down her face.

Arkas sighed. "I did not kill that *thing* you think of as your sister if it makes you happy. Actually, she's out scouring the countryside for you right now with that imbecile *father* of yours. We lost them hours ago, but I have a man keeping an eye on the two of them." He leaned in closer to the trembling girl and whispered: "I can have them both killed anytime I wish."

"NO!" Iona shrieked. "Please, I beg you!"

"Relax," he said. He reached up and gently stroked the side of her head with his right hand, running the two fingers he still had through her hair, which she endured in silence. "I left them alive for *you*." He cast her a hard smile. So many of the poor folk he had had in his dungeons thought of themselves as selfless souls, but when he had shown them true pain, most lost all concern for their children and loved ones and became obsessed only with their own survival. Still, a few prisoners here and there had surprised him, holding fast to their innocence through any degree of suffering, yet confessing immediately and offering their own lives the minute he threatened their loved ones. *Courage...* This girl had that kind of soul—illogical, but simple to manipulate. "That will be our contract," he said. "You will do whatever you are told and make no attempt to escape, and I will allow that fat little man and the mute freak to continue to breathe."

"Uh!" the girl whimpered. She processed his words for several heartbeats and then whispered: "I...I'll do *anything*."

Arkas blinked at her. *She meant the words.* He almost respected the little slave girl in that moment, and it made him uncomfortable. He turned away from her sickeningly sincere brown eyes and reminded himself that she was a tool, and one that he would use mercilessly.

"Is that... uh...*him*, boss?" Dunlin said from the front of the cart.

Arkas sensed a sharp jolt of fear from his subordinate. He shut his eyes and sent out his Starborn senses, and almost immediately he perceived the swell of trapped dragon's power tattooed into the hulking mass of unnatural flesh. "Yes, that is Gorlick," he said with a grin.

Arkas had kept his half-ogre companion separate from his other servants for several reasons, not the least of which being that Gorlick disliked being around men whom he perceived to be sniggering at his appearance when he was not looking. Arkas's other comrades were crass men—the kind Gorlick might rip into a half dozen pieces over the wrong choice of words.

"Do not look him in the eyes," he said in a soft voice to Dunlin.

"Y-yeah," Dunlin said in a raspy whisper, and he shrank in his seat on the cart.

"Come over here, my friend," Arkas shouted. He rose and gazed over the sidewall of the cart to see the massive cloaked figure emerge from the trees and come bounding toward them.

Dunlin's breathing quickened, and he whispered: "Make sure he knows... I'm a friend."

"Relax," Arkas said. "I have no intention of driving this cart back myself." He turned and extended his left hand to Iona and said: "Stand up. There is someone I wish you to meet."

The girl's face paled as she extended her hand and allowed him to pull her up. When she looked over the cart wall and saw Gorlick coming, she drew in a gasp and stumbled backward.

"You'll have to get used to my associate," Arkas said, gazing down at her. "Get back up." This time he did not extend his hand but sent invisible tendrils of magic out around the girl and brought her forcefully back to a standing position. By the time she was on her feet, Gorlick was at the side of the cart, glaring at her with bulbous yellow eyes from under his hood.

"Who the hell's this?" Gorlick grunted.

"This is Iona," Arkas said in a calm voice. "She is what the Norn sent me to find."

"What?!" the half-ogre snarled. He leaned in closer, looking Iona up and down. Arkas was still holding her with his magic, but she had enough freedom of movement to tremble and breathe very quickly under Gorlick's gaze. "A girl? Are you having a laugh with me?" His voice started to rise.

"Afraid not," Arkas said. "This *girl* is the weapon I was promised." As he spoke the words, he cocked his head at Iona. Trembling though she was, the little slave was listening to this exchange and trying to make sense of her situation. *That could be dangerous.* Her mind was incredibly easy to gaze into, which could be a problem if he were forced to bring her around other telepaths. Arkas raised his hand and whispered: "*Anaskath Niung.*" A translucent swirl of magic leaped from his hand and shot directly into Iona's forehead. She let out a brief whimper, and then her eyes rolled back into her head as her mind entered a magical trance. With her in this state, Arkas was able to reach inside her brain and obliterate the last few seconds of memory.

"We shouldn't tell her what she is," Arkas said.

Gorlick peered at the girl and muttered: "And what is she?"

Arkas let out an exasperated sigh. "I haven't completely deciphered that yet. There is power unlike anything I've ever seen inside her—it's not magic, it's...*stronger* than magic."

Gorlick stared at Iona for a few seconds longer, then grunted: "Is she dangerous?"

"I don't think so," Arkas said. "She had a knife to her throat, and she did nothing. I was going to kill the person she loved most, and she did *nothing*. The energy inside her doesn't respond to anything she thinks or feels—it doesn't even protect her from my magic." He met Gorlick's asymmetrical eyes. "All the same, this simple slave girl may have more power in her than even the great dragon."

Gorlick frowned. "How? Why?"

"I don't know."

"Can you bend her power to your will?"

"Not yet," Arkas said, shaking his head. In truth, he had almost no more idea how to wield the energy inside the girl than she did. Trying to channel and manipulate it with his magic was a bit like trying to shape an anvil with his fingers. *He did not have the strength.* Still, he had her for a reason. Of that much, Arkas was certain.

"How long'll it take you to figure it out, you think?" Gorlick said.

"No idea," Arkas admitted. "Until that time, we'll need to hang on to her—keep her hidden." He sighed at the half-ogre. "She will stay with you."

"WHAT?!" Gorlick snapped. "I don't want to care for some damned girl—"

"You won't have to care for her," Arkas said, cutting his friend off. "Quite the reverse, actually. Iona's a trained house slave, and she's well used to cooking and cleaning. Your *home* would benefit a great deal from her touch I think."

The half-ogre's lips curled back, revealing his thick, jagged teeth as he snarled: "I don't want another person out there with me!"

"WELL TOO GODS-DAMNED BAD!" Arkas snapped back.

Gorlick let out something like a low growl, and as he did, the dark hood fell away. Arkas gazed upon his handiwork. Deep blue tattoos covered every part of Gorlick's bulbous face.

Arkas had followed the basic foundational runes the Onkai and Nemesai used, but he had taken the so-called "apotheosis" process much further. The half-ogre's body was far more resilient than that of any human, and so Arkas had imbued him with far, far more ink from the dragon's tears than anyone would dare put upon a man. Gorlick was so terribly strong now, and his flesh so difficult to harm even with battle magic, that Arkas wondered at times if his creation could overpower him. Still, he stared hard into the enormous yellow eyes, knowing better than to show fear to the monster.

"This slave is very possibly the most powerful weapon in the world," he said in a calmer voice. "Gods know why, but she is. We would be insane to throw her away, and I cannot bring her back with me to the Nemesai. Cromlic is slipping, but he's still one of the most powerful telepaths in the world." Arkas dared to put a hand on his massive friend's shoulder and added: "I need Iona where no one can find her, and with someone with enough strength to guard her. Placing her with you is the best option on both counts." He squeezed the dense flesh and said: "Please, my friend."

Gorlick's jaw clenched, and his brown-stained fangs gnashed against one another for a few seconds. Then he looked to the side and muttered: "I'll work her hard."

"That's fine," Arkas said. "You cannot beat her though—at least not much. I need her healthy, and also, I'm not certain what would happen if you killed her. You and your home and several of the surrounding *mountains* could be obliterated in half a second."

"Hmm," Gorlick grunted.

"Dunlin will bring you supplies every so often," Arkas said.

"W-what?" Dunlin said, his tattooed face going a little pale as he turned to face Arkas. "I—I would really prefer not to—"

"You will bring them supplies," Arkas said in an icy voice. "A fitting response to that is *yes, sir,*" he narrowed his eyes, "or have you suddenly become insubordinate?"

"Uh... no, sir," Dunlin said in a dry whisper. "I'll do whatever you command, sir."

Arkas stared at the man for a moment, considering the possibility of burning his skin in a few carefully selected places. *Perhaps later.* He turned back to Gorlick. "Can you get her back to the hideout by yourself?"

The half breed stared at Iona, whose eyes were still rolled back in her head, and he gave a low chuckle. "I think I can manage."

"Good. I knew I could count on you." He shifted his gaze back to the girl but continued speaking to Gorlick: "Do not tell her anything about who I am or why she's important. I took her from her family to serve you—my secret soldier. If she starts to ask too many questions, just threaten to kill her sister and father. She'll shut her mouth then."

"Got it," Gorlick said with a slight nod.

Arkas willed the collection of spectrals he had assembled to dissipate from Iona's mind. After a few seconds, her eyes rolled forward again, and she blinked several times. She looked at Arkas, and then at Gorlick, whose grotesque face was now plain for her to see. A gasp of terror escaped her lips.

"This is your new master, Iona," Arkas said, gesturing to his friend.

"W-what?" she whimpered, looking Gorlick up and down.

"I suggest you refrain from staring," he sighed. Iona lowered her gaze but continued to pant. Arkas spoke to her in a gentle voice: "This is what you need to do to keep Hervin and *Livia* alive. Can you serve my friend here or not?"

"I... y-yes," Iona whispered, tears dripping from her eyes onto the cart floor.

"Good," he said. "It's a few days' travel where you are headed. You'll go with Gorlick now. I have other business to attend to."

Iona bit her lip, hesitating, and then she said in a small voice without looking up: "Why kidnap me? You look like you could afford a dozen slaves with ease. Why attack—"

"Stop," said Arkas, and he flicked his wrist and sent his magic down into one of the floorboards near Iona's feet. It ripped up in another explosion of wooden shrapnel, and she jerked back from it with a shriek. "No questions," he whispered. "None at all, or I punish your family. Just do as you're told. Can you adapt to that?"

"Yes," Iona whispered.

"Good." He turned to Gorlick. "Take her then. I'll send Dunlin in a week or so, and I'll be out myself in a month."

"Mh," Gorlick grunted. He reached out two enormous hands and took Iona by the shoulders, lifting her as though she were weightless. She whimpered but made no attempt to struggle as he placed her in a seated position on his right shoulder. "She better be a good cook," he snarled, and then he turned with the sobbing girl and walked back toward the trees.

Arkas stared at them, a cold frustration creeping through his body. Nearly five years he had waited for this *weapon,* and it was a silly little girl with power he had no idea how to access. It troubled him to think that a brilliant Starborn like his father, *or Cassian,* might have no trouble at all finding a way to use Iona if they ever got their hands on—*No!* Arkas would poison her or cut her throat before he would let anyone else have her. But anyhow, there was no need. The girl was a puzzle, and despite what Cassian and the others thought, Arkas was not stupid, or weak. Soon he would kill them all.

CHAPTER 20: GRANDFATHER SPIRIT

"Relax," Gretis whispered into Kota's ear. "You have spent years learning to quiet your mind. That is all this is."

Kota drew in slowly, trying to comply. He was sitting atop his meditation blanket, his hands and arms in their usual position. He had spent hundreds of hours in this pose, relaxing his body, focusing on his breathing and the beat of his heart, and letting his thoughts pass into obscurity. His animus complicated that abandonment. It leaped out from him of its own free will and carried back pulses of the world around him. Kota could feel Gretis standing behind him. He felt her lips move as she spoke and the subtle movements and tension in her legs and back as she bent down. It was not like sight or sound, but something more like a sense of the world he might gain from touching if only he had tens of thousands of fingers reaching out in every direction at once.

"I am sorry," she whispered. "I can tell this is difficult for you."

"You are being so nice," Kota said with a dark laugh. "It is unnerving."

He felt Gretis's mouth curl into a smirk behind him. "Would you prefer I be stern and callous?"

"That would at least be something familiar. All of this is so alien."

"I can only imagine," she said with a slight laugh. "Your animus is developing so much faster than mine did that I have very little idea how to go about your instruction. I dare say the difference between the two of us is akin to the difference between a normal sorcerer and a Starborn."

Kota tensed as his power surged with new sensation. "I can feel the disturbance your breath makes in the air when you speak."

"Can you?" she said, the amusement plain in her tone. "That is excellent. Such perception shall become immensely useful." He felt her walk around behind him and then lean in and peer down. She lifted her hand behind his head and lifted two fingers and whispered: "How many fingers am I holding up?"

"Two, but your forefinger is a little closer to my hair. I can also feel that you are concealing a small dagger in your right boot and an even smaller one is strapped to a thin leather sheath under your sleeve."

"Now you are showing off."

"I might as well take some pleasure in this. My head feels like it is going to split open." He turned and opened his eyes to look at her, and it was a relief to remember he could see. "Was it like this for you?"

"No," Gretis said with a shrug. "My animus sense came on so gradually there was no point at which I was overwhelmed." She knelt down in front of him so that they were eye to eye and said: "This is a gift, Kota. Followers of the Sansrit path work their whole lives to reach the level of connection you have managed to acquire without even trying."

Kota gazed down at the edge of the blanket where it rested unevenly over the dirt and dried leaves. "I understand the advantages this will bring in many combat situations. I will try to be strong." He found it impossible to hide the anguish in his voice completely. He had slept very little the night before. His animus sense had kept leaping down through the soil and carrying back the movement of worms and other insects far below.

Gretis gave him a sly smile and stood up. She drew the dagger he had felt in her boot, which was a simple bit of finely honed steel within a thinly carved wooden handle. Gretis cradled the hilt in her right hand while she reached down and picked up a small acorn with her left. As she rolled the brown mass between her thumb and forefinger, she said: "Kota, I think you only begin to guess at the possibilities. Perhaps I can inspire you with a small demonstration."

Gretis rose and held the acorn up so that he could see it. "I would like you to think about the Onkai soldier for a moment. He has roughly three times the strength of a normal man and can move and react far faster as well. The strength comes from the tattoos in the body of course, but the enhanced precision of movement and reflexes come from the markings on the scalp. I could not possibly explain the specifics of how the process works, but long ago the legendary Starborn, Dracus Mobius, discovered that he could stimulate specific areas of the brain through carefully controlled magic. However it works, the tattoos grant the Onkai accelerated perceptions and enhanced control over his muscles that probably exemplify the furthest limits of what the human mind can achieve. However, as you have already seen, a powerful Sansrit Master can move and react even faster, but that is only the beginning."

Kota remembered catching the arrow and then the stone. He gazed at the acorn in Gretis's hand, wondering where this was leading, and to move things along he muttered: "Please explain."

“Observe,” Gretis said, and she tossed the acorn behind her back, sending it sailing toward a tree no thicker than Kota's forearm. As it flew, Gretis calmly adjusted her grip on her thin knife, and then, just before the acorn hit the trunk, she snapped her wrist behind her backward without looking. A fraction of a second later, the blade struck the acorn dead-center, pinning it to the tree. Gretis winked at Kota and then drew the second, smaller knife from under her right sleeve. Again without looking, she flicked her wrist behind her back. The second dagger whipped in a blur to the outstretched handle of the first where it stuck itself, tip first.

Kota gaped. Gretis was deadlier than she had ever let on to him. With precision like that, she could kill nearly anyone in the blink of an eye. All he could think to say is: "How did you do that?"

The woman answered him only with a hint of a smile and then walked over and pulled her knives away from the tree. She tucked the smaller one back into the leather sheath under her sleeve and then returned to Kota and held out the larger blade to him, handle first.

Taking the knife, Kota said: "What is this for?"

Gretis hunched down in front of him and fished around on the ground until she found a thin twig. This she brought back up and held out in front of Kota between two fists and said: "Cut this stick in half."

"All right," Kota said. He raised the blade and brought it down in a quick slash, but to his shock, the small twig did not split. It stopped the knife as if it were a piece of steel. Confused, he reached out and touched the tiny stick, which Gretis calmly allowed him to do. It was indeed a simple piece of brittle wood. A young child could snap it between his fingers. "Why couldn't I cut it?" he asked.

"Answer that yourself," she said in a soft voice. She held the twig up closer to him, still clutching it between her two fists. Kota hesitated, then attempted to reach out with his new sense around the wood. His animus responded immediately to his mind and sent tiny pulses of itself out to the tiny target. An image of the thin piece of wood formed in Kota's mind, but it felt no different from any of the hundreds of others on the ground.

Confused, he muttered: "I can't feel—"

"Focus on your target," Gretis whispered. "Just relax. Take your time."

Kota had trouble conceptualizing how to 'focus' his animus sense. It was unendingly leaping in all directions. Still, his teacher had told him to try, and so he did. He shut his eyes and slowed his breathing. The piece of wood was there before him, as were Gretis's two hands. Kota tried to block everything else out and will his energy to the small point. To his surprise, it subtly began to obey. The sensations from all around faded away and what remained became vastly more detailed. He perceived every tiny groove in the small twig. He felt its brittleness and its dryness. Then, as he probed deeper, he felt a tingling sensation that set his new sense afire. There was an energy inside the sliver of wood, and it was flowing back and forth between Gretis's hands.

"You feel it, don't you?" she said.

"Yes," Kota whispered. "Is that your animus?"

"It is."

Kota opened his eyes and looked at her. "You can stretch it outside of yourself?"

"I can do *many* things with it." She held out her left hand and said: "Give me the knife." He handed her the weapon, and she said: "Observe again with your new sense."

Kota shut his eyes once more and willed his animus to focus on the blade in Gretis's hand. Within a few seconds, he felt the tingle of her power pulsing within her flesh. The power stretched slowly out around the knife, taking the shape of the blade. Gretis picked up a larger stick from the ground that was roughly the width of her thumb and brought the dagger to it in a slow movement. There was no snap. The knife's edge slid through the wood like it was nothing but air, and the bottom half dropped in silence away.

"What you have inside you, Kota, is a kind of magic," she said as she tossed away her newly made stump and slipped her dagger back into her boot. "It is not like the energy sorcerers wield, which is directed by the intellect. Your power is far more primal, and it is *alive*." She sighed softly and added: "In your case, it is *quite* tremendous. Already your animus dwarfs my own, but at the moment you can only tap into a fraction of it. Think of our duel yesterday."

Kota thought upon the swordplay of which the two of them had engaged. His body had moved with a strength and speed that it had never known, but he had failed to land even a glancing blow against Gretis. For his part, she had not touched him with her sword either. Whenever she came close to striking him, his animus had taken control, and he had dodged or parried faster than he could imagine, but it only seemed to work in defense.

"You have to learn to direct your power and at the same time surrender to it. It is an art that I cannot truly teach you. You must *feel* it out and develop it for yourself. Until you do, you are far too dangerous to return to society."

Kota frowned at her. "I thought... after what happened with those people—when I did not hurt them, I mean—that you determined I was *not* the dangerous creature you had been fearing."

Gretis met his eyes and said: "There is no *rage* deep within your spirit. Still, your animus is unbelievably powerful, and at your current level, it can and will respond unpredictably to your emotions. When you and I duel, your spirit refuses to injure my body." She gave him a kind smile and said: "It is held in check by your love for me. But with others..." Gretis grimaced and whispered: "Your animus has no concept of moral complexity. If you were to become angry with someone—even over something small—it might make a split second determination that that person was an enemy. You could rip a man's throat out before you even realized what you were doing."

Kota remembered his hand snapping up to meet the stone without his having any control over it. He gazed down at that appendage and said: "How do I ensure I will not be a danger to others?"

"By learning control," she said slowly. "I will help you."

"How long do you think it will take me?"

"I don't know. There has not been one like you in thousands of years."

Kota lifted his head and peered at her, her words triggering a thought in his mind. "Will you tell me the rest of the story about my people?"

Gretis let out a soft laugh and replied: "As you wish, young warrior." She walked over to the hut they had built and drew out her own meditation blanket, which she brought back and set in front of him. Gretis seated herself upon it and folded her legs, and then said in the rolling voice she used for storytelling: "I believe we left off with the great defender spirits bonding with a tribe of humans in the wilderness, did we not?"

"Yes," Kota said.

She sighed. "That first generation possessed incredible power—power as you now hold. In that age, before humans came to acquire sorcery, there was little that could stand against your ancestors. They were strong enough even to challenge the elves for supremacy in the world. That is not, however, what they chose to do.

"The mightiest of all the ancient spirits infused its essence into the chief of the ancient tribe, a shamalak whom we know only as Nataka." Kota took in a sharp breath. *He knew the name.* His father had whispered it to him many times when they had looked up at the stars in the night. Nataka was the grandfather—the oldest and strongest of the spirits that were said to watch over the shamalak people.

"That figure of legend is said to have lived for several hundred years, and he grew very wise in that time. Nataka saw that the children born to his new race of people inherited all the physical characteristics of their parents, yet they did not inherently know how to channel the power in their spirits—that, in fact, no creature in the world inherently possessed this ability. He also saw that some of his people had begun to want more than to simply live in peace with nature. They fell prey to—" Gretis's expression became grim, "*human* desires, and they possessed the power to take virtually whatever they wanted from the other beings around them. Some of the shamalak even became dominated by dangerous emotions, as *my son* did. They became a danger, and Nataka decided that the power of the ancient spirits could not be allowed to run rampant. He ordered that none of the young shamalak be trained to harness their spiritual energy." She gave a little shrug. "There are two different versions of what happened next."

"What are they?" Kota said.

"In one version, the tribe obeyed Nataka's decree. The generation who wielded the power hunted the new breed of demons that were beginning to appear in the world, but after a time they died away. Before Nataka passed on, he decided that connection to the spirit world was too important to be lost completely to history. He went on a long pilgrimage and found humans who did not possess spirits on par with his own but whom he judged to be wise and trustworthy. He gathered them together and taught them all how to bridge the connection between mind and animus. In the language his tribe spoke—a tongue older even than Dhavic—the spirit was called the *Sahansrit*. Thus, this first generation he trained took on the title of 'Sansrit Masters' to honor him."

Kota considered this story, and then asked: "What is the second version of what happened?"

"Virtually the same as the first save that not *all* the shamalak in Nataka's tribe chose to obey the command. A few traveled far into the east. It is rumored that they developed their own form of what we think of as Sansrit Mastery."

"What do you believe?" Kota said.

"I do not know," Gretis said with a shrug. "If I accept the story of Nataka as true in the first place, then it seems logical that at least one or two of your people would disobey, but then if there were a group of shamalak running around with abilities like my own or greater, I might assume they would have made themselves known to history in some way. Whatever the case, it does not alter the truth of my existence or my connection to my own spirit."

Kota extended his claws and gazed at them, and he remembered the indentations they had made in the rock the day before. He had pierced solid stone without even realizing it. "I think the point of the story then is that the power of the Sansrit is too dangerous in my people's hands."

"That is indeed one way to look at it."

Kota glanced up at her. "What is another?"

"That your people were wise enough and strong enough to do what was right—that they chose to surrender their power rather than to use it to dominate."

Kota gave a small laugh. "I suppose I like that one better." He gazed into his teacher's eyes and said: "All the same, why have you gone against Nataka's ancient decree? Why teach a shamalak the ways of the Sansrit?"

Gretis's mouth tightened. "I do not think you are quite ready to learn *that* part yet. For now, you must simply trust me."

"I do trust you," Kota said, though he was disappointed with her answer.

"Then let us continue," Gretis said. She walked over to a bag she had resting against a tree and drew out a long strip of cloth. Holding it up, she said: "I think we will begin using this. From now on you will spend half of every day blindfolded, so that you may only be guided by your animus." The woman gave a dark little chuckle and said: "Actually, I have heard of Sansrit followers choosing to permanently blind themselves to become one with their new senses, but I think you and I are not quite so extreme."

Kota took the blindfold from her and tied it around his head, covering his eyes. He found he could still see light through the fabric, but no more detail than that. "What should I do for this training?"

"Simple tasks will do for now. You will go and gather firewood for our camp, and then wash our clothes and linens in the river." Kota felt his teacher's lips curl as she added: "I think you will find the way your new sense reacts to flowing water to be quite... *disconcerting* at first. We will train a bit this afternoon, and then, if you feel ready, you will go and hunt tonight."

"Hunt," Kota whispered. The thought of tracking and killing an animal without the use of his eyes seemed an impossible task. How could he aim his bow?

"Try to relax," Gretis said, putting a hand on his shoulder and squeezing gently. "You have gone through a profound awakening that very few ever experience. There are so many things you will discover about the spirits of this world, and about yourself. Be strong. It will take you time to understand it and to adjust, but I will be here with you every step of the way."

"How will we know when I am ready to return to society?"

A smirk played across Gretis's smooth features, and she said: "We will know you have learned control when you can defeat me in single combat."

CHAPTER 21: THE EMPIRE'S NEW COMMANDER

Cassian paced slowly over the light grass in front of his assembled troop of men, with Titus prancing in as delicate a gait as a dragon his size could manage behind him. Three hundred and fifty pairs of eyes were focused on the two of them. The soldiers were eager to know why they had been summoned, though many already had a fair idea and were bursting with excitement.

"Good afternoon," Cassian said, projecting his voice to every corner of the assemblage. "I sense your general did not share the purpose of this assembly. The reason is quite simple and yet immensely consequential to the rest of your lives: You are all now *mine.*"

Cassian gazed around. There were thrills , confusion, and apprehension leaking out of the minds around him, and yet every soldier was perfectly upright and at attention. The shadows of Romulus's harsh disciplinary policies would linger for some time to come. That might prove an advantage.

"I have chosen each of you individually to become members of my personal guard. This is not because you are especially talented in combat. I picked you because, of all the soldiers in this camp, I believe you are most capable of adhering to the moral standards to which I intend to hold my soldiers. I am *not* Romulus. My men will not steal from cowering peasants nor commit rape. You are to be the first of a new kind of army—one that can be trusted and respected for more than the number of men you have killed. Together, we will be better than that.

"You need not concern yourselves with the prowess you have demonstrated on the battlefield until now. I will *make you* into the finest fighting force that has ever existed. I have many new combat formations and tactics that I have developed with my mentor, the great General Somar Dojinko. We will drill together for six hours a day, every day, until I am satisfied that you have mastered them to perfection." Cassian sensed dismay at this decree, but he knew he would soon turn his soldiers' feelings entirely around.

"It is important to understand going in that I expect *perfect* discipline. You will hold exactly to the formations I set you in under *all* circumstances. I will shape you into precise tools that I may conduct telepathically while I fly above on my dragon, and you will learn to respond instantly to my projected thoughts." Cassian spoke to them all through his mind: <In this manner, we shall become organized on a level no army has ever been before.>

He returned to verbal communication: "As I shape your skills, I will also bestow each of you with mystical gifts. Over the years, I have worked closely with the Onkai order, and I took time to study the magical runes they utilize. Many of you are probably aware that Dracus Mobius, the infamous Starborn and first bishop of the Onkai, declared the system of tattoos he invented to be *holy*, and that using them to empower a state army would henceforth be considered heresy. I have developed my own system that does not belong to the church, but which will bestow nearly exactly the same effects. Over the next several months I will imbue every fighting man in my personal guard with this power."

There were enormous waves of exhilaration. Cassian let his new soldiers' imaginations run for a moment with the knowledge that they would become as powerful as the legendary Onkai, and then he explained the great drawback: "This power shall come at a cost. As I said, I have very high moral standards. The markings will contain a spell woven into them that I may activate at any time from nearly anywhere in this world. With a thought, I will be able to cause you immense suffering, or even bring about your deaths. Let me be quite clear in stating that abuse of your new strength will be met with immediate and *terrible* consequence. This will be our contract. I will tolerate neither dissent nor desertion. You will obey my commands and live up to my ideals absolutely."

He paused again, letting the men weigh what he had just said. When he judged the time was right, he went on: "I give all this to you as a choice. I selected more men than I need on purpose. If any of you do not wish to be part of my personal guard, you may return to Romulus's service without consequence from me. Know that if you stay, you are almost certainly committing yourself for life. I *will* be the next emperor of Denigoth." Cassian spoke the words with confidence, knowing the effect they would have. "You will come with me through everything I face. This force shall be a relatively small contingent in the scope of the Denigoth military, but you will be more effective than an army many times your size. We will have a systematic hierarchy of command that can easily incorporate troops and even legions from other Generals when we need them, but you will be my most elegant and exact unit. Moreover, you will be my officers in reshaping this empire."

Cassian could feel the near hysterical excitement in his men now. He stared at the faces in front, watching as Somar had taught him to watch, as well as using the full telepathic gifts of his Starborn mind. He felt far more optimism than doubt. Every sense told him that three hundred and fifty men had already made the decision to follow his command. Cassian had known they would. He had sought very specific qualities in picking them all out. After a moment of silence, he breathed in deeply, then said: "I say this to you all: if you would go, go *now*, for it is the only chance I will give you."

Along their rows, the men were perfectly still. Cassian picked up sounds and images from various minds within the group, most of which involved imagining fighting with mystically enhanced strength and speed. Some were anticipating growing rich under the future emperor's command. Others were thinking about becoming the moral paragons described in the speech. Whatever their motivations, not a single man moved.

"I see," said Cassian with a soft chuckle, letting his voice carry all over. "So be it then." *The thing was done, just like that.*

"SOLDIERS!" he yelled, and three hundred and fifty bodies stiffened and stood taller. "We will begin drilling at sunrise. Set your gear at the ready. I will expect you out of your tents, dressed, armed, and in exact formation within six minutes of when you hear the horn. Do *not* come late, and do *not* come to me with excuses. Is that clear?"

There was a resounding "YES, SIR!" The men cried in near perfect unison.

"Excellent!" Cassian shouted, gazing around at what would soon be his elite, personal army. His heart, still numb from Dimitris's death, felt a tremble of excitement. His destiny had truly begun.

CHAPTER 22:
A SISTER'S DETERMINATION

Livia felt a deadness in her heart as Hervin drew the cart up to the eleventh inn on the path north. The sun had risen high into the morning horizon and... *nothing.* She was sure they had lost Iona's captors hours ago. There were so many winding roads through the hills that split in dozens of places. *Had it been foolish to rush out like this?* That thought pained her. They might have gone to one of the local hunters and paid to borrow a tracking dog, but then... what would she have used to give the hound a scent? Livia knew enough about hunting animals to understand that they needed a basis for sniffing out quarry, and that they could only track something that continuously touched the ground. If Iona had been laid in a cart, a dog could not be used to find her. Livia might have done far better with a search party, but then who would leave their homes in the middle of the night for a former slave?

"I'm sure we'll find something here," Hervin muttered as he stepped down off the cart. He moved in quaking steps to the wooden post in front of the inn and proceeded to tie the reigns of their horses to it.

Livia could not even manage an encouraging smile for him. *Iona was gone.* She could feel it. Gods but it wasn't fair! Hervin had revealed that he had adopted both of them and sent the cow away, and for the first time in her life, Livia had been truly happy. All that joy had been an illusion. The pain she felt now was far worse than anything Lady Sondal had ever done to her.

Still, she stepped down from the cart and gazed at the 'Limping Stallion' inn. It was a strange name, perhaps chosen as some secret joke the owners had. The building was two stories tall and was in reasonably good shape for a roadside inn. Livia had studied maps of this area and knew that there was a town a half day's ride east, and this inn was set up to cater to those traveling between cities. It had horse troughs with relatively clean looking water, which the flustered Hervin had failed to take advantage of, tired and thirsty as their horses must be after a full night's riding.

Livia went around to the back of the cart and reached under the blankets to slide out the image she had drawn of Iona's captor. She had shown it to dozens of people, none of whom had recognized the face. As Livia looked at it now, she wondered if it were an adequate drawing. She had felt confident about it at first, but now, after so much failure, she noticed dozens of tiny imperfections. *Gods, was this all hopeless?* A feeling of despair washed over Livia, and she became so lost in it that the sound of footsteps to the left failed at first to register.

"Hello!" a loud male voice said.

She gave a little jump and looked up to see a large man in fine green and brown linens walking toward her from the direction of the outhouse to the side of the inn. Livia blinked at him, automatically scanning for danger the way she had trained herself to do during years of whippings from Lady Sondal. The man was at least ten years older than she, and though he was smiling, there was something troubling in his dark eyes. He was quite tall and built like a fighter, with thick, knotted limbs, and he wore a sword on his belt with a gold-laced pommel that probably cost more than both her horses. *He was an aristocrat—maybe even a lord.* As Livia registered all of this, she also noted that he had maneuvered himself between her and the entrance to the inn, *where Hervin was.*

"Good morning," the man said, lifting an eyebrow. He took several steps toward her.

Livia cast him a terse smile as if to say, *'Good morning, please leave me alone.'* He continued to move closer. She looked down into the cart, instinctively feeling the need for a weapon—even a small one—to be on hand. She had left her bag in the front of the cart, in which she had packed a small dagger in case there was trouble on the road. Livia gazed stupidly down at her simple dress—the one that did not have extra pockets for things such as knives. She had nothing on hand.

"Former slave, eh?" the man chuckled. He drew near enough for her to catch the all too familiar stench of wine.

Livia snatched up her drawing, cast the man a second tense smile and started to walk past him, but she was forced to stop when his arm shot out, and he leaned into the side of Hervin's cart, barring her path.

"Where you going?" he said, the grin still on his face. "Hang around a few minutes. My name's Calvis Suleeman, and I'm a *baron,* so maybe don't be so quick to brush me off."

Livia cast him a cold stare, trying not to tremble. She was furious that this noble-born ass would trouble her now, but also frightened of the look he was giving her. His smile...*did this baron think he was being charming?* No, he would not care—not with a slave girl. She glanced at the entrance to the inn. *Hervin should have waited for her!* It was not as if she could scream out like a normal young woman.

"You're just gorgeous!" Calvis chuckled. He leaned in, and Livia flinched back, but he moved remarkably fast and got an enormous arm on the other side of her. She began to breathe very quickly and turned and glanced at the door to the inn again. *It was still closed.*

"Why are you so quiet?" Calvis sighed. He reached up and brushed a thick finger over the part of her cheek where her tattoos were. "Who freed you?" She flinched away from his hand, but this only seemed to amuse him. "Must have been an imbecile. You'd fetch five or six *Thousand* desseks in a capital city brothel." He leaned in closer to her face, so that his hot, drunken breath assaulted her nostrils. "Maybe you're a runaway slave, and this isn't a real freedom mark. If I thought that were the case, well..." the nobleman cast her a smirk, "it would be my duty as a baron to place you under arrest."

Livia's jaw clenched. She thought of the magic—the *tiny shred* of power buried somewhere inside her. She reached for it, feeling desperate, but it refused to come as it had the day before. Only a vague tingle traveled through her right hand, and before it could manifest into any kind of external force, a mind-shattering surge of pain erupted through her. Livia's knees weakened, and she stumbled. The baron caught her, taking her shoulders in his hands

"What's wrong?" he said with a soft laugh. "Did my words make you nervous? I must say, that is a bit suspicious." His eyes stared hard into hers for a moment, and then they began to travel down. His smile broadened along the way until he suddenly blinked several times at her midsection, and his expression contorted into confusion. "Prince Arkas?" he muttered, and he took a step back from her. She followed his gaze down and realized that her drawing had unfolded in her hands. "Gods, I... I'd know that face anywhere," the man muttered. He gazed back up into her eyes and said: "Why do *you* have a portrait of the Emperor's son?"

Livia gazed down again at her drawing. *Arkas Adronicus? The Starborn?!*

"Oh shit!" Calvis muttered, taking a visibly nervous step back from her, his eyes going wide. He looked her up and down as if seeing her anew and said: "Are you... are you his mistress or something?" Livia had never seen a face grow pale so quickly. "Actually, I don't need to know! I... I have a-absolutely nothing but respect for the royal family—and prince Arkas himself!" The man cast a nervous look around, as if expecting danger, and then he put up his hands in a pleading gesture and whimpered: "N-no trouble, p-please, I—I have a wife and two sons!" He turned then and ran toward the inn's stables, which were about sixty paces to the right.

Livia watched him go, but her mind was entirely elsewhere. *Iona had been abducted by a Starborn?* She gazed down at her drawing once more. Could it be a mistake? The fear on her would-be attacker's face had been so real—he had been entirely convinced that her sketch was of Prince Arkas. Livia's hands began to tremble, and she dropped the drawing onto the grass. *The son of the Emperor!* The weight of that notion crushed her mind. How the hell was she going to get Iona back from such a person? He could have both her and Hervin executed if they so much as cast him a disrespectful glance.

Livia tried desperately to think. *Prince Arkas was Starborn.* If she remembered correctly, he was also a high ranking member of the Nemesai order. Her heart nearly exploded in her chest. *Was Iona in a Nemesai cell?* She shut her eyes and remembered the words the young man had said: '*Are you the weapon*?' Why would the Nemesai think that Iona was a weapon? Why would Arkas not take her to the local Nemesai temple for interrogation rather than abscond with her to some distant place in the North? Why had Livia not been arrested as well—or Hervin? If the order suspected heresy, it was normal for them to interrogate everyone surrounding the crime.

None of the facts made sense on this front, but that did not mean this was not a religious arrest of some kind. If Iona were perceived as some kind of important *weapon,* ridiculous as the idea seemed, would the order not send its most capable agent to apprehend her? A Starborn was undoubtedly that, but what kind of weapon could Iona be, and against whom? Livia's fingers went to her temples, and she started to rub. There was no way to decipher the motives with what she knew. Still, Iona's life hung in the balance, which meant decisions needed to be made.

Livia shut her eyes and focused. She and Hervin had lost Prince Arkas in the night, but perhaps that did not matter so much now that she knew who he was. Starborn were easy to find. They drew attention wherever they went. Still, even if she knew precisely where he was and also where he was keeping Iona—which would likely be in a Nemesai stronghold—what could be done? Livia had some power that seemed to react to the magic of others, but it was unpredictable at best. Without another sorcerer around, she had barely managed to crumple up a single piece of paper and toss it across a room, and the effort had nearly killed her. Just now, when a man was threatening to assault her, she had not been able to muster any kind of offense.

Livia had no experience in combat or subterfuge whatsoever, and her enemy was a Starborn prince with virtually limitless wealth, and there was the even more significant enemy of the Nemesai Order itself. Against such opponents, she was as nothing, even with whatever strange abilities lay inside her, but... *there was a person in the world who had defeated both Prince Arkas and the Nemesai Bishop himself.*

"Livia?" Hervin's voice came accompanied by the creaking of hinges. She turned to see him walking out the doorway to the inn, a sorrowful look on his face. "N-no one has seen anyone matching the description I gave," he muttered, "but I still think we should show the sketch." He walked to her and said: "Sorry, I should have waited for you before rushing in. Did you need to use the privy?"

Livia glanced at the outhouse, her mind flashing for just an instant to the man who probably would have raped her, but she pushed all that away. Instead, she walked to the bag at the front of the cart and drew out her paper and pencil, and wrote:

I know who has Iona, and I think I know what our best chance is to get her back.

Hervin stared at the note for a few seconds after she handed it to him, and then exclaimed: "Who?! What do we need to do?"

Livia grimaced as she took the sheet back and wrote more:

I'm going to get involved with some dangerous people. I need you not to ask any questions. You know almost nothing about what is going on. That may save you if I am caught.

"WHAT?!" Hervin exclaimed after reading the words. For the first time since she could remember, his face filled with anger at her. "What are you talking about? I adopted you both! You don't get to face danger to find Iona and keep it secret from me!"

Livia stared at him. *Of course he was angry. He had a right to be.* Hervin's feelings were not what mattered most though. He had never even been able to stand up to his own wife. Her kindly adoptive father would never be able to face a Nemesai inquisitor. *She could though.* Livia had good reason to believe her mind was a dangerous thing to invade, and her powers would either come when the time came, or they would kill her. Either way, no one would learn anything from her she did not want known.

She snatched the paper from Hervin's hand and wrote again:

I love you. That is why if you do not agree to leave this to me, I will run away, and you may never see me again. It breaks my heart to write this, but you must agree now, or I will leave you right here.

When she finished writing her hand was trembling, and a set of tears had run down her cheeks, but she felt utterly determined as she held the note up for him to read.

Hervin read the words and then, in a frightened voice, said: "Are... are you sure?" Livia swallowed and gave him a decisive nod. His face took on a sad, defeated expression, and he muttered: "A-alright."

Her heart ached, knowing the pain she was causing her... *father,* but this had to be done. She leaned forward and planted a kiss on his forehead, and then pointed to the cart.

"W-where are we going?" Hervin murmured. Livia shook her head to the left, indicating the direction of south. He squinted at her. "Do you mean back home?" She nodded. Her father drew in a very slow breath. Frustration played in his eyes, and then his thick lips pressed hard together, and he began walking to the driver's seat of the cart. Livia stepped around to the other side and climbed up next to him.

Hervin set the horses into a slow, tired trot back home and did not speak for a very long time. That was probably for the best. It gave Livia time to think. *What would it take to infiltrate the Cassianites?* She could read and write very well, and she more or less ran most aspects of Hervin's trade business, which meant access to supply lines and goods in which notes and secret literature could be concealed. She was smart—much smarter than the pair of fools that had been handing out Asango's pamphlets. If the Cassianites could be convinced to trust her, she could make herself very useful to them, and in turn, they could help her find out where Iona was. That might take time, and the thought troubled her, but this was the only realistic path of which she could think to get Iona out of the hands of Prince Arkas.

Livia blinked as another thought entered her mind. There was still the Sansrit witch, Lady Gretis. The woman might help her, but then again even a Sansrit Master might not side with a slave girl she had met one time against both the Nemesai Order and the son of the Emperor of Denigoth. Livia did not know, but she could write a letter—*a very carefully worded letter*—exploring the possibility. This was a secondary plan though. For the moment, she would find a way to join the damned Cassianites. They got people away from the Nemesai all the time, or so she had heard. It was worth the risk to join their ranks. Hell, she would find a way to get an audience with Cassian Asango himself if that was what it took!

CHAPTER 23: KOTA'S BURDEN

Glavius gazed at what appeared to be four parallel claw marks in solid stone. He hoped to the gods that they had been made by Kota. There had been a handful of alleged sightings of a brown-skinned demon demonstrating impossible feats of strength and speed, though it never attacked anyone. Glavius had been on this trail for weeks, but this was the first time he had discovered any real evidence that this was the correct path. Still, as he looked at the deep gashes in the rock, there was a deep feeling of apprehension. If there were a powerful demonic creature roaming about, he was not at all prepared.

Glavius rested a gloved right hand on the hilt of his sword in silence, gazing around. He was deep into the Tagason mountains, where very little was mapped, and he had elected to leave his horse in the town to the west because the terrain had become so uneven. That had been many hours ago. Now, trees and birds and gods know what else surrounded him on all sides. Evening would come soon, and he might spend the night alone in the wilderness, but then again, perhaps not.

After several more minutes of searching, Glavius came across the stump of a tree a little wider than his waist. The trunk had been carried off, which of course meant that a person rather than natural causes had felled the tree, but that was not what was interesting. The slice in the wood was straight and clean, as if something had slashed through it in a single cut. He had seen Gretis perform incredible feats of strength, but never anything on that level. *Could it have been Kota?*

Glavius gazed back in the direction of the deep gashes in the stone and swallowed, wondering if what he was about to do was incredibly stupid, and then he moved his left hand to the horn on his belt, drew it up, and blew. The low, unmelodious sound of the bullhorn tore through the peace of the forest with such sharpness that dozens of birds shot into the sky from all around. Glavius slid his sword halfway out of its scabbard as he turned slowly around, gazing in all directions. There was nothing—nigh a sign of movement on the ground or from anywhere for several moments. He hoped they were near enough that they had at least heard the first blast, if not close enough to trace it back. Gods knew Kota's ears were insanely acute. Still, no response came as the minutes dragged on, and Glavius finally decided to risk a second blow. He drew in a slow breath, and then moved to horn to his lips once more.

"No, don't blow that damned thing again!" a familiar voice shouted from the right. Glavius whirled to see Lady Gretis step around a large tree, a calm smile on her face. She looked the same as ever, seeming not to have aged a day in the year and a half since he had last seen her. "It is wonderful to see you, my old pupil."

"Hah!" Glavius laughed, bringing a gloved hand to his forehead. "Thank the Gods! I've been searching for weeks!"

"Oh?" she said, raising an eyebrow. "We have been right here—at least most of the time."

"Well it's damn good to see you," he said, grinning as his eyes scanned about. "Where's Kota?"

"He was not in a position to abandon his task when you blasted your obnoxious horn," Gretis said, and then she gestured through the trees. "You are welcome to come and see him. I think he has grown very lonely for his old friends."

Glavius swallowed. He had crucial things to tell them both, but after a year and a half, there were a few questions he could not resist asking as they began to move together. "Did you... unlock Kota's power—or whatever the hell you call it?"

"Oh yes, we accomplished that almost immediately after we left."

Glavius tried to read her serene expression as they walked, *which was impossible*. He had no idea how Sansrit training worked, and he doubted she would reveal much in conversation. *Still, there was no harm in trying*. "Can you at least tell me why you kept him away so long?"

"I have not kept him at all," Gretis said, her voice smooth and patient. "I encouraged Kota to return to the temple many months ago, but he insisted on remaining away."

"Why?"

Gretis's face became somber. "Kota has grown very, *very* powerful—more so than I think either of us expected. He's afraid of returning to the company of normal folk."

They walked for perhaps a quarter of an hour with little more conversation other than Gretis asking questions about Otho and the goings-on of the temple. Eventually, they came to a small clearing in the forest where Glavius saw two very large animal skin tents built near to a flowing stream. Around them was a clean and orderly campsite. Cooking utensils sat drying in a neat pile atop a blanket, with small sections of cloth laid over them to protect from dust. There was another mat upon which rested a large assortment of knives and swords, each polished to a shimmering patina. In one of the tents, Glavius saw books—dozens and dozens of them—stacked in neat piles, and there was a thick stack of papyrus paper as well held in place by a rock. The top sheet had a great deal of writing on it, and several charcoal pencils rested at the center of the page. There was also a somewhat worn cornerstone set against the back wall.

"You've been out here this whole time—just the two of you?" Glavius said.

"We have traveled to nearby settlements here and there and encountered occasional caravans. Kota and I needed supplies after all. But for the most part, yes, we've been out here, where there was no one for him to hurt." She gestured past the stream and said: "He can tell you himself. It will do him good to talk to a friend."

Curious, Glavius stepped up to the edge of the stream and gazed in the direction she was pointing. On the other side, past a handful of trees, he spotted Kota, walking slowly down the side of a small mountain, carrying a boulder directly above his head that was *twice as tall as his body and larger still in width!*

“HOLY SHIT!” Glavius exclaimed. No twenty Onkai could lift a mass of rock that size, but Kota was plodding along, the great stone bouncing with each step he took. Glavius gaped as he walked closer, barely noticing as his boots sank into the stream. The display of strength was unreal, like the stories the older Onkai told of the power of the Demon King.

Glavius drew closer and closer and more details came into view. Kota's claws and indeed his fingers had penetrated into the stone, and there was a crunching sound as his sweating friend took each step. The claws on Kota's feet were extended as well and were biting into the mountain face beneath. *Was that for traction?!*

When Glavius was within a few dozen steps, Kota wheezed out without turning his head: "Hello, Glavius!" He sounded friendly, if strangely nervous. "I'm almost done. I can't set it down until I get to the bottom." Kota made his way to the bottom of the slope where he came to a clearing of dirt and grass, at the center of which a large hole had been dug. His feet sank up to the ankles in the soft earth as he trudged forward with the impossible weight held over his head to the edge of the pit where he slowly brought the boulder down over his head. It occurred to Glavius distantly that the rock should have crumbled free of Kota's fingers under its own tremendous weight, but it did not. Somehow, his shamalak friend was able to lower the thing gently into its hole.

"Sorry," Kota finally said, whirling around with a timid smile of teeth and fangs. The simple look on his face did a great deal to assuage Glavius's fears that his dear comrade had been changed by this awesome power. *The kind, humble young man was still there.*

"I've missed you, little brother," Glavius said, and he darted forward, extending his hand.

Kota's grin widened, and his own hand shot out, but he noticeably hesitated before gripping Glavius, drawing in an uneasy breath.

"Worried you're gonna break my arm?" Glavius chuckled.

Kota let go and said: "A little." *It was strange to see fear in the silver eyes.* Kota had always been so brave and full of hope. "I... I've missed you a great deal too." He grinned. "Nobody's made fun of me in over a year."

"How long you been carrying that thing?" Glavius said, gesturing to the massive boulder.

"Ah," Kota sighed, "about a month. I was carrying a smaller one before, but I keep... getting stronger."

"You're amazing!" Glavius said, and he clapped Kota on the arm—or tried to—the movement was cut short with such abruptness that it took Glavius a second to realize that Kota's left hand had snapped up and caught his wrist. It had happened almost too fast for his eyes to register.

"S-sorry," Kota said, letting go of Glavius's hand and shrinking back a step.

"It's alright," Glavius said, trying not to let the nerves show in his voice. "You didn't hurt me."

"You're my friend," Kota whispered, gazing down at the hand he had just drawn away. "It understands at least that much."

"What does?"

"My animu—"

"Kota!" Gretis's voice snapped. Glavius whirled around to see her standing a few paces behind him. She was staring with a hard expression at Kota. "There are sacred rules to what you may reveal to the uninitiated."

"Rules I made in the first place," Kota said in a quiet voice, and he lifted his eyes to meet hers, "my first incarnation that is." These incredibly perplexing words seemed to steal some of the fire from Gretis's eyes. She hesitated, and Kota went on:

"Glavius is my friend—maybe my best friend. I trust him completely."

For a long moment, Gretis and Kota stared at one another, and then finally the Blade Witch said in a quiet voice: "Do as you like," and turned back toward the campsite.

"Wait," Glavius said. She paused but did not turn. He whirled back to Kota and said: "I want to know whatever it is that you have to tell me, but I came here to deliver important news to both of you."

Gretis spun slowly back around and said: "What is your news?"

Glavius reached into his bag and drew out one of several papyrus scrolls he had packed. "First, a girl named Livia has been trying to contact you almost since the day you left." Gretis's face paled a little at the name—something Glavius had never seen before. "She's sent dozens of letters to your home and even to the temple asking your whereabouts."

"Is that one of her letters?" Gretis said, eyeing the paper he held.

"Yes," Glavius said. "Would you like to—"

She darted forward and snatched it before he could even begin extending his arm, and as fast as he could blink, she had broken the wax seal and had the thing open. He watched her face as she read it and saw more color drain from her skin. As soon as the Blade Witch finished, she looked up at Kota and said: "I... I think I have to go south for a time."

Kota was about to say something to this, but Glavius held up a hand. "There's more." He swallowed, a little nervous about what kind of reaction his next words might produce in his friend. "We've gotten reports—*unconfirmed mind you*—that the Demon Lord Narakum has been attacking shamalak tribes near..." he swallowed and gazed into Kota's silver eyes, "near where Cassian Asango met you almost seven years ago." He watched his best friend's bronze face fill with horror. Kota began to breathe very quickly, and blood vessels began to stand up under his skin around his eyes. Feeling uneasy,

Glavius went on: "Like I said, this is unconfirmed. We don't have any real lines of communication with your people. Hell, nobody even knows where any of the tribes are—"

"I know where they are!" Kota said in a sharp hiss. He looked at Gretis. "The demons are trying to get to me, aren't they?"

Her face twitched, and she said in a low voice: "There is no way to know." He glared at her, and after a brief pause, she conceded: "But yes, you are most likely the reason."

"And I'm up here *hiding*!" he said, and the last word sounded lower than the others, almost like the snarl of a wolf. He looked at Glavius. "Gods! How long did it take you to find us out here?" He put his forehead into his hands, his fingers curling around tufts of dark hair. "Hundreds of my people could be dead by now!"

Glavius held up a hand. "Otho sent search parties before I left. For all I know they've already subdued the threat—if there even was one."

Kota looked at him for a few seconds, then said: "I have to go."

"Kota," Gretis said in a very soft voice, "you are not ready to face a Demon Lord yet."

"It's what I was born to do," he whispered. "My people are being killed because of me. Do you honestly think I could just play cornerstone up here with you and carry rocks up and down a mountain while they're slaughtered by demons?"

Gretis gazed down at the dirt beneath her feet, pausing for a few heartbeats before murmuring: "No."

"Go do whatever you have to do about this Livia and her letters. I will go to my tribe."

"I'll go with you," Glavius said.

Kota pursed his lips, looking at him. "I thank you, but I can travel much faster on my own, and," he swallowed, "lives are at stake."

"No, Kota," Gretis said in a somber voice. "You must not rush into this."

He stared at her, an incredulous look on his face. "What do you mean?"

Her eyes shifted to Glavius for a fraction of a second and then returned to her pupil as she whispered: "It is true that these attacks—if they are indeed real—are most likely being conducted to draw you out. That is good reason to proceed with caution."

Kota grimaced, and said in a voice that sounded desperate: "I can't let them die—not when I can save them!"

"Are you so certain that is what you will do—*save them*?" She moved to Kota and put a hand on his shoulder. "You remember what happened to you the last several times you encountered demons. What do you think will happen now, all your terrible strength and speed?" She leaned into his face and whispered: "You have become more lethal perhaps than even *you* realize. What will happen when you cannot think? Neither one of us knows how your animus will react when you come into contact with a Demon Lord." She lowered her head and sighed: "You might kill everything in your path."

Kota shut his eyes and drew in several very slow breaths, a pained look on his face. Finally, he said: "What would you have me do?"

Gretis gazed down at the letter in her hand, appearing troubled for a brief instant, but then her expression hardened. "We will go together. Before we do though, we must commune and seek clarity of mind." She gestured to Glavius without looking and said: "If you truly wish to confide your secrets in your friend here, then he may as well participate." She cocked her head and said: "Glavius, you cocky little imbecile, I think you could be of great help to your friend right now if you have the courage."

Glavius blinked and murmured: "I... I have no idea what the hell the two of you are talking about." He shook his head. His very perceptions of reality felt somewhat strained at the moment. "You both sound like insane heretics babbling horse-shit that would make the Nemesai turn red, but..." he sighed and looked at Kota, "your animuh, or whatever the hell you call it, was right: I damn-well am your friend." He turned to Gretis, and several dozen instances of her knocking the hell out of him flashed through his mind as he grunted: "I got courage, *Blade Witch*."

This drew a wry grin from her dark lips. "All right then," she whispered. "Let us prepare."

Gretis directed Glavius to gather a great deal of dry wood, which he did over the next hour or so as the sun set. In truth, he was glad to have a simple task to perform as his mind attempted to unravel the conversation that Gretis and Kota had had. Dozens of questions flooded his thoughts, but he was not sure he wanted the answers to them. It had taken him many years to learn one religious ideology, and he did not particularly wish to trample over all that tedious work. Still, his sense of wonder had been ignited, and he quietly admitted to himself that he was quite curious at what the two Sansrit were going to do.

When evening came, Glavius followed further instructions and set a roaring bonfire going in the center of the camp. Kota, who was in the midst of carefully grinding bits of plants, said: "How are things at the temple?" He sounded distracted, and of course troubled. Glavius could only imagine the thoughts that must be running through his mind.

"Darius is taking over more and more administrative duties. I may as well mention that the party of Nemesai who took you prisoner were attacked by a mysterious group of men in masks."

"Oh?" Gretis said, looking up from a table upon which she had laid out an assortment of strangely colored powders. Her eyes narrowed in suspicion. "Men in masks?"

"So I hear," Glavius said with a suppressed grin. "I was not there of course. This is all conjecture. Anyhow, they were attacked. Of course, a Starborn had recently shattered all their crossbows, and, as we all know, Nemesai are complete shite with swords, so they were subdued in seconds."

"No one was killed?" Gretis said, her voice tinged with dark amusement.

"No," Glavius sighed, "but the leader.... I heard he got it pretty bad. It seems that one of the bandits forced him to eat several pieces of dog excrement." Glavius shook his head. "Terrible shame to do such a thing to a man of the church. I heard they made him chew every bite."

Kota's face twitched just a little with humor, and Gretis sighed: "What did Otho do?"

Glavius shrugged. "He said it was not the Onkai's business to police banditry." He chuckled and added: "On a completely unrelated note, I was given a promotion and a sizable bonus immediately following these events."

"I see," Gretis said. She rose from her table, carrying a large clay urn in each hand. "Well then, shall we begin, gentlemen?"

Kota rose with a handful of freshly chopped herbs which he carried over and tossed into the fire. The flame shifted instantly from orange to purple where the substance touched, and the air took on an acrid scent of something like flowers mixed with alcohol and soap. Gretis knelt down in front of the fire, placing the jars in front of her. She reached into the first one and brought out a handful of light gray powder, which she tossed into the fire. There was a hiss and then an explosion of purely white smoke.

"Breathe normally," she said, looking at Glavius. "We are only going a little way in."

"In where?" he said.

She gave him a playful smirk. "The spirit world."

"Yeah..." Glavius muttered, and he inhaled in the smoke. It seemed to tingle in his lungs. He watched Kota sit down in front of the bonfire, crossing his legs and placing his hands on his knees, palms facing up. "Should I—" Glavius muttered, turning to the Blade Witch, but he saw she had assumed the same pose. "Just like our sword training," he muttered, "Don't tell me what to do. Just watch me flounder and have a nice chuckle."

"Just sit down," Kota said without opening his eyes. "You'll understand in a few moments."

"You're as bad as she is," Glavius murmured, rolling his eyes, but he sat as instructed. The scents of the fire were growing pungent, and as he drew them in, a feeling of relaxation began to wash over him—a profound sense of peace. *It was actually quite wonderful.* Minutes passed, and his muscles lost their many tensions, giving way to a deep warmth that did not seem to be coming from the fire, but inside of him.

"Glavius," Gretis whispered.

He felt so entirely calm that it did not alarm him immediately when he opened his eyes and saw the Blade Witch as a figure shrouded in blue, translucent fire. He blinked, and then looked again. The flame did not dance around her in wisps, but had a distinctive shape, with curves and angles. It took him a moment to piece the image together, for it felt as though his tether to reality was slipping by the second, but he finally deciphered the form of a wolf sitting back on its haunches. It was tall—taller than Lady Gretis herself—and its form was large enough that she sat within it with legs still crossed in front of her. Glavius panted as he stared at her, so serene within this creature's glowing body, and then her eyes opened very suddenly, and two orbs of blue fire stared out at him.

"You can see it, can't you?" she said with a chuckle, gesturing up to the wolf. "I always suspected you had a strong spirit of your own."

Glavius might have panicked, but the sense of tranquility the smoke had granted him was still present. "What am I seeing?" he managed to say, and he was surprised at how soft his voice was.

"This is a part of the person I am," she said. "I used to think it was so mighty, but then I saw *his* spirit." She gestured to the right.

Glavius turned his head and let out a gasp as he beheld a mountain of blue flame, wide and vast, stretching up above the trees. This burning mass also had a distinctive shape, with monstrous limbs and a fierce, lion-like head far above, but Glavius did not look at these things. In the center of the inferno of power sat Kota, bathed in blue light. His legs were crossed like Gretis's, his hands still resting half open on his knees, palms up.

"Kota bears a terrible burden," Gretis said. Glavius turned to see her stand up and walk toward him, the wolf-spirit rising up on its limbs and moving with her, its head hovering just above hers. "Perhaps he was right to share these truths with you." She sighed. "I cannot guide him forever. What if I were to die? There is far too much for him to face alone."

Glavius turned back to Kota and swallowed. This moment was beyond insane, and yet it all felt incredibly natural somehow, like he was finally seeing something that the deepest parts of his soul had always perceived. In a whisper, he said: "What will he face?"

Gretis put a hand on his shoulder, and the burning paw of the wolf moved with it. When it touched him, the sensation was hot and wild and alive. "The animus that resides in Kota is older than the human race—even more ancient than the elves and the Great Dragon. It was born of nature itself to hunt and kill demons, and the fact that it has returned now..." Her fingers tightened on Glavius's shoulder. "The demons are going to come again, Glavius—maybe in greater force than ever before. I see no other conclusion."

"Gods!" he whispered.

"Kota has a remarkable heart," she went on. "His courage and his goodness keep all that tremendous power in check, but he still needs help to remain centered, especially now that he is going to face a creature of hell." She drew her hand away and gestured to Kota. "Let us aid him."

Gretis walked toward Kota, her wolf spirit continuing to move with her. As she passed through the outer barrier of Kota's animus, strange sparks of white and emerald green flashed for a few seconds as the smaller spirit was enveloped by the larger. Untroubled by this, the woman walked to Kota's side and sat down next to him, putting a hand on top of his. He grasped it, and there was a quickening of the vast swell of energy around him.

"Come," Gretis said, her voice friendly and inviting.

"Uh-h-h," Glavius grunted, staring at the impossible sight.

"You said you had *courage*, did you not?"

"I guess I did," Glavius muttered. He drew in a very deep breath, his mind spinning, and then he walked forward. When he came to the outer shell of Kota's animus, he reached out a hand and touched it. A sensation of intangible warmth and power coursed through his fingertips. It felt strange, but it did not hurt him. *The hell with it.* He stepped inside and was immediately engulfed within the spirit, a feeling like hot wind blowing against him. It tingled and made his limbs tremble.

"Closer," Gretis said. "Take his hand."

Glavius looked at Kota. "Does he... can he hear what you're saying right now?"

"Probably not," she said, her voice light. "His connection to the spirit world is far, *far* more intense than yours or mine. All the same, we can help him. Take his hand."

Glavius sat down next to Kota, feeling more than a little unsure of what he was doing. He tentatively put his hand on Kota's. The fingers instantly curled around his, and something deep within Glavius seemed to come alive. "GODS!" he panted as a blazing power he had never known crackled through every cell in his body.

"Remain calm," Gretis said in a serene voice.

Calm? Glavius's heart and mind were stretching in dozens of directions at once. He could *feel* the energy in the grass beneath him, in the trees and bushes in the forest. He could also feel the beast all around him—*Kota's animus*—and its primal feelings of anger.

Demons! The spirit raged to destroy them all. It could not stand their unnatural presence. There was a burning desire for violence, and at its center was Kota. He was trying to control the beast, and he was afraid.

"I believe in you, my friend," Glavius said, and he gripped Kota's hand tighter.

"We can help him calm the creature," Gretis whispered.

"How?"

"All living things have a spirit, and not all are violent. There is peace all around us. Help me draw it to him."

He looked around, feeling stupid. "I... I don't know—"

"Close your eyes, Glavius," she said. "Listen to your spirit. You are connected to it as you have never been before."

He swallowed and did as he was told. When he shut his eyes, he did not perceive darkness, but swirling patterns of light all around him, flowing like slow currents.

"Start with the grass," he heard Gretis say.

Glavius lowered his fingers to the soft, wet grass beneath him and immediately felt the gentle tingle of its energy. He felt... tranquility... it was quiet but profoundly beautiful. Somehow, he was able to will some of that energy into himself, and as it seeped slowly up his arm, he felt his inner tension melt away. *What was it to be a blade of grass*? There was no fear. No anger. Never in his life had Glavius felt so calm, and as he considered this, he felt some of that wonderful bliss flow down his other arm into Kota.

"Yes," he heard Gretis whisper. "Keep going."

Glavius's lingering thoughts faded away and all became feeling. His animus was energy unto itself, but it was also a conduit. He could sense spiritual life all around him and could reach out and draw it in. Slowly, he lost himself in the process until there was no perception of time or even his individuality. *There were only the spirits.*

Sometime much later he heard Kota's voice say his name, and he slowly opened his eyes to see morning light creeping in through the trees, illuminating his friend's face.

"Thank you," Kota said.

"What?" Glavius murmured, shaking his head. "What the hell?" He blinked several times. "It's morning?" He looked down at his hands. They were no longer glowing. His spirit no longer seemed to crackle inside. *Had it even been real?* He looked up at Kota and said: "I'm feeling... a bit confused."

"Yeah," Kota sighed, "this is all fairly disconcerting. I want you to know though that you helped me. I was starting to lose my center. Thank you."

"I don't even... know what I did," Glavius muttered.

"Something to contemplate on the trip home," Gretis's voice said from behind. He turned to see her strapping a dagger to her right calf. She had three swords on her belt and was wearing a leather vest that had at least ten throwing blades in sewn-in sheaths. With a sigh, she glanced up at him and said: "I am afraid Kota and I must go on ahead."

"I understand," Glavius said, thinking of the poor shamalak tribe.

"You did quite well with your first encounter with the spirit world," Gretis said with a slight nod that almost seemed to be a gesture of respect.

"Yeah," Glavius said, finally rising. "So... I might as well ask: will I develop Sansrit abilities now?"

This elicited a small burst of laughter from the Blade Witch. "Not nearly, dear boy, but..." She looked him up and down, "*perhaps* we might consider a new course of training sessions together when this is all over."

Glavius grinned stupidly. "Yeah, all your spirit stuff isn't so hard." He turned to Kota, who was holding up an extremely large sword and inspecting it. His heart sank a little as he whispered: "You're going to go face whatever's down there now."

"I must," Kota said, turning to face him.

"You're the best friend I've ever had," Glavius said without thinking.

Kota cast him a wide grin, displaying all four of his fangs. "I'll see you again, my brother." He chuckled and added: "Don't beat on anymore Nemesai while I'm gone."

"Only if I see any," Glavius laughed back. It was good to see his friend smile. He understood now the incredible weight Kota carried. *The demons were returning.* That revelation hung like a terrible weight on Glavius's heart, but there was a fighting chance. The bright-eyed little shamalak he had met almost seven years ago had very possibly become the greatest warrior the world had ever seen. It was an honor to be his friend and, whatever forces of Hell came, Glavius would gladly die by Kota's side.

CHAPTER 24: LONE ASSASSIN

Soulic carefully poured water into the brass goblet on Cassian Asango's desk, wearing a tired look as he gazed down at the withered hands his Elokien was projecting as his appendages. It was still irritating after two months of this daily act to move slowly and keep himself hunched throughout the day. He had spent several weeks observing Asango's infamous tutor, Somar Dojinko, carefully picking up every idiosyncrasy to emulate. Soulic even looked like the old bastard. All of this was because he had deciphered that the Starborn thought of Dojinko as a second father and had guessed correctly that Cassian might have a soft spot for someone who reminded him of the old man. Every day was a carefully crafted, carefully improvised performance, but that would all be over in the next few minutes.

"Here you are, my lord," Soulic said, hearing his words distorted by the Elokien's enchantments to reflect a grating, elderly voice.

"Thank you," Asango said, looking up from his maps for a fraction of a second and making eye contact. The Starborn had been engrossed for most of the morning in his tactical plans. He had papers strewn all over his war table and beautifully detailed images and lists. Soulic found the way Cassian 'wrote' to be quite fascinating. All he seemed to have to do was think and letters seared into the page in elegant calligraphy.

"Will there be anything else, sir?"

"Please tell the kitchen I will take my lunch in my tent, and that I would like it as soon as possible." He did not look up this second time, though Soulic did note the *'please.'* Asango was polite to his servants, even when he was in a foul mood. That was a point in his favor at least.

"Absolutely, my lord." Soulic turned to leave, and as he did, he felt a psychic tendril reach out from the Starborn to probe his thoughts. He gave no resistance but allowed Asango to see the false thoughts and memories that had been meticulously synthesized in his mind. Soulic had spent nearly half a year in the far east, outside of Denigoth's borders, where a group of sorcerers had meticulously created pockets in his psyche to store artificial personas. He had practiced this art against some of the best telepaths in the world before moving on to a Starborn. As Cassian's tendril penetrated into this outer shell, Soulic concentrated on his servant persona and found that it was thinking about how best to slice the skin from potatoes—probably a memory or thought pattern stolen from a particularly dull subject. It seemed to be no more interesting to Asango than it was to Soulic, for the Starborn abandoned his probing after a few seconds and returned to his planning.

Opening the tent flap door, Soulic moved outside into the heart of Cassian's war camp. The way the Starborn's 'personal guard' was run was another point in his favor. The soldiers, most of whom were covered from head to foot in deep gray runes that augmented their strength and speed, did not conduct themselves like fighting men Soulic had encountered before. They refrained from heavy drinking in the evenings and bullying local peasants as they moved about the countryside. He had hardly even heard any cursing from them, but found they conducted themselves as gentlemen in the classic sense of the word that was more imagined than real in the empire.

Yet they were ruthless killers. Soulic had to remind himself of that every time he started growing too fond of the Starborn. Cassian's men had slaughtered hundreds, perhaps even thousands in the efficient tactical style that had made Asango a living legend and had earned him the rank of General at such a young age. Most military leaders from other countries now refused to fight him. They had heard the stories, as many had, of the young Starborn descending from the sky on his dragon and killing the leader of any force that opposed him, leaving the army in disarray. Asango's voice would then come from all around, offering terms of surrender. Soulic had to admit that Cassian was incredibly generous to his enemies when they surrendered, but that was likely only a strategy to encourage others to come quietly. Soulic refused to believe that there was anything magnanimous in a Denigoth conqueror.

He approached the kitchen, which was more or less a large cluster of mobile iron stoves and wooden tables with cooks moving about. The small army was very well supplied at all times. Cassian had a superbly organized supply chain, not to mention he could use spells to make fruit and vegetables to grow from seeds to full maturity in a few days when in a pinch.

"The General would like his meal in his tent at your convenience," Soulic said to the barrel-chested fellow he knew to be head of the kitchen. The man looked sharply at Soulic and then gave a quick nod. "Just a moment, sir."

Soulic smiled and sat down at one of the nearby mess tables, acting as a tired old man would. Some of the men cast quick glances at him here and there. In one respect, he had achieved something to which many of them desperately aspired: He was close to Asango. This was terribly amusing given that he was about to kill the little bastard. He wondered at times why he was doing it. Was it because Cassian was a rising star in the Denigoth military, or was it because he had been the one who brought Kota into the human world, and ultimately to Soulic's mother? He *hated* that she had replaced him, and with a *damned shamalak!* Would Kota cry when he found out Asango had been killed because of him? Soulic shook his head. *This was because Cassian was a symbol of Denigoth conquest. Nothing more.*

The head cook placed a steaming bowl of a bean and meat stew and a handful of boiled vegetables on a wooden tray accompanied by utensils. "Please tell the General that we did not get our fish shipment this morning, else he would have his favorite lunch." The cook had a guilty tone in his voice, though there was no fear behind it. *Asango did not punish his men over such trivialities like some commanders.*

Soulic picked up the food and carried it back to Cassian's tent. As he came to the door, he stopped and took out the small ceramic phial from inside his coat and poured its contents into the Starborn's soup. His stomach twisted just a little. *He liked Asango.* There was also the fact that if he killed this Starborn, either Telemachus Vale, or the monster, Arkas Adronicus, would eventually become emperor, which would likely mean that slavery would continue in Denigoth, as would the brutal punishment of *sin.* This almost gave Soulic pause, but he found himself stirring in the poison nonetheless. It was yanthum, one of the most horrible toxins he knew.

"The shipment of fish did not come, my lord," Soulic said as he entered the tent.

"That's a shame," Cassian replied. "That smells good enough anyhow. Place it on my desk please."

"Yes, sir." Soulic placed the tray on the small desk near Cassian's bed. The young man continued to glance down at his maps. Soulic moved quietly to the door. When it happened, visitors would need to be turned away. He could use his Elokien to take Asango's form, but he had no desire to exploit such a trick. Once the Starborn was dead, a quick exit would be best.

Finally, Cassian rose from his war table. He took a slow, deep breath and then tilted his head from side to side, eliciting a handful of pops from his neck. "Beef stew," he said with a smile. He walked over to his desk and sat down. "Tovor," he said, using the name Soulic had given him, "please go and take your own lunch, or you are welcome to eat in here if you like."

"Thank you, my lord, but I am not hungry just now. I prefer to take your dishes back as soon as you finish, if you would not mind."

"I appreciate your dedication to cleanliness," said Cassian with a little smile. Soulic felt the Starborn's psychic tendrils brush against his mind once again. The telepathically implanted false-self met the probe, and Asango observed a simple set of thoughts from a kind old man who wanted to please his noble master and keep a tidy tent.

"Hmm," Cassian grunted, and then he picked up his spoon and ate several mouthfuls of the stew. Soulic suppressed the urge to smile. The church had been trying for over a decade to kill this young man. Soulic's hand subtly slid inside his coat and thumbed the tip of the short sword in his belt. It rested concealed from sight within the veil of his Elokien as it had for many weeks.

"Tell me, Tovor, did you ever have any sons?" Cassian said.

"No, my lord. I never found a wife who quite suited me."

"Any brothers or sisters then?"

"No, my lord, I was an only child."

"As was I." Cassian took another mouthful of his soup. He was in the midst of swallowing it when his jaw suddenly tightened and let out a surprised grunt. With a sharp convulsion, he spat the soup all over his desk, and then he hunched forward, grabbing on to the edges of his table to steady himself. His breathing turned to furious hissing, and he glared up with wide eyes.

"Are you alright, my lord?" said Soulic, not bothering to feign concern in his voice. He drew his short sword from its hiding place slowly, letting the Starborn see it. Cassian's body began to shake wildly. Soulic watched him and said: "I am truly sorry, but you are too dangerous to allow to live." He sent a mental command to the Elokien, and the illusion unfurled around him, revealing his true form.

"What—what?" Cassian shrieked between convulsions. He looked at the sword and exclaimed: "Stop!" He raised a hand, but Soulic thrust the blade immediately into the Starborn's chest. The chair in which the young Starborn had been sitting jerked back, knocked by the tip of the weapon. *The sword had passed through his body with no more resistance than air!*

"No hesitation at all," Cassian's voice came from behind. Soulic whirled to see his victim standing directly behind him, looking perfectly fine. "I was hoping we could come to an understanding naturally, Soulic."

Every muscle in the Sansrit warrior's body tensed in rage and fear. In an instant, he made his decision and slashed at Asango's face. The weapon bounced away as a translucent wall of magical energy shimmered in the air, letting off a high pitched whining sound. Cassian stared through it, his eyes cold and calm. *The son of a bitch had not even flinched!*

Soulic's blood ran hot for the kill. The barrier was made of magic, and he had overcome sorcery before. He drew out his elven dagger from its concealed place in his shirt. Released from the sheath that secreted its powerful enchantments, the Odessian Blade blazed yellow light and hissed in the air. Soulic rammed it into Cassian's shimmering wall. Golden sparks popped from the collision as the dagger, whose name roughly translated into *spell drinker,* bit into the shield. Soulic's animus rippled power and speed through his limb as he drew the weapon back and slashed again, and then again, and then again.

Cassian stared with maddening composure at the blazing onslaught. On the tenth slash, the Starborn raised his hand and made a whipping gesture, and Soulic felt several of the bones in his right hand snap. He let out a scream, dropping the weapon. It floated, hilt first, through the translucent shield, and Cassian took it in his hand.

"You bastard!" Soulic snarled. The Starborn had ripped through the protection of his animus as if it were nothing. Truly, Asango was every bit as powerful as people said. He could kill Soulic at any time and was only toying with him.

"Not toying," Cassian said. "I was fairly certain you had at least one surprise for me." His eyes shifted to the Odessian blade in his hand, and then back to Soulic. "Any others?"

Soulic took a moment to breathe, surprised that Asango was choosing to speak with him rather than break more of his bones, or just kill him outright. He took the opportunity to send his animus sense out behind him to see if anyone were outside. He perceived at least twenty men, all with weapons drawn. *The Starborn had planned all of this!*

"There is no escape," Cassian said in a grim voice.

"Yeah, I gathered that," Soulic said with a low growl. His sword-hand was broken, but he had learned to fight with his left appendage. He subtly adjusted his footing.

"I would prefer it if you surrendered quietly."

"Go to Hell!" Soulic hissed, and he yanked another dagger from his belt and slashed at Cassian's face. It came as no shock that the blade bounced harmlessly away. He expected his arm to be shattered, but the young Starborn whispered something inscrutable, and there was a tiny flash of lightning that burst from his hand. Every muscle in Soulic's body suddenly convulsed in pain as the electricity struck his chest. He dropped to the carpeted floor of the tent, his flesh on fire.

"Do not try to rise," Cassian whispered, stepping over him.

Soulic gazed up, feeling a sense of resignation that he was going to die. He was surprised at how calming that thought was. "When did you know?" he managed to rasp out, curious at where he had erred.

"The moment I met you," Cassian said with a slight shrug. "The false mind you have crammed into your brain is... admittedly quite an impressive bit of work, but it is not the first time I have seen the tactic. The finest assassins in the world have been coming to kill me since I was eleven.

"My heart breaks for you," Soulic snarled. "How difficult it must have been growing up as a disgustingly wealthy aristocrat gifted with near god-like power." He did not care about dragging out these last moments. With a final glare, he said: "That's all I wanted to know. Get on with it."

Cassian sighed, a slight frown on his face. "How disappointing. I was hoping I might win you over with enough time. Our philosophies are not *that* dissimilar. Tell me, what made you decide to act today?"

The calm in Asango's voice was gut-wrenching. "I grew sick of serving you – of listening to you talk!"

"Huh," Cassian grunted, seeming amused by the words. "If you are trying to provoke me, I have no need or desire to kill you here. You know my one-time-friend Kota, after all, and your mother... I might wish to seek an alliance with her at some point. No, if I cannot reason with you, I shall send you to the capital to meet justice. You have murdered several imperial officers and a general. I do not particularly approve of the gruesome modes of execution reserved for men who commit crimes against the military, but I doubt anyone will accept my recommendation for a quick death."

Soulic smirked. "You think you can scare me? I'm not some peasant in awe of a Starborn. I see you for the self-righteous, hypocritical cutthroat you are!"

"I appreciate that," Cassian said with a hint of a dark grin. He knelt down over Soulic and said: "And no, I do not think I can *scare* you, Soulic. Your heart is far too consumed by anger to bother with fear. I have seen all the terrible things you have done, and I saw why."

"You don't know *anything* about me!" Soulic was becoming acutely aware of the fact that he could not move. Cassian's invisible magic was holding him in place.

"I *do* know, actually. You are not terribly complicated. A Denigoth military official raped your mother. You want to punish your father and everyone like him." Soulic glared up, enraged that the Starborn could steal these things from his mind, but Cassian leaned in still closer and said in a soft voice: "I want to help you, Soulic, because I understand how you feel, and I hate all the things you hate."

"You *are* what I hate! You've been running around committing murder for more than a year, just doing whatever you want to the weak!"

Cassian sighed. "Neither my men nor I have killed a single person who was not trying to kill us, nor have we taken food from starving peasants, taken slaves, or committed rape. On the contrary, we have redistributed a great deal of wealth from the *rulers* we have deposed, and many peasant families are eating now who would have otherwise starved." His face contorted a little. "Still, I grant you that military conquest in any form is ugly business."

"But I'm sure you have a wonderfully composed justification to that ugliness!" Soulic laughed. His power was returning slowly. *Perhaps if he could keep the Starborn talking a little longer...*

"I doubt anything I might say would do much good with you, would it? Not with your rigid, childish sense of justice."

Soulic took a breath. *Just a little longer.* "How many have you killed in the name of your empire?"

The Starborn chuckled. "You do not give up, do you? I admire that. However, I have been studying your animus for weeks, and I know how quickly it can generate energy." Just then the flap to Cassian's tent opened, and a man in a black robe Soulic had never seen before stepped inside holding a small metallic bucket. Cassian nodded to him and held out his left hand, and the man reached into a concealed pocket in his chest and drew out a pair of tongs, which he gave to Cassian. Soulic watched with unease as the Starborn reached into the bucket with those tongs and carefully drew out an inky black leech with streaks of brilliant blue curling about the length of its body. Soulic recognized it instantly.

"NO!" he hissed, glaring at Cassian. "Just kill me!"

"You are far too useful to simply kill," Cassian said. He knelt back down, holding the squirming leech with his tongs. The Starborn pointed at Soulic's chest, and his shirt instantly ripped open, revealing his bare chest. Then Asango lowered the leech.

"STOP!" Soulic screamed, and he tried to thrash against the magic, *which was impossible.* Cassian placed the slug down on his sternum, and there was an immediate tingling sensation followed by a sharp feeling of coldness. Soulic felt the energies of his animus begin to drain into that icy void. Power was pulled quickly from every corner of his body, and after only a few seconds it was completely gone.

"Interesting," Cassian said in a soft voice, peering down at him. "I was not certain that would work on a Sansrit warrior, but apparently to the leaches, your *animus's* power is enough like a sorcerer's magic."

Soulic found that he was free to move his hands, and he reached immediately for the slug on his chest, but when his fingers touched it, he discovered that the slimy, soft thing Cassian had placed on him had become quite solid. Instinctively, he dug at it with his fingernails, but it was like trying to claw at solid steel, and as soon as he made the attempt, a mind shattering level of pain erupted in seemingly every nerve in his body at once. For all his Sansrit training, Soulic could not help screaming out.

"I apologize for what you must be going through," Cassian sighed. "Amanthian leeches are the stuff of my nightmares. I have a recurring dream of the Nemesai Bishop putting them on me and draining away my power while he smirks down."

Soulic was able to lift his head enough to glance at the hideous creature. He could feel it drawing out his animus's energy as fast as it was generated, leaving him weak and helpless. He rolled up onto his knees and bared his teeth like an animal. "Just execute me! I'm never going to serve you."

"You will," staring into Soulic's eyes, "because I am going to make you a bargain."

"You can't *buy me*, Starborn!"

"I can tell you who your father is."

Soulic froze. "T-that's not possible! How could you know?"

"I know an old man who was a corporal at the time of your conception. I wrote to him, asking if he knew who took Princess Angretta as a prize, and I received an answer. He is alive—the man who raped your mother."

Soulic trembled. Even with its power drained away, his animus could still bristle with hatred. Asango could be lying, but the prospect of finally finding the man was too irresistible. "Tell me. I'll assassinate anyone you want—I don't care who!"

"I know you would," Cassian said, his face appearing... *disappointed.* "We shall have to work on that." He peered at Soulic. "Actually, I want to keep you in reserve for a time. If things go as I hope over the next several weeks, I will have achieved enough victories for the empire to go to the capital and be named crown prince." The Starborn rolled his eyes. "I expect my enemies to act against me then. They have had plenty of time to lay their traps, and I am certain they have been studying my tactics, my powers, and all my resources this entire time." He cast Soulic a slight grin. "I doubt anyone will expect me to have a Sansrit in my retinue though. In a crucial moment, such things can be the difference between life and death."

"And you're just going to trust me to be your bodyguard?"

"Of course not," Cassian laughed, "I would not trust you with *anything* as you are now." His face became deathly cold as he added: "Which is why I am going to do a bit of tinkering on you. Your *animus* puts up remarkable defenses around your mind, yet I am confident I can get through them."

Soulic edged back. "I don't want you in my head!"

"You are a *very* deadly killer who is ruled by an insane sense of right and wrong," Cassian said, stepping forward and raising his hand. "I cannot have you running around as you have been, and anyhow I am not asking your permission."

Soulic tried to run, but he found once again that his body could not move, and this time his animus could not help him at all. He stared, unable even to flinch as Cassian's hand moved to his forehead. Just before it touched, he snapped: "I don't care what you do to me, as long as I get to kill my father. Swear it, Starborn!"

Asango paused, seeming to consider the request. "I am not going to give you license to break into a man's house and hack him to death, but... when I have the power, I will grant you justice."

"That's not good enou—" Soulic lost all connection to whatever it was he was trying to say as Cassian's fingers touched his forehead. Psychic strength like nothing he had ever imagined pried into his mind, obliterating all thought. It was almost peaceful, save for the sense that something alien had taken control. Even his animus stopped raging and fell silent, *like a dog before its master.*

CHAPTER 25: SLAVE OF THE WEST

Livia stared at the illustration that lay on the desk in Hervin's back office, her eyes narrowing as they traveled the details. The figure of Prince Arkas was marked by a slightly exaggerated right hand with three missing fingers, so the people would recognize him. He stood with a vicious, predatory grin next to a boy who hung by his wrists, stripped down to only pants and looking terrified. They were in a Nemesai cell together—Livia's best guess at the layout of such a room—with a table in the corner littered with instruments of torture. Off to the right was Bishop Cromlic, whom Livia had never seen. She had heard descriptions of an elderly man with a thick beard, and she had improvised. Arkas's face was burned into her mind though... She had seen it hundreds of nights in her dreams. Always her drawings captured the evil of that face. It was her victory over him that thousands—perhaps tens of thousands all over the empire had seen her work. For this particular illustration, with the frightened child and the eager princely torturer, she wrote the words: "So much easier when my opponent is not Cassian Asango." It was important to keep the captions short. The purpose of drawing the images was to speak to the countless peasants in the Empire who could not read. The words were for the small handful in most villages who *could,* so they might pass on the message. When Livia was satisfied with her work, she signed the sheet with the name the empire had come to know her by: *'Slave of the West.'*

"Are you finished?" Domor said, perking up from his chair in the corner. Livia raised her head and nodded at the burly dwarf. He grinned, hopped down from the chair, and scurried across the room on his short legs. She watched him, eager for a reaction to her work. Domor leaned over the desk, which was only a little shorter than he was, and gazed at the picture. After a few seconds, his thick lips curled into a smile, and he let out a deep-throated chuckle. "You sure hate that little bastard prince."

Livia tapped the dwarf on the shoulder three times. He turned and looked up to see her questioning look. They had been working together long enough that he knew immediately what she was asking.

"I can make the plate by tomorrow morning," he said.

Livia frowned and exhaled loudly through her nostrils. This was the closest she could get to vocalizing exasperation without a voice. If Domor took until morning, that would likely mean some of the work would take place at night, in candlelight, when he would be drunk. That would mean the plate would have errors, and when they used it in the printing press, her painstaking satire would be riddled with smudges and imperfections. If she could get him to complete the task before his nightly guzzle of wine though, every detail would be replicated with the almost magical precision of a dwarven craftsman.

"I..." Domor said, shrinking a little under her gaze. "Maybe by tonight?"

Livia smiled and cast him a polite nod. This drew a grin from the dwarf's heavily creased face. He was just a little infatuated with her, she knew. She handed him the cartoon and let her lips curl up just a little higher. Livia had never put much energy into *flirting,* but there was perhaps no harm in just a tiny play upon his affections to help keep him motivated.

"I—I'll take it to my shop," he said, the side of his mouth twitching a little as he looked at her. The dwarf turned and walked out the back exit of Hervin's shop, and Livia watched him go. There was always a little flutter in her heart when Cassianites walked in and out of that door. So far as she knew, the Nemesai had no idea that the infamous *Slave of the West* resided in her town, let alone that the defiant voice who had inflamed the empire belonged to a female mute. There was a delicious irony in that.

Just before the door swung shut, Domor's mannerisms changed. The town knew him as a perpetual drunk, and so he wobbled as he walked, reaching out and catching himself here and there and making slow blinks of confusion. He could play the part well, bellowing out crude and salacious remarks at uncontrolled volume, or making ornery threats at anyone who looked at him wrong. Dwarves were dangerous. People knew that and left them alone unless there was very good reason to do otherwise.

Once she was alone, Livia gazed down at the sheet of blank parchment still on her desk, her mind running through several dozen topics of criticism to level at the Nemesai and the '*Claw Hand Prince.'* She wondered at times if Cassian Asango had read any of her essays on slavery or religious intolerance. More than once, Livia had imagined him sitting in his war camp, having a chuckle at her latest piece of work. So far as she knew, she had become one of the most well-known voices in his movement while he was gone. *Did he know that? Would such a man care about the thoughts of a crippled, former slave?*

Livia blinked and shook her head, throwing off these tangential thoughts. Her eyes moved to the map that hung on the left wall of the office. Arkas Adronicus was most likely hiding Iona somewhere in the Vakathy Region. She had extrapolated through secret letters within the Cassianite network that the horrid Prince disappeared to this uninhabited corner of the empire roughly once a month. No one knew exactly where he went though, and the territory was incredibly vast and largely unmapped. It was suicide to attempt to follow a Starborn in the wilderness who did not wish to be followed. Without the distractions of a populated area, their telepathic senses could supposedly register any intrusion with incredible accuracy. Even Livia herself, while possibly immune to having her mind read, had no reason to believe she would be undetectable to Arkas. Still, following him into the uncharted forest seemed to be all she had. The Cassianites kept track of who was in the cells of the Nemesai temples, and if the information they had given her was correct, no girl named Iona, nor any female in the empire matching her description or age had been among the unfortunate prisoners of the order since the abduction.

Livia wondered, as she often did, whether her little sister was dead. The thought filled her with guilt that she had not done more. It had taken a great deal of time and resources to rise as high as she had within the Cassianites, and she still was uncertain how much pull she had in the organization. Asango would return from the battlefield soon. *Perhaps... after all she had done to help his movement, he might see her.*

"Livia?" Hervin's voice rang through the several walls between the office and the front of the store. She shot up immediately and moved to the floor board in the back corner of the room, which she quickly opened, stuffed all evidence of her political writings inside, and then resealed. Then she moved to the door to the office and walked through to the storeroom amongst all the meticulously inventoried stock. Several dozen clay pots rested amidst this inventory with concealed chambers holding hundreds of inflammatory pamphlets. Her most recent essay on aristocratic abuse of power was planned to hit the streets of every major city in the western half of the empire soon. That brought a smile to her lips as she lifted the bar on the heavy wooden door and stepped through to the front, where she saw a nervously smiling Hervin standing next to several extremely well-dressed individuals.

"This is my daughter," he said, with a somewhat quaking gesture of his arm.

"Ah," a tall man with a thick, gray beard grunted, casting Livia a smile of yellowed teeth. He was wearing a black, silken tunic that was beautifully stitched. A gold chain as thick as a man's finger hung from his neck, ornamented at the center with a red sapphire encased in still more gold. This obviously wealthy man stepped forward and said: "Your father has been going on about your cleverness, my dear." There was a subtle tone in his voice that did not quite match the friendliness of his words. It seemed to communicate that she and her father were *amusing,* but not important.

"This is Lord Baradon," Hervin said, almost huffing out the words.

Livia's heart quickened a touch. The man before her owned the very ground she stood upon, and all the countryside for at least a day's walk in any direction but the ocean. She swallowed and immediately dropped into a curtsy, lowering her head and lifting the sides of her skirt, which suddenly seemed very poor and tattered.

When Livia rose again, she saw that a younger version of Lord Baradon had stepped forward and was also smiling at her. He looked to be a year or two older than herself at most. The young man was tall, and broad-shouldered, with dark hair cut short. He wore a deep green tunic and a matching green cape that ended at his knees. His deep blue eyes scanned Livia up and down, and he said: "I had heard quite a few whispers about the *silent slave,* and her unmatched gorgeousness." These words were followed by a marked increase in the intensity of his grin.

Livia blushed a little. The compliment was not quite gentlemanly, but not nearly so rude as some of the things men said to her. This young man was almost certainly Simius Baradon, the son of the lord. He did not have a bad reputation so far as she knew, but she had heard he was a sorcerer, which could be dangerous. Swallowing, Livia gave him an ambiguous nod and then gazed at Hervin with a questioning look, hoping to shift attention away from herself.

"Lord Baradon requires a new supplier of wine for his home," Hervin said.

Livia frowned. She and Hervin did trade in wine, but it was only a small part of their business—a section she had been gradually shrinking since the cow had gone from the home. Surely the lord could find more obvious suppliers.

Baradon seemed to be able to interpret her expression, for he said: "I'm afraid I have very little taste for what the local merchants bring in. My preference—my *passion* really—is for wine from the Tilsian vineyards." He let out a sigh. "I had a supplier, but he went and died, poor fellow. Anyhow, I would be a much happier man if I could have a steady flow of the stuff once more." He turned to Hervin. "I don't need much. Can you manage five barrels a month?"

Livia suppressed a gasp. *Five barrels a month!* That would take an enormous bit of figuring out. She and Hervin had contacts who traveled through the Tilsian Valley, but their trips were seasonal, not monthly. Delivery routes would have to be negotiated with multiple parties, and they had never dealt in wine by the barrel before. After years of enduring the cow's drunken cruelty, Livia had refused to ever touch a drop herself, and thus she knew virtually nothing about vintage, pricing, authenticity, rules for storage, and so on. *Still, this was the wealthiest customer they could ever ask for.* It would be complicated, but she supposed she could work everything out.

Livia glanced at Hervin and subtly extended two fingers on her left hand and made a fist with her right. He recognized the signals and said in as smooth a voice as he could: "I estimate it will take two weeks to put a system together."

<You run things here, don't you?> Livia heard a voice exactly like that of the lord's son say, but as her eyes moved to his face, she did not see his lips moving. He was casting her a flirty smile, and the look in his eyes confirmed that she had not imagined the words, which meant... *telepathy.* Her stomach twisted.

<I was wondering how this nervous little fool managed to run the most successful trade business in the city,> Simius continued in her mind. *He was showing off.*

Livia tried not to fidget as she returned his smile. She remembered, well over a year ago now, ripping the Nemesai sorcerer's mind to shreds. The vision of him writhing in pain on the city floor sent a shiver through her, and just as it did, she felt the same little tingle in the back of her head that came when that horrible man had tried to gaze into her thoughts. *Was Simius trying to read her mind?*

<By the gods,> Simius telepathically whispered. He was staring at her with wide eyes, his right eyebrow raised above the left. <You learned occlusion? How? Holy Hell, your mind is a *fortress*! Who taught you?>

Livia's heart began to thump very fast. She had not been ready at all for this. *Her deepest secret exposed*—at least... part of it was. She could see the intrigue in Simius's eyes. That was dangerous. He might have questions for her—questions to which she would not be able to provide satisfying answers.

"Shall we estimate two hundred desseks a month?" Lord Baradon said to Hervin. Livia shifted her gaze to him and realized that she had just missed an entire conversation between her father and this man. Hervin was repeatedly glancing at her out of the corner of his eye, looking for some signal. She blinked, trying to separate the anxiety from her intellect. She ran through a series of quick calculations in her mind as best she could in her flustered state, and then coughed—a signal to Hervin to increase the price.

"I estimate it would be closer to... *two-fifty*?" Hervin muttered, looking unsure of himself. He had never been a strong negotiator, but since Iona had been kidnapped, he had lost all confidence. The Lord frowned at this offer, and Livia sniffled twice, indicating that Hervin had gone up too high. He fidgeted and said: "Actually I think two-thirty might do the trick."

Livia gazed at the Lord, watching his eyes, and then she reached up and scratched her right temple with her index finger, signaling that the man would accept this number. All the while, she was aware that the lord's son was staring at her unabashedly. There was an expression of deep amusement on his face.

"I'll consult with my accountant on this price," Lord Baradon said, his voice stern but even. Livia could see that he was already comfortable with the amount. *He wanted his wine very much, and in the end, he could afford to pay for it.*

<You're a fascinating creature,> Simius whispered in her mind. <I can't believe it took me this long to discover you.>

She gazed into the young aristocrat's deep, blue eyes, and saw undisguised *desire.* It was not the first time she had perceived this in a man toward her, but in the son of a lord it was far more dangerous. Simius Baradon, the heir to the fief in which she had spent her whole life, was not someone she could casually spurn. If moved to sufficient anger, he could destroy her life and Hervin's—maybe even have them killed. As she gazed at the young aristocrat, her nigh infallible sense of people told her he was not the kind to humbly accept the rejection of a former slave.

"Well, please send word as soon as you have the shipping worked out," Lord Baradon said. He did not hold out his hand but stood still as Hervin gave him a bow. Then he turned to his son and said: "Shall we move on to other business?"

"Let's be off," Simius said with a grin. The two of them moved to leave, the father stepping ahead of his son. Just as the lord passed out the door, Simius drew a silver coin from his pocket, turned, and sent it spinning through the air with his thumb to Livia. As came whipping forward, she heard his voice in her mind: <I would like to have dinner with you some night soon. Buy a nice dress. I would love to see you in green.> Even through the strange resonance of the telepathic communication, there was something in his voice that made her cringe inside. *Entitlement.*

She caught the coin as the young nobleman closed the door to the shop, and Hervin turned and looked at her, exclaiming: "What was that about?"

Livia gazed down at the fifty-dessek piece in her hand, giving Hervin a shrug combined with a sufficient iciness in her expression to advise that she did not wish to communicate just then. Her mind was traveling in dozens of different directions at once. Simius had not been overly crude. He had a touch of charm to him and had shown interest in her intelligence rather than simple, base desire for her like so many others. Still, Livia did not fool herself for an instant into thinking his intentions with her were honorable. She could never be his wife. He was going to be a lord. At best, she could be his mistress—a life many young peasant girls would covet given that Simius was a handsome young noble with wealth and power. It was not a fate Livia wished though. She had spent over a year denouncing the aristocracy. The Baradon family had its absurd riches at the expense of the peasants beneath them, and they provided little to nothing in exchange for the taxes and rent they exacted. *No, she would not be some nobleman's whore.*

There was also the matter that she might very well kill Simius. Livia had nearly brought death to a Starborn a year and a half ago. She *still* did not understand how her power worked—if it could even be called 'power.' She had tried hundreds of times to focus her mind, trying to reach back to that moment she managed to crumple the paper through... *magic?* Nothing had come from her efforts but the pain. Twice in her life, whatever force lay inside her had come to her defense, both times against attackers using sorcery: one mental, one physical. Livia had formed dozens of wild theories about what her power might be, none of which correlated to anything in the tomes on sorcery she had spent hundreds of hours reading. What she did know was that her power did not seem to obey her commands, which suggested there was very little chance she could will it to stop if it went on the attack.

Livia quieted her breathing as she stepped back into the storeroom, still clutching Simius's coin in her palm. Her blood was running cold. The young nobleman would know about the Nemesai whose memories had been eviscerated. He did not have enough information at present to make any real connection from that event to Livia, but if he probed—if he somehow discovered *any* of what she could do, it might spark some extremely dangerous speculations.

Gods, why was this happening now? Livia almost trembled as she imagined how close she might be to rescuing her sister. Had the time come to run? There was the money Lady Gretis had given her years ago to facilitate travel, and she had contacts now. Disappearing might actually be feasible.

Livia stepped through the second doorway into the back office and sat down at the desk. Plans needed to be made. She did not need to abandon Hervin yet, but that could change very soon. The focus for the moment should remain on impressing members of the Cassianites with her provocative messages to the people. Simius was ultimately just one more variable in the insane gamble she was taking. All of it was in the hope that she could convince Cassian Asango to help her retrieve Iona. It hurt how much Livia was afraid he would not be the hero she imagined, but she would continue to risk her life on the hope that he was.

CHAPTER 26: THE NAKAWA TRIBE

"This is it," Kota said, and Gretis heard the unease in his voice. He was staring at a series of subtle claw-marks on the side of a tree she would never have noticed had he not pointed them out. The sun was high in the sky above them, and the forest was alive with the sounds of birds and furry things. Her pupil reached up and ran his fingers over the gashes and whispered: "My tribe."

"Where are they?" Gretis said. She stood behind Kota, her hand on the hilt of her sword. She could not sense the presence of demons, but some dark creatures were more difficult to detect than others.

"Wait," Kota said, and as if in response to this there was a howl from deep within the forest. It was higher pitched than any sound Kota might have made, and Gretis thought she detected an ever so subtle trace of *fear* within it. She had spent quite a bit of time amongst various shamalak tribes and had learned several different dialects of their language, yet she had never quite deciphered the howls. There were changes in pitch and rhythm too subtle for her human ears to detect.

"They ask us to throw our weapons down," Kota said, drawing the long sword from his belt and throwing it to the forest floor several paces in front of him.

Gretis lifted an eyebrow. "Really? Is *that* all they ask?" She gave a soft chuckle and, unlike Kota, did not commence disarming.

He stared at her. "They're afraid. There is no harm in doing as they request." She saw the same look of guilt on his face that he had displayed throughout their entire journey. Kota felt *responsible* for whatever attacks had been inflicted upon his people in search of him.

"There is gods-damn plenty of harm if you and I are attacked and we don't have our swords ready," Gretis said. She craned her neck to stare into her pupil's towering form and snapped: "You're not returning as Kota, the eleven-year-old. I will not see you endanger yourself over some misplaced sense of obedience to your tribe."

There was a crackle of dried leaves, and Gretis cocked her head to see six shamalak archers emerge from brush around them, each with an arrow nocked and aimed at her from various angles. She met their silver eyes, one-by-one, and saw fear mingled with anger. The archers formed slowly around her and Kota, never lowering their arrows, and then a group of three additional warriors, each of an age with Kota, emerged from the center of the brush before them. These ones were shirtless like their brethren, yet they carried imperial military swords and shields, albeit quite old looking ones. *Perhaps they had traded with the empire?* Whatever the case, imperial steel was a definite improvement over the crude iron and stone weapons she knew the shamalak tribes to possess.

"We come in peace," Kota said in his native tongue. Gretis had not heard him utter a single word of the shamalak language in years, but he spoke every syllable with an easy precision.

One of the swordsmen—a youth with a square face with a scar on his right cheek—bellowed: "Kota?" His metallic eyes narrowed, and then all the apprehension left his face, replaced by an expression of excitement. "KOTA!" He threw down his blade and shield and ran forward.

"Narok!" Kota exclaimed, and the two figures embraced, both grinning wide enough to display fangs. Several of the warriors around them lowered their weapons, though most did not. One swordsman in particular, Gretis noted, was glaring at Kota. His muscles were tense—almost trembling with what seemed like anger. Much of his right ear was missing, its tip looking to have been bitten off from the uneven scarred edges.

"Do not embrace this traitor!" the glaring shamalak said in his native tongue. Kota and his apparent old friend stepped apart. Narok whirled to face the speaker, whose lips twitched back, revealing many teeth as he snarled: "He's the reason our brothers are dead!" The warrior pointed the tip of his weapon at Kota and cast him a furious scowl. "Deny it, *brother!* Deny that the demons are here for *you*!"

Kota's face lost all of its good humor. He stared at his accuser, somber and guilt-stricken. "I know little of these attacks, but perhaps they have been for my sake. I have come to find out."

The words elicited bewildered looks from some of the warriors. Narok seemed to be less apprehensive with his old friend than the others. He looked Kota up and down and said: "W-we all heard the stories you passed to our tribe years ago." His expression filled with pain as he added: "After the first... attack, we were told that the *great warrior* had one moon to appear, or they would kill dozens more—all of our children."

"They cut down twenty of us before we even knew what was happening!" snarled the shamalak with the dismembered ear. He lowered his shield enough that Gretis noticed dozens of deep scars on his shoulders, biceps, and chest. He took several huffing breaths, seeming to hold himself back from simply attacking, and then shouted: "My brother, Tequin, died because of you*!* He was sixteen winters old!"

"I... I'm sorry," Kota said, his face stricken with horror. He turned and gazed at Gretis, as if to ask what to do. She had never seen him in so much pain, and something tightened within her reflexively.

"What is your name, warrior?" she asked the scarred shamalak in his own tongue.

The swordsman paused, his eyebrows rising as he stared at her. After a brief moment, he grunted: "Skillen."

"Well, Skillen, *I* took Kota away from your tribe to train him," Gretis said in a loud voice. She gazed around, meeting the eyes of every warrior. "If not for me, he would have returned to you all years ago." Her animus sense detected the tightening of muscles amongst her audience. She readied herself for an attack. "None of you have the authority to execute visitors to the tribe, let alone a full member." She gestured to Kota. "This is a matter for the elders. You will—"

"Do not speak of our traditions as if you know them!" Skillen hissed, and he took several steps closer to Gretis, the tip of his sword now pointed at her.

Her animus pulsed eagerly. It would be a simple matter to rip out her blade, focus her energy through it, and slash Skillen's sword in half before he could even flinch, yet Gretis held this urge in check. The warrior before her was angry, but he had a right to be. She knew well the pain of seeing a younger sibling killed. Thus, instead of attacking, she stepped toward Skillen so that his blade was only a finger's length from the tip of her nose and looked into his eyes. "I am horribly sorry for your brother, warrior. I promise you, the ones who cut him down will die."

Skillen's furious expression faltered a little, revealing a flash of the pain that lay beneath it. "Y-you cannot fight these... *things.* No one can! They killed a group of Onkai soldiers like they were nothing."

"WHAT?!" Gretis shouted, her animus coalescing through her lungs and vocal cords so that the word came out with tremendous volume, and every shamalak but Kota flinched. "Where? When!"

"Yesterday," Kota's friend, Narok, said. He blinked, staring down at the leaves beneath his bare feet. "A troop of Onkai found our tribe. We called Kota's grandfather to translate to them for us, but..." his face contorted, and Gretis had the sense that he was reliving a horrible moment, "The demons magic user—he came out of the shadows and attacked the Onkai with fire. Several died right away, but the ones who could still fight...

a *monster* unlike anything I've ever imagined dropped from the sky and hacked them to pieces." Narok's bronze skin went ashen as he spoke. "It was bigger than any creature in the world, and the way it moved! That beast hacked all the rest of the Onkai to pieces in one—maybe *two* heartbeats."

Gretis's memory flashed to her battle with the Demon Lord Rakathon years ago. Even with the full power of her animus and a fair bit more summoned from the heart of the world, she had only been able to annoy him for a few minutes before he beat her within a hair of her life. She recalled the feeling of his massive hand around her throat—*Gods but he had been strong!*

"Some of our tribe..." Narok went on, his voice filled pain, "it was as though they were driven uncontrollably into a rage as soon as the big demon appeared. He killed them all first."

Kota's breathing grew rough. Gretis glanced at him and saw veins standing up on his arms and neck.

"Where are the Onkai now?" she said.

"We wrapped their bodies," Narok murmured, and then added in a quieter voice: "*What was left of them.*"

She turned to Kota, switching back to Tethric as she said: "This is the second encroachment into the Denigoth Empire in less than a decade. It seems the Demon King is no longer abiding by the terms Emperor Tacitus laid down."

Kota blinked. She had never told him about her battle with Rakathon, as any complete discussion of the encounter would lead to the topic of Iona, whom Gretis suspected to be the Messiah spoken of in the Enumis—a subject that would place far too much weight upon Kota's already overburdened mind. Still, he knew that demons had attacked her, and that they were not simple, corrupted creatures roaming the countryside but soldiers of the Demon King, and Kota was educated enough to know what that meant.

"Are they starting another war?" he said, also in the human tongue.

"I do not know," she replied, sweeping the bewildered shamalak tribesmen around them with her eyes. "I think that they are focused on eliminating you to the point they are willing to risk the consequences. Attacking Onkai soldiers..." she grimaced, "We must get word to Otho, and to the Denigoth Imperium."

"What are you two talking about?" Skillen grunted in the shamalak tongue.

"War," Gretis answered him, her voice cold. "Take us to the elders."

Skillen's face twitched in irritation, but Narok turned and gestured with his left arm to a path in the trees. "Yes, I think they will wish to speak with you."

"Kota, pick up your sword," Gretis said.

The shamalak around the two of them fidgeted as Kota glanced down at his weapon. After a brief pause, he looked at Gretis and said: "No."

"You heard them say it!" she snapped. "Demons are in this forest!" Kota only stared at her, stone-faced, and so she exclaimed: "Gods-dammit!" She darted over and snatched up the weapon herself. Before any of the shamalak around her could react, she looked at her stubborn apprentice and said aloud: "Kota, advise your tribesmen not to attempt to disarm me."

Kota frowned at her but muttered: "This woman is more dangerous than an Onkai. She could kill all of you right now if she wished."

The swordsmen around her tensed, and a few of them edged back.

"I came here to slaughter demons, not shamalak," she said, meeting each of their eyes. "You would do *far* better to have me as an ally, which is what I came to be."

"Some of us have heard stories of you from the North," Narok said in a voice that was remarkably gracious, given the circumstances, "stories that predate your meeting Kota, *Blade Witch*." His eyebrow raised as he asked: "You are the same 'Gretis' who visited the Sorius Tribe in the northern plains, are you not?"

"I am."

"You may enter our village without disarming," he said, giving her a nod.

"Thank you," Gretis said, nodding back.

Skillen and the other warriors said nothing as Gretis and Kota began to walk with Narok. They filed in behind in silence. Just to be safe, Gretis kept Kota's sword out, pointing the blade down at an angle as she walked so that it hovered just above the ground. She was not concerned merely with the angry warriors around her. *The demons had a magic user.* Gretis had heard of but never encountered Nathrets—sorcerers who sacrificed their souls for increased arcane power. Kota had met one years ago, but he had had an extremely talented Starborn with him, and, from what Gretis had deciphered from the reports, that one had been a weak specimen. *This Nathret could be centuries old and far, far stronger.* Its power, combined with that of an Archdemon and its servants, was likely too great a force for Kota and herself to take on.

"Have any of the tribe tried to flee this forest?" Kota said. His voice mirrored the nerves in her stomach.

"A few," Narok whispered. "We heard their screams shortly after. The sorcerer brought back one of their heads. He's not afraid of us—not of the whole tribe. He dropped the head at the feet of the elders and told them next time three children would die for every adult who tries to run."

The edge of the shamalak village came into view through the trees, and Gretis saw dozens upon dozens of triangular animal skin structures surrounding fire pits dug in the ground bordered with stones. The village had been built in a clearing next to a flowing river. As she and Kota stepped into its borders, hundreds of nervous silver eyes stared at them. Women hugged young children close to them, while many others gripped weapons. Some had bows and arrows, some swords, some carved wooden spears, and some simply curled their fingers, extending their claws. For all of this display of hostility though, Gretis pitied them. This tribe had been terrorized for weeks, and they were ultimately powerless to defend themselves. She looked at the gaunt, disheveled faces and understood how far they had fallen. Gretis had spent time among shamalak in the past, and though every tribe had their own idiosyncrasies, they were overall a remarkably kind and happy people. This lot was utterly miserable. There were abandoned basket weaving projects lying in the dirt, old clay pots lying in cracked pieces on the ground, and many other details that bespoke of hopelessness.

They ambled toward the center of the village where a large canopy constructed of thick tree limbs rested. The floor of the open structure was covered in many blankets. Four very old shamalak—two males and two females—sat upon those blankets under the shade, their thin bodies wrapped in animal skins. They watched the visitors to the village approach, glancing at Gretis, though their attention, like the rest of the tribe's, was chiefly focused on their long lost member.

Kota stepped ahead of the others and moved to the front of the canopy, which visibly made several warriors nearby fidget, but he dropped into a kneel, fists on the forest floor, his head bowed low. "Honored Elders," he said aloud in his native tongue, "I, Kota, son of Keema, return to my tribe. I have seen my spirit and learned the truth of myself."

The four elder shamalak stared at him in silence, and he remained perfectly still. Finally, the most wizened of them, a wrinkled woman whose hair had gone entirely white, spoke in a creaking voice: "You return to us with honor, Kota, son of Keema. You return to us a man."

There was a low snarl to the left. Gretis turned to see a very large shamalak male who appeared to be in his mid-thirties bounding forward. He had a great battle ax in his right hand and a wooden shield in the other. Unlike the other shamalak around her, this one had bone-white face paint around the angles of his hawk-like face. From this, and the multi-stranded necklace of beads and animal fangs that hung down his broad chest, she guessed this to be the tribe's chief.

"So you finally show your face," the leader bellowed as he stepped up to Kota's still kneeling form and glared down. "At least you have *that* much courage."

"I know what has happened," Kota said in a grave voice, keeping his head bowed. "I know members of this tribe have been killed by those in pursuit of me."

The arm holding the ax near Kota's head trembled at these words, and the chief's bronze face grew a touch redder. "Women and children," he said. He leaned in. "Have you come to surrender yourself to the demons to end this slaughter?"

"No," Kota said, "I have come to kill them."

"Have you really?" the chief grunted in exasperation. "*No one* can kill those things."

"Nonetheless, I will try," Kota said.

The chief stiffened and said in a sharp voice: "Kota, if you are still a member of this tribe, then rise."

Kota rose to his feet and met the leader's eyes with a solemn look. The two of them were of a height with one another, though the chief's body was thicker while Kota's was leaner and more defined. For a long moment, the white-painted shamalak stared at Kota, and there was silence all throughout the village. He seemed to see something that met his approval, for eventually, he lowered his ax. His voice lost only a little of its hard edge though as he said: "Many a warrior would have stayed away were he in your place. I can see in your eyes that you have returned as a man. Still," his face grimaced, "it would probably be best for the tribe for me to bind your wrists and ankles and hand you over to the monsters."

Gretis fidgeted, and the fingers of her right hand curled around the hilt of her sword, but Kota gave no reaction at all. He stared at the chief, unblinking until the female elder spoke: "Kota has committed no crime. To hand him over to those evil creatures would be an act of cowardice and would bring shame upon the tribe."

Two shamalak emerged from the crowd then, one male and one female. They were older than Kota, and, as Gretis gazed at them, she saw parts of her pupil's features in each of them. The male, tall and quite strong for one with hair so silver, moved to Kota's right side, and the woman to his left, and each stood facing the chief. "We stand with our son," the male said. "Whatever judgment you pass upon him, you must deliver to us as well." There was a rumble of whispers through the crowd, but Gretis did not listen to them. She was focused on the hint of a grin that played across Kota's somber features as his mother and father, after so many years apart, were willing to lay their lives down for him. In that moment, his mother cast a quick glance back at Gretis. Under her thick mane of dark hair spangled with gray, the shamalak woman's eyes studied her. There was a touch of resentment in them, for Gretis had stolen Kota away from her, but there also seemed to be respect—perhaps even a bit of appreciation.

The chief drew in a deep breath, gazing at the trio before him, and then said: "The elders are correct. You have committed no crime," his silver eyes moved to Gretis, "though your actions have cost this tribe many lives."

"Kota's actions have not caused *any* of this," Gretis said aloud, stepping forward and facing the leader's hard stare. "Nor have mine for that matter. Kota is the subject of a very old prophecy. He is destined to become a great enemy to demonkind, and they would have sought to kill him whether he trained with me or not. Fortunately for all of you and for this world, I *did* train him." Kota's father turned to face her. He was handsome in the way that Kota was, though he had three diagonal scars that ran parallel through his left eye socket, which had been rendered into an empty pit. He cast her a nod of respect, which spurred her on. She turned her head slowly, meeting the stares of the rest of the tribe as she said aloud: "Demons do *not* honor their bargains. If you were to hand Kota over to those hideous creatures, they would slaughter you all for nothing more than the taste of your flesh." The words elicited murmurs from all around.

"I am so sorry for the losses you've suffered," Kota said, following Gretis's example and facing the rest of the tribe. "I will—" he broke off, suddenly twitching, and then he cocked his head up and sniffed at the air. In a sudden blur, he shot toward Gretis. Almost before she registered the movement, Kota had his sword back from her hands, and he sprang upward so fast and that the chief and even his parents flinched back. The leap carried him up at least five times his own height before the claws on his left hand slashed down into the trunk of a tree in an explosion of bark that redoubled that momentum. Gretis gazed up into the treetops above, her heart beginning to pound as she saw a shadowy figure perched up high on a branch. It too appeared to have a sword out.

Kota flew at this figure as the branches billowed in the wind above them. It was difficult to make out the details of what happened next. There was an inhuman snarl, then a loud clank of metal striking metal, and then three *hacks* in the air in quick succession. Something round dropped from the branches—a mass of gray and black. It hit the ground and bounced, and Gretis saw the fur and the ghastly teeth and eyes of blood red. *It was the head of a demon.* The face was like that of a tiger with ashen gray fur with black stripes.

Three more shapes dropped from the branches then. One was a severed limb of leather armor and black claws, one was a breast-plated torso with the remaining arm still clutching a black sword, and one was the demon's lower half—a pair of furry legs that bent in reverse with metallic thigh and shin guards. Finally, Kota dropped down from full height of the treetops into a crouch. His right hand held his sword out to the side. Black blood dripped from the weapon's edge and off a spatter across his face. He was huffing.

"Kota!" Gretis shouted. Her sword was already in her hand, though she could not recall consciously drawing it.

Her pupil looked up at her. *He could recognize his own name.* That was a good sign. She watched him, looking for the beast.

"I can't smell any others," he said, his words coming in the human tongue, though at a deeper pitch than usual.

"Spirits around us!" the chief exclaimed. He stared at Kota with wide eyes, which, Gretis noticed, most the tribe was now doing. "H-how did you—"

Kota silenced the leader with a sharp grunt and a raised hand, hooked claws extended, veins standing up under the skin. His eyes narrowed as he whispered: "We're being watched."

Gretis could not help gazing about, despite the fact that her animus—far keener than her human eyes—detected nothing in their immediate surroundings. "Where?"

Kota looked at her, his jaw trembling as he spoke. "In the sky and in the trees... I can feel them now, but I can't reach them without abandoning this tribe." He gazed around at his people. Most of the shamalak were gawking, awed by the feat of strength and speed they had just witnessed. They spoke to one another in hushed voices, yet most fell silent as Kota spoke again: "They have scouts watching every conceivable route of escape.

"Of course we do!" a loud, male voice shouted in Tethric from the left. Gretis whirled and saw a man in a thick black robe standing at the edge of the village. The first thing she noticed about him was the pale, green-tinged skin. He looked to be perhaps forty, with wizened eyes but a lean and healthy build. He had a shaven head and face, and his lips were curled into a slight grin that had no warmth to it—*no humanity*. There were two shamalak children just in front of him—one a girl who looked to be about seven and the other a boy perhaps a year older. Both were on their hands and knees, trembling. The man's thin, veiny hands were held up just behind the pair, and Gretis's animus perceived tendrils of potent magic reaching from him to the young hostages.

This was the nathret the tribesmen had described. Gretis's stomach twisted that this one was bold enough to enter the village with Kota in it. *What did that mean?*

The whole of the tribe stared at the demon sorcerer in deathly silence, and more than a few of them shrank away from him. The nathret seemed to notice this, for a smirk appeared on his face as his eyes darted about. He took a step in Kota's direction, and as he did the two children slid forward, their knees and hands scraping along the dirt. Neither child seemed able to move much, but from the way they whimpered and from the tears that fell from their eyes, Gretis judged that they were most likely in severe pain.

"Let them go," Kota said in a dangerous growl, and he ran at the enemy.

"I'LL KILL THEM BOTH!" the sorcerer shouted, and he whipped his hands up. The children rose up like marionettes on strings, each squealing in pain. They floated a head or so above the ground, and Kota halted, bringing his bounding momentum to a skidding halt on the ground. Gretis stared in surprise. *He was able to stop himself? How was this nathret affecting his animus?*

A rumbling growl escaped through Kota's teeth before he snarled: "If those children die, I'll cut you to shreds!"

The sorcerer raised his right hand and the girl rose a litter higher and let out a shriek. "Throw away your weapon," he said in an icy voice, and he made a two-fingered gesture to his male hostage. The boy's arms spread involuntarily, and he began to scream in pain.

"All right!" Kota shouted, and flung his sword to the left.

“Good,” the nathret hissed. His left hand relaxed and the boy's arms fell back to his sides, his screams dying into whimpers

“I warn you,” Kota grunted through his teeth, “I don’t need weapons to—“

"Do not speak," the nathret said. "Just stand there." The muscles in Kota's face twitched. Gretis could tell that the sorcerer was studying her pupil with all his senses, and so she took the opportunity to study him with hers. Pieces of her animus whisked toward the nathret and immediately carried back an impression of terrible magical strength. It made her tremble inside. She recalled her encounter with the Starborn, Telemachus Vale, a year and a half before, and the power she had felt in him. *Was this demon that strong?* Perhaps not, though he was damned close.

<You know something valuable, Sansrit witch,> the sorcerer's voice hissed abruptly in Gretis's skull. She felt vicious psychic tendrils prying at her mind. By reflex, her mental walls came up. She had begun training in occlusion at the age of six in her father's palace, and her animus provided its own defenses against psychic invasion, yet still, she sensed the nathret take something.

"Iona," he said aloud, with a vicious grin. Gretis felt the blood leave her face. *Had she just cost the human race its savior?* The sorcerer stared at her with dull green eyes that seemed intelligent and alive, yet vacuously empty. "Where is she?" he said. A tiny wave of relief washed over her, but then the nathret chuckled: "You'll reveal everything soon enough, foolish little Sansrit witch."

Kota snarled, and the sorcerer turned his attention back to him. "We were concerned you would bring Onkai with you if you came, but it appears you are a remarkably stupid creature."

"You've come to make demands, I assume," Kota said, "So make them."

This only brought another predatory smile to the nathret. He gazed around at the tribesmen, seemingly unconcerned by the ones with bows and arrows. Not one of them was even daring to aim at him. He spoke aloud to them in their own tongue with perfect enunciation: "Every single one of you will be slaughtered tonight! We shall leave no one alive!"

Gretis saw fear permeate the rage in Kota's face. Through his teeth, he said in a voice that sounded almost desperate: "What do you want?"

The sorcerer's grin widened. "There is no bargain for us to strike." He stepped forward and put his hand on the shamalak girl's shoulder, and she shrieked in fright. "That is your fault of course. You are simply too strong, *shamalak.*" He looked Kota up and down. "All that primal power—I honestly don't know if the darkest magic I have would be enough to kill you. That is why all these *people* must die tonight."

“What do you mean?” Kota said, sounding desperate.

“Imbecile,” the nathret hissed. He raised his right hand and gestured to the severed head of the demon Kota had killed moments before. "The second you catch the scent of any of my... *more primal* brethren, you will lose all control and attack. You are incapable of surrender. We knew that, and so we always planned to exterminate this village. Perhaps some part of you will still be driven to protect these pathetic creatures." He gestured around. "It *could* yield us an easy victory." The sorcerer gave a little shrug. "Who knows? Either way, every one of these filthy mongrels will be dead by morning.

Kota, perhaps along with his animus, let out a growl so loud and deep that Gretis felt it in the ground beneath her feet. *This rage had been intended,* she realized. The nathret was taunting Kota, but why?

"Which one of these vermin is your mother?" the nathret said, raising an eyebrow, and then he pointed. "Her?" An orb of green fire the size of a man's head formed in front his finger tip and shot forward, tearing through the air at Kota's mother so fast that she did not even have time to scream. Gretis faintly registered a blurred shape moving alongside the thing kicking up a spray of dirt, and then there was an explosion of emerald flame. She screamed and ran forward. *It all happened so fast.* The green ball burst into a conflagration of emerald fire that sent waves of heat out. Then the flame died away, revealing Kota standing with outstretched arms in front of his mother. His chest was charred black, and smoke was rising off his skin, and yet... *he was whole.* His animus had protected him, and it was crackling for a fight. This inspired Gretis, and she whirled around to face the nathret, *but he was not there.*

"He's gone," Kota said in a gravelly voice. "I don't know how. My animus can't find him—like he just vanished."

Gretis blinked at the two shamalak children. Both were sobbing, but they were alive. *Thank the gods!* She swallowed and turned back to Kota. His parents were at his side, and his mother was tracing the blackened spots on his skin with her finger. In a bewildered whisper, she asked: "How are you unhurt?"

Gretis put her hand on the woman's wrist and said: "There's no time to explain any of this." She gazed at Kota and saw the fear in his blackened face. Her own mind was racing in terrible directions. *They knew Iona's name now... because of her!* The Nathret had come here and revealed his plan of attack. *Why?* Was this a feint of some kind? What would be the point? If his dark forces were going to launch a surprise attack, they would have no need of subterfuge. No—his words had to be some kind of twisted mind-game focused upon Kota, which meant she needed to assume they were true. The rest... *she would have to figure that out later.*

Gretis drew in a deep breath, aligning her mind to the impossible task before her. "The demons are only waiting until nightfall because they will be strongest then," she said. "It is not enough time to get any of these people to real safety, nor is there time to get word to anyone who can help us."

"What do we do?" Kota said. It hurt to hear the uncertainty in his voice—*the fear.*

"What we can," Gretis snapped. She turned to the chief, who was leaning a hand against the side of a tree, an utterly bewildered look on his face. "What is your name?" she demanded.

"What?" the chief muttered. It took him a few heartbeats to focus on her and respond. "Tarook," he finally said.

"Chief Tarook, I need you to gather every warrior over the age of thirteen you have and line them up there!" she pointed to an empty space between the trees and the tents, and the chief followed her gesture with his eyes. "I want everyone else there!" she pointed to a second space of bare earth, and again the chief gazed at where she indicated.

"W-what are you planning to have us do?" the he said after a moment.

"We're going to prepare for battle," she answered.

CHAPTER 27: EMPEROR TACITUS

The afternoon was bright and beautiful, the scents of freshly cooked bread and meats permeated the air, and the sound of music, laughter, and cheering echoed in every direction. Somar stood in the center of the bustling town square amidst a crowd of mostly peasants, watching as the great General Cassian Asango finally rode into Denigoth's capital on his vaunted dragon.

This was a momentous day, and Somar had set out on the road more than a month before in anticipation of it. His pupil had surpassed all of his expectations upon the field of battle. Cassian's exploits were well known, though some were too difficult to believe, even for Somar. Allegedly, the boy had taken Kyromanth—a massive walled city that no Denigothian general, including Somar himself, had been able to capture—a*nd he had taken it in a single day*. No one seemed to know how he had done it, but there were dozens of theories. Whatever the case, Cassian's reputation was now second only to Tacitus himself—at least among the common folk. The boy had continued to anger and frighten the empire's nobility and, of course, the Nemesai. This was part of the reason why Somar had chosen to view his pupil's grand entry on the ground with the commoners who loved him rather than from some lofty balcony from in of the city's towering buildings as one of his status might demand.

Somar made out the dragon first. Titus had grown since last he had laid eyes on the creature. Cassian was only a dark shape atop its majestic gray form, but from their relative size to one another, Somar could tell that Titus was now significantly taller than a horse. The dragon moved just a little awkwardly over the street, though no one seemed to notice.

The scraping 'clacks' of its claws over the paver stones were nearly imperceptible amidst the roar of the crowd. Cassian had become a legend. As Somar drew nearer, he saw the fierce grin on his former pupil's face. The young general raised his fist and shouted toward one side of the street, and men, women, and children all screamed in response. This drew a chuckle from Somar.

There were twenty men on each side of Cassian. They were tall, armored figures, and as they drew nearer, Somar could see the vaunted markings on their faces that the boy had etched into their skin with the dragon's tears they had gathered together years ago. The men were forming a wall around Cassian, which Somar thought to be a sensible enough precaution. He wondered how many assassination attempts there had been in the field, and how many were now to come. The Nemesai were likely growing desperate.

Suddenly Cassian's eyes locked onto Somar's, his matured features instantly shaping into a wide grin. The boy had sensed him of course, even amidst these tens of thousands of minds. <Hello, old man,> Cassian's voice whispered in his mind. <Please come and meet me in the palace. I have so much to tell you.>

Being unable to answer in kind, Somar replied with a nod. Cassian's eyes instantly shifted back to the crowd, and Somar sighed. The two of them had written to one another only a handful of times since they parted, yet it seemed their bond was as strong as the day they had parted. He felt a tingle of pride as he watched his beloved pupil bask in the people's love.

"Have you ever seen anyone so pleased with himself?" a feminine voice full of mirth said from behind him in an exotic, yet strangely familiar accent. Somar felt his eyes widen as he turned and saw the beautiful, now far more mature face of Keska Ethedrine, Cassian's sister Starborn. She was an utter vision, her dark skin complimented by a dress of gleaming orange strewn with diamonds hanging from an intricate web of thin silver chain. Her full lips were curled into a playful smirk, as if she were amused by all that was going on around her.

"We decided to follow you down to the streets," Telemachus said. He was standing next to Keska, though Somar had not noticed him at first. The third Starborn stood tall and handsome as ever—almost beautiful really—dressed in a finely embroidered tunic of green and black cut to a perfect fit of his upper body.

"How did you know I was here?" Somar said, hearing the delight in his voice at seeing this pair.

"Ah," Telemachus grunted, and his smile took on a nervous edge.

"He has had men following you since you entered the city," Keska said.

"Well before that actually," Telemachus sighed, rolling his eyes. "We've been... *concerned* that the local Nemesai contingent might *take an interest* in you, given your relationship with our brother."

"Not to mention the fact that I took military action against Bishop Cromlic when he came to arrest Cassian," Somar said with a dry chuckle. "Yes, similar thoughts occurred to me as well. I *did* travel with quite a few of Cassian's soldiers, as I'm sure you know."

"Yet you came down to the streets alone," Telemachus said, frowning just a little. Somar raised an eyebrow at the handsome Starborn. *Why was Telemachus so concerned for him?* The two of them had only spoken once nearly seven years ago. Still, he heard genuine worry in the Starborn's voice as he added: "You should not be taking such risks."

With a chuckle, Somar gestured toward Cassian, who was still very near, and said: "Somehow I felt safe knowing that the great General Asango and his dragon, as well as a contingent of his tattooed soldiers, would only be thirty paces away."

"He makes a fair point," Keska said, turning and facing Telemachus with a playful smirk.

"He does," Telemachus muttered, his eyes fixed on Cassian, who had now passed them in the street and was cantering away upon his dragon. "All the same, there our brother goes, and here you still are. He cannot protect you at all times, and it is not something upon which you should depend."

Somar stared at Telemachus and saw the focus in the young man's eyes. "I sense perhaps you have a plan to save me from my own foolishness."

Telemachus's expression immediately softened, and he said: "I would never call you 'foolish,' sir, but yes, I do have a plan." He gestured to his right, and Somar followed the direction with his eyes and saw an empty alleyway behind the back of the parade crowd. "Might we ask you to walk with us for a few moments, old man?" It vaguely registered to Somar at that moment that the finely dressed pair of Starborn should have drawn stares from all around, but no one was paying them any attention. *Sorcery of some kind?*

Somar glanced at Keska and saw that most of the humor had left her visage, yet enough was still present as to make him feel at ease. Even without this though, he trusted both of these people. Years ago, when he met each of them, he had judged them to be individuals of excellent character.

"All right," Somar said. He started walking, and Keska fell into step next to him, with Telemachus moving to his other side.

The three of them broke away from the already dissipating crowd and walked together in silence for a time. They strode through one of the poorer sections of the capital almost thoughtlessly. Somar knew that such an incredible public event as Cassian's arrival would elicit a fair amount of crime. Even mildly clever thieves would know that nearly every citizen's attention would be on the legendary young man, as would the attention of the city guards. Indeed, the streets and many of the shops they passed appeared entirely empty. It might have been dangerous to walk amidst such an environment as a group of only three, but then two of Somar's three were Starborn. He could scarcely imagine what a pair of them could accomplish together.

They eventually made their way into the resplendent northern district, where Telemachus led them down several streets of massive, lavishly built structures to seemingly the largest and finest of them all. It was a structure of white marble brick, decorated in metal plates with strange symbols of the arcane. Three tall men in full armor stood around the door, unmoving, each hefting a silver-tipped spear.

"Hello," Telemachus said with a careless gesture to the nearest of the guards. The man immediately saluted him. Telemachus nodded and lifted his hand, and a massive wooden door swung open.

"Is this your home?" Somar asked as he stepped into a vast and beautiful chamber. There were sculptures and books in display cases and well-preserved specimens of exotic animals Somar did not begin to recognize - and he considered his knowledge of the world to be quite replete.

"As much as you might say the Obsidian Guild is *mine*, yes, this is my home," Telemachus said. His tone was not one of boasting so much as amusement. The young Starborn had become the official head of the insanely wealthy organization of sorcerers some time ago, Somar knew. "The guild owns houses all over the empire, as well as in other nations, of course. We have several properties within the dwarven kingdoms, and there is an ancient contractual agreement to several rooms within an elven palace in the northern lands, though I have not attempted a visit, nor has anyone in the guild in the last two hundred and thirty or so years."

"Ah, I have often heard rumors that the order was still secretly dealing with the elves," Somar said. "I suppose people love to imagine such conspiracies."

"Oh we've never stopped dealing with them," Telemachus replied with a chuckle. "We receive requests once or twice a year. There was actually one such solicitation to steal the

Elokien talisman Cassian came to possess some years ago, but the guild does not act against Starborn, even for the elves."

Somar suddenly felt a tinge of suspicion. "You're being remarkably free with information. As I understand it, the Obsidian Guild is a viciously secretive organization."

"Yes, it is," said Telemachus with a playful grin. "I definitely should not be revealing secret dealings with elves, but I am. Tell me, Golden General, how do you assess the situation?"

Somar stared at Telemachus, studying his face, and then Keska's. "Cassian knows I am here," he said, reassuring himself of his safety, though truthfully, he felt no need. "You brought me to this place for a reason – *this place specifically*. Not simply to avoid being heard – Starborn can accomplish that anywhere." Somar blinked. "It can't be... Do you wish me to join the order?"

"Exactly correct," Telemachus said.

"Well, I cannot guess why," Somar laughed. "Is the sorcerer's gift not a prerequisite for membership?"

"Bah," Telemachus grunted with a dismissive gesture. "The knowledge you have—your experience in politics and strategy—you are a remarkably suitable candidate, and we'll be damn lucky to get you."

Somar's frowned. "Was this at Cassian's behest?"

"Actually, this is a compromise we are trying to work out with him," Keska said. She was resting comfortably on a sofa, her form gracefully draped.

"The truth is that protecting you would be a great liability to him," Telemachus said.

"Oh?" Somar murmured. "Assuming I have any real importance, do you think him so incapable?"

"Dear man," Keska said, her voice taking on a serious tone yet somehow remaining relaxed at the same time, "If Nemesai Inquisitors were to lay a hand on you, Cassian would probably kill them. Bishop Cromlic knows this well, and it is not altogether unthinkable that he might sacrifice a few of his men to elicit a *reaction* from our brother sufficient to call not only for his arrest by the church but by the empire itself."

"Yes-s-s," Somar muttered. This line of thought was not unfamiliar to him, but he had assumed that Cassian's retinue of tattooed soldiers would be more than enough to deter Nemesai inquisitors. Protection from Telemachus had several advantages over that scenario though, not the least of which being that the young man had a far more even temper than Cassian. There was also the fact that the Nemesai could not afford additional enemies, and the Obsidian Guild had a vast network of wealth and power at its disposal, not to mention that Telemachus himself was a Starborn, just like Cassian, with presumable access to the guild's legendary archive of spells.

"It would be best if you moved into this building," Telemachus said. "I'll provide you with the finest accommodations of course."

"And you can visit me again in Aloria," Keska purred.

Somar shifted his gaze back and forth between the fascinating couple. "I think the two of you have invested far too much thought into the wellbeing of a simple old man."

"Your safety is important to us," Telemachus said, and then he added with a sigh: "Our brother needs... *stabilizing influences*."

"Are you sure you do not mean *supervision*?"

This elicited a soft chuckle from Keska, but Telemachus said in a stern voice: "You know as well as anyone how he is, and the capital is a far different venue than a battlefield, with different rules and different dangers and consequences."

"And you think I can control him?" Somar said.

"Cassian would have killed Bishop Cromlic if not for you," Telemachus said in a grim voice.

This gave Somar pause, and he thought back to that visceral day nearly seven years ago when Cassian had Cromlic on his knees in front of hundreds of onlookers. There had indeed been murder in the boy's eyes. Somar recalled grabbing his pupil by the arm. When Cassian had glared up at him—a sixteen-year-old boy wielding so much destructive power—it had taken quite a bit of Somar's courage to stare back and say all he had said.

He gazed at Telemachus. The handsome young man might be emperor if not for Cassian. Gods knew not even Cromlic himself had endorsed Prince Arkas for the job. *Did Telemachus truly have no hunger for the throne at all?* No, he was too kind—too virtuous and gentle to reign over the violent factions of the Denigoth Empire, and he probably knew it. Somar glanced at the girl. *She could do it.* Cassian had said more than once over the years that Keska was the most formidable of his siblings. Charming and elegant as she was, Somar thought he could see something quite dangerous within those dark honey eyes.

"So I am to spend the remainder of my life in the company of one Starborn or another," Somar said.

"Are we such terrible company?" Keska laughed, lifting an eyebrow.

"You can be... *overwhelming* at times," Somar replied, and he was satisfied to see a playful smirk play across the female Starborn's face. She opened her mouth to speak but then closed it, her eyes suddenly narrowing and her head cocking to the side. Whatever had affected her so suddenly seemed also to have touched Telemachus, for he frowned and stared down at the floor, breathing through his nose. Somar did not question this, having had enough experience with Cassian's telepathic flashes as to know that the two of them were focused on something he could not detect. After a moment, Keska gazed back up at him and said: "Your presence is requested in the palace."

"Cassian called to you?" he said.

"No," Telemachus said with a slight edge to his voice. "Emperor Tacitus asks for you."

Somar drew in a sharp breath, straightening by reflex. *The Emperor...* Old and jaded though he was, he felt a flutter in his stomach. "Now?"

"Yes," Telemachus said with a nod.

"I suppose I should be off then," Somar said.

Telemachus glanced at the door and said in an even icier voice: "He has sent an escort for you."

Somar glanced down the ornate hallway and saw one of the Obsidian Guild's guards step through the thick doorway. The hulking man's face had gone a few shades paler under his helmet. Breathing nervously, he managed to mutter: "My lord—"

"We know," Telemachus said. "Master Dojinko will go with them."

"Y-yes," the soldier grunted, and he blinked at Somar.

Craith... There was little else that would cause even Starborn to lose their good humor. Somar smiled at the poor soldier and said: "Yes, I'll be off with them." He walked past the man through to the doorway and then stepped out to see ten dark and silent figures standing perfectly still in the street, swords sheathed at their waists. He glanced at their deathlike masks of polished metal, which obscured the soulless eyes beneath. Each of them was tall and broad-shouldered and clad in black leather armor with an outer layer of ring mail. This was complimented with black boots, black gloves, and black hoods that surrounded the metallic faces they showed to the world. Not a speck of their flesh showed anywhere, which was part of their terrifying mystique.

Even Somar, who had managed to become part of the upper echelons of the Denigoth military, knew little of these creatures. Supposedly, they had been human once, but Emperor Nihilin, a notoriously powerful and ruthless Starborn of the fourth century, had developed a means to strip away the souls of men and fill them instead with dark magic. Craith did not, or *could not* speak, and demonstrated nothing but cold, mechanical obedience to their emperor. Somar knew that even demons feared these unfeeling things. If ordered, a craith would stand in a single spot for two hundred years, never moving, never resting or needing food or water, tear his own arm off without uttering the slightest hiss of pain—so the stories went. Somar had seen groups of them in action in the demon war long ago and witnessed the terrifying combination of their massive physical strength combined with an inhuman lack of fear or hesitation. Many considered them to be more lethal even than Onkai.

One of the craith stepped forward when it saw Somar and held up a scroll in its right hand. He took and opened it. In elegant calligraphy, he read:

Your presence is requested as soon as possible in the throne room, old friend.

-Tacitus

"Let's go then," Somar said, gazing at the silver mask of the one who had handed him the scroll.

The creatures said nothing, yet three of them immediately moved behind him, three moved in front of him, and the remaining pair moved to his sides. All of it was coordinated and executed without so much as a glance at one another, as if they were of a single mind. Somar drew in a nervous breath and began to walk, and immediately the silent killers moved with him, matching his pace with an eerie precision. He found a strange bit of humor to the situation. It was said that the Starborn emperor could see through his craiths' eyes. Somar doubted anyone in the world would dare attack him at that moment.

The walk to the palace went quickly. Somar knew the capital well and maneuvered through the streets with ease despite his tight-knit entourage that blocked portions of his view in every direction. Here and there, he watched peasants, and even well-dressed folk shrink from the craith procession. Everyone who lived so close to the palace knew them by sight of course. Emperor Tacitus did not deploy his special force often from what Somar had heard, but when he did, there was a very strong implication that trouble was not to be made.

Cassian's parade had presumably ended some time ago, leaving a lingering swell of people in its wake that grew thicker as they neared the palace. Crowds parted immediately as the craith approached. A few eyes here and there cast nervous glances at Somar through their armored bodies, but not even the Imperial Guard slowed them as they approached the palace entrance. Somar paused when he saw the palace, the craith pausing with him as his eyes scanned the vaunted walls. This building was the greatest seat of power the human world had ever seen.

He strode with his entourage into the entry hall, where the polished stone floor was adorned with a thick red carpet that was wonderfully soft to walk upon. The craith never broke their protective formation, yet Somar was still able to appreciate the opulence around him. They passed massive paintings and sculptures of past Starborn emperors and notable heroes of Denigoth's history. Through an open window, he gazed down at the courtyard where a group of extremely well-dressed children ran giggling inside of an enormous hedge maze. Somar was so enthralled by this that he hardly noticed when they came around a bend, and Cassian, standing before the tremendous throne room doors, whirled to face him.

"Hello again, old man," his pupil said, a wry grin on his face despite the presence of the craith.

Somar looked the boy up and down, and, peering so closely, was not sure he could continue to think of Cassian as a *boy.* The smooth, youthful face had become tanned and almost rugged, and there was neatly shaved but still present stubble that defined the bone structure of his jaw. Most of all though, Cassian had the eyes of one who had recently faced battle—intense and unblinking, like those of a wolf.

The craith soldiers stepped aside, allowing Somar a path to his former pupil, which he immediately took. The two gripped each other's wrists, grinning.

"He awaits us inside," Cassian said, gesturing to the throne room entryway with a backward nod. There was excitement in his voice. Years of both their lives had led to this day.

"Why in the world am I here?" Somar said.

Cassian sighed and rolled his eyes. "Have you not figured it out? They all see you as a means to rein me in. I assume my dear brother Telemachus has been whispering his concerns in our emperor's ears for years." He smirked. "Tell me, did he wait a whole five minutes before launching into his fears about what I am going to do now that I am in *the capital?*"

"You might count yourself lucky that you have a brother who cares so much about your wellbeing," Somar said.

"He...is important to me," Cassian said, and some of the sarcasm left his voice as he spoke. Then the young man's eyes shifted toward the thick wooden doorway, and he whispered: "Emperor Tacitus has entered the throne room." To Somar's surprise, the boy tensed and shut his eyes, and his whole body shook for a heartbeat. Then an awed smile crossed his face. "I had almost forgotten how much power that man radiates—Holy Hell!"

Two of the craith stepped past them and opened the doors, and Somar saw the Great Tacitus Adronicus perhaps twenty steps forward, sitting on a regal throne of wood, silver, and the bones of dragons. At seventy-two years old, the man still looked strong and robust. His hair was somehow more black than silver, and deep blue eyes that were entirely alert held them in a piercing stare.

The Emperor wore a fairly simple garb of black with golden threaded embroidery. Other than that, he did not decorate himself in any way with jewels or even a crown, despite the fact that he was the most powerful human being in the world, *in more than one respect.*

Tacitus sat, straight-backed, as Cassian walked across the expanse of red carpet between them and knelt. Somar followed and took a place at his pupil's side, lowering his head. He was vaguely aware that some fifty craith were positioned throughout the vast throne room, some next to tapestries, some standing to the sides of the throne, and many others concealed.

"I am honored to kneel before you, my Emperor," Cassian said aloud.

"Rise, Cassian," Tacitus said. His voice was a charming rumble of finely aged masculine strength. "You as well, my old friend."

Somar pushed his aged body up with not quite so much grace or ease as his pupil, but he bore the pain in his knees in silence, *for this was the Emperor of Denigoth.*

Tacitus stood from his throne and walked down the eight or so steps until he was level with Cassian and said: "I have enjoyed watching your campaigns these last years, my boy." He chuckled: "You have quite a unique way of doing things." Cassian gave a slight nod to this but said nothing. The emperor stepped around him slowly, seeming to appraise him. "We both know why you have come to the capital. Before we arrive at any discussion of your *crown,* I would like to ask you a few questions. Please answer them honestly."

"Yes, your grace," Cassian said.

Tacitus paused at Cassian's left side and said: "Tell me, how many people do you suppose wish to kill you at this very moment?"

Cassian answered in an even voice: "I have made many enemies on the battlefield. I imagine many thousands would love to see my head cut from my body."

"You speak of peasants first," Tacitus said, sounding vaguely amused. "Such stock are of little threat to one such as you. How many people *capable* of killing you wish to see you dead?"

"Bishop Cromlic and your son come immediately to mind," Cassian said. Somar watched Tacitus's eyes as Cassian spoke of the man's offspring. He could read nothing in them. Cassian went on: "I also imagine that many of this empire's wealthier citizens – particularly the older generation – are threatened by my economic and societal views. I suppose Romulus would turn on me in a second if he were presented with the right circumstances."

"Yes, you have collected an extremely impressive list of enemies for one so young," the Emperor said, a serious expression in his domineering features. "Who are your allies?"

"As far as true allies, I would count my dragon, of course, Telemachus, Keska, my personal guard, and Somar Dojinko here," said Cassian.

"No one else?"

"They are all who are truly loyal to me and also resourceful enough to help me against my *impressive list of enemies*."

Tacitus raised an eyebrow. "You do not count me as an ally?"

Cassian stared into his emperor's eyes. "I never have. No."

Tacitus chuckled. "I think that is one of the reasons you have long been my favorite. You do not expect anything you have not earned." He put a hand on Cassian's shoulder. "The throne of Denigoth most certainly needs to be earned. You understood that better I think than Dimitris ever did." Whatever humor had been in Cassian's face vanished at the mention of his dead brother. Tacitus went on: "You are the strongest of your generation, Cassian. I knew that long before Dimitris challenged you." He lowered his hand from the boy's shoulder and said in a harsher voice: "Strength is not enough though. I have watched you throw my empire into an unprecedented uproar. You make speeches and publish writings that display an unbridled contempt not only for the church but most of the upper class. It is all very bold and uncompromising, and it displays a deeply concerning lack of tact or prudence."

Cassian said nothing to this but met his emperor's gaze. Somar knew his former pupil well enough to guess that he would have launched into a fierce argument with anyone else in the world over such words.

Tacitus stared at Cassian for a long moment, seeming to study him with cold dispassion. "Your weakness, my boy, is in the honesty of your heart." He smiled, but it was a dark and callous smile. "You are simply not built for falseness of any kind, and people - even uneducated peasants - can sense that. It is inspiring, but it limits you. When all of these wealthy and powerful men of the court with - shall we say *flexible* moral stature - finally see that you cannot be bribed or flattered or played in any way, they will *not* admire you. They will despise you with a passion and even a righteous conviction of which you cannot conceive."

"What do you suggest I do?" Cassian said, his voice cold but even.

"I suggest you *evolve*," Tacitus said. "Politics is an immensely different game than open warfare." He leaned in almost uncomfortably close to Cassian's face and said: "Tell me, do you believe you are the first Starborn in history to notice corruption? Why do you think we who have come before you have governed as we have? Were we all fools? Do you believe yourself to be the only one of us who has ever possessed integrity?"

Cassian answered immediately: "I believe their practices were appropriate and necessary to keeping order in less advanced times, but—"

"I do not need to hear your rigid philosophical theories," Tacitus said. "I know you have read as many historical texts as most of my grand historians, but you studied them all through the myopic lens of an angry young man convinced that he knew better than the rest of the world. You are very clever, Cassian, so clever in fact that you've never had to be wise. Here you are, finally, in the heart of the Denigoth Empire. Perhaps it would be prudent to look around and study things a bit before you tell us all how unenlightened we are."

"I have only ever shown you respect, my emperor," Cassian said, not entirely concealing his irritation as he spoke. "Of course I will do as you wish."

"Splendid," Tacitus said without smiling.

"This *evolution* you wish me to undergo - is it your condition for naming me crown prince?"

"No, that was merely an old man's advice," the Emperor said. "If you wish a specific criterion, a crown prince cannot have the church itself as an open enemy, nor any order therein. Bring the matter to a close."

Cassian stiffened slightly. "Do you mean I must make peace?"

Tacitus sighed. "I shall give you another piece of advice, since you merit that much. The Nemesai are a brutal, antiquated body that our people become less and less tolerant of every year. Still, they are a *holy* order. Even you must understand the importance religion plays in our people's lives – in their codes of morality and their tolerance for the hardships of their fragile lives. A *wise* ruler must handle religion delicately. Perhaps the time finally *has* come to do away with the Nemesai, but a brilliant emperor could accomplish that feat without attacking them head on and plunging his empire into civil war."

"What do you suggest I do?"

"I suggest you use that fine intellect of yours and overcome the problem." There was a subtle edge to his voice. "We both know if you were not a Starborn, your head would have been severed years ago for the things you have said and written. Even with all your power, you dare not walk the capital streets without a dozen of your personal guard around you. Bring the matter to a close, Cassian, and do it without murdering a bishop of the church. The day you show me you can accomplish that, I will name you as my heir."

"Understood," Cassian replied, though his eyebrows knitted together. After a moment, he said: "I have a question for you, my Emperor, if I may ask it."

"Yes?" Tacitus said, sounding a bit amused.

"Why did you make me kill my brother?" Somar felt his stomach twist. What his pupil was asking effectively amounted to an accusation leveled at the most dangerous man in the world.

Tacitus stared at Cassian for a long moment, then answered: "I had my reasons."

"What were they?"

"Perhaps I shall tell you someday."

Cassian met the Emperor's eyes for a few heartbeats, then said: "Thank you for taking the time to speak to me, Great Tacitus. I will think very hard on all you have said."

Tacitus nodded and then turned to Somar. "You must help him keep a level head, old friend."

"I... will do my best, your grace," Somar said.

"Good," Tacitus said, and he gave them a nod. "I shall see you both at the banquet tonight, and then I am afraid I must leave for a few weeks. I have some urgent business in the West." He turned to Cassian and said: "Upon my return, I expect you to report progress on these matters."

"Understood, your grace," Cassian said.

"Good day, gentlemen," Tacitus said.

Cassian and Somar knelt before the emperor once more and then left the room together. When they came back out the wooden doors, Somar noted that the craith were gone. *Was that a symbol that Tacitus's protection was now gone?*

"Well *that* was wonderful," Cassian said with an exasperated sigh.

Somar gazed at the young man. "Tell me, now that the Emperor has made himself clear, will you at least *entertain* the idea of making peace with Cromlic?"

Cassian turned, his eyes narrowing in anger as he said: "Not a chance in hell."

Somar swallowed. He had had a year and a half vacation from the boy and all of his extremism, but once again fate had brought them together. His mind stretched back to the words the great dragon had whispered into his mind while Cassian faced the white fire. Somar found that he was no less afraid now of the darkness Promethiock had spoken about overtaking his pupil than he had been years ago, and a sickly feeling in his gut told him that the prophesied moment when Cassian's enemies would overtake him might be very close at hand.

CHAPTER 28:
THE SLAVE HIDDEN AWAY

"IONA!!!"

The inhumanly deep voice jolted her out of sleep as it had hundreds of times before. Iona shot up in her cot and shouted by reflex: "Coming!" She gave the response before even opening her eyes. Her master's temper could be terrifying, and he disliked when she did not answer his call immediately.

"I'm outside," he said in a more subdued snarl.

Iona blinked, taking in the dull, early morning light through the cracks in the thatched roof above her head. Then she bounced off the cot, letting her feet slap down on the still morning-wet dirt that was the floor of her home. She could hear Gorlick outside. He was huffing in his thick, wet way of breathing, and there was a scraping sound of something being dragged through the soil and plants outside.

Iona felt a hot tingle of nerves in her stomach. *He had killed something.* It might be a bear, or a deer, or a tradesman who had been unlucky enough to wander too close.

"*Please don't let it be human,*" she said in the softest whisper she could manage.

"WHAT?" Gorlick's voice snarled through the hovel's wall of hay and hardened mud.

"Nothing!" Iona shouted. She dashed out of her tiny quarters and into the main room of the house, her legs dancing around the enormous table upon which Gorlick did most of his skinning. She cast a quick look at her kitchen—the cleanest section of the home by far—and took a quick mental note of how much wood there was on hand for the stove. *Not enough—not if he is bringing home something large.*

Iona ran out to the doorway and caught sight of the enormous black dog, and it caught sight of her in turn and bared its teeth, letting out a dangerous growl. *Why did it still hate her?* The beast took a step forward, continuing to snarl, causing her to cringe in the doorway. Boar, as Gorlick had named the creature for its strangely flat snout, was less like a dog and more like a horse, with the long, powerful legs and a broad back. She had come to suspect that Gorlick had produced Boar by breeding a normal dog with some supernatural beast to produce a hulking half-breed, perhaps so that he could have something like himself.

"DOWN!" Gorlick snapped, and the tremendous hound lowered the back half of his body to the ground. The creature continued to glare at Iona with its yellow eyes, lips curled back.

Knowing this was the best she could expect from the beast, Iona turned to Gorlick. Of all things, he had a dead grizzly bear, which he was holding by the back of the neck as he dragged its limp form along. Iona had grown so used to Gorlick's hulking form over her many months with him that she seldom stopped to consider it, but for a brief second, she gaped at how much larger he was than the bear, and it made her cringe inside.

"He was huntin' my deer," Gorlick muttered as he shoved the animals limp form down onto the ground. "I guess you get the new blanket you 'been wantin'."

"Y-yes, thank you, master," Iona said, gazing at the corpse. She guessed he would take several days to skin it, and while he did the body would sit in the house. There would be dozens of flies, and... *the smell...* Such things never bothered Gorlick. He had not even had an oven when she first came to live with him and was entirely comfortable eating raw meat.

"Were you out all night?" Iona asked.

"Yeah," he grunted. "Fry me some eggs. I want... eight. Put some salt on 'em, eh?"

"Of course, sir," she said with a nod.

"Good girl," he muttered, and his bulbous, tattooed features relaxed. It was strange to Iona that she did not fear

Gorlick more. He could crush her skull in one hand, but he had never once hurt her. In that respect at least, the half-ogre was a kinder master than Lady Sondal had been. There was always the understanding between them though that if she ever tried to run, he would take a trip south, and Hervin and Livia would die, so Iona had forced herself to make peace with staying, and life was tolerable.

She watched her master pick the bear's carcass back up as if it weighed no more than a pillow and stroll back to the shack with his dog trotting behind. When they were gone, she turned and headed around to the back of the house. Morning sunlight glinted off the metallic sections of the chicken coop that faced the east. Gorlick had built the thing tying sticks together with pieces of armor he had... *acquired* from armed men who had been unfortunate enough to come upon him in the forest. Boar was excellent at keeping forest predators away from the chickens, but the armor plating kept *him* away from *them* at night.

"Good morning," Iona said, smiling down at her feathered little friends. There were nine birds, and they all scurried up as the coup door opened. She opened the wooden crate nearby and grabbed a handful of dried corn before letting the chickens out. She liked to wake them with a treat. It built trust.

After the chickens went to eating, Iona crawled inside the coup and gathered up eight eggs, pulling them into her apron, and then crawled back out on knees and one hand. Rising with the bounty, she moved to her garden, which was a sizable square of fenced earth behind the house. Iona was glad she had finally convinced Gorlick to make it for her. It had not taken him long. He had built the fence by shoving thick tree limbs into the ground and then tilled the earth in a few minutes by merely digging his enormous hands in and dragging them along.

She untied the uneven gate of tied sticks and stepped inside. *Her potatoes were coming in!* That was exciting. Between the chard, tomatoes, carrots, and all the mustard and dill that were so abundant in the forest, Iona was adding more and more variety to the food she and Gorlick ate. He would pretend he did not care of course, but she knew he did. He had built the garden after all, and she had caught him secretly inspecting the plants more than once.

Iona gathered up a few bits of chard and tomato into her apron and then stepped back out of the garden. She was careful to tie the door behind her, knowing that Boar would trounce everything if given a chance. Ingredients in hand, she walked back toward the house to perform one of her favorite actions in the world: *cooking.* It was good to be able to stay in practice. She wanted to keep her skills up for the day when she might... *return to Hervin and Livia.* Iona swallowed, shaking off a swell of emotion. Gorlick did not like it when she cried.

Straightening, Iona walked to the front of the house, but when she did, she saw something that caused her entire soul to shiver in fear. *It was him!*

The young sorcerer with the missing fingers was riding slowly toward her on a black horse. When he saw her, his cruel face twisted into a smile. Iona felt her heart flutter in her chest, and she took several unconscious steps backward, and her hand lost its grip on her apron, letting all her ingredients spill out onto the ground Nothing in the world frightened her more than this young man. His name started to flash through her mind but then vanished. She thought she had learned it—*more than once*—by accident, but he had ripped it from her memory each time, leaving a dull, stinging haze in its stead. She could always recall the pain though. This young man had performed dozens of 'experiments,' as he called them, on her. He had drawn her blood, pierced into the deepest recesses of her consciousness, and cast strange spells that burned and tingled wildly, all in an attempt to draw 'it' out, *whatever 'it' was*. Every one of those experiments had ended in a fit of rage from the young sorcerer. Iona had dull, sometimes nonsensical memories of all of it. More than once, he had demanded she admit she was the Messiah and was hiding it from him. *He was insane...*

"Hello, Iona," the young man said.

"H-hello," she managed to squeak. She had started to tremble.

Boar came padding out of the shack and let loose a growl at the visitor, arching his back.

"Shut your ugly face!" the sorcerer snapped, and he waved a black-gloved hand in the dog's direction, hissing some inscrutable words. The air in front of Boar's snout suddenly burst into a puff of orange fire, and the hound let out a terrified yelp and leaped back. This drew a smirk from the young man. He dismounted his horse and chuckled at the now very skittish looking beast: "You've got to be about the most hideous animal in the world." His gaze returned to Iona. "How are you being treated?"

"She's being treated fine," Gorlick's voice snapped from out of the shack. He stepped out of the doorway, an uncharacteristi-cally wary look on his tattooed face.

"Is she?" the sorcerer said, staring hard back at the hulking creature. "Your grotesque mutt has gotten even bigger since last I came. I'm not sure I trust it around my prize."

"Boar doesn't kill anything I don't tell him to," Gorlick snapped.

"Hmm," the young man grunted. "We shall have to talk about this later."

"You brought supplies?" Gorlick said, and his bulbous eyes scanned the young man and his horse, which only had a few small saddle bags attached.

"Do I look like a delivery boy? Dunlin will be by soon, like always."

Dunlin was another of the young sorcerer's subordinates, a large man who brought a cart full of supplies every other week or so. He had tattoos like her master, though they were not nearly so thick. Iona disliked the way Dunlin leered at her when he was there, but she knew the man was utterly terrified of Gorlick, so she made sure never to stray too far from her master when he was near.

"Why are you here then?" Gorlick said. There always seemed to be an underlying tension between these two, yet at the same time, the young man seemed to be her master's only friend.

"I felt the need to make sure the two of you were well," the sorcerer said. A smirk came across his pale face as he added: "We're about to make our move. In two days, my brother falls."

"I've heard *that* before," Gorlick said with a low sigh.

"This time, things are different. He can't beat what we have planned. I don't even think my father could."

"Maybe, but Cassian's a dangerous little bastard. Make sure you don't underestimate 'im like last time."

Cassian? Iona blinked. *Wasn't that the name of the Starborn Livia had been so enamored with?* As this thought passed through her mind, the sorcerer turned and glared at her, and she felt a sudden searing pain in the front of her head.

"Hahhh!" she squealed as whatever had just been passing through her mind vanished. Iona blinked several times after it was over and involuntary tears rolled from her eyes. She sniffled, looking at him, begging with her eyes: *no more.*

"Relax," he said with a sigh, "the less you understand, the less danger you're in."

"Yes, sir," she whimpered.

The young man turned back to Gorlick. "And you, watch your mouth."

"Mhh," Gorlick grunted, narrowing his eyes.

The sorcerer stared at him for a moment, then said: "No one's come around looking for her?"

"Ain't seen anyone in months except that little piss-weasel, Dunlin," Gorlick said. "If I had, I would'a taken care of 'em."

The young man frowned. "Don't grow overly confident."

This seemed to irritate Gorlick, for his lips curled back a little as he replied: "You doubting me?"

"No," the sorcerer said quickly. *He seemed to be at least somewhat afraid of Gorlick.* "Gods know you could probably kill an entire platoon of Onkai with your bare hands, but all the brute power in the world does nothing to pierce elven enchantments, nor can it fool the eyes of the Norn. Enemies may come here that you cannot even perceive."

"We have to worry about things like that now?" Gorlick growled.

"We're not exactly playing for low stakes, are we?" The sorcerer's dark eyes moved to Iona, and he made a sharp gesture at her, which made her flinch. No magic leaped from his hand, but instead, he spoke: "You know what I think she is, Gorlick. I believe it more every day."

"Shouldn't you be *kneeling* then?" the half-ogre muttered, rolling his enormous eyes.

"Why the hell would I do that?" he said, casting Iona a sneering look. "I'm an *abomination*, remember?" She knew the sorcerer hated her, but the reason was confusing – it was as if she represented something for him.

<*You have no idea,*> the young man whispered into her mind, seeming to respond directly to her thoughts. He took a step toward her, and she shrank back. "Why in the world did they choose you? You're so weak and pathetic! I know you dream about returning to your precious *Hervin* and that *thing* you think of as your sister. I want you to know that you'll never see either of them again." Iona backed up against the wall of Gorlick's shack and flattened herself there, shivering. The young man moved closer and said: "I don't care if you're meant to save this world. If I can't become emperor, then it can all burn." He glared up at the sky and shouted: "CAN YOU HEAR ME, NORN? IF I CAN'T USE HER, I'LL KILL HER!"

"Hey!" Gorlick shouted, "Calm the hell down!"

Iona's heart was racing at terror-stricken speed. She squeaked: "I—I don't—whatever you think I am—"

"Shhh," the sorcerer whispered, and he held up two gloved fingers and touched them gently to the tip of her forehead. Her fear evaporated instantly, overtaken and consumed by a white-hot pain. Then a dull confusion overlay the last few moments. When the hand drew away, it was like waking from a dream where all the details that had seemed so real and vibrant slipped away as her eyes opened. Iona blinked, feeling a terrible throbbing in her skull. Then she realized that the strange young man was in front of her. *When had he come? What had he taken?* She had no idea...

CHAPTER 29: THE COMING DEMONS

"How many of them do you think we can protect?" Kota said in a quiet voice. He was careful to speak in the human tongue as he said this. There were many extremely acute shamalak ears nearby, and he had the sense not to add to the fear that already pervaded his tribe.

None, Gretis thought but said instead: "I don't know."

They had made their way to the caves in the side of the mountain the Nakawa tribe called: "Hrothma." According to several elders, this was the most ideal defensive position the local countryside had to offer. There were numerous large stones at the foot of the mountain sticking up out of the ground, which would provide plenty of opportunities for Kota and Gretis to maneuver around and between barriers and hopefully avoid being surrounded by the enemy's likely large numbers. Most of the caves went back no more than twenty paces at the farthest, and they were narrow and short. Gretis had directed the woman and children, and many of the men, into seven of these small caverns, but they could scarcely be seen behind the wall of spears that stuck up and outward in the cave-mouths like the prickled backs of porcupines. Every able-bodied shamalak in the tribe had spent hours carving wooden spear after spear for this task, and there were close to a thousand of them in the dirt. This was by no means a superb defense against an army of demons, but it would slow attackers down, and the swordsmen of the tribe had been carefully divided amongst each cave. Quite a few of them had Denigoth military blades and even shields, and they had been instructed to lie in the breaks between the spear clusters and attack cautiously.

Gretis had also carefully stationed shamalak archers surrounding the clearing that would be the battlefield. Most of them were perched upon branches, concealed behind leaves and pine needles, each one with several quivers packed to bursting with arrows. They had been instructed not to fire until Kota had engaged the enemy directly, so as not to give away their positions until the confusion of battle had set in.

She and Kota were the main defense. This terrible notion loomed in Gretis's mind as she watched the light begin to disappear behind the treetops in front of them. How could they be enough? The tribe would die tonight, and likely so would she and Kota. They could not leave though. Kota would never abandon his people, and Gretis would never abandon him, so there they were.

"How are we doing?" a low voice said from behind in shamalak.

Gretis turned to see Keema, Kota's father, standing behind them. His aged face was troubled, yet not terrified.

"I'm sorry... for all of this," Kota said, his voice tight. He gazed down at his father's feet. The two of them had not spoken to Gretis's knowledge throughout all the preparation for battle. These were the first words they had shared in nearly ten years.

To her surprise, the wizened shamalak grinned at his son, revealing yellowed fangs. "You got real strong, didn't you?" he said. The old man reached up and put a hand on Kota's right arm and squeezed the thick muscle. Kota's animus made no defensive move at all – *an unusual reaction*. "When I saw you kill that demon... I've never been prouder of anything in my life." He turned his toothy grin on Gretis and said: "I'm so grateful to you for all you've done for my son."

She saw the defiance in the old shamalak's smile, and it lifted her heart. He was determined to be gracious in the face of death. Despite the fact that he was an elder, he had a blade dangling from his left hand and had insisted on fighting with the young warriors. She saw where Kota had gotten his courage.

"He was the best student I ever could have hoped for," Gretis said, responding to the man in his own language.

Keema's smile widened, and he turned back to Kota. "The *messengers* you sent from the Dentha tribe told me you were learning how to write like humans can. You should have sent me a letter, you little shit." He slapped his son's arm, and once more the animus gave no reaction at all.

The trace of a grin appeared on Kota's face. "You can't read, father."

"Then you could come tell me what it said someday," the old man chuckled.

Kota's face constricted. "I'm sorry I didn't send you anything. I'm sorry for bringing all this death on the tribe!"

"What are you *sorry* for?" Keema said, rolling his silver eyes. "Being born? If that is what brought these monsters, then your mother and I are to blame far more than you." He glared at the trees from which the demons were soon to emerge. "You did *nothing* wrong, my son. I see you standing here, ready to face an entire army of the darkest things in this world to protect your people." His gaze grew very intense. "The *courage* of that—the *honor!* I want you to know that you've filled your father's heart with pride, and if I die tonight after seeing my son stand so brave and strong, I'll have had a better life than any man I know."

Kota did not speak for a moment, though the muscles in his throat clenched several times. Gretis knew he held his father in the deepest respect, and these words would mean a great deal to him. Finally, Kota managed to say: "Thank you, father."

Keema sighed up at the stars. "Your mother wouldn't come over with me. She said you'd have to talk to her when the battle is over—well, she *commands* it." He took a few steps back toward the others and said: "I'll do my best to keep her safe. Give those demon bastards every bit of hell you can, my son!"

"I will," Kota said, and a touch of steel had returned to his voice.

Keema nodded and disappeared behind a cluster of spears. Kota watched him in silence. His father's words seemed to have granted him a measure of peace, but it had to battle against an overwhelming sense of doom and responsibility that could not be expunged.

Gretis took a slow breath, then said: "The nathret told you your tribe would be killed to get under your skin—to throw you off balance."

"I know," Kota said in a solemn whisper. "Seeing that does me no good though." He turned and stared into her eyes. "He didn't trigger my animus—even though he was a demon. You know what that means, don't you?"

He had figured it out... all of it... Of course he had. For all of Kota's primal strength, he was a wonderfully intelligent young man. Gretis met his eyes and said: "It means he can slip around you on the battlefield without you even knowing."

"He can kill my whole tribe," Kota said, his voice low and grave. "The spears won't do anything against his demonic sorcery, and once I catch the stink of the more primal demons, I'll go into a frenzy and won't be able to think about protecting anyone."

"And you know *why* he wishes to slaughter your people." It was not a question.

"He understands what I am," Kota said, gazing down at the leaves at his feet. "You've been warning me for years about how dangerous I could become if I ever let myself be consumed by anger. The nathret wants to push me to such rage that even if I survive the onslaught of demons, I'll lose myself." Kota raised his right hand in front of his face and gave a little flick of his fingers. The hooked claws appeared instantly, warping out from his nails into sharp talons. "If he can make me into a feral beast, his kind won't have to worry about me anymore. I'll cause such a ruckus that the Starborn will come—my old friend, Cassian, and perhaps his brothers and sister. They'll kill me. They'll have to."

"Kota looked up at her again, and there was pain in his silver eyes as he gestured to the caves and said: "I want you to promise me you'll protect them—*not me*—when the time comes."

Gretis felt her throat constrict. *This was all wrong.* "Kota, you cannot fight an entire army of demons on your own."

"I have to try," he said through clenched teeth.

Gretis could not speak just then. It was impossible to tell him that his life was worth more than that of his tribe, *but it was...* He was meant to fight in the apocalypse—to stand between the darkness and the light in the most important battle the world would ever see, yet he had been manipulated into certain death through his love for the people who raised him. Kota's life would end this night because... *he was such a good man.* Gretis felt as though her heart were going to burst from her chest.

"I know you're burning to tell me to flee," he said. "I thank you for not saying it." He swallowed. "You've always been so kind to me."

A pair of tears welled up in Gretis's eyes. "I was horrible to you in the early years."

"Never," Kota said, grinning his wonderful smile. "I loved every minute of our training." He started to say something else, but then his eyes widened. He turned toward the forest, his right hand dropping smoothly to the hilt of his sword. "*They're coming,*" he whispered.

Gretis shook her head, whipping the tears from her face. She could not yet feel the demons approaching as Kota could, but if he said the enemy was coming, then they were. After a few tense heartbeats, she heard the sound of crunching and snapping in the distance—the noise of a large group crashing through the forest. As she slid her sword out of its hilt, some part of her mind flashed to the last moments of her childhood, when the Denigoth army was approaching the edge of her city.

"*They will not be able to breach our walls,"* her father had assured her in a voice that had almost seemed calm. They were the last words he had ever spoken to her. Shortly thereafter, the horrible slaughter began upon her beautiful, tranquil home. The shamalak behind her had far less protection than her own people had had, and the enemy coming was far crueler.

Just as Gretis began to sink into despair, she felt the energy of Kota's animus burn like roaring fire in defiance of the demon horde. She turned and glanced at him. His lips were curled back, bearing his fangs that seemed thicker and longer than they had only a moment before. Veins stood up on his neck, around his eyes, and his limbs were trembling with dangerous excitement. Each breath he took was like the rumbling growl of a forest cat. *He had not given up!* Kota's spirit had come alive, and it would fight with everything that it was. This was the truest courage she had ever witnessed, and she found it stoked the flames in her own soul. She turned back toward the wall of trees, gripping her weapon and seeing that perhaps the fierce pounding of her heart was something to be embraced. *This would be the fight of her life!*

The first wave came then. Six demons in black armor with gray, tiger-like faces emerged from the trees, their eyes glowing blood red. Kota bolted at them instantly, kicking up a spray of dirt. In the blink of an eye, he came at the foremost of the demons, which had an ebony-black blade raised over its head. The sword came at Kota, and his own sword knocked it to the side with enough force to throw the demon to the left. Without hesitation, he delivered a diagonal slash, slicing the creature it in two at the navel. *The young warrior was moving so fast!* Before his first victim had hit the ground, he had knocked away another ebony blade and cleaved the head off the second closest enemy with a one-handed slash while his opposite hand brought up a dagger behind his back and blocked the edge of a battle ax. Kota whirled on this attacker, slicing through both its legs just above the knees. The demon let out a scream as Kota kicked its dismembered body at two of its comrades, knocking them off balance. With a snarl he whipped at the three of them, silver blade moving so fast it could only be seen in glints of light. Gretis ran forward to cover his back, gaping at what she was seeing. *Kota was a hurricane of steel and death!* Demon limbs flew sloshing about in the air.

By the time she got to him, the blur of motion had ended, and Kota stood over the creatures, his face and chest dripping with their dark blood. He turned and looked at her, and she could swear his silver eyes were glowing in the darkness. He raised his sword and pointed it back toward the caves and managed to snarl out a single word: "PROTECT!"

Gretis sensed motion from the right and turned to see a battle ax spinning directly at her. Kota moved into its path in a blur and caught the thing by the handle with his left hand. He glanced back over his shoulder and growled: "GO!" so loud that his voice resonated in her bones.

She turned back toward the caves and saw, with horror, that a few of the tiger-faced-monsters had moved around them. Arrows were flying from the archers in the trees. One struck a demon in the shoulder. The monster snarled and tore the projectile away, and then started bounding straight for its source. Gretis broke into a desperate run. Behind her, she heard roars and screams and the sound of metal meeting metal with incomprehensible force, but none of that could be allowed to matter at the moment. *She had her target.*

As Gretis whipped over the wet grass, her hand moved to the grip on one of the daggers pocketed in her vest. She yanked it free and then called upon her animus to feel out the trajectory, angle, and distance, and then execute a precise throw. The blade whistled from her fingers and struck the base of the creature's skull an instant later, burying itself up to the hilt. Her victim stumbled forward mid-bound and began to gyrate and thrash upon the ground. Supernatural though the demon was, its flesh still obeyed many physiological principals, and she had just sliced directly into the connection between its brain and the rest of its body.

Gretis sprang over the battlefield and came upon the creature, watching it jerk for half a heartbeat before she focused the energy of her animus into her sword. There was a swell of power in the metal, and perhaps a high-pitched whine as she slashed through the steel-hard bones of the neck. With a black spray, the head rolled free of the body.

There was no time to savor victory. Enemies were everywhere. Gretis glared around and saw at least ten of the snarling monsters coming at her in the night, eyes burning red. Their beastly faces displayed nothing but hatred and bloodlust. Three were coming from the right, two from the left, and five head-on. They let out monstrous roars as they raised their black weapons.

I die then... The words whispered up from the pit of her soul, yet just as they did, she heard a grizzly crunching sound behind her followed immediately by an ear-splitting scream that could only have been emitted from the throat of one of these tiger-demons, and she felt a wild grin touch her face. *Kota was still alive, and he was fighting on!* She slid her sword back into its scabbard and ran her hands up the front of her vest, drawing a throwing knife between each of her fingers in smooth, fluid motion. Then Gretis shut her eyes and gave her body over to her animus. It had no fear at all, even now. The ancient spirit simply perceived the oncoming threats and reacted. Her left hand flicked, and the first blade flew away. She felt but did not see the dagger spin in the air and burry itself in the eye socket of the nearest beast.

The battle grew more chaotic by the second. A sword came slashing from behind, and Gretis's leaped upward, her feet barely clearing the ark. She somersaulted over several of her attackers' heads and came to a smooth drop behind them. *Move faster!* She rose in a whirl, each of her hands sent a dagger flying. One took a demon in the back of the knee while the second sank into the base of a particularly large demon's neck. This one dropped to the ground, already convulsing.

"Is that the best you can do?" she shouted. It was a damned fool thing to say, but her blood was running hot in her veins.

Almost immediately, a chilling answer came as a psychic hiss in her mind: <Oh no, foolish wretch, we can do far, far, *far* better.> It was the voice of the nathret.

Gretis suddenly detected a swell of corrupt energy far beyond that of the creatures around her. It was above her. Time almost seemed to slow as she looked up and saw the utterly titanic horror descending from the night sky.

"Oh gods," she rasped, the words spilling from her without thought. The tiger-like giant was bigger than Rakathon had been—*much bigger!* It floated down on wings that blotted out sections of the stars. The clawed feet touched almost gracefully down on the grass perhaps a dozen paces in front of Gretis, and the creature cast its burning red gaze down at her. She thought she saw a vague amusement as the black lips drew back, revealing teeth that could rip away the top third of her body in a single bite.

There was no point in trying to fight such an enemy, nor even to run, and perhaps the Archdemon had a strange power to keep her from acting, for she stood transfixed as it drew a sword that seemed sufficient to knock in a castle wall and cocked it back for a strike.

A roar so loud it shook Gretis's bones erupted across the battlefield. The monstrous fiend turned its head, as did Gretis. Kota stood amidst a sea of eviscerated demons, sword raised. His eyes glowed unmistakably now in a brilliant silver-blue that lit up the night around him, bathing the remains of his victims. Gretis gaped. *How many had he managed to kill in the last few moments! Thirty? Forty?*

The Archdemon covered the thirty paces between itself and Kota in two quick strides, raising its blade to answer Kota's challenge. *No!* Gretis screamed inside. Kota stood possessed by his animus, unable to turn away from a foe that hopelessly outmatched him. A memory flashed of the moment Gretis had tried to parry a single slash from the Demon Lord Rakathon and was hurled back into a tree so hard her spine had nearly broken. *The creature rushing at Kota was far stronger than that!*

Gretis stared in horror as the Archdemon cocked back its massive weapon and brought it down in a diagonal slash. Kota swung his sword in response. The two blades clashed, and the sound was something like thunder congealed with an avalanche of heavy stone all focused into one great 'CLANG' that jolted every bone in Gretis's body. Yet... to her utter bewilderment... the tremendous ebony blade was knocked back.

The Archdemon's features seemed to take on a look of shock. Gretis could hardly wrap her mind around what she had just seen. Even if Kota could match the incalculable strength of the monster before him, his body—so much lighter and smaller—should have been knocked to the side like a hard-kicked pinecone. *Could his animus somehow root his form to the ground?* And as she rolled this in her mind, it also registered that the heavy weapon the demon brandished would have had far more inertia than Kota's human-sized sword, and to counter that force, Kota would have had to swing with even greater strength! *Was that even possible?*

A second diagonal slash from the Archdemon's sword came immediately, and Kota knocked it away with another explosive block, and then his left hand moved in a blur to his belt and whipped back out toward his opponent. A dagger flew into the monster's neck so fast that the handle disappeared within the fur. There was a gurgled roar of pain, and then the Demon Lord made a low sweep with its sword. Kota leaped up fully above the creature's head, and he hurled a second dagger which struck somewhere in the thing's shoulder. The Archdemon roared and slashed, and Kota managed to block the tremendous blade once more, but this time his body went sailing through the air. He disappeared into the darkness of the forest, and Gretis heard several loud cracks like the sound of tree limbs snapping.

"No!" she shrieked as the Archdemon let out a triumphant cackle and dropped to all four paws on the ground, facing the direction Kota had been thrown. It somehow kept a grip on its sword as ghastly black claws bit into the dirt. Then the monster arched its spine and charged toward the trees.

A boulder *the size of a cow* flew out of the forest and struck the Demon Lord in the face, resulting in an explosion of crag and dust that managed to knock it fully onto its back. Kota sprang from the trees in a magnificent arching leap and landed on the monster's chest, thrusting his sword deep into the sternum. The thick metal armor that covered his enemy's torso seemed to mean nothing to his strength, for he yanked his weapon out and then stabbed again, then again, then again, burying the blade to the hilt each time. The Archdemon gurgled out cries of pain as black blood spurted up from its wounds, and Kota continued to hack and stab. He cut his way up the chest and then raised his weapon up over the throat. Gretis felt raw spiritual energy gather in the sword and the blade erupted in blue fire.

A bolt of lightning came from somewhere in the darkness and struck Kota in the chest with *PFFT* sound that sent him tumbling over the wet grass toward the caves. Gretis let out a scream and bolted across the battlefield toward him. Fear set her animus afire, and she moved so fast that the world around her blurred. Even so, she registered the dark smoke that was puffing off Kota's scorched chest. He had burned away too much of his animus's power in the fight. *It had not been able to protect him.*

As fast as Gretis was moving, the surrounding demons got to her pupil first. He rose just as a black arrow struck his shoulder. It ripped through his flesh and came out the other side. Kota roared and stumbled back. One of the lesser demons rushed at him, leaping and bringing its sword down at his skull. He managed to bat the attack away and slice the creature in half at the waist, but a second enemy came from behind. Kota whirled, but too slowly, and a lateral slash bit into the side of his right leg.

"BASTARD!" Gretis screamed, coming upon the demon and hacking open its stomach. Before it could even stumble back, she had its head off. Blood spattered on her skin as she turned to face more of them. *Kota's life must be saved!* Gretis was ready to fight and die to protect him. Still, her animus-sense detected leaking blood from multiple points on his body, and there were so many enemies left. Her eyes panned across the battlefield. The Archdemon was slowly rising from the grass. The black blood that had been gushing out only a brief moment before now barely trickled.

"You could never have won," a cruel voice said from her left. Gretis cocked her head and saw the nathret standing only a dozen paces away, his right hand raised in front of him, palm up, as an orb of green fire the size of a head floated above it. He cast her a smile bathed in emerald light and said: "I offer you your life, Sansrit witch. All you need do is kill the vermin behind you. Just cut his throat."

Gretis grunted in anger and flung a knife at the nathret's chest. In an almost relaxed motion, he gestured with his left hand, and the dagger altered course into the side of the mountain. She gritted her teeth, then hissed: "You and I in single combat. Let us fight to the death."

"You wish to purchase that shamalak a few extra moments of life?" the nathret laughed. "Why? Why die for him?"

Because I love him more than my own son, Gretis thought. She said nothing though but took a step toward. "Face me!"

The nathret grinned. "You silly little wretch. I have no honor upon which you can play. You have already shown me how quickly you can move. What reason would I have to let you dance around my magic when it is so much easier to make you come to me?" He raised his right hand, and the blazing green orb he had manifested rose with it, seeming to aim at the mouth of a cave. "Come!" he shouted, and ten of the tiger-demons rushed immediately to his side. "If she moves to attack me, cut her down, and then the *warrior* behind her." The nathret gestured toward the cave mouth with his eyes and said: "There are thirteen vermin children back there. Shall we see what their flesh smells like when it burns?"

"I'm sorry, Kota," Gretis hissed through her teeth, "It was an honor to be your teacher!" She sprang at the cluster of demons before her, weapon raised, knowing that this was the last moment of her life.

Her leap was cut abruptly short, and she was forced back down to her feet by a hand on her shoulder from behind—*Kota's hand.* Gretis glanced back and saw him with eyes shut, his head lowered. Then she felt a surge of energy. It was strange... like communing with the spirits. *What was he doing?* The feeling was subtle at first, but then... Gretis gasped aloud as she felt a doorway to the spirit world rip open—no, *dozens* of doorways! They were all around, and as they opened, power came rushing out.

A chorus of roars erupted from the caves. Gretis perceived a swell of motion within accompanied by power. *What was happening? What had Kota done?* At least a dozen shamalak came rushing out of the cave nearest her. Three of them had swords, five of them had taken spears from the cave floor, and the rest simply had claws extended, and... *every single one of them had an animus blazing inside!* They rushed at the cluster of demons before Gretis in a frenzy, stabbing and hacking and slashing with wild preternatural speed.

"STOP!" the Nathret shrieked as five of his brethren fell to the mob. The attack had been too unexpected and come on too quickly even for preternatural demons. A second wave of animus-driven shamalak emerged from the caves on the heels of the first. They did not emit the kind of energy that Kota did—in fact, most of them were well below Gretis in power—but there were dozens upon dozens of them all rushing forward in a mad bloodlust. Gretis cast another look back at Kota. He continued to grip her, eyes shut, his breathing deep and hard. He was the vortex of all this spiritual power.

Arrows flew at the nathret from behind. He whirled around and whipped them away with a quick wave of his hand, but as he did, three shamalak children, no more than twelve at the oldest, leaped on him. One sank its claws into his shoulders and bit the side of his neck. Another drove a spear into his left thigh, while a third simply clawed wildly at his ribs.

"GYAHH!!" the demon sorcerer screamed. "How DARE you!" He shut his eyes and began to hiss out a spell.

Kota's grip loosened on Gretis's shoulder, as if granting her leave to act. She pulled free and dashed at the nathret. He opened his pale eyes suddenly, finishing his conjuration, and an explosion of emerald magic burst from his form in every direction. The shamalak children were flung away. His power hit Gretis as well—an expanding wall of concussive force—but the animus within her met it and tore through. She came out the other side she slashed into the horrid man's stomach so deep she felt the blade knick his spine. The sorcerer let out a gurgling squeal, and his eyes went deathly wide. Gretis glared at him for a brief instant, and then she swung her blade a second time. His head came away with surprising ease.

The shamalak children, having already recovered from the telekinetic blast, grinned up at her, frenzied growls escaping through their teeth. They seemed to understand she was an ally, or perhaps... *one of their pack.*

Still more shamalak rushed from the caves. *There was an army!* Men, women, and children took up spears and rushed the few remaining demons strewn about the battlefield, moving with preternatural speed. Gretis watched one tiger-faced demon bat away three of the pointed ends only to be impaled by five more.

She turned back to Kota. *He was gone*. Gretis whirled, her eyes instinctively falling on the Archdemon. She just managed to see Kota knock away a swing of the leader's tremendous sword as twenty or so shamalak came snarling in. Most leaped at the titanic monster from behind, hacking and stabbing at the back of his legs, while others clawed their way up his body and began to bite and slash at the sinew of his neck. The Archdemon shrieked in agony and fell to one knee. Kota sprang forward—the arrow still sticking out of his shoulder—and swung his blade. The Archdemon's head ripped off onto the grass, and Gretis breathed a great sigh of relief.

Kota fell back down to his knees, gasping. His eyes lost all of their luminescence immediately, and he began to wheeze. Gretis sprinted to him, her mind already shifting from role of warrior to healer. "Don't try to move!" she shouted.

"Holy Gods this hurts!" He reached up for the arrow in his chest.

"NO!" Gretis snapped, slapping his hand. He glared up at her, and the irritation in his eyes—*rather than dying agony*—came as a wonderful relief. "I'll get the arrow out of you," she said in a softer voice, and as she spoke her animus detected something—a diminishing of power from all around. The shamalak around her were returning to themselves, the primal spirits within them vanishing back into the spirit world. Some of them were staring at their own blood-soaked claws in wonder, while others murmured whispers of confusion to one another. *They were not Sansrit Masters.* What Kota had done was incredible, but it seemed it could only be sustained for a few precious moments.

"There are other injuries," Kota rasped. "See to them before me."

Gretis swept the field of battle with her eyes. A few shamalak had sustained cuts and bruises, but somehow... it seemed that not a single one of them lay dead. Their attack had been so unanticipated and so quick and decisive that even their injuries seemed minimal. She turned back to Kota. "No one is gushing blood, and your people are remarkably resilient to infection. *You* have a gods-damned arrow through your chest. I will see to you first."

Kota cocked his head up at her, a scowl on his black-soaked face, but Gretis only smiled at him. *He was alive!* It had seemed certain just a few moments before that her wonderful pupil would die a brutal death. Her throat caught, and a pair of tears formed in her eyes. When Kota saw this, his face lost all of its severity, and he pressed his lips together.

"You saved everyone," she whispered. "How did you do it—open all those doorways?"

Kota shrugged then winced at the pain it caused him. "I have no idea," he rasped. "I didn't even know what I was doing. My animus... parts of it I'd never felt before came alive in the presence of the Archdemon."

Gretis gazed at the arrow tip protruding from the back of Kota's shoulder. If he were a normal mortal, he would be leaking a great deal of blood, but there was not even a trickle. The gash in his leg was similarly vacant of fluid. That was fascinating. His wounds had been inflicted by demons, and the terrible psychic residue of attacks from things so evil interfered with an animus's ability to heal flesh, but Kota had the most powerful animus in the world. If it could do this much, then perhaps, with deep meditation, it might also be able to restore his damaged tissue.

“You did well, young warrior,” Gretis whispered.

Kota gazed at members of his tribe, many of whom were staring at him with looks of wonder in their silver eyes. "This could have been a massacre," he said in a somber voice, staring with a contemplative look. "An Onkai search party should arrive here within a week or so to find their... *fallen brothers.* I'm going to ask them to help me protect and hide my tribe."

"How would they do that?" Gretis asked, frowning.

"I want to take all of the Nakawa back to Temple Town with us."

"Ah," Gretis murmured, imagining how the townspeople would react to an entire tribe of shamalak amongst them. There would be panic and anger. It had taken the simple folk years to grow used to Kota, and he had been a kind, humble boy who spoke Tethric passably well and was quick to assimilate to human culture. An entire tribe of bronze-skinned, silver-eyed people who only spoke an incomprehensible tongue and did not worship the gods... *that might be a very different matter.* "How will you convince Otho to accept this?"

"Well for one, I'll show him the Archdemon I killed," Kota said, gesturing with his still good arm to the tremendous corpse on the ground and its accompanying head. "Hopefully that will convince him that I'm worth something to the order as an ally—enough to pay a bit of a price."

"You wish to reveal yourself then?" Gretis said, raising an eyebrow. "Otho would no longer be able to keep your secret. He would have to explain to the order and the town folk *why* they must welcome a strange people."

"My anonymity is far less important than their lives," Kota said. "If the tribe isn't protected, this will happen again... to get to *me.* I cannot stay here and watch over them indefinitely." He sighed. "As you like to remind me, I have a *destiny.* This is a reasonable bargain for Otho if I can kill powerful Demon Lords for him."

"You have a point," Gretis said.

Kota grunted and rose to his feet. "We should meet with the Starborn as well and tell them what has happened here. I think Cassian might see me—if he still remembers me at this point."

"Yes," Gretis whispered, and her mind returned as it had many times before to the pieces of the prophecy she had not revealed to Kota—the parts that almost certainly pertained to Cassian Asango, *The Destroyer.* She could not conceal this dark secret from her apprentice much longer. *Perhaps she had waited too long already...*

Kota blinked, then looked sharply at her as if he had just remembered something. "Is the nathret dead?"

"Yes, quite dead."

"Good," he whispered. He reached up and rubbed his right temple with his fingers. "What was he talking to you about this morning anyhow? Who is... *Iona*?"

Gretis's stomach tensed at the name, remembering suddenly that the holy child had been stolen away. Kota gazed at her, expecting an answer, and she longed to give him one. Livia's letter had been carefully worded, but it seemed to imply Nemesai involvement—an obstacle far too great for nearly anyone to overcome, *but not for Kota.* It would be so easy to convince him to help, noble young man that he was. But... the Norn's warning about Iona lingered in her mind: *You may do nothing to help her. If you try, you will only bring disaster.*

"She is—" Gretis hesitated, feeling a flutter in her heart.

"KOTA!" a deep, feminine voice cried from the left.

They both turned to see Kota's mother marching through the crowd. She was utterly covered in black blood. The old shamalak woman seemed to have wiped a great deal from her face, but smears remained around her mouth. *She had attacked with claws and teeth,* like the most feral of the tribe.

"How bad are your wounds?" the woman shouted in her native tongue, her voice fierce.

"I will live, mother," Kota shouted back.

The woman dashed to her son. There were still bits of flesh caught in her claws as she knelt down. "You have an *arrow* through your body!"

"It is fine," Kota whispered. "My spirit will heal me."

His mother stared at the wound a moment longer, and then gazed around at the tribesmen that surrounded them. "What... happened to us?" she asked in a distant voice.

"The Grandfather Spirit," Kota said back in a soft whisper, the shamalak words rolling off his tongue with reverence. "He helped me save the tribe."

"Nataka," his mother said, blinking, "he is in you?"

"There is... much I want to tell you, mother," Kota wheezed.

The woman peered at him and then her silver eyes moved to Gretis. "You're not going to leave that arrow in him, are you?" There almost seemed to be accusation in her voice. "I had heard you were something of a healer."

"Of course not," Gretis answered, more than a little relieved at the change of subject.

"What an ugly wound," the woman grunted, and then she cast another look around. "I want to help. Tell me what to do."

"Alright then," Gretis said, her mind aligning to the task at hand. "I stowed most of my supplies in the center-most of the caves. Please have someone bring them to me. Assign someone else to start a fire and boil water. I'll need light, so either start a fire or bring me torches. Have the wounded sit together in a group and do your best to arrange them from most injured to least."

Kota's mother drew in a sharp breath, then nodded and turned back to her people and began to call out orders like a military commander. Her husband—Kota's father—was helping an elder to his feet. He watched his wife out of the corner of his eye with an expression of pride, and perhaps amusement. Gretis noticed Kota was watching her with the same look, and she felt her heart lighten just a little. There was anxiety around every corner, but this was a good moment. Kota had done the impossible, and he had done it out of love for his family and his people. Did that not prove that there was hope left in the world? Did it not prove that the forces of good were worth believing in?

CHAPTER 30: HIS MOST HATED ENEMY

Cassian gazed at his reflection in the gleaming hand-mirror the palace servants had left on his side table. He was sitting on the edge of his bed with his pants draped to his waist, the upper half of his body uncovered. The morning light was just beginning to flow in through his open window, illuminating his features unevenly so that parts of his face were in shadow. He stared into his own eyes. They were hard, fierce eyes—a little too devoid of... *something*. He had not gazed at his reflection the whole time he had been in military command, and finally doing so made him feel *reflective*. There was a pervading sadness that ached from deep inside. What was it? What in particular of the countless regrets he had stuffed away was now tugging at his heart? Cassian had long since made the decision to bear all the pain his journey cost him. There were moments though, once in a great while, when he wondered if the price had been too great.

Dimitris...

Cassian turned as he felt Soulic begin to stir from the antechamber just outside his door. The obnoxious bastard would come in in a moment. Cassian stood and pulled his tunic over his chest just as Soulic muttered through the door: "Has thy most regal, arrogant self deigned to awaken yet?"

Cassian felt the faintest traces of a smile play across his face as he answered: "He has." Soulic was proving to be a fine squire for many reasons. Cassian had long suffered irritation at how his servants endlessly praised him and scraped for his approval, but no such problem existed here. "Did the attendants bring tea?"

The door shot open, and Soulic entered, a tired look on his face. "Yes," he grunted, tilting his head from side to side and eliciting several loud pops from his neck. The man ambled over, carrying a steaming ceramic teapot and a cup on top of a tray in his hands. "I had a few sips and I'm still alive, so if they poisoned it, they're using something slow."

"Flirting with suicide, are you?" Cassian yawned.

"Slavery can drive a man to such things," Soulic muttered as he set the tray down on Cassian's side table. "Shall I pour you a cup, *my lord*?" The touch of venom in his voice was measured, amounting to sarcasm rather than open hostility. The Sansrit warrior's animus had somehow protected his mind from the full scope of Cassian's psychic control, leaving him enough free will to speak his mind however he pleased.

"No," Cassian said, rising and stepping to the side table. He reached down and poured himself a cup of tea and brought it to his lips. If there were poison or sedatives in the concoction, as there had been in many drinks and meals Cassian had been served over the years, he could counter the effects with healing spells long enough to analyze the foreign alchemical compounds and then break them down. The tea was still hot and had a bitter taste to it, and after several sips, Cassian felt his mind sharpen. "You came in late last night. Who were you this time?"

"An old lady," Soulic sighed. He had knelt down on the stone floor and commenced to polish his boots with a brush. It was a bit unorthodox to do such a thing in the presence of a high-ranking lord of course, but Cassian did not mind. If nothing else, his murderous new companion kept himself impeccably clean and well dressed, which was a subtle communication of high standards to the rest of the imperial court. "I overheard new rumors about you. The Nemesai have put forth claims that you worship demons in this tower, and that you and I are lovers."

Cassian laughed aloud. "At least they are conducting themselves with a modicum of class."

"I actually overheard several conversations on the second point," Soulic said with an eye roll. "Each one involved a question about why you still aren't married or even engaged." He cocked his head at Cassian. "I am a bit curious myself why you have not chosen a bride. Surely you could have your pick of nigh any maiden in the empire."

Cassian gazed down and said in a quiet voice: "I can bear their rumors." He did not care to explain his feelings to Soulic, but the thought of marriage to anyone other than Thalice sickened him. His bond to her ran deeper than perhaps any human could understand. Still, his people would expect him to marry eventually. Offers of betrothal from the most powerful families in the empire had been coming in for years. *Was it time*?

He turned to Soulic. "Anything else to report?" There was a touch of hesitation, and Cassian sensed a psychic struggle in his servant's mind. *Soulic was trying to hide something.* Cassian sharpened his voice and said: "Answer me."

The Sansrit warrior stiffened, drawing in a sharp breath through his nose before hissing: "I *may have*... stumbled upon a handful of Nemesai slapping around a woman accused of prostitution in the street." He grimaced. "They utilized their normal vocabulary of *whore* and *slut* and proclaimed they were going to stone her to death. I... *may have* picked up a stone myself and..." he drew in a second deep breath and then muttered: "I kept the beating mostly to their arms and legs. They're still alive."

Cassian rolled his eyes, wondering if he needed to focus harder on restricting the man's free will. "Did anyone see?"

"Possibly," Soulic said with a shrug. "I changed images a few times before I came back though—in discrete hiding places of course."

Cassian shut his eyes and forced himself to say in an even voice: "Did you attack them as the old woman?"

"Yeah," Soulic chuckled. "Shocked the hell out of them."

"Almost everyone in the empire knows I have an Elokien," Cassian said with a sigh of irritation. "Perhaps you can imagine that a decrepit old woman strong enough to overpower a pair of tattooed Nemesai, who happens to have appeared shortly after I arrive in the capital, might bring a bit of suspicion my way?"

Soulic raised his right eyebrow. "Would you have me let them assault that poor girl? You did not see them—the way they were grinning as they beat her." His expression flashed to something dangerous as he added: "The religious condemnations were nonsense. It was an excuse to put their hands on a pretty girl and scare the hell out of her. Probably made them feel *powerful."*

"You are quite possibly correct," Cassian said, forming his fingers into a steeple in front of his chest. "On one hand, I am happy to see *any* Nemesai denied their self-righteous bullying. On the other though," Cassian raised his right hand and reached an invisible tendril of magic through the air. He felt for the metallic shape that dangled within Soulic's silken shirt and gave it a sharp, precise yank. The Elokien burst through the buttons and cloth and flew directly into Cassian's palm. He closed his fingers around it and said: "Beating men half to death—even cruel men—is a crude and unintelligent answer to the problems in this empire, and I will not have you running around making these decisions as *you* see fit."

Soulic glared, and Cassian sensed the violent anger within the man boiling up. "What would *You* have done?!" he snarled.

"Me? I would have used my mental powers to make the men feel a nauseating revulsion at what they were doing, and I would accomplish this without their knowing I was anywhere near them."

"I'm not a telepath."

"Nor are you discrete, or really very thoughtful when it comes to these matters. For the time being, you are not permitted to traverse the capital streets at night."

For a moment, Soulic stared at him with a look of pure hatred, but then, remarkably, the expression shifted to that of a dark grin, and the Sansrit warrior chuckled. "For all your talk, you'd rather do it the way I did it, wouldn't you? I can see it in your eyes. They *deserve* what they got." He tapped his right temple with two fingers and said: "Why don't you take a look inside? I don't mind. You can see how good it felt to beat the shite out of those bullies—to see their cruel smiles turn to terror."

"A kind offer," Cassian said, rolling his eyes and rising. It was true that the notion of simply stopping the Nemesai by force had entered his thoughts many, many times over the years, but such action would draw sympathy for his enemies from the people—perhaps even garner them support. He would end the Nemesai reign in a way that left their order forever gone from the world, and that required patience and calculation.

"You can take my Elokien," Soulic muttered as he slipped on his boots, "but if I see a man hurting a woman, I'm gonna hurt him. That's the way it is, *My Lord*."

"Hmm," Cassian grunted. He had studied his companion's mind enough to know that Soulic had a limitless hatred for men who put their hands on women. This was due to the assault on his mother, which Cassian—at least to an extent—could respect. He decided to drop the matter for the time being.

Cassian finished dressing in silence and then said: "Let us go and get some breakfast. There is a great deal to be done today." The two of them left his room and walked down the winding stone stairway and then down a long hall toward the castle's main dining hall. When he drew near to the vast chamber, he sensed something... *wrong*. Soulic too seemed to detect something, for his hand was on the hilt of his sword, and he was glaring at the thick wooden doors ahead of them. Cassian focused his senses and attempted to decipher the odd feeling.

This time of morning, the dining hall should have been bustling with people, but there was no great sea of thought and emotion through the doors. There was... *coldness...* It took Cassian a moment to associate the feeling, but when he did, he realized he was detecting the emperor's craith soldiers—many of them. Craith minds possessed no errant thought at all, but only an emotionless and mechanical drive to carry out orders. Cassian wondered why so many of them had been summoned to the mess hall, and then he sensed two additional minds within the room that he had felt before, years ago. They belonged to Bishop Cromlic, and Prince Arkas.

The doors flew open quite suddenly, and Cromlic stood at the center of the dining gall amidst a small ocean of armored craith. There was a dangerous eagerness on his face. Cassian stared back. He had not come into contact with the Bishop since that now infamous day nearly seven years ago when Cassian had defeated the Nemesai force in his village and laid a curse upon the man's mind. Arkas stood to the side, his face pale and sweating. Unlike the bishop, Arkas's fractured mind could not wholly conceal its emotions from Cassian's perception, and it was emitting something like... excitement.

"Good morning, Lord Cassian," Cromlic shouted in a voice that radiated confidence.

"What is this?" Soulic whispered, glaring about at the dozens upon dozens of craith throughout the room.

"I wonder that myself," Cassian said. He stepped forward into the chamber, refusing to show fear. Craith served the emperor, not the church. The most likely reason they were here was to prevent a conflict erupting between the Bishop and himself. *Why?* Did the disgusting old man have some new atrocity to reveal—something he seemed bursting at the seams to say? Whatever it was, Cassian was not afraid to hear it.

Soulic moved into the dining hall along with him, driven by an irresistible compulsion to protect Cassian's life, yet as he did, he whispered in a low hiss: "You're out of your mind walking in here."

With a cordial smile, Cromlic gestured to two steaming plates on the table to the right of him. "We ordered the staff to make you eggs and bacon. I heard that was what you usually ask for."

"He has something dangerous planned," Soulic whispered.

Cassian glanced briefly around the room. The craith were positioned in a wide square around the two men, standing perfectly still and straight, arms at their sides. He could not read either of his opponents' minds—at least not immediately.

"You seem to have gone to a great deal of trouble for this meeting," Cassian said, gesturing around.

"It was no trouble for *you,*" the Bishop said.

"We should leave," Soulic whispered.

"Why are you here?" Cassian said, drawing nearer to the table.

"So brisk and direct," Cromlic said, the sides of his mouth curling up and revealing yellowed, almost green teeth. He gestured to the bench across from him and said: "Won't you sit?"

"I cannot think of two people in all the world with whom I would find it so repugnant to eat," Cassian said, staring into Arkas's eyes, and then into the Bishop's. *What were they hiding?*

"That is disappointing," Cromlic said, and he waved his hand. The table between them slid to the left clearing a path. He moved toward Cassian, his eyes blazing with dangerous confidence. "Food or no food, heretic, you and I have a matter of extreme importance to discuss."

Soulic slid his sword halfway out of its scabbard, and as soon as it did the Craith in the room moved closer, every one of them setting a hand on the hilt of his weapon.

"Calm down," Cassian said, pressing the back of his hand against Soulic's chest. The Sansrit warrior hesitated, but then lowered his sword back into its sheath. The craith remained perfectly still only a short distance away. Cassian looked at

Cromlic and said: "If you have something to say to me, then out with it."

"As you wish," the Bishop said, his cruel smile growing. "Cassian Asango, I charge you with heresy against the gods! After all these years, I give you this one final chance to confess freely."

Cassian blinked. There had to be more to this meeting than another heresy charge. *How could they enforce it?* There was something he did not see yet. To find out, he played along and said: "Confess to what? What are my crimes?"

"The list is quite long. You have spoken direct blasphemy, incited resistance to the holy authority of the church, and defamed an acting bishop."

Cassian was unable to resist responding: "Yes, I did all of those things, and will *continue* to do so."

The Bishop's sneering eyes grew more intense. "Well then, by divine right of Balthar, God of Justice, I arrest you. Seize him!"

At these words, every craith in the room rushed forward. Cassian was so shocked that he barely managed to hiss "Dasak!" A translucent sphere of energy whirled up around him an instant before the first pair of metal gauntlets moved to grab him. They struck against his shield and, when their limbs were knocked back, they yanked silver swords from their scabbards in near perfect unison and came again. To Cassian's left, Soulic was attacked by three craith at once, each slashing at him from a different angle. Soulic moved in a blur, contorting his body and dodging away while managing to hack through the neck of the nearest of his opponents. There was no spray of blood, and the creature gave no reaction to its wound, but only lunged at Soulic just as swiftly a second time. Cassian had only an instant to perceive all of this, for at least twenty of the silent killers ran at him at once from different directions, all with swords raised.

<What is this?!> he telepathically shouted to the Emperor, whom he felt watching at that very moment from far away. No

answer came. Cassian's hand whipped into his pocket and closed around the Elokien he had confiscated from Soulic. He willed the enchantments within both it and the one around his neck to activate, forming a mental picture of what he wished to project. A dozen different phantoms of himself appeared throughout the room while his own image became obfuscated within a cocoon of simulated transparency, essentially rendering him invisible.

The craith were not fooled. They stepped through his projections and continued to rush at him, stabbing at what should have been impossible to perceive. Cassian redoubled his protective spell while telepathically calling to his men, who were in the village outside: <I am under attack in the palace! Come to the dining hall!>

Cassian willed his body to rise above the heads of his enemies, but the six craith closest to him leaped with preternatural speed and delivered a barrage of slashes into his shield. No sooner had the first wave begun to drop to the floor than a second leaped over their heads. Again, weapons slammed with preternatural strength into Cassian's barrier, causing him to strain to hold his defense. He could feel his power draining away by the second, and the craith kept coming.

In the midst of this impossible onslaught, Cassian glared up at the stone ceiling. *If he could blast a hole and soar up through it*—the instant this thought entered his mind, he felt an unearthly swell of energy below him. Six figures in black stood amongst the others holding perfectly still, their heads lowered, and their right hands raised in his direction. Six beams of silvery energy erupted from their palms in a hiss of power and bit into Cassian's shield. Their combined magic crackled against the cocoon, and though his barrier thwarted the beams from striking into his flesh, he felt their deathly magic pulling him back down to the floor.

Liches... There had long been stories of Starborn emperors of the past inducting fallen enemy sorcerers into the ranks of the craith, but Cassian had never believed such beings, after having so much of their humanity stripped away, could still wield magic. *His assumptions had been quite wrong...* The power coming off these undead creatures bit into his shield with shocking strength.

As Cassian's feet were forced to the floor, blades struck his translucent shield over, and over, and over—sometimes three in a second. He was surrounded on all sides. In the midst of this, his eyes fell on Cromlic and Arkas, who were standing very near to one another and chanting. Cassian felt the tingle of electrical energy gathering around them. To his left, Soulic was fighting hard. Several heads and arms of craith lay around him, but the Sansrit warrior was also growing weaker and weaker. Cassian weighed all of this in his mind for an instant, and then he focused upon his two human opponents. *Arkas was closer.*

<Soulic, kill Bishop Cromlic,> he commanded.

Instantly, the Sansrit warrior darted through the cluster of craith he had been fighting and sprang in front of the Bishop. His sword slashed, and Cromlic screamed "Dasak!" in terror. His shield came up just in time to save his head from being cleaved, but Soulic simply attacked again and again. Cassian turned his attention to Arkas, who had an orb of blazing orange light the size of a human head crackling in front of his right hand. *There was so little time to act!* The protective sphere around Cassian's form shimmered white in cascading ripples every time a craith blade struck it, and they were hitting now like raindrops in a storm.

Cassian willed his body forward, not bothering to waste precious time forming a spell but raising his right hand and willing raw magic into a tremendous invisible blade in the air. He whipped his arm and sliced through at least twenty craith in an eye-blink, cutting through their swords, armor, flesh, and bones. He lurched over the dismembered chunks as they hit the floor and came at his true victim.

Arkas shrieked, and his clumsy control over whatever offensive spell he was forming fumbled. Cassian mentally wrestled control of it and willed it back into the little fool's hand. The flashing cloud rebounded, engulfing and burning away outstretched fingers. Arkas let loose an ear-splitting scream and jerked back a charred, smoking stump.

<Die, you horrid little monster!> Cassian telepathically cried as he raised his hand with the death stroke. His *brother* gaped at him with wide eyes and made a sound that sounded remarkably like the squeal of a pig.

There was a crackle in the air, and Cassian felt offensive magic coming at him from six different directions at once. His mind shifted to defense instantly, abandoning the long belated killing of Arkas, *for the moment.* He whirled to face the liches, who held up gauntleted hands in front of their chests. White beams from each of them struck once more into Cassian's protective cocoon with power that had a cold, macabre resonance to it.

As he glared at them, he saw more and more craith charging in through the doorways. *There were hundreds!* Most of them bore swords, but a few here and there raised their hands and joined their lich brothers, sending terrible, unending beams of power to collide with Cassian's dwindling barrier, and he became aware then of how much of his strength he had used, and how little was left.

His soldiers were coming, but at that moment he made a calculation: a massive armed force attempting to enter the imperial palace could not save him. If the Emperor were on the side of Cromlic, which he seemed to be, Cassian's personal guard would be cut down by the palace archers well before they managed to break in. *They would just be throwing their lives away...*

<Why have you betrayed me?!> Cassian's mind shouted to his emperor. Again, no answer came. Dozens upon dozens of craith attacked him from all sides. His shield was struck ten or even twenty times a second by their ghastly black blades. It was too much too fast. He turned and saw a handful of the dark soldiers holding Soulic's limp body up by the shoulders, one

gripping his hair. Cromlic was still alive—in fact the Bishop was casting him a vicious grin.

To hell with it then! The stubborn, defiant part of Cassian's mind cried out. He had only seconds to live, but in those seconds, much could be done. He closed his eyes and whispered: "Arathelmos Kiavass Sorokai!" invoking the names of the darkest and most powerful spectral entities he knew. Years ago, he had invented a spell that would be considered forbidden by any school of magic in the world. *Self-sacrifice*—the exchange of his life for one brilliant instant of destructive power. If he had to die, then his end could at least be spent killing Cromlic and the little wretch Arkas. He had always known it might end like this...

Thalice's face flashed through his mind as he felt the awesome swell of energy begin. *It was good to have been loved.* A smile crossed his face as he put his hands together.

<CASSIAN, STOP!> Emperor Tacitus's psychic voice shouted in his mind.

Cassian hesitated, and the spell, held together only by his will, faltered. He opened his eyes and watched the golden corona of energy between his hands vanish along with the last of his strength, and then the silver blades of the craith finally pierced through his barrier.

They did not kill him. A hundred swords returned to their scabbards as soon as Cassian dropped to his knees, and instead cold, powerful hands took hold of every limb of his body and lifted him to a standing position. One craith stepped in front of him from the sea of black cloth and silver armor with two iron manacles in his hands, each with a deep hole in the side. Cassian knew instantly what these were. He stared without words as the craith clapped the first one and then the other. A second dark figure stepped forward and pulled a black pouch from its belt that moved and twisted. The craith inserted gloved fingers and drew out a hissing, squirming Amanthian leech and brought it to Cassian's right manacle. Almost immediately, he felt its cold, slimy form latch onto his skin, and then the tiny flickers of magic still left inside him began to drain away. When the craith drew another leech and put it on his left manacle, this drain syphoning became even more pronounced.

"This was always your destiny," Cromlic cackled. Cassian shifted his eyes to the old bishop. The man was drunk with victory after so many years. *His grin was sickening.* He leaned in very close to Cassian's face and hissed: "Are you confused, Starborn*?* Do you wonder why the craith would attack you upon my order?"

Cassian said nothing. He was trying to feel for his men, but his psychic senses were painfully dulled. Somewhere behind him, he could hear Arkas sobbing in pain on the floor.

The Bishop's smile broadened, revealing his hideous teeth once again. "As I am certain you know, it was Emperor Coronitus who invented the process by which a man can be turned into a craith." Cromlic cast a sweeping gesture at the black figures that surrounded the two of them, and then he reached forward and grabbed a handful of the hair above Cassian's brow. "Despite all his power, Coronitus was a devout servant of the gods, unlike *you!*" He shook Cassian's head. Cassian continued to stare into the bloodshot eyes as some of the old man's spittle hit his cheek. "Being *wise,*" Cromlic went on, "the great emperor knew he was a mortal and might die at any time or even become incapacitated, and so he gave his craith a secondary directive in their hierarchy of obedience." Cromlic leaned in very close to Cassian's face as he hissed: "So long as the orders did not directly counteract the emperor's own, the bishops of the church were granted power to command the craith." Cromlic leaned in still closer so that Cassian was forced to endure his hot breath. "Coronitus did *not* grant the authority to command his army to the other Starborn, for he understood that such power belongs rightfully to those who have dedicated their LIVES to the CHURCH!" he gave Cassian's head a furious jerk," and not simply to men born with POWER—men who might have no RESPECT for moral responsibility at all."

"Kill him!" Arkas screamed from behind. The little bastard was whimpering in pain as he stumbled into view, clutching the hideous new stump to his chest. "Kill him now!"

Cromlic's eyes widened, and he trembled for an instant, seeming to consider the suggestion, but then wheezed out "I am afraid we cannot oblige you in that just yet, Prince Arkas." His dark eyes shifted to Cassian. "The Nemesai have business with this heretic, but do not worry, his fate from this moment forward will be more terrible than you can imagine."

Cassian could vaguely feel his men now, rallying outside the castle walls, but everything was dull and distant. Soulic was lying on the ground next to him, and it was difficult to tell if the man were alive. *They would both be dead soon.* Cassian drew in a slow breath shutting his eyes and resigning himself. The Emperor had betrayed him, and all was lost, so he gave one final telepathic command to his soldiers outside: <I am taken, and you cannot save me. Execute plan Elyria.>

CHAPTER 31: LIVIA'S SUITOR

Ally in the west,

I have news that I believe will excite you! We recently managed to get closer to Prince Arkas than we ever had before on one of his excursions into the countryside. An agent of ours, inspired by your essay on the doctrines of freedom, volunteered to help. I shall, of course, not name him in this letter, but he is highly skilled at avoiding the perceptions of sorcerers, and, as our intelligence has suggested on previous occasions, the claw-hand-prince seems to be the least adept of this generation's Starborn. Our man was able to follow Arkas to the edge of a large forest hill, where he disappeared into a cluster of trees.

It was not safe to follow further, for it was obvious that the prince's destination lay within, and there have been numerous sightings from travelers in this area of a monstrous creature that looks much like an ogre but wears a thick cloak and wields a tremendous ax. Our agent found quite a few footprints on this hill which he described as: "inhumanly large." He also found a second set of trucks that often accompanied this set. These were small and bare-foot, so of course, they did not match the fine boots Arkas was seen wearing.

Livia felt a swell of excitement seep up through her stomach as she read this last sentence. The tracks had to belong to Iona, though the massive creature that guarded her—what in the world was he? She swallowed and read on:

> *Our agent created a map for you, which you will have noticed I folded in with this note. Prince Arkas stayed upon this hill for two days. In that time, our man glimpsed a hulking figure through the trees here and there but never caught direct sight of it. He heard it several times bounding through the trees at a crunching, thunderous pace. There was also an unnaturally large dog with a strangely shaped face prowling the parimeter, which might well have detected our agent had he not laid a powder of his own concoction over his tracks to mask his scent.*
>
> *We strongly suggest that any course of action be taken while the Starborn is away. Our agent also suggests employing archers, armed soldiers, and sorcerers if possible. An entire trade caravan disappeared in the area several months ago, and our intelligence indicates that the group had more than twenty armed men guarding it. Local authorities ascribed the disappearance to banditry or mutiny among the mercenary guard, but our agent discovered a cluster of long-dead corpses in the forest. I have no desire to fill this letter with gruesome detail, but he said that many of the bodies had been torn apart so horribly that even their skeletal remains were difficult to identify as human.*
>
> *That is all I have for now. You have proven an inspiring figure in our cause. I pray that you tread very carefully. Best of luck,*

Your friend,
--Yellow Dog.

Livia frowned down at the paper. It was ironic that the *'yellow dog'* implored her to be cautious when he—*or she*—was using the prince's name openly and including the map and letter in the same package. *How stupid!* If the envelope had fallen into the wrong hands, then Arkas would almost certainly be notified that he was being followed, which would cause all sorts of problems. Still, the letter had arrived safely, and Livia had nearly everything she needed to finally act. Her hands trembled as she reread the note, studying the description of Iona's jailor over and over. Arkas had an *enormous monster* guarding Iona... *Why?*

Livia was troubled, yet at the same, this letter was the strongest tangible evidence she had acquired that her sister was alive. As she thought on this, her heart swelled so painfully in her chest. She missed the sweet little Iona. What in the hell were Arkas and this creature doing to her?

Livia slowly folded the note, handling the paper as if it were something holy. She knew she would read it many, many more times, as was her practice with all the notes and scraps of information she had managed to acquire on Prince Arkas's movements. It was enormously dangerous to keep such documents anywhere near her. The words in this letter alone were more than enough to justify her execution. Once she had memorized every line and taken careful notes, selecting out keywords while keeping her notations vague and inscrutable, she would burn this letter. That would likely take three or four days.

Livia gazed over at the back door to her office. The morning light was just beginning to show in through the edges. She would need to prep the shop for the day and then go and cook breakfast for Hervin and herself. The two of them had been financially well-off over the last year—especially given the absence of the cow and her expensive wine habit—but Livia had abstained from hiring additional help. Every spare dessek was saved to secret stashes in preparation for hiring mercenaries if her attempts to elicit help from Cassian Asango failed. Livia still had not managed to make contact with anyone in Asango's inner circle, and without an introduction, she was just some mute girl trying for a one-on-one meeting with the future ruler of Denigoth. It could be suicide to announce herself as the 'Slave of the West' who had been mass-producing seditious and even heretical pamphlets, though that might be her only chance.

There was a sudden knock at the door, and by reflex Livia bent down, her hands darting to the removable floorboard beneath her desk where she kept dangerous documents. Like herself, this hiding place was quite silent, with the wood carefully whittled to be thinner than its brother pieces except at the very top where it caught between them. She slipped the note amidst a few other scraps of documentation and was on her feet facing the door within a single heartbeat, years of experience with the cow having taught her proper habits of secrecy.

Livia walked to the back entrance to the shop and lifted the small bar holding the door shut. As the dense wooden mass creaked open, she blinked at the sight of Simius, the noble-born sorcerer who had somewhat aggressively flirted with her a week before. He stared through the crack at her, a grin on his handsome face.

"Livia!" he exclaimed. "I've missed you. May I come in?"

She said nothing. It was troubling that he had come. She had hoped that her note had dissuaded him from further romantic pursuits, but the look in his eyes said differently. If anything, he seemed more eager than before.

"There was no need to send the coin back," Simius said with a chuckle, holding up the silver piece he had given her. "It was yours—a gift."

Livia tensed. She had no desire for such a *gift,* and all that it might imply.

"Please, may we converse a bit?" he said, flashing his nearly perfect teeth, "in whatever medium you prefer of course. I assure you I can read and am happy to do so to know your mind." His smile flickered on the right side very slowly, as if to emphasize his sculpted cheekbones. Livia had to admit to herself, Simius was quite handsome, and there was a charm to his voice and every mannerism that was impossible to ignore entirely. "Please, I beg you," he continued, "after I read your letter, I was unable to think of anything else—in fact ever since we *met,* I have thought of little else. Won't you speak to me just for a few moments?"

Livia hesitated. She knew how dangerous it was to refuse the son of her overlord. Simius could destroy both her and Hervin's life with a few words to his father. At the same time, his expecting to be let into her private office with no witnesses was quite audacious. Any onlookers might well assume that he had come to bed her. Several in the town thought of her as a whore already, even though she was past the age of twenty and had never even kissed a boy on the lips.

With a foot blocking the door from opening further—*though gods knew what that could do against a sorcerer*—Livia drew out the latest of her sheets of paper from her pocket as well as her current charcoal pencil and wrote:

I have no interest in this romance.
Please leave me in peace.

She held the paper up for him, and he glanced at it and then peered at her. Livia gave a small flinch as she felt his psychic tendrils attempt to prod into her mind. He seemed to notice her reaction, for his mouth twitched, revealing a hint of fascination.

"How do you do it?" he whispered, looking her up and down. "I've met grand master sorcerers who can't block as well as you. It is... *unreal* how talented you are."

Livia stared into Simius's eyes as a piece of his attraction to her fell into place. She was a puzzle to him. He could read virtually everyone in the city, but not her. It was almost charming to be... *intriguing* to a clever, handsome nobleman, but there was something behind all his smiles that she did not like.

"Come on a walk with me," he said. "Please?"

Livia shook her head and pressed against the door, sliding it shut. She reached down for the wooden bar to secure it when she heard his telepathic voice whisper inside her head: <Why is that dwarf always coming and going from your shop?> Every muscle in her body seemed to constrict at once. She looked at the still closed door as the voice came again: <I asked him why he came to see you so often. He said it was to buy wine—a reasonable enough explanation given that everyone knows that stubby little creature for a drunk, except... he never seems to have any wine when he leaves here.>

Livia felt twisting barbs creep up from her stomach and into her heart and limbs, and even into the skin on her face. She had given Domor bottles of wine as part of their cover at first when he had begun making prints of the essays and pictures she made for the Cassianites, but the dwarf had guzzled them down and produced shoddy work. *Why had she not resorted to giving him urns filled with water?* Livia had wanted to keep her damned costs down... Gods that was stupid!

She turned and looked at the door again. *What could Simius know*? Dwarf minds were nearly impossible for sorcerers to read... *weren't they?* As she considered this, the bar lifted of its own accord and whisked to the right, and then the door swung open. Simius stepped inside, meeting her gaze.

"Are you having a romantic affair with that stunted warthog?" he said, lifting an eyebrow.

Livia remained still, offering no answer. If Simius were simply jealous, that would make matters far simpler. She tried to look embarrassed by the question, cringing and glancing away. Simius watched her do this, and he seemed to find dark amusement in it.

"I *thought* it was an affair," he said, staring at her with unblinking eyes, "at first. However, I've had my telepathy since the age of four, and I have quite a bit of experience looking into people." His gaze narrowed. "I've observed hundreds of secret trysts between men and women, men and men, and so on. I know the sorts of people who carry on clandestine affairs, and you are *not* that sort—certainly not with a crass, alcohol ridden dwarf who leers at every female he sees." The nobleman took a step forward, causing Livia to edge back. "Knowing this, I find myself wondering *why* you have secret meetings with such a creature—ones for which the two of you have taken the time to construct excuses."

She felt his eyes boring into her, daring her to answer. Her hands began to tremble at her sides, and she closed her fingers into fists to stifle it.

"You look nervous," he said, nodding. He gestured toward the seat by the desk and said: "Please sit down."

Livia's head was swimming. *Was this the end of all her efforts?* She ambled to the chair and sank into it, all the while feeling the eyes of the young sorcerer upon her.

He moved to her and put a hand on her shoulder, and as he did Livia gave a little jump. *Would this be the moment?* She felt truly threatened now. Would her power finally come to her aid as it had against Arkas? Simius leaned down until his mouth was alongside her right ear and whispered: "Dwarf minds are exceptionally difficult to read, but you can catch little pieces under the right circumstances. Getting them drunk can be quite helpful, for example."

Livia felt the blood drain away from her face and leave a painful tingling in its stead. And then Simius added five words that made her heart nearly burst within her chest: "You work for the Cassianites."

She shot up from her chair and wriggled free of his hand, stumbling back against her desk and nearly toppling with it back onto the floor. This drew an amused chuckle from Simius, who seemed remarkably relaxed for having just uncovered sedition against the church in his father's territory.

"Hey-y-y," he said in a suddenly very gentle voice, "you have no need to be so afraid. I am... *something* at least of a fan of Asango. Gods know he's probably about to become the crown prince of the empire—if he hasn't already." Simius looked her up and down. "I want you to know I understand. You were a slave. Of course, you would support his ideas."

Livia stared at the young nobleman, trying to ascertain what was happening. How much did he know? Why was he not calling for the city guards? *Why was he smiling at her like that?* She gazed around the room and inadvertently noted that his right foot was directly on top of the floorboard that hid all her secret documents.

"It is all right," Simius said, moving closer. "I can help you." His grin brightened. "I did not understand why you would reject my advances—actually it drove me a little mad." He let out a soft chuckle. "But you were just protecting yourself and what you were doing." Simius brought his hands up and gently grasped her by her upper arms. "Now that all is clear, I can protect you, and we can be together."

Livia was so baffled by these words that she just stood there for a long moment, gazing at the aristocrat's utterly shameless eyes. His expression was seemingly so light and friendly, but she saw what lay underneath. He had not precisely threatened her, but there was no need now. They both knew that he had all the excuse required to throw her in his father's dungeon or... *hand her over to the Nemesai.* The way he was staring at her—the look in his eyes—was so... *possessive.*

"I'd like us to have dinner," he said, and then with a little smirk added: "tonight." *It sounded almost like a command.* He reached into his pocket and drew out the silver piece once more. "Take this."

Livia's hand trembled as it rose to take the coin. She did not know what else to do.

The door creaked open behind Simius rather abruptly, and a burly guard staggered in, panting. The man had his sword and shield out, and his face was dripping with sweat. When his eyes fell on Simius, he bellowed: "Thank the gods, I must have asked half the town where you were! Y-your father sent me to find you. "

"What is it?" Simius said, his voice suddenly quite sharp. Wide-eyed, the soldier started to speak, then hesitated, glancing at Livia. Simius said in an impatient tone: "Don't worry about her. Tell me what's going on."

The guard swallowed. "The Nemesai Temple down the hill, sir, it's... it's been destroyed!"

"WHAT?!" Simius snapped. "What do you mean?"

"I—I mean it's nothing but a pile of rubble, my lord. The whole thing was burned, but it isn't just that. Every statue was smashed—everything in the place was completely destroyed. And the Nemesai themselves—*they're gone*—at least we're fairly sure they are. There wasn't a single body in the rubble. We questioned a few tradesmen who were near the temple last night. They said they heard sounds of grunts and screams, but they thought it was just men being interrogated inside the walls."

Simius's fists balled at his sides, and he fidgeted. "You're telling me that someone... *abducted* Nemesai inquisitors?"

"Uh..." the soldier grunted, looking nervous, "I don't know, sir—it looks like it."

Simius gazed down at the floor, taking seething breaths through his nose. "Why didn't anyone report the fire last night?"

"Nobody saw any fire, sir," the soldier said, his face growing even paler than before. "It was like the whole thing was done with... *sorcery.*"

"Gods," Simius panted. He put his hand against his forehead, suddenly panting. "Are there any tracks? Any evidence at all of who did this?"

The guard fidgeted. "Well, sir, it's a common road that runs by their temple, so there are tracks going all over the place and we have no way of telling what's what. But there was a piece of evidence... it was *everywhere,* sir."

"What was it?" Simius whispered.

"A single word painted on the stones over and over again. I can't read, but your father said it was '*Elyria.*'"

"Elyria?" Simius hissed. "What the hell does that mean!"

"I—I don't know, sir."

The young nobleman's face was growing redder. "What about dogs? Has anyone thought to set dogs tracking these men?"

The soldier hesitated, casting another nervous glance at Livia, then said: "Your father... wasn't sure if he s-should, sir. I mean, anyone who could do this to a Nemesai temple—who *would* do it—we aren't sure we would have the resources to fight them."

"I see," Simius whispered. He stood still for a moment and then turned his head rather suddenly toward Livia, a dangerous look in his eyes. His psychic voice hissed into her mind: <Do you know anything about this?>

Utterly bewildered, Livia shook her head.

He glared at her, and she felt his psychic tendrils lash at her mind...*harmlessly.* This seemed to infuriate him, and his telepathic voice snapped within her skull: <Do you know what could happen to my family over this? Do you know what the Emperor does to lords who fail to keep order in their territory?> He turned to his guard and said: "I would like you to keep an eye on this girl for me while I go and see my father. She is *not* to leave this building. If she tries, arrest her." Simius glanced over at Livia, his expression still more suspicious, and added: "Her *father* should come in in the next hour or so. *If* she somehow manages to disappear, even for a moment, I would like you to pick up something heavy and beat Hervin Sondal until he can't move. If she still does not reappear then, cut his head off."

Livia gasped. Simius glared back at her, watching her tremble against her desk, and then he turned to the soldier again. "I would like you *not* to reveal what I just commanded you to do to anyone." He walked over to the man, who was cowering a little despite the fact that he was significantly larger than Simius. "So long as the girl stays here and doesn't give you any trouble, you will not give an explanation as to why you hung about outside this shop. If your tongue slips on this subject, I'll cut it out of your throat. Is that clear?"

"Y-yes, sir," the guard managed to rasp.

Simius turned back to Livia. <I hope you are not lying to me, my dear. If you are, I'll have to kill you.> Without another word, he spun and headed out the door and into the streets, leaving Livia with the guard, who stood gaping at her, nearly as bewildered as she was.

Livia just breathed for a long moment, trying to slow the wild jitter of her heart. All of this *was* happening! Her life, as well as Hervin's life, could come to an end at the slightest misstep—*no, that was an underestimation*! Her life was likely forfeit already. She gazed down to the floorboard. The map to Iona—*Gods, she had come so close!*

Livia clenched her fists. There was no room for self-doubt—nothing in the world to do but grit her teeth and try. She had to figure out what was going on. What in the world did 'Elyria' mean?

CHAPTER 32:
A TWISTING OF DESTINY

Kota breathed in the slow rhythm Gretis had taught him, feeling his spiritual energy swirl within his body. He sat upon a flat stone section that was warm from the sun, his eyes shut. Meditation was easiest atop a mountain like this, where his animus sense was not disturbed by the endless chaos of the ever-changing world. Kota had a pristine mental image of a few insects crawling about and the occasional bird gliding by, but for the most part there was only the gentle wind and the solid rock that had remained much as it was for countless thousands of years and would continue to do so long after he passed into the next life.

His wounds were nearly mended. For three days he had sat in this same pose, surrendering his mind and body to the animus within him, and in that time, it had burned away the corruptive energies left behind by the demonic weapons. The beast wanted him healed and strong, for, he sensed through a deep instinct he barely understood, it was preparing his flesh to battle an even greater threat in the days to come.

Kota's senses tickled, and then his mind locked on Gretis, who was traversing the rocky path up to him. The energy flowing inside of her familiar animus felt wild and alive. He observed in silence as she drew nearer and nearer, and then he caught the scent of freshly cooked meat in the air.

"Are you hungry yet?" she said from a dozen steps behind.

"A little," he answered without opening his eyes. "Not much really. My animus seems to have... slowed everything down inside my body."

Gretis paused at this, and he felt a series of pulses from her energy reach out to his chest and then return to her. "Your heart is beating so slow you should be dead," she said, her voice carrying a measure of concern that was overshadowed by what seemed to be fascination.

"It is a little strange," he whispered. "There are times when I go perhaps a quarter of an hour without taking a breath—maybe longer."

"I... think you should eat," she said after a moment.

"As you wish," Kota said, and he opened his eyes. His animus shift shifted inside of him, accelerating his bodily functions to their normal state. As he rose, he noticed that the shoulder that had been pierced by a demon's arrow now hurt little more than a light bruise. His leg was a touch worse, for the gash in it had been quite deep, and yet, hour after hour, he had felt the animus pushing through the demonic corruption and knitting the muscle fiber and other tissue back together. He could probably run on it now.

"How is the tribe?" Kota said.

"Still asking questions," Gretis said, "Many, *many* questions."

Kota grinned as he reached out and took the plate of steaming food from her, which he noted held pheasant speckled with a pinch of salt and some of Gretis's wonderfully sharp red pepper. "I'm sure you've been frustrating them with vague and confusing answers."

"Of course," she said in a mirthful tone. "I am sworn to keep the mysteries of the Sansrit path secret, *as are you.*"

Kota sighed mid-chew into his meat. He was not certain how he felt about the secrecy of his art, now that demons were encroaching back into mortal lands. The 'oath' that he had taken was essentially to his past self, *Nataka,* the founder of Sansrit Philosophy. Only... he was not truly that man—at least if he accepted Gretis's teachings on the division between soul, mind, and animus. Many hours of meditation atop the mountain had been dedicated to the question of whether he essentially was Nataka reborn or something else. If the former, might that not grant him the right to decide for himself what was right? Now that demons were returning, surely the ancient knowledge should be restored to the world and his people. Then again, Nataka was a legendary figure that had lived for hundreds of years before constructing the edicts of Sansrit Philosophy. If Kota had only inherited the power and not the ancient chieftain's wisdom, then what right did he have to override thousands of years of tradition laid out by the greatest man in his people's history?

"Decisions," Gretis whispered.

He cast her a little smile of respect, acknowledging her prowess at guessing his thoughts. After swallowing his food, he said: "I will keep to my oath at least for the time being."

"Until what?" she asked, raising an eyebrow. "What is your threshold?"

"I don't know."

Gretis looked at him for a moment and then said: "A fine enough answer, I suppose. I make no claim to know the correct path at this point myself. I can tell you that such choices are not to be made lightly, but you already know this." She grinned suddenly and reached out and touched the side of his face. "You're not my student anymore, are you? It is no longer my place to tell you what to do."

Kota swallowed. "If you had not been here, I would have died in the battle, and even if I lived, my tribe would surely all be dead."

Gretis smirked. "Yes, I am not altogether useless just yet." Her expression grew more somber as she added: "But you *are* the warrior of prophecy—the one we of the Sansrit have been awaiting for over twenty centuries. Gods, Kota, you defeated an Archdemon in single combat! I wonder if even your friend Cassian could have done that." He noted a change in her face—in the tone of voice and pace of her heart as she spoke this last sentence. "I think... the time has come for the two of us to have a talk about him—*Asango.*"

"Cassian?" Kota said, staring at Gretis. Her skin had gone just a touch pale.

"The... prophecy that allowed me to recognize you for what you are," she said, speaking slowly, "it also speaks of *him*."

"What?" Kota said, blinking at her. "How? Starborn didn't exist when those words were written."

"No, but the Norn did, and the description she gave could be nothing other than a Starborn human." Gretis drew in a slow breath, gazing down at the mountain face beneath them both. Kota had rarely ever seen her so nervous. "Your friend Cassian has... *the potential* to become the greatest evil this world has ever seen—something vastly more terrible even than the Demon King himself." She paused, giving him time to digest these words.

Kota's mind flashed to the moment seven years ago when the fascinating human boy had bowed to him in the forest. They had only met the one time, but those few days, hunting a nathret to a dead elven city, were deeply ingrained in Kota's memory. They changed who he was and set him on the course to Gretis and his destiny. Cassian had saved Kota's life—*saved all of their lives*—after knowingly walking into a deathtrap to rescue a handful of peasant children. It was chilling to think that the noble Starborn he remembered could ever become a force of evil.

"Has the *potential*?" Kota finally said, fixing his eyes on Gretis's. "Does that mean this may not come to pass?"

"Perhaps," Gretis said in a somber whisper. "The wording is not entirely clear, and the prophecy was transcribed in a dialect of Dhavic far older than even the scholars study, but several things are clear, Kota. The first is that your fate and his are intrinsically interwoven. A moment will come when you will have to—"

Kota suddenly lost track of what Gretis was saying as his animus locked on to something foul. A split second later his nostrils caught a putrid, death-ridden scent in the air. He rose, scarcely conscious of drawing his sword from his belt as the attacker descended from behind. Kota spun, whipping his blade into the path of a black sword aimed at his right shoulder. The demon—a black and oily bat-like thing—let loose a metallic shriek as it flapped its great wings and dodged toward the sky. Kota was faster though, his legs catapulting him upward. He caught one of the monster's thin, rat-like ankles in his left hand and yanked while his other limb guided his sword to its mark. The demon had dark leather armor and ring mail over its torso, but Kota's blade sliced through it with ease, cleaving the bone and sinew and splitting the hellish creature in half at the waist.

Kota fell with the corpse, and by the time his feet touched down on the mountaintop, he was himself again. His heart was beating hard, and he was suddenly aware of the spatter of black blood all over his chest, which somehow felt warm and ice-cold at the same time. Gretis had her sword out and was glaring around at the sky, searching for more enemies. Kota followed her example, but when he looked up, he saw only a handful of clouds drifting under the sun. *Where the hell had the creature come from?*

"Remarkable," a deep, oaky voice said from almost directly behind the two of them. Kota whirled, utterly astonished that someone could sneak so close, and saw an elderly man with a thick beard of gray-speckled black—*a man that somehow did not seem to exist to Kota's animus sense.* He wore fine, dark robes, and there was a thick silver chain that hung around his neck that housed a brilliant green jewel. His wizened eyes were not focused on Kota but staring down at the upper half of the demon, which lay face down in a mess of its own blood. "Your instincts—your reflexes, speed, and power are awe-inspiring, my boy." The man looked up and cast him a grin.

"Who are you?" Gretis said, tilting her sword toward the old man.

"Tacitus Adronicus, Starborn of the Eighteenth Generation, and of course, current Emperor of the Denigoth Empire," he said, meeting her gaze with a relaxed expression. He took a step toward them both, and Kota's animus sense felt—*he could not conceptualize what he felt.* The power showed itself only for an instant, but it utterly dwarfed anything he had ever perceived before, including even the Archdemon he had faced. "You are a remarkable young man, Kota," the Emperor said. His tone was cordial, yet there was a coldness to it.

"Emperor Tacitus," Kota said, finding his voice, and he dropped to one knee and lowered his head in respect. *Gretis did not though.* She stood staring at the old man, and from the furious beat of her heart and the constriction of her muscles, Kota realized that she was afraid. He looked up at her and saw that her face had gone several shades paler.

"You've done an excellent job of tucking him away this last year," Tacitus said, eyeing Gretis. He took another step toward them both, and it almost seemed to Kota's senses that the world itself shifted. The Emperor moved with his hands folded behind his back, hunching just a little forward, like a feeble old man. He sighed and squinted up at the clouds as he said: "I've had a hell of a time finding you two."

Gretis stuttered: "Y-you're—"

"Yes, I am," Tacitus said, shifting his gaze back to her, all the humor draining from his face. "I am... *very sorry,* my dear. Please know that I hold you in the very deepest respect," his glance shifted to Kota, "both of you."

Gretis turned to Kota, a look of horror on her face as she shouted: "RUN!"

"There is no running," Tacitus said, his hand snapping up, and suddenly Kota felt an incomprehensible force wrap around his body, enveloping every part of him. He was yanked to a standing position before the Emperor, and though his animus filled his body with all its strength and willed him to move, it was useless. Gretis stood next to him in a rigid pose, her arms locked to her sides as if they too were being squeezed.

"I want you to know that I will *not* kill him," Tacitus said, looking at Gretis and gesturing to Kota. "I have a use for him actually."

"Y-you b-bastard!" Gretis managed to hiss through her teeth. Her face had gone quite red.

This elicited a chuckle from the Emperor. "So simple it all must seem to you," he said. "All the *moral clarity* you must have felt, hidden away for so many years in your little home in the woods. You have no conception at all of what it is like to bear the responsibility of the largest empire in history on your shoulders." Tacitus shook his head. "I rule over very nearly the entire human race. Can you even *imagine* the scope of such a burden?" He let out a gruff sigh. "I have no wish to hurt either of you, but there is far more at stake than the lives of two Sansrit masters."

"Let Kota go!" Gretis managed to snarl. "Please! I am the only one who has read the prophecy!"

The muscles in The Emperor's jaw contracted as if he was hesitating, and then he said in a grim voice: "I cannot allow even the chance that he fulfill his destiny. Your student shall have to come with me. You, however," he whispered, a sorrowful look crossing his face, "I need something for the Onkai to find, so that poor Bishop Otho will stop searching for the two of you. His attention will be needed elsewhere very soon." The Emperor stared at Gretis with any icy expression as he continued: "I am afraid a demon managed to get the better of you."

He raised his right hand, and the black sword that had belonged to the dismembered bat-creature lifted up off the ground. It turned slowly in the air until the blade was pointed at Gretis, and then it lurched forward. An internal scream of rage erupted from Kota, and all the power of his animus boiled up, yet still, he was unable to move as the weapon flew into Gretis's stomach. A shrill gasp escaped her as the sword buried itself up to the hilt. Her eyes went wide, and she dropped to her knees, suddenly free of the Emperor's impossibly powerful grip.

Kota growled through his teeth, straining even harder. The Emperor turned to him as Gretis fell forward into a pool of her own blood. Kota heard every rasping breath she drew—every duller, slower beat of her heart, and he could not believe it. *Gretis was dying!*

"It is a hard thing," Tacitus said, looking him in the eyes. "I had to watch *everyone* I loved die in the war." He stepped in front of Gretis, obscuring Kota's view of her. The rasping drew to a slow stop then.

"WHY?" Kota managed to snarl through his fangs. A pair of tears dripped down his face.

"The greater good," Tacitus said, unblinking. "I do not expect you to grasp that. How could you? You cannot fathom the things I know." He walked forward and put a hand on Kota's shoulder. "I can feel how badly you want to attack me right now, and I do not blame you in the slightest. She was such a fine woman, *Princess Angretta.*"

A growl emitted from Kota's throat. *If he could just get one hand free...*

"Before I dispel your soul, I wish you to know that I am sparing your tribe," Tacitus whispered, and he turned his head just a little to the right, nodding back in the direction of the Nakawa village. "My liches are obliterating their memories of the past few days, and the other craith are removing all the carcasses of all the demons. Your parents, I'm afraid, shall never learn what happened to you, but they will be alive. It is a mercy, and it is all I can offer you now."

Kota saw figures in black and silver rise from the sides of the mountain. His animus sense, it seemed, was somehow being suppressed along with his strength, but these creatures had a subtle, disgusting scent about them that reminded him of death.

The Emperor raised his hand to Kota's forehead and pressed his thumb down as he began to chant. Almost immediately, Kota felt a swell of cold, unworldly energy move through him. It flowed to every part of his being, and then, gradually, it began to pull. He felt a sense of separation—like everything that made him who he was being drawn out of the vessel that was his body.

"I sincerely hope you can join your teacher in whatever form of *heaven* the two of you find," Tacitus whispered.

Kota began to feel a sense of peace. *His time in the world was over.* His concerns did not matter any longer, for he could do nothing to affect them. Then something visceral happened that he did not at first understand. The familiar force of his animus reached up around what seemed to be his *soul* and pulled it back, tearing through the Emperor's magic. All sense of disembodiment shattered, and Kota was again staring into the eyes of Tacitus Adronicus, alert and awake.

"*How the HELL—*" The Emperor shouted. He looked Kota up and down with an almost stupefied expression. After a brief moment, he pursed his lips under his thick mustache and shook his head. "Your *animus* is stronger than I ever guessed, my boy. It is trying to help you, but it most certainly *is not.*" The old man cast him a dark, contemplative stare, and then hissed: "I am afraid you are going to be trapped in there. I wanted this to be painless, but the normal means do not work on you, so I shall have to reach from somewhere much... *darker.*" The Emperor began to chant again.

Kota felt an icy force rip into him, and immediately he felt sick. It was foul and vicious, stinging his nerves as it took control. Whatever invisible power Tacitus had been using to hold him in place vanished away, yet even as it did Kota still could not twitch a muscle. His gaze shifted suddenly, his eyes turning of their own accord. He watched his own hand come up, claws extended. The fingers twiddled for an instant, and he felt them move, but the action was driven by the cruel, alien power that now resided within him.

"Can you still hear me, shamalak?" Tacitus said. Kota gave no response, *for he could not.* The Emperor peered at him for a moment, then turned and looked at one of the black figures. It moved forward as if commanded by his thoughts, carrying a bundle in its gauntleted hands. Kota watched his own hand reach out slowly and take something metallic from the top of this bundle and raise it up: *a silver mask.* The thing was heavy, and it had thick leather straps that had been boiled to hardness and riveted to fit around the back of a skull. Against all internal desire, Kota drew the mask up over his head and slid it down until his eyes were peering out through the cold, rectangular slits.

The Emperor gazed at him for a brief moment, then said: "Finish putting on your uniform, craith. We have much to do."

CHAPTER 33: A VISIT TO THE NEMESAI

As Tacitus stepped onto the finely carved stone steps to the Nemesai temple, he glanced back at the dragon that stood less than a hundred paces away. Instantly, the thing's yellow eyes turned to him, blazing like twin suns in the night. Titus, as Cassian had named the creature, was quite an imposing figure. No peasants stood near it, though everyone gawked from a distance. By all reports, the beast of legend had not moved for over three days. It seemed to have no need to eat or sleep or even drink water. Instead, it glared at the temple, hour after hour, letting the *fearless* men of the Nemesai Order know that it could attack anytime it wished. The dragon wanted its master—*its father*—Cassian, back.

"Hello, your majesty," said an oily skinned-man in his late twenties with a thin, almost rat-like face marked in dark tattoos. The Nemesai's pale blue eyes nervously flicked over Tacitus's shoulder to the dragon for an instant, then swept the fifteen craith the Emperor had brought to this meeting. He had enough respect at least not to meet his ruler's eyes but shifted his gaze to the stones below as he whispered: "It is an honor to meet you, your grace."

"Yes," Tacitus muttered, not bothering to ask for the man's name. "I would speak with your bishop. Is he available?"

"He is, sir," the young man answered. He cast the craith another uneasy glance and then whispered: "I'll take you to him immediately."

Tacitus gave an aloof nod but said nothing. He let the fellow lead him in through the doors and up through the narrow hall, quietly sighing to himself. Nemesai temples were such dreary places. Tacitus quickly found himself surrounded by dark stone lit only by a handful of wall candles. They eventually arrived in a large chamber where six men stood together near the flames of a fireplace, whispering. They all turned, and he saw the eyes of his son lock on his and then fidget away, while those of Bishop Cromlic fixed firmly.

"My Emperor," Cromlic said, and he dropped immediately into a bow that was mirrored by every man in the room.

Tacitus stepped forward, and his craith slipped silently in behind him and fanned about the back of the room. Nearest was his favorite and most powerful slave, Kota, who took up a position just to his right.

"Good evening, gentlemen," he said. "I understand you are having some difficulty with your prisoner.

With this invitation to speak granted, the heads rose. Tacitus sensed resentment in several of the holy men, which was an unwise attitude to display toward the Emperor of Denigoth.

"Trouble, yes," Cromlic said, the muscles in his face tensing. He gestured to a large table with chairs set about to the left and said: "Would you honor us by taking a seat, your grace?"

"No," Tacitus answered, and his eyes moved to the face of his son and then the empty sleeve where the boy's right arm should be. *So pathetic...* The jokes were already being whispered around the court of Arkas's *second* crippled limb from Cassian. At least the little weakling had had enough pride not to come pleading to the throne room for help. "My main purpose for being here is to visit Asango, but if you have something you wish to say, good Bishop, then speak."

Cromlic drew in a nervous breath through his nostrils, then said in a forcibly calm voice: "I must renew my request for your leave to kill the young man."

Tacitus gave the Bishop a level look. "You are not to cause Asango any permanent damage. That is my will."

"Your Grace," an exceptionally tall Nemesai said in a booming voice. *The man actually dared to raise his voice to his emperor.* "We have received reports that several of our temples have been destroyed! Men of the church—*Holy Men*—have been dragged away in the night!"

"I am aware," Tacitus said.

The speaker's tattooed face reddened. "And while all this was happening, that little heretic is *laughing* at us from his cell! Never has this order stood for such insolence!"

"Father," Arkas said, his face pale and sweat-soaked, "Cassian is able to fight the leeches somehow. It shouldn't be possible, but he's managed to hold on to almost all of his telepathy." Arkas swallowed, "He penetrated the minds of the last several inquisitors we sent to his cell. He taunts them, whispers things in their minds, and... makes them feel whatever they're doing to him."

And you are too afraid to go down and face him, even now, Tacitus thought, glaring at his coward of a son.

The tall Nemesai broke in again: "Tomaris, one of the most dedicated veterans of our order ran out *Screaming* from Asango's cell. It took me hours to calm him down. He was going to *hang* himself!"

"That heretic is never going to confess," Cromlic said in a grim whisper. "He is far too dangerous to hold in a cell. Execution is the only logical answer, and by theocratic law, we have the right to—"

"No," Tacitus said in a calm, but authoritative voice, "you may not end his life."

The belligerent Nemesai took yet another step toward Tacitus, a look of fury on his face as he shouted: "With all due respect, not even an Emperor may command the church in its holy business! It is time that you—"

Tacitus had but to think it, and six of his craith sprang across the room at the man. He managed the beginning of a terrified scream before the first blade entered his chest cavity. The second sword took his head off in a grotesque spray of blood, and a third sliced the remaining mass of his body in half at the waist. Cromlic and his men jerked away from the violence, gasping and shrieking as they huddled back to a corner of the room as the craith continued to hack away, shattering bones and rending flesh until there was nothing left but a sickening mess.

"You men of the Nemesai seem to lack a fundamental understanding of your place in this world," Tacitus said, his voice remaining calm. He stepped toward them, and his craith darted to his sides, fresh blood and even bits of sinew dripping from their weapons. "I can understand the place from where your difficulty arises." He willed his servants forward, and several of the holy men began to shriek and tremble, *including his son.* "You see yourselves as the living avatars of a god, and thus your actions are sacrosanct—perhaps even *above* the authority of your Emperor. The obvious problem with this is that you are only men, and men are sacks of meat that can be slashed and gutted when they anger their ruler." His craith lurched further forward at his silent command and raised the tips of their blades to the throats of Nemesai. Tacitus detected the scent of urine in the air.

He gazed at Cromlic, who was flattened against the wall. To the Bishop's credit, he was the calmest in the group, though his skin was quite pale. Tacitus spoke directly to him: "It is my *command* that Asango shall not be killed." His gaze shifted to his son as he added: "*Anyone* who defies me in this will be put to death." He willed his craith to edge their blades a little closer as he added in a soft voice: "If you men hold religious convictions that might drive you to disobey me, you need not speak. Simply *think it,* and I shall know."

There was a moment of terrified tense silence as Tacitus stared at the Nemesai, scanning their minds. For all their ruthlessness and cruelty, they were cowards all of them, even the bishop. *Of course, they were.* Ten thousand of them were not worth a single Cassian.

"Good," Tacitus said. "I will go and speak with Asango now." Without another word, he walked to the stone stairway that led down into the dungeons. The Emperor felt just a little on edge as he descended the steps. Killing a man of the church was not a casual matter, and indeed not a step he would take under normal circumstances, but the Nemesai needed to be shown how far he was willing to go. They were only aware of attacks on a few of their temples at the moment. Soon they would learn the true scope of Cassian's 'Plan Elyria.'

A letter written in Cassian's sharp calligraphy had arrived a few days ago, explaining everything in brazen detail. The boy had carefully studied his enemy, assessing the strengths and weaknesses of each temple, learning the number of men on hand at any time, analyzing guard movements, proximity to local militia, policies toward intruders, and so on. For a longer time than anyone might have guessed, he had been quietly stationing elite soldiers he had gathered during his military conquests. The Nemesai had had no idea of course. For years they had been chasing the 'Cassianites,' trying to stamp out all the seditious and heretical writings Cassian and his followers had been circulating. The boy had played them perfectly. They were watching his right hand, never suspecting that his left was doing something far, far more dangerous.

"*If you are reading this, then every Nemesai temple on the continent lies in ruins save the one in the capital,*" the letter had begun. Tacitus had not doubted the words, absurd as the claim was. Cassian never lied. The operation had been executed in a single night. The boy had somehow created a spell to allow his sorcerers to communicate telepathically over distances as great as Starborn, and this had let them coordinate attacks upon all fifty-eight Nemesai temples on the continent at once. All of the order's gold had been seized, all their buildings and fields destroyed, their cattle stolen, their deeds and documents burned. The Nemesai Order was effectively obliterated. It would take a century to recover all they had lost, and then there was the matter of all the holy men. *The letter had not revealed what had been done with them...*

Tacitus stepped down into the dungeon, and immediately his mind attuned to the swell of fear in the chamber of bars and stone. In the dim light of poorly maintained wall torches,

Tacitus passed cells of doomed men and women. These were the ones who had not confessed immediately to whatever sins of which they had been accused. Some of them were supporters of Cassian's views, and some had been fairly rich but poorly connected in political terms, which made them attractive targets for the wealth-seizing inquisitors. Only one person in the entire dungeon was an actual heretic, so far as Tacitus could decipher: *Asango.*

The boy's cell was in the very back of the dungeon. His room was secluded from all the others by especially thick walls and a solid steel door. Tacitus willed the lock of this barrier to open with a thought. As it swung open, he gazed down the steps to the sunken floor and saw Cassian sitting on a pile of hay, staring up at him.

"Hello, my Emperor," the boy said, squinting. Cassian had no tunic or shirt, and Tacitus immediately noticed that six additional leeches had been placed at various points on his chest and arms. They swelled and contracted with a slow rhythm between large welts and open wounds from whipping. Cassian's handsome face was dirty, but his eyes had lost none of their alertness or confidence.

"Hello, Lord Asango," Tacitus said.

"Telemachus and I were just in the middle of a game of telepathic cornerstone," the boy said, his voice remarkably calm, "but I should be happy to put that on hiatus for you, your grace."

Tacitus chuckled. Cassian had no self-pity whatsoever. " Poor Telemachus. He wishes desperately to see you freed."

"But of course you commanded him not to come to my aid. Will you sit, great Emperor?" The boy gestured to a wooden chair across from him, the shackles on his wrists clinking as he did. The chains on his arms traveled up to thick pulleys and looped back down to cranks on the wall so that he could be hoisted up off his feet at any time.

Tacitus took a seat upon the chair. "They are feeding you at least?"

"Yes, thanks to your express orders, but then you already knew that." There was hatred just under the surface of Cassian's pleasant voice. He had cut his mind off from Tacitus's in the first hour of his captivity. There was no longer trust between them and might never be again. "That display above was interesting. Killing a priest. Not even I have ever gone so far."

Tacitus gave a casual shrug, then said: "Let us not speak of that imbecile when there are far more important matters at hand." He leaned forward and said: "I have many questions, as you might imagine. I suppose my first is: *why the name Elyria*?"

The faintest trace of a grin crossed the boy's bruised face. "I learned the name from a very old document I... *acquired* from the Nemesai. Elyria was officially the first person they ever executed." Cassian gazed down at a brown leech on his stomach, whose corpulent little body was expanding and contracting at a slow interval. "She was a priestess in a now dead religion known as Parakha. The Nemesai tortured her for over a week to *bring her to the light,* but she defied them at every step. On the last day of her life, one of her inquisitors leaned into her face to shout some condemnation, but she leaned in herself and bit down on his nose." Cassian chuckled as he added: "The woman actually managed to tear most of it off. They immediately killed her of course, but the wound she delivered to her tormentor became infected. Healing spells were not as developed in those days, and the man ended up dying in a fever-ridden delirium."

"And this woman fascinated you," Tacitus said.

Cassian shrugged, causing his chains to clink. "I have no idea who she was—maybe a horrible woman—but she stood up for herself in the face of death, and I respect that."

"Where are all the Nemesai your men took? Are they dead?"

"Not dead," the boy said, gazing again at the leech.

"Where are they?"

"I shall never tell," Cassian whispered.

Tacitus stared at the boy for a few heartbeats, then said: "I could rip it from your mind."

Cassian looked up directly into his eyes and said: "I doubt it."

Tacitus's mouth shifted into a hard grin at this challenge. "Resigned yourself to die, have you?"

"Resigned myself to *live,* actually," Cassian said without blinking, "exactly according to my heart, and to hell with the consequences."

Tacitus found himself chuckling. *The boy who had survived Promethiock's fire.* Cassian's gall was impossible not to like. Was his fear truly burned away? The Emperor decided to let the matter drop for the moment and said: "We have something else to discuss."

"What might that be?"

"Your intentions."

Cassian smiled, displaying the perfect white teeth that lay under his filthy lips. "My intentions," he said slowly. He blinked at the shackles on his wrists and then locked eyes with Tacitus once more. "Why the hell am I still alive? What are *your* intentions, my Emperor?" He spoke the words in a tone that would have warranted death for *any* other man in the world.

"To do what is right for my empire."

"I find that to be more of a vague justification than an answer. You do not seem to want these men in robes to kill me at the moment, yet you did not come here to free me. There is only a small number of possible outcomes to this situation."

"Yes-s-s, you have gotten yourself into quite a bit of trouble, Asango, after I took the time to caution you to end the conflict."

"I would have ended it soon enough on my terms if a secret rule to the craith army had not *mysteriously* appeared after centuries of obscurity. I know Cromlic had no idea he could command your undead killers until recently because years ago I had a look inside his sickening mind." Cassian said nothing further, but his eyes burned with accusation.

"Hmm," Tacitus grunted. "If you have something to say—"

"Did you arrange for all of this to happen?"

The Emperor sighed. "Has it not crossed your mind that the Bishop was desperate for a means to destroy you and was putting every possible resource toward that end, including the scribes in his archives?"

"It has. Did you arrange for all of this to happen?"

"I did not, but when it *did* happen, I reacted exactly as I warned you I would. Perhaps you might be grateful that I am keeping you from death."

Cassian stared at him for several tense, silent seconds, then said: "What is your aim in all of this?"

"*You* are my aim, Cassian," Tacitus replied, looking into the boy's fierce eyes. "I do not wish to see you die as a martyr in this cell, which, near as I can tell, is *your aim*."

Cassian gave a cavalier shrug. "What is the alternative?"

The Emperor held out his hand and gave a psychic command to his favorite new craith. Kota placed a neatly rolled scroll into Tacitus's palm. As this transpired, Cassian's eyes flicked to the enthralled form of his shamalak companion from years ago, and his brow furrowed. A tingle of nerves rose in The Emperor's stomach. *It had been a mistake to bring Kota here.* After a few seconds though, Cassian blinked and looked away, evidently not sensing his old friend.

"The alternative is to make you my heir," Tacitus said, "*for a price*." He held out the scroll, and Cassian's dirty hand reached out and took it.

He opened the scroll and began to read, but after a few seconds he gave a dark chuckle and gazed up at Tacitus. "You actually came here to entice me to confess? To repent of my *sins* to that man?"

"I did. You have inflicted *monumental* consequence on the Nemesai for your parents' lives. Now it is time to swallow a bit of pride and move forward."

"And kneel at his feet?" Cassian said. "Tell me, my Emperor, how will you possibly justify freeing me after my soldiers took men of the church prisoner?"

"You said these *men of the church* are still alive, and I believe you. Set them free."

"And what of the destruction?" the boy asked, raising an eyebrow. "My men burned down temples—*holy places*!"

"Cromlic exceeded his authority when he took a living miracle prisoner and proceeded to torture him. There were bound to be repercussions for such an action." Tacitus shrugged. "This is a fair compromise. Your confession and repentance will bring peace to the empire. The Nemesai order will still exist, but only as a shadow of what they were."

"And you believe Cromlic would accept this *compromise*?"

"If I command it."

Cassian gazed at some spot on the wall for a long moment, unmoving, and then he turned back and said: "No."

"Gods be damned, you idiot boy!" Tacitus said, his voice rising in anger. The enormity of his power pulsed outward, threatening to kill everyone within the walls of the church with a single unchecked thought. "I am offering you your life!"

"What will the Nemesai inquisitors do when I free them? Will they simply shrug and give up their lives' work?" Cassian chuckled, "No, I think they will immediately begin strangling the people of this empire to rebuild their temples and their grotesque horde of wealth."

"Cromlic will rebuild either way."

"Will he?" the boy said with the hint of a smirk. "The Bishop cannot tattoo his men without dragon's tears, and I have taken all of his away. Who will get him more, *your son?* Do you think that pathetic little coward will brave the dangers of the Great Dragon's lair? Do you think Promethiock would tolerate his presence?" Cassian shook his head. "No, the Nemesai will not be replenishing their numbers in any meaningful way for many, *many* years, and in that time an entire generation will come up who will have lived without the oppressive rule of a *moral policing force*. I doubt they will accept the kidnappings and torture when the order finally attempts to re-establish itself."

"This *generation* you speak of will still have slavery. No one will enact all your ideas for public education. None of your high-minded plans will be ushered in because you will be a long-rotted corpse in the ground."

"I will not inflict the Nemesai on the people again now that they have been removed," Cassian said. "I would rather die."

Tacitus gritted his teeth, staring at the boy. He took a moment to remember that he was thrice this young man's age and that Cassian had yet to even begin to discover that of which he was truly capable. When the Emperor spoke again, it was in a subdued voice: "I think you and I both require a bit of time to think." He rose from his chair and turned toward the metal door. The nearest craith pulled it open.

"Wait," Cassian said, and his right hand snapped up. To Tacitus's astonishment, a tiny sliver of magic shot toward the door, colliding with it and causing it to shut.

He stared at the boy. *With seven leeches on his body! By the Gods Cassian's mind was strong!* Tacitus let out a soft chuckle. "Quite impressive. Can you free yourself?"

"Not yet," the boy said, the veins standing up around his eyes. It had taken him enormous effort to do what he had just done. "The Nemesai think that adding leaches is like laying more and more weight on my back, but it is a bit more like adding another variable to an equation." He glared into Tacitus's eyes and said: "I like puzzles, but there is one that has been grating in my mind for a long time now, and I want an answer for it: Why did you instigate a fight to the death between Dimitris and me?"

Tacitus blinked. *Why not tell him the truth?*

"I did it for you, Cassian," he said in a soft voice. "You and Dimitris were always going to fight. There was no other possible outcome given who you both were. The Nemesai had plans to manipulate the duel to their candidate's advantage—

ways you were not anticipating. I took control and made the match happen on fair terms because I wanted you to have a chance."

Cassian stared at him. *For once, the boy had nothing to say.*

Tacitus drew in a slow breath and added: "Sometimes an Emperor must do things he finds ugly for the greater good." The boy still said nothing, and Tacitus turned back toward the door and willed his craith to open it once more. He stepped into the hall but then turned back. "You have three days to reconsider my offer, Cassian. If you cannot see reason in that time, I will let the bishop slit your throat." He let the words sink in and then added: "Cromlic used to boast about killing your parents. He described a great satisfaction in particular at watching the life leave your mother's eyes. Will you allow him to feel that joy again with you?"

The muscles in Cassian's face constricted. His mind was a veritable fortress even now, yet Tacitus felt vicious anger seep out from it.

"Think on the matter," the Emperor said, and then he turned and left the room. As he walked back through the hall of suffering, a grin crossed his face. The Nemesai were performing their role even better than he had hoped. More and more, they were twisting the boy into a *viper*.

CHAPTER 34: IONA'S POWER

Arkas dropped from his horse onto dirt and leaves, his heart pounding. He was covered in a slimy sheen of sweat despite the cool night air. The long ride had failed to calm his nerves. There had only been the sickening fear coupled with the throbbing from the right arm he no longer possessed. He had rolled his father's visit over again and again in his mind and reached the conclusion that Cassian would be freed. If that happened, Arkas would never reach the throne. Instead, according to the Norn's prophecy, Cassian would kill him.

"Who's there?" the inhumanly deep voice rumbled from within the shack ahead. Gorlick seemed to notice Arkas at the same instant as his dog, for the hideous black beast came darting out of the house and ran straight at Arkas in a barking frenzy.

"SHUT UP!" Arkas snapped. *Gods how he hated dogs!* Using his left hand as a focal point, he willed out an invisible hand of magic and caught the stupid beast by its throat in mid-stride. He flung it to the right, sending the whimpering thing fifteen paces into the side of a tree.

"What the HELL you doin'?" Gorlick's voice boomed from within the hovel, and then he stepped out like an angry giant, glaring down at Arkas. "You think you can just—" The half-ogre stopped short and his eyes went wide. "What happened to yer arm?"

"ASANGO!" Arkas screamed, holding up the wrapped stump. "It's time! Where is the slave?"

"She's..." Gorlick grunted, still gaping at Arkas's wound, "she's down by the creek."

"You let her run around unattended?" Arkas snapped.

Gorlick's hideously bulbous face contorted into a glare. "Yeah, I let her go all the *time*. Where the hell's she gonna run?"

Arkas hesitated. The half-ogre was too valuable an ally to battle over such a matter, and, inwardly, his tremendous friend made him a touch nervous so up close. "You're probably right," he said in a low voice, twitching as he spoke the words.

The heavy muscles in Gorlick's shoulders slumped, and he muttered "Yeah, I know what I'm doin'."

Arkas turned in the direction of the creek and immediately reached out with a psychic tendril. He found Iona's mind within seconds through the trees—innocent and remarkably free of anger and self-pity for a girl enslaved to a horrible half-ogre. She was focused on a small fish that was swimming up the brook. Arkas saw it through her eyes and felt her simple joy at dipping her feet in the cold water.

"Stupid peasant," he hissed as he made his way over the uneven terrain, weaving through the thick trees. Arkas did not move quietly, and when he stepped out from the foliage, Iona was already looking in his direction. Her gentle blue eyes widened when she saw him, and she took a nervous step backward into the stream.

"Careful!" Arkas snapped.

"Uh!" Iona grunted, and then she glanced down at her foot in the flowing water, staring as if she had forgotten for an instant where she was. Trembling, she stepped forward onto the bank and said in a nervous voice: "S-sorry, sir." Her gaze fixed suddenly upon his arm, and he sensed a feeling of horror come over her that she was afraid to voice.

Arkas glared at her. When he had first acquired this Iona, many months ago now, he had felt his path to the throne was assured, yet after dozens upon dozens of hours of experimentation, he had found no way to harness the elusive power residing within her. Absolutely *nothing* he had tried had even drawn a reaction from it.

"Let's have no more lies," Arkas rasped as he moved toward her. He could feel the little slave's fear. *Did it surpass his own?* For a brief moment, his anger melted away, and a sad, desperate hope he had thought long gone bubbled up. "If... if you've been hiding what you are from me, now is the last chance to speak." He was not sure whether he was addressing Iona herself, or the transcendent force within her.

"I..." the girl muttered, staring at him with the same look of confusion this line of inquiry always elicited, "I don't know w-what you're—"

"PLEASE!" Arkas shouted without thinking. He thrust the wrapped stump of his arm in front of her and said: "I know you can heal me!" His words spilled out like those of a lunatic, yet he did not care. "The scholars call Starborn 'living miracles,' but it isn't true! *YOU* are a miracle! I can feel it every time I'm near you! Please, just—just give me back my arm, and I'll let you free!"

Iona stared at his dismembered limb, her face growing pale. "I... I d-don't know what you want me to do," she whispered.

Arkas could feel every corner of her mind, and he sensed no deceit at all, *but how could that be true?* How could anyone stand to be so close to such vast power and not understand how to wield it? The Norn had set him on this path with this foolish girl to drive him mad!

"COME OUT!" he screamed, causing Iona to flinch back. *What was it that burned so brilliant inside this idiot girl? A celestial entity? A sleeping god?* "Am I supposed to kill her to bring you forth?"

Iona shrieked at these ravings and dropped to her knees. She held up her hands in a pathetic defensive gesture and whimpered: "Please! I don't know what you're talking about!"

Arkas trembled in rage. *There was no more time for games!* "I tried to be patient," he said in a dry whisper. "I tried to be kind." He reached down with his clumsy left hand to the inner pocket of his coat. His fingers closed around the icy hilt of the weapon he had brought, and slowly, nervously, he pulled it out.

'Teskathian,' his father's scholars called the dagger, a name that offered no translation even from the oldest dialects of Dhavic. It had belonged to Daibok, the Demon King himself. Arkas's father had ripped the thing from the monster's hand in their legendary battle. Teskathian had been used for untold centuries in blood sacrifices to the powers of hell. Arkas had only seen the blade drawn free from its black scabbard once and beheld its molten glow. The dagger had felt to his senses like a piece of damnation itself—sickening and terribly potent. It was the perfect weapon with which to threaten, and perhaps *even kill* a messiah.

"I'll give you one final chance," Arkas hissed, holding up the still sheathed knife.

Iona blinked out tears and squealed: "Oh Gods! What are you going to do?"

"Fine then!" he hissed, and he willed a thread of his magic to wrap around the black, metallic scabbard that held the weapon's power in check and yanked it away. The red-orange glow of the jagged blade burned free, radiating instant heat like a blacksmith's forge. He drew the dagger back, coiling his muscles, and cried: "NOW, YOU'RE GOING TO—"

Iona rose from the ground, and her eyes turned suddenly to orbs of blazing white light. Arkas felt power on a level he had never imagined flowing with her. With a scream, he fell back onto his hands, dropping the demonic weapon. He quickly broke into a desperate scramble away. The energy flowing off the little slave could rip through his magic and eradicate every cell in his body in an instant.

Arkas wailed in fear as Iona's right hand lifted, and a then beam of brilliant white erupted from her palm at the ground between the two them. Her power tore into the earth, throwing up an explosion of dirt and stone that would have killed Arkas had his magic not formed up into a protective cocoon at the speed of thought. He watched bewildered as dozens of rocks shattered against his shield. For a long moment, he cringed with eyes shut at what might come next, but as sweat dripped down his face, he realized that the massive energy had vanished.

The cloud of dirt took a long moment to dissipate. When Arkas could finally peer through it, he saw Iona, still standing in the same position. She was blinking slowly, a dazed look on her now filthy face. Her limbs were slackened, and she was teetering from side to side, looking as though she would drop at any second.

"W-what... w-what happened?" the girl moaned, and then she slumped down to the ground, all the strength seeming to leave her. She panted, barely able to hold her head up off the ground, but then her eyes fell on the destruction in front of her, and she let out a gasp.

Arkas took an uneasy step forward and saw what Iona saw: a charred crater in the ground large enough to bury Gorlick and five or six like him. The little slave had wreaked this destruction in half a second, and, Arkas sensed, it had been done with only the tiniest fraction of the power that resided within her—power that was once more resting quietly, *doing nothing.*

"What h-happened?" Iona squeaked again in a weak voice, and she stared at Arkas with a look of fear. He could read thoughts in her frightened mind. She believed *he* had done this...

Arkas stared at her and then gazed once more into the blackened hole between them. If any trace of the hellish weapon he had brought remained, he could neither see nor feel it. His body was still trembling, but his anxiety was subsiding as a revelation dawned very slowly in his mind.

"The *hell's* going on?" Gorlick's voice boomed from behind, and Arkas heard the crunching sound of his enormous friend bounding over the forest floor. The half-ogre emerged a few seconds later with his ax in hand, huffing through his thick teeth. A surprising impression leaped from his companion's mind: *Gorlick cared about Iona...* Perhaps it was not a kind or unselfish sort of affection, but he was genuinely frightened—

and enraged—at the idea that she might have been hurt. Apparently, the half-ogre liked having a servant to cook and clean for him, and who had grown so used to his grotesque features that she no longer cringed at the sight of him.

Seeing into Gorlick's mind brought Arkas out of his stupor. He swallowed dryly and got to his feet, meeting the brute's harsh stare. "We've had a breakthrough," he rasped.

"What?" Gorlick snapped.

"I think..." Arkas wheezed, staring at the ground and shaking his head slowly, "I think I finally know what she is." His thoughts were still racing—what he had perceived in that flash of light was virtually undeniable. The idea of playing with such power... *Perhaps this was going too far, even for him.* What horrible damnation would await Arkas when his heart finally ceased beating, and he faced divine judgment? Still, these fears were not what sickened him most.

All of it was beginning to make sense... Arkas understood what his father had done to him now, *and why.* The secrets of the empire, the demon war, the deaths of the last generation of Starborn... they fit together perfectly into a stomach-turning mosaic. He did not know Cassian's role in all of it, but he had a guess, and if it proved correct, then the heretic would soon be freed, which meant the Norn's wretched prophecy would come to pass. Cassian would kill him.

"I'm just his stepping stone," Arkas whispered, and he felt tears of bitterness well up in his eyes.

"What h-happened to the ground?" Iona said in a small squeak from the ground.

"Yeah, what the hell happened?" Gorlick snapped.

"I have to think," Arkas said, meeting the half-ogre's bulbous eyes. "This is... this is bigger than I ever thought."

"What are you babbling about?" Gorlick snorted.

"Heaven," Arkas said, sweat dripping down his face, "*and Hell.*"

"You're startin' to sound like a damn lunatic."

"Yeah," Arkas whispered, putting his remaining hand on his forehead and running his fingers through his hair. "Gorlick... do you think... do you think there's anything good in me at all?"

There was a brief moment of silence, and then the low answer: "No."

The word seemed to tighten all that was shaking inside Arkas. He drew in a slow breath and said: "Neither do I." His eyes shifted to the trembling slave, but he continued to speak to Gorlick: "I'm going to send Dunlin when the time is right. Make sure Iona is ready to leave at a moment's notice."

"Why? What are you planning?"

"I'm going to kill *all* the Starborn. Everyone except me." It felt good to say the words. There was clarity in it. If his father really were going to free Asango, then there would be an inevitable gathering—a feast perhaps to celebrate the terms the Emperor and the heretic had finally reached. Telemachus would be there, and Keska—she had been on her way to her own country but had almost certainly turned back when she learned what had befallen her precious *brother*, Cassian. With any luck, they would all be in the same place, and then, with some careful planning, Arkas could have Dunlin bring Iona into the room. *He would be far away of course.*

Arkas stared down at the large crater in the ground. How many hundreds of times greater would the reaction be if he arranged things just right? How many thousands of people would die? He would gladly sacrifice all of them to kill the four people that stood between him and the throne.

"I may need you in the capital when the time comes," Arkas said to his companion. "I don't know what the damned craith will do once my father dies. They may try to kill me. Hell, staying alive now is going to be quite a challenge."

"Yeah," Gorlick muttered with a nod. For the first time Arkas had ever seen, the monstrous half-breed looked... *uneasy.* "Iona," he whispered, gesturing to the still terrified slave girl, "what you got planned... is it gonna hurt her?"

Arkas stared at his friend for a brief moment before the lie came to his lips: "Not at all." In truth, he did not know, but he doubted her frail body would survive.

"Good," Gorlick muttered.

Arkas questioned one more time if he were making the correct decision. Once he started down this path, there would be no going back. Even so, he had little choice. The Nemesai order was all but eradicated. He could not look to them for protection—not if Cassian Asango walked free.

"Be ready to come at a moment's notice," Arkas hissed. "This is going to get ugly."

CHAPTER 35:
A SECRET MISSION

"You're telling me that *twenty* of our men are dead?" Glavius shouted. He glared around at the Onkai soldiers spread all over the forest clearing. There were shamalak as well—dozens of men, women, and children. It was a sight he would have found fascinating at another time, but right now he felt little beyond the anger and fear boiling up in the pit of his stomach. "Did anyone find Kota or Lady Gretis?"

Corafin, a captain equal in rank to Glavius, fidgeted and said: "Y-you should talk to Legate Darius." Three infantry soldiers flanked the man, and Glavius knew each of them.

"Answer the gods-damned question," he said through his teeth.

Tormin, a young soldier Glavius had rescued once from a Kothla Demon, stepped forward and said: "We found... *Lady Gretis,* sir." Before his captain could stop him, the youth pointed to a field tent that had two guards standing close together at the door.

"Is she hurt?" Glavius said. The young soldier's face paled at the question, and Glavius lunged toward him, shouting: "Is she dead?!"

Tormin started to answer, but his captain stepped in front of him, casting Glavius a stern, if sympathetic look as he said: "You need to speak to Legate Darius."

"You can tell him I'm here," Glavius grunted as he turned into a brisk walk toward the tent. When he moved within a dozen paces of the entrance, both of the guards straightened up, their gloved hands moving subtly to their sword hilts.

"Captain Glavius," the taller of the two said, giving a slight nod, "if you wish to enter this tent, you need to speak to Legate

Darius. He left orders not to admit *anyone* without his express permission."

"Where the hell is he?" Glavius said, glancing around. Darius was a smart, capable leader, and probably one of the few men Glavius looked up to in his life. Unfortunately, he could not seem to spot the man.

"The Legate is interviewing shamalak in the hills, where they found—" the soldier hesitated just long enough to send Glavius's nerves even further on edge, "he's trying to get them to track for us, sir."

"Good idea," Glavius hissed with a shrug. He started to walk toward the tent door.

"Sir!" the larger guard snapped, and he drew his sword from the scabbard at his side. "We have orders to—"

"Get out of my way, soldier," Glavius said in a deathly cold voice, staring the young man in the eyes. He did not know this pair, but they would know him. Glavius currently held the informal title of finest swordsman in the Onkai Order. Whoever these young, tattooed boys were, they had seen him fight in the sparring pits and developed a healthy fear of his skill. Their eyes told him this, and he might have felt terrible under nearly any other circumstance bullying brothers of The Order, but it was Lady Gretis inside that tent—the closest thing he had had to a mother since he was five.

The soldier on the left edged away from the door, and then his partner nervously mirrored him. Glavius looked from one to the other as he said: "You can inform Darius I'm here—tell him I pulled rank on you. He can have me whipped if he wants. I don't care."

"Yes, sir," the taller Onkai said with a nod.

Glavius stepped past the pair and untied the knot on the tent opening and then drew back the thick brown flaps. He was not sure what he might find, but as he stepped inside of the small room onto the blanketed floor, his blood turned to ice. *Silence...* the absence of any of the minute sounds living beings produced. This struck him an instant before his eyes fell on a white sheet laid over the shape of a corpse on the floor of the tent. He stared at it in shocked horror. *Gretis could not be dead!* She was the *Blade Witch*—the impossibly skilled, incomprehensibly fast warrior who knew more about swordplay than any ten Onkai soldiers—the wise and stern woman who could dance between the role of a serene master sage and a wild and lethal force held in check only by an unshakable sense of what was right.

Glavius knelt down slowly, his heart a painful lump in his chest as he reached out and drew the sheet away. There she lay, crouched and still gripping the hilt of the sword that had been driven into her gut. *Why had they not taken it out?* His eyes welled up as he stared at the black blade sticking out of the back of his teacher. Her blood was crusted to the sides...

In a daze, he peered around at the face. Gretis's eyes were shut, and her expression was remarkably tranquil. Seeing the woman's face brought finality to his disbelief. *She was dead—truly dead!* Glavius's sense of where he was grew... *fuzzy.* Rage erupted inside him, and he whirled and bolted for the door of the tent.

"GODS!" he cried, stumbling out onto the grass. His anger was too much to contain, and he rammed his fist downward. Dirt sprayed as his rune-enhanced arm tore nearly up to the elbow into the warm earth. He yanked it back out only to thrust his left fist into the ground where it struck a large rock deep within. The impact might have shattered a normal human hand, but it only served to fuel Glavius's rage. "GODS DAMMIT!" he cried, punching over and over, thrashing and tearing at the dark soil as if he could take his revenge from it.

"Glavius!" a sharp voice came from somewhere amidst the blur of the world around him, and then he felt a hand grip his right shoulder and yank. He was flipped onto his back where found himself suddenly staring up at Legate Darius.

"She's Dead!" Glavius blurted without thought, and more tears rolled out of his eyes.

Darius clenched his jaw, and then extended a hand, saying: "Get up, soldier."

Glavius reached out by reflex. Distantly, he felt his fingers close around the wrist of his commanding officer, and the muscles in his arm engage reflexively to the pulling force. He rose to his feet and gazed into Darius's eyes, whispering in a chalky voice: "Where's Kota?"

"Let's talk," the Legate said, gesturing to the tent where Gretis's body still lay.

"Sir," Glavius snapped, not moving, "Where... is... Kota?" His hand moved to the hilt of his sword. "Tell me what you know right now, or I'll go search myself!"

There was a frustrated sigh from Darius, and then the man's fist came so fast and unexpectedly that Glavius could not dodge it. It slammed into his right cheekbone, knocking him on to the ground. Before he could even catch his breath, the bottom of Darius's boot was pressed firmly into his neck. The Legate stared down, a cold look on his face as he said: "I need you to compose yourself, soldier. There is some small chance you can be of use to your friend if you can pull yourself together." He lifted his boot, and once again held out a hand.

Glavius stared up at his attacker, not caring at all about the punch but focusing on the possibility that he could be of help to Kota. "Yes, sir," he said, reaching up and taking Darius's hand a second time. When he was on his feet again, the Legate gestured to the tent, and this time Glavius walked toward it, despite the anxiety of having to gaze at Gretis's body a second time.

"I want everyone on evening prayers," Darius said as they fell into step with one another. "Pray for the dead."

The Legate opened the tent flap and stepped inside ahead. Glavius hesitated for a brief moment, and then followed. He tried not to look at the corpse, but the tip of the dark blade caught in the corner of his vision, and he choked back a violent burst of sobbing.

"Sir," he, managed to grunt, "why do you have her laid out like this with the sword still inside. She should be—" he paused as he saw Darius hold out his hand and slowly lower it, indicating that he should speak in a much quieter voice. Glavius stiffened, his muscles tensing before he swallowed and went on in a whisper: "She deserves better than this, sir."

"Look at the body," Darius said in a hushed voice, his eyes deathly serious. "Look *closely.*"

Glavius hesitated, then turned to Gretis's remains. At first, he had no idea why Darius would possibly make him look at the corpse a second time, but then he noticed something... *was wrong.* Her skin was of the same complexion he had seen only a few days before—a living, human color. Her eyes were shut, and they had not swollen as those of a long-dead body did. What was more, Gretis's lips had not curled back in the normal pattern of death but still looked smooth and supple.

"I've had this body in here for over a day," Darius whispered. "It doesn't decay or rot." He sniffed at the air and said: "You ever smelled a corpse this fresh that didn't make you want to puke your innards out, soldier?"

Glavius swallowed, his heart starting to race. "No, sir."

"Neither have I." Darius knelt down next to Gretis and said: "There's *warmth* coming off her. It isn't much, but if you look for it, it's there." Glavius grew very excited and opened his mouth, but the Legate said in a quick whisper: "Before you start bellowing, realize that there are dozens of shamalak outside, and we should assume that each of them can hear as well as Kota."

Glavius hesitated, and he became aware of the chanting of his brothers outside. Darius had ordered them into evening prayer early to drown out this conversation. *Why*? Yet this question was not nearly as important as the more immediate one.

"Gretis is a-alive?" Glavius whispered.

"Gods know how, but she isn't quite dead," Darius whispered. "That means you and I need to be very, very careful."

Glavius dropped to his knees next to his commanding officer. "What's going on, sir?"

"I don't know, but there are a handful of things that bother me about this situation. The whole shamalak tribe seems to have seen our men die at the hands of a small group of demons. I know this because I interviewed one after another. I used a translator named Narok—an old friend of Kota's. Every time one of them described the attack, he got a glazed over look in his eyes—*every single one*, whether it was a man, woman, or child." Darius rolled his eyes. "They're the ones that directed me to Gretis's body, yet when I ask these shamalak if they can track Kota—whom none of them report having seen—they all say the same three words: 'Nia voro gas." It roughly translates into something like: "Cannot find the scent." The Legate rolled his eyes. "I took over a dozen of them up there, each one individually, and I received the same answer, word-for-word, every time, and each tribesman had the same glassy-eyed-look. Does that suggest anything to you, Captain?"

Glavius felt himself frown. He understood little of psychic warfare, but he recalled a distant lecture he had heard from a Lucinian monk on memory tampering, and how the victims sometimes caught a strange, detached expression and were prone to repeating the same phrases over and over when describing events that had been psychically inserted into their minds.

"You think an entire tribe of shamalak had their memories altered?" he said.

"That was my guess, and so I took a very close look at the battlefield, and I found something that made the hair on the back of my neck stand up." Darius took in a dry swallow and said: "I almost missed it, but the dirt was especially loose in quite a few places—almost like a hole had been there that was recently filled in. Being as careful as I could not to let anyone see, I poked at a few of these sections with my boots. All the holes I found were in roughly the same shape—the imprint of a clawed foot almost the size...of a man's body."

Glavius's eyes widened. "An Archdemon," he said in a dry voice.

"Yes, the biggest one we've seen on this continent since the demon war. The shamalak did not report seeing an enormous monster. They only described a handful of lesser creatures of hell led by a nathret. That means that everything we are seeing here is a deception—a carefully painted picture set out for *us* to tell a false story."

By unthinking reflex, Glavius glanced behind him, looking at the tent door, and again he heard the chanting of his brothers outside. Glavius understood now the reason for Darius's caution. "Do you know why, sir?"

"*Why* is not entirely clear, though we can at least guess that part of the reason was to avoid the massive response our order would make if we found clear evidence of a powerful Archdemon in Denigoth. I think that *who* did this is a more important matter for the moment." Darius glanced at Gretis's still form as he said: "Depending on the skill and talent of the telepath involved, it can take hours or even days to alter an individual's memories. Starborn can do it much faster, but even then—an *entire tribe* with pre-programmed responses..."

"Hold on," Glavius said, putting a hand on the legate's shoulder. "Do you think that one of the starborn was involved?"

Darius grimaced. "I don't know, but we shouldn't dismiss it as a possibility—not with a telepathic feat on this level. I know that Keska Ethedrine and Arkas Adronicus left the capital recently and are roaming about the countryside, and..." the Legate hesitated, his tattooed face almost seeming to pale as he said: "Actually, I heard reports that the Emperor left as well."

"Tacitus?!" Glavius almost shouted.

"I'm certainly not jumping to any conclusions with him," Darius said quickly. "Why the hell would The Emperor of

Denigoth bother with a bunch of shamalak in the wilderness? Then again, why would any of them? In truth, the only starborn I know wasn't here is Cassian Asango, and that's because he was locked in a Nemesai cell when this would have happened."

"What?" Glavius hissed, jerking.

"You haven't heard?" Darius said.

"No, sir," Glavius said, shaking his head. "A starborn in a cell? Are... are they going to kill him? Would Otho let them?"

"I don't know the answer to that, but," he swallowed, "have you passed by any Nemesai temples on your way here?"

"I kept to the country roads, sir."

"Hmmm," Darius grunted, pursing his lips. "I might as well tell you that—so far as I know and can extrapolate—Cassian Asango's men have destroyed every temple on the continent, and all the attending Nemesai are... *missing."*

"Holy shit!" Glavius hissed. His eyes widened, and though he was a servant of the church and was bound to stand on the side of any of the orders against outside force, his first instinct was to smile. "Asango is one dangerous son of a bitch!"

"Dangerous enough to be killed," Darius whispered. "There will be no question now as to whether Cromlic can execute him. For all I know, my old comrade's head has already been cut off, but as troubling as that is, you and I have more pressing concerns."

"Yeah," Glavius muttered, still overwhelmed by what he had just heard. He looked at the Legate and was grateful that the man was here. In the face of all of this madness, Darius was smart, cautious, and level-headed.

"All the evidence most likely points to either a significant number of sorcerers from the empire colluding with the forces of hell, or that the demon king has more nathret under his command than anyone has guessed, and they are operating in Denigoth." Darius cocked his head and looked into Glavius's eyes "I'm fairly sure you know as well as I do that Kota was no ordinary shamalak—he wasn't even ordinary by the terms of the Sansrit. The fact that he was here—that this was *his tribe*—cannot be a coincidence."

"No..." Glavius whispered, staring down at the tent floor. "Sir, what do we do? Do you think he's dead?"

"We haven't found a body," Darius sighed. "I haven't found anything really beyond what I've just told you. There doesn't seem to be much here that can tell us what truly happened," his eyes shifted once again to Gretis's body, "except *her*."

Glavius hunched forward on his knees toward Gretis, looking down at her. Despite the sword through her gut, she seemed remarkably tranquil. He knew more about what an animus could do than most, having recently become aware that one lived inside him. To an extent, they could heal the flesh, but this... He realized why Darius had left the sword through her gut. If it were pulled free, her innards would spill out.

Glavius clenched his jaw. "What can we do for her, sir?"

"Very little," Darius said. "That's a demonic blade. Our healers can't do anything for her wounds." He leaned in toward Glavius and said in an even quieter voice: "That's why I'm sending you on a secret mission. You're going to go *to the elves*."

"Sir?" Glavius grunted, staring at the legate, stiffening in surprise.

"It's a long shot, but it's all we have at the moment. In some of the old texts, there are reports that elves have a way of breaking the corruption of demon-inflicted-wounds. If that can be done, then maybe..." he glanced at Gretis's body, his face looking gravely uncertain. "Like I said, it's a long shot, but it's all we have."

"Would the elves even help us? They haven't in centuries."

"One did," Darius muttered. "You will recall that girl who appeared in our temple years ago on Kota's behalf."

Glavius blinked. Of course he recalled Thalice Corostine. Every young man present that day in the temple remembered her. The absurdly lovely elf was the chief subject of most of their dreams and romantic fantasies. She had become a legend spoken of to new recruits who had not been lucky enough to gaze upon her unworldly beauty.

"In private quarters that night, Thalice invited Kota and Gretis to come to her home," Darius said. "It's possible she would help Gretis now. We have to try."

"Yes we do," Glavius said, his muscles tightening. "I'll take her right now."

"No, you won't," Darius said with a low sigh. "Whoever did all of this has a strong interest in keeping whatever Gretis might have to say a secret, and we should assume that, with everything they have managed to pull off here, they will have some means of keeping an eye on us to make sure we swallow what they've served us." Darius put a hand very, very gently on Gretis's shoulder and said: "Her heart isn't even beating. I doubt it would take much to tip her fully into death. You and I aren't sorcerers, Glavius. We might not even know if someone nearby cast a spell to tie up this *loose end*." He shook his head. "No, we are going to be extremely careful. I have men building a coffin in the forest. You and I are going to bring it in here and fill it with sand. Then we're going to load it into the back of a cart so everyone can see. In consequence for your *outburst* a few minutes ago, I'm going to assign you packing duty. You're going to collapse this tent and load it and all of its contents into a wagon. You'll do this while I give a speech to our men and the tribe about the dead and friendship and cooperation between our two peoples, so that as many eyes as possible are off you."

Glavius drew in a deep breath, considering his instructions. "Sir, what if there are telepaths about reading our thoughts right now?"

"If there are, then we are already doomed to fail," Darius said with a grim shrug, "but I don't think we're being observed that way. I've had all of this in my mind for more than a day, and I'm still alive. Until the moment we are defeated, we need to assume that success is possible and press forward, for there is far too much at stake to hesitate."

"Yes, sir," Glavius said with a nod.

Darius pursed his lips. "You're right to be worried about telepaths though. That's why I'm not telling the men any of this. You and I... we're the only ones. It's the best we can do. When this troop sets out for the Northern Temple, you and I are going to have a heated argument. You'll accuse me of not looking hard enough for Kota. Most of the men know how friendly you two were, so it will be plausible. I'll become frustrated with you and send you on some humiliating errand to the Southern Temple, saying that I'm sick of you. You'll sulk and head south for at least an hour, and then turn east. You'll keep to the back roads as much as possible, avoiding all large cities where sorcerers might lurk."

Darius reached into the collar of his shirt and drew out a small, corked vial, which hung from a leather cord about his neck. He pulled it up and off his head and held it out to Glavius. "This is a potion made from elf's blood—one of the last the order has. Otho made me take it before he sent me here on the chance that something might have happened to Kota or Gretis. There's not much, so you'll need to ration it. I've been putting a drop in Gretis's mouth every few hours to try to help along whatever's keeping her alive. I have no idea whether it's doing a damned thing, but I want you to keep it up."

"Yes, sir," Glavius said, accepting the vial. He stared at it for a brief moment, then whispered: "How will I find the elven city, sir?"

"I've already drawn you a map," Darius said. Glavius felt his eyes go wide at these words, but before he could ask, the Legate said: "We've always known where a few of their cities are. The higher ranked members of the order are shown documents with many closely held secrets about our immortal friends." Darius gazed up at the ceiling, a tired look on his face. "We stay away from them out of respect for the treaty our predecessors signed hundreds of years ago. I don't *technically* have the authority to send a soldier into their lands. You should know... they may kill you on sight."

"I understand, sir," Glavius said, his voice perfectly calm. *Of course he would risk his life for Kota and Gretis.* They would do no less for him.

"All right then," Darius said, nodding. He reached into a pocket in his jacket and drew out a small, neatly rolled scroll. "I'm a fair hand at drawing. Hopefully you can follow this." As Glavius took the scroll, Darius patted him on the shoulder and said: "I'm glad you made it here, Glavius." The tiniest of smiles touched the Legate's cold, serious face as he added: "I hope you live. If you do, you'll be the first human to set foot in a populated elven city in over three hundred years."

Glavius smirked. "I'll try not to die then, sir."

CHAPTER 36: SACRIFICE

"You do not have to do this," Telemachus said, his expression contorted in pain. The young man's hand was on Somar's shoulder, clutching tightly. "Cassian would not want you to die."

The air was cold and thick in the vault below the Obsidian Order's headquarters in the capital. It was an expansive room filled with hundreds upon hundreds of books and arcane treasures gathered by the order's many powerful members throughout the centuries.

"Do not dare let him know," Somar said sharply. "You will give me that respect, Telemachus, won't you?"

The Starborn swallowed dryly. "I will, but in return, let me debate this with you once more before you go forward."

Somar smiled at the smooth featured young man. *He was so unlike Cassian.* Telemachus was averse to making threats or flaunting his awesome power. Rather, he sought out the noblest parts of men and inspired them. Somar had come to respect these qualities enormously, but this was not a time for kindness. Bishop Cromlic had Cassian in a torture cell.

"There is nothing to debate," Somar said with a chuckle, smiling. "This is my choice, without regret. I have outlived many finer men than myself. From peasant to Imperial General to even Senator, and then finally tutor to the most remarkable person I have ever met... My life has been a grand adventure, and I am grateful for all of it, but I am quite old now. No desire burns within me to cling to a few more years when I could use my life to save *him*."

Telemachus grimaced. "All Cassian has to do is sign a piece of paper and kneel."

"And he never will," Somar sighed, "nor would I wish him to."

"Your life is worth more than my brother's damned pride!"

"You know this is about far more than that," Somar said in a gentle voice. "It is principal and conviction. The Nemesai are *wrong,* and Cassian is doing what no one else in the world is willing to do in standing up to them."

"And you wish to die so that he can *what*? The instant my brother steps out of his cell, he will be a criminal—the most infamous one in the world."

"Perhaps," Somar exhaled, "and perhaps not. Some men manage to rise above the law, and I don't think you or I can possibly say what the Emperor will do."

Telemachus frowned but said nothing. This was not the first time Somar had noted that the young man appeared unsettled by the actions and tendencies of his Emperor.

"Please help Cassian as much as you can when this is over," Somar said. "I believe there is a reason there are five starborn rather than one. You are so many of the things that Cassian is not, and yet he is much that you are not."

Telemachus swallowed. "Well, the person that *I am* does not approve of this course of action."

Somar gripped the young man's shoulder, and for an instant, he let his mental guard down so that Telemachus could feel his resolve. "This is what I want," he whispered.

The starborn youth stared into his eyes for a long moment and then nodded with a grim expression. He reached into a pocket in his fine silken robe and withdrew a shiny black pill the size of an almond. Somar took it.

"This is smaller than I thought," he whispered as he rolled the cool, smooth mass in his hand. "Are you sure it will be enough?"

"No need to worry about that," Telemachus said with a dejected sigh. "It is *unbelievably* potent."

"And you're certain Cromlic will not be able to detect the magic inside?"

"The pill is coated with a mixture of amber and lead, which will poison you by the way, though that will be the least of your worries."

"How do I activate it?"

Grimacing slightly, Telemachus muttered: "When the time comes, slip it between your teeth and bite down. You *should* have two to three minutes before your heart explodes, but I can't be certain of that, given your age."

"I understand," Somar said. He reached up and slipped the little pill under his tongue. It felt strange and unnaturally cold in his mouth, but he knew he would not have to hold it there long.

"Goodbye, my friend," Somar said, practicing speaking with the deathly object in his mouth.

"Goodbye, old man," Telemachus whispered, gazing down at the white marble floor.

Somar drew in a breath through his nostrils and turned around, and as he did, he felt a small thrill. Even now, in his feeble and aching form, he could affect the fate of the world. What he was about to do would be written of for centuries. He scrambled up the white marble stairs and out the great beautifully carved ebony doorway of the Obsidian Guild into the capital streets. His mind was racing faster than it had in years, and he perceived everything around him in vivid, colorful detail. The night was calm and quiet in the wealthy square where the guild's headquarters sat, but to the east, where the Nemesai were holding Cassian, the distant sound of shouting echoed. The peasants were furious that their savior had been abducted, and now that they had learned the Nemesai were too frightened to venture out and face the dragon in the street, many had begun to gather and shout and even throw things at the temple. *Cassian was already winning.*

Somar walked in a slow gait, his hood drawn back. His movements were likely already being watched. Cromlic was desperate to apprehend him, and the Nemesai had spies and informers all throughout the city. They had been waiting for him to step away from Telemachus, *and now he had.* Just to be certain he caught his unseen observers' attention though, Somar drew out the bottle of wine he had stuffed in the pocket of his robe, pulled the cork, and took a quick drink, making sure not to swallow the pill. Then he shouted: "You bassstards!" in his loudest, most slurred baritone. "Where is Cassssssian?!" He took another sip, purposely spilling wine on his chest, and then bellowed: "NEMESAI S-S-SCUM!" Then he stumbled forward and let loose a string of obscenities loud and horrible enough to get the attention of everyone within several blocks.

He had only to wait a moment before he heard the patter of footsteps behind him, and a fierce, authoritative male voice shout: "Somar Dojinko!"

"WHAT?!" Somar shouted, spinning clumsily around to see five men in dark robes, the closest of which had the distinctive markings of the Nemesai on his face. "Don't come near meee, bastards!" he hissed, taking a defiant sip of the wine and then smashing the bottle on the ground and glaring.

"Take him!" the inquisitor shouted. The other cloaked figures dashed at Somar and grabbed him by the arms and hair, and then the leader stepped forward and leaned into Somar's face. With a smirk, the man said: "You picked a terrible time to wander off drunk, old man." He slapped Somar across the face with a gloved hand. The blow was hard, carrying enough augmented strength to burst several dozen blood vessels around Somar's cheekbone. It might have hurt less if he hadn't been clutching his teeth to keep the pill in place. The inquisitor went on: "I can't believe how foolish you are, *Great General* of the Imperial Army." He cast a quick gaze around then and then said aloud: "We need to get him back to the church before that starborn realizes what's happing. Tie his hands and search him."

A bag was thrown over Somar's head from behind, and he felt his wrists being bound while strong hands moved around his body in cruel, humiliating ways. They found nothing. As soon as the search was over, Somar was forcibly marched down the street with rough shoves and slaps to the head amidst brief instructions. After a few moments, he was lifted under the arms into the back of what seemed to be a wagon, which promptly began to roll over the bumpy capital streets. Somar knew he was being taken directly to the Nemesai Temple by the increasing volume of shouting in the air from the peasants—shouts for Cassian's freedom.

"These idiots are going to attack the cart!" a voice said furiously to Somar's left.

"No they won't," the leader's voice replied. "We have steel and crossbows, and they know it. Don't be such a coward."

The inquisitor was evidently correct, as Somar's cart wheeled through a furious cacophony of threatening screams, but they did not so much as slow down. Somar heard the sound of gates opening and then being closed from behind after they had rolled further. They came to a stop, and a moment later he was gripped by his wrists and brought out of the cart. Without words, his captors led him on a long, cold walk. The ground under his feet seemed to be slick, wet grass at first, then later it became hard stone, and then he was stepping down stairs. Eventually, Somar was halted by a sharp jerk at his right arm.

"Keep him here," the leader said in an excited voice, and Somar heard the man's boots slap across the floor. A door opened some distance away and then closed again. There was the sound of muffled voices for perhaps half a minute, and then the door opened again.

"Lord Dojinko!" Bishop Cromlic's unmistakable voice boomed. It had a tone of cruel delight in it that might have caused Somar to bristle were he not planning to do what he was. Eager footsteps moved toward him, and suddenly the bag was yanked from his head, and he was standing eye-to-eye with Cassian's worst enemy. "I am so very, *very* glad to have you as my guest, old friend," the Bishop almost cackled, displaying a great many of his yellowed teeth as he spoke.

Somar could not resist returning the grin and saying: "Bishop Cromlic, it is so nice to see you like this—not cowering at my pupil's feet and begging for your life, I mean."

A hard slap came to the back of Somar's head, and again he nearly lost the pill. A deep voice from behind said: "Shall I cut his disrespectful tongue out, sir?"

"Not just yet," Cromlic said, breathing hard through open lips. He leaned into Somar's face. "Yes, it must have been quite a thrill for you two heretics to attack a Bishop of the church. Unfortunately, all your prideful sinning has come to an end."

Not quite yet, Somar thought but did not say as he met the terrible man's stare. "I suppose you'll want to put me in front of Cassian now, so you can get the most out of torturing me. Shall we get on with it?"

The Bishop's face lost all its cruel humor, and he said in an icy voice: "*Your pupil* will see all that defiance crushed and broken. Before I'm done with you, you'll beg him to confess just to bring an end to your suffering."

"We shall see," Somar said.

"Bring this fool," Cromlic hissed. Somar's lack of fear was infuriating him. The old man huffed and twitched as he walked down a dim hall lit by wall candles. Somar was forced to walk behind. They went together through a heavy steel door at the hall's end and down a dark, winding stairway until he finally emerged into an enormous room full of cells and torture implements. Along the way, Somar had listened carefully to the footsteps behind him. From what he could tell, there were only two Nemesai in the room other than Cromlic. *That was good.*

Sweat dripped off Somar's face as they stepped down the row of cells. In the dim torchlight, he could see frightened souls hiding behind bars, and slowed to look at them. The smell of the place might have been horrible, but his heart was beating far too quickly in his feeble chest for such things to matter. He was in a dreamlike state. Every sense was heightened, and all input blended together. These were his last moments.

"Don't linger!" the Nemesai said from behind. Somar felt the tip of a blade poke him in his back just below the left shoulder, and he winced at a shallow stab into his skin as his captor added: "Hurry up."

"Certainly," Somar said through gritted teeth, quickening his pace.

Cassian's voice came suddenly into his mind: <What are you doing here! Why did Telemachus let them take you!>

Unable to answer in kind, Somar used his voice: "It is all right, Cassian." His words echoed down the dim hall, and he felt another blow to the back of his head in punishment.

"Do not TOUCH him!" Cassian's voice cried through a small grating in a thick metal door.

"Be careful," the Bishop said, his deep voice filled with amusement. "We want our new guest conscious."

"Yes, sir," the inquisitor said, and then Somar felt his hair being gripped from behind. "Don't speak again unless you are told to, old man."

The Bishop walked forward and fished a key out of a concealed pocket in his robes, which he slipped into a hole in the door. Then the old sorcerer brought the door open with a wave of his hand and said: "Good evening, Lord Asango, we have brought you a guest."

Somar heard the sounds of chains clinking along with Cassian shouting: "You smirking idiot! Do you think I cannot attack you even now? I have agents all around this church, as well as my DRAGON! If you hurt him, this place will be burned to the ground in minutes!"

Some of the glee left the Bishop's face, and he glared into the cell. "Always so dangerous. I do not believe you, boy." He made a quick gesture with his hand, and Somar was forcibly marched forward to the cell door. Cassian came into view, covered in leeches, scabs, and bruises. Cromlic's hand raised in front of Somar's face, and he whispered: "*Rahazak*!" A swirling ball of blue fire formed hovering above the man's palm. "I am the one making *threats* now, Asango, and you will finally listen!"

Cassian rose, chains clinking, and Somar saw in his eyes that he meant to attack. Even now, he had some hidden power, *but it would not be enough*. The dragon's prophecy had been quite clear. Without Somar's help, the boy would die.

"Wait!" Somar said in a loud, authoritative voice.

For a brief moment, both Cassian and the Bishop froze. Somar looked at his pupil as he slipped the pill between his teeth and bit down. A fiery hot liquid squirted out in his mouth, and he swallowed. It burned and tingled on the way down, and then his body began to feel terrifyingly hot.

"I want you to know that I did this willingly," he said, staring at his beloved pupil. "Telemachus tried very hard to talk me out of it, but when we went down into the island of death together, and I looked into the Great Dragon's eyes, he told me this moment would come, and I would have this choice to make."

The Bishop moved the flame closer to Somar's face and hissed: "What are you talking about, you blubbering old fool?"

Somar felt the raw magic infusing his decrepit body with raw, tremendous power. It was different than anything he had been expecting. Greater. Every muscle, every nerve was on fire, and it was wonderful!

"What have you done?!" Cassian said, his emerald eyes going wide.

Somar smiled and snapped the rope that had been holding his wrists as if it were thin paper. His body moved more quickly than it ever had in his life. With one hand, he gripped Cromlic's outstretched wrist, easily overpowering the strength in the shocked Bishop's body and twisting his arm. Whatever spell the man had conjured dissipated into nothingness as he shrieked in pain. Keeping his grip on Cromlic, Somar whirled in half a second on the men behind him and delivered a closed-fisted-blow to the closer one's face. He felt bone crunch under the force of his knuckles, and the man fell to the ground and began to convulse. The second Nemesai fumbled for his sword, but Somar head-butted him right between the eyes. That one dropped to the ground next to his fallen brother, a limp mass.

Cromlic wriggled and hissed: "Get off me, you—GHH!"

Somar caught the vile man by the throat and lifted him up off the floor. The Bishop seemed as light as a child's doll. He jerked and clutched at Somar's hand.

"Cassian," Somar said, unable to stifle a laugh. "Is this what you feel like all the time? This power is absurd!"

"It will kill you," Cassian said. His face was a pale contortion of pain.

"Oh yes, but I knew it would." He squeezed Cromlic's neck, cutting off the airflow completely. The hissing turned to a gurgle. "I'm sorry, but I cannot let you kill this man. You hate him far too much. If you murder in hatred, it mutilates your soul. This I know." Somar squeezed harder until he felt a crunch. He let go, and the Bishop fell dead upon the floor.

Cassian stared down at Cromlic's body, transfixed by it. It was the first time Somar had ever seen the boy rendered speechless.

"I take your darkest sin from you, my son," Somar wheezed. He walked forward. His body was already beginning to deteriorate. He could feel bone and muscle burning. *The pleasure was becoming pain!* He reached out and grabbed a leech in each hand from Cassian's chest and said with a dark chuckle: "Brace yourself, boy." He yanked.

"SHHHK!" Cassian shrieked, his body trembling wildly as skin and perhaps even a bit of muscle tissue came away. He took several incredibly rapid breaths and then said: "Hurry, get them all off! Maybe I can still save you!"

The old man's fingers closed around two more leaches and ripped them away. This time Cassian was silent, but Somar was beginning to hiss with pain. He did not understand anatomy the way Cassian did, but he knew instinctively that his body was ceasing to function. The unfiltered magic coursing through him was ripping his insides apart. *There were only seconds left!*

In quick succession, Somar grabbed the last three leeches and yanked them away, and then he fell to the floor, a panting, sweat-soaked heap.

"NO!" Cassian shouted. His shackles ripped away from his skin with a furious metallic snap. Somar smiled. *The boy had all his power back*. "WHY DID YOU DO THIS! I never asked you to help me!"

Somar felt his body going very still. The pain was receding. He felt warm and at peace. "This is a good death," he managed to whisper.

Cassian gripped his hand, though Somar barely felt it. The boy whispered: "You are the only—" he broke off, and tears dropped from his eyes, "You were more a father to me than my own ever was."

"Thank you, Cassian," Somar softly exhaled. His vision was going black. "I think that our time together... was my favorite part of my life." He blinked, trying to see the boy, but he could not. It was difficult to speak—difficult even to remember what words were. "Do not.... die. Be strong, Cassian. Always... be... strong."

Somar lost all connection to where he was. Cassian faded away, and warm, immense light appeared before him, drawing him in. It was the most beautiful thing he had ever seen...

CHAPTER 37: HIS DESTINY

Cassian stared down at the old man's lifeless body. His best friend was.... *gone,* the way his mother had been gone. They were stolen away into a realm that all of Cassian's immense gifts could not reach, and the sickening pain of that finality was overwhelming.

"I understand why you did what you did," he whispered to the dead form, imagining that somewhere, Somar's soul was watching him. "We were the same, you and I, in our hearts if not in our circumstances. You understood everything I have done, and perhaps now... you will understand everything I am about to do."

Cassian rose slowly as the last of his tears fell. He was enveloped in something beyond rage. By merely thinking it, he summoned spectral entities to heal his many wounds. They obeyed his will as they never had before. The constant mental battle with the leeches seemed to have honed his control over magic to new heights, *or perhaps it was just the unbridled focus of hate.*

Cassian stepped out of his cell and gazed down the length of the Nemesai dungeon. Twenty-six sets of iron bars lay before him in a long row, many holding prisoners. He raised his hands, extending his fingers as he sent dozens of invisible tendrils of his power into and around the poles, and then he brought his hands together in a sudden clap. All the metallic bars ripped out of the mortar and collided into one another at the hall's center in a thunderous crash.

<Do not be afraid,> Cassian said in a telepathic whisper as he reached into the minds of the suddenly terrified prisoners. <All of you are free to return to your families without fear of the Nemesai. *I will take care of them.*>

There was a clinking to his right, and Cassian turned his head to see Soulic tugging on his chains as if to draw attention to himself. The man had been shackled to the wall as Cassian had been, but his injuries were far more extensive. Cassian flicked his wrist, sending twin slivers of magic from his fingers focused into thin blades. They slashed through the joints in Soulic's shackles with ease, and the Sansrit warrior stumbled forward as half rings of metal dropped at his feet.

Soulic forced himself up without words and walked toward Cassian. His naked chest was covered in still open wounds, and he looked thinner than he had been when they entered. The Nemesai had barely fed him at all, and he had been put through a hell even worse than Cassian had. Through all of it, the swordsman had not said a word—not given the Nemesai so much as the satisfaction of a whimper.

"Can you fix these?" Soulic rasped, holding up his arms. Both hands had crooked, broken fingers.

"Yes," Cassian replied. He held up his own hand and thought—*not spoke*—a spell. The small bones in Soulic's fingers snapped back together and into their proper places. The warrior's horribly bruised face remained expressionless as the magic knitted the hard and soft pieces of the fingers into working order.

"Leeches," Soulic said, tilting his head to the side. He had been given two. One was on the side of his neck, and the other was on his right pectoral muscle. Cassian waved his fingers, willing tendrils of power out with tightly controlled precision. The pulsing leeches emitted horrid screams as their bulbous bodies were sliced in half. Soulic finally displayed a touch of emotion by breathing a sigh of relief. He wagged his neck from side to side, eliciting several pops from the bones inside, and then said: "What's our play?"

Cassian glanced back at Somar's lifeless body, then said: "I am going to destroy this place—wipe it from the face of the world."

"Sounds about right," Soulic said in a vicious hiss. He walked past Cassian to one of the Nemesai soldiers Somar had killed and snatched the man's sword. He held it up in front of his face for a moment, looking closely at it and waving it in the air as if to gauge the weight and balance. Then he shrugged, lowered the weapon to his side, and said: "Ready when you are."

"Your father's name is Gaius Norvelian," Cassian said.

Soulic froze at these words and stared at Cassian through the black bruises around his eyes.

Cassian glanced around at the prisoners still crouching nervously in their cells. They were not certain what to do. Each of them had suffered along with Soulic and himself. Up in the temple rooms, the Nemesai were starting to stir. The thick ceiling above his head had muffled the sound, but the inquisitors had heard something, and they would soon come to investigate.

"The man is seventy-nine years old," Cassian went on. "Lord Norvelian is in poor health. Among his afflictions is a significant degradation of his mind. He is given to fits of screaming and paranoia—very possibly the result of reliving old battles and... *sins.*"

"Why are you telling me this?" Soulic said.

"I promised I would reveal his identity if you served me, and after this," he gestured around the dungeon, "you have given me more than enough. You may leave my service now. Come here, and I will remove the psychic tampering I did to your mind."

Soulic gazed down at the stone floor for a long moment, breathing softly, and then he looked up at Cassian and said: "No thank you."

Cassian frowned at him. The man's animus was quickly regaining its strength, and thus its defenses around his thoughts were returning. Rather than attempt to breach them, Cassian said: "Why not?"

Soulic drew in a deep breath. "I've had some time to think during this... *experience*, and, if I'm honest with myself, I'm a mad dog. I need a collar around my neck, or I'm a danger to the world. You're a good fit to hold the leash. I doubt I could ever find anyone better." He gazed down at the Nemesai body beneath his feet and sighed: "Besides, I don't think it would bring me much satisfaction to murder a crazy old man—not when I've finally found something to hate even more!" He kicked the Nemesai in the chest, and, with a crunch, the lifeless form sailed a dozen paces in the air until it collided with the wall and bounced.

"It may be unwise to continue serving me," Cassian said.

They heard footsteps above, and a gruff voice shout: "What the hell happened down there?"

Soulic glanced at the door to the upper chambers. "If you destroy this temple, how will the Emperor react?"

"He may be a bit cross with me," Cassian said, "and, by extension, you."

Soulic frowned for a few seconds, looking thoughtful, and then he shrugged. "Let's do it anyway. What are your orders?"

They heard the crossbar to the dungeon entrance being slid open, and Cassian saw a young soldier in his mind's eye.

<GET BACK!> he said in a psychic shout into the man's mind. The Nemesai leaped away from the door in terror.

Cassian looked at Soulic. "Our Elokiens are being kept on the third floor of this structure in a wooden chest. If we somehow make it through this, I would prefer not to have to fish them out of the rubble."

Soulic lifted his stolen sword and gently touched the tip with his finger as if to gauge the sharpness. "How many are up there?"

"Twenty-two," Cassian said. "Four have gathered in front of the door thus far. Another eighteen are rushing down from the upper levels."

"Twenty-two it is," Soulic said, his voice taking on a strange, almost beastly cadence, and Cassian felt the power of the man's animus begin to flare.

"Just a moment," Cassian said. Soulic could certainly outfight a handful of Nemesai, but these odds were somewhat ridiculous. Cassian gazed up at the ceiling and focused his magic upon the air, mentally forming the cracking field he had developed long ago to expand and amplify the vibrations of his voice many hundreds of times over, and then he spoke aloud: "This is Cassian Asango. Bishop Cromlic is dead. The Nemesai order has come to an end. I am going to destroy this horrid place. I know all of you cruel men can hear me. I grant you one brief moment to run away with your wicked lives. You have sixty seconds." He sensed a psychic explosion of fear above him as the soldiers of the church panicked, trying to decide what to do.

"You have a gift for subtlety," said Soulic, gazing at him with a raised eyebrow.

Cassian turned and walked to the nearest empty cell, raised his hand, and then began to chant. Nearly two years ago, he had seen Dimitris cast the Drathnakal—the most destructive spell known to man. Cassian had not heard the words his brother whispered, but somehow, they came to him now, as if drawn from the ether of the universe. He felt a massive swell of his own power leap from his hand and become absorbed into a cacophony of whirring spectral forces. He focused them into a battering ram of spinning energy that glinted every conceivable color to an almost blinding level in the darkness of the dungeon. When it was ready, he sent his construction forward. The spell ripped through the stonework, obliterating everything in its path. Remaining in control, Cassian curved the Drathnakal upward, and within a few thunderous seconds, he had carved a tunnel up and out of the temple to the streets of the capital. The spell continued its path even after he let go, soaring up into the sky, and there came a collective awe from hundreds of the minds of peasants that had come to protest for him.

<It is time to leave the temple now,> he telepathically whispered to the men and women who had shared his imprisonment. <Stand up, please.>

Nervously, one-by-one, the prisoners did as they were told. Cassian watched a feeble old man in tattered rags come to him first, and then a slender girl a few years younger than himself. They had bruises of course and looked half starved.

"ASANGO!" a deep shout boomed through the door from above.

"Ah-h, there's that bastard," Soulic said with a vicious smirk. Cassian recognized the voice from above as belonging to Sebastos, the remarkably tall high inquisitor who had spent dozens of hours inflicting pain on his Sansrit companion.

Soulic walked to the mess of bars in the center of the dungeon and snatched one up in his hands. He moved to the foot of the stairway and cocked the long piece of iron back like a javelin and shut his eyes, breathing softly as he adjusted the angle of his shot to whatever his animus was sensing. "SEBASTOS!" he shouted suddenly, and then he sent the bar flying. It tore a hole through the thick wood and disappeared through it, and immediately after came one of the loudest screams Cassian had ever heard.

A fierce grin played across Soulic's bruised features as the Nemesai's groans grew quieter until they twisted into a sickening gurgle.

Cassian turned back to the other prisoners, who were cowering at this new show of violence. "Go," he said to them in a gentle but authoritative voice, gesturing toward the exit he had drilled in the wall. They timidly moved at his command and disappeared up the rough pathway of charred stone and soil. When the last of them was gone, Cassian turned to Soulic and said: "You may go now."

"Bye," Soulic said, and he raised his sword and ran up at what was left of the door. The mad Sansrit warrior burst through it in a spray of splinters and then began to attack. Cassian did not bother to follow the battle. Nearly every Nemesai in the temple had fled now, and the few left were no match for Soulic. Instead, he shut his eyes and reached out to his dragon, whom he could sense only a few hundred paces away, clawing eagerly at the ground.

<Titus, COME!> Cassian felt the creature bolt forward and leap into the air, spreading his wings. The dragon sent forth a blast of white fire that shattered a section of the temple's eastern wall and then folded its wings and whipped through the resulting hole. Cassian felt the dragon land on the floor above his head. He raised his hand and sent a burst of invisible concussive force upward, and his power ripped through the wood and stone. Then he willed his body to rise, and after a few seconds he was eye level with his beloved pet. The dragon leaned into his face, its hot, sulfurous breath stinging his skin.

"I have missed you," he said, running his hands over the rough scales. The dragon nuzzled his forehead for a few heartbeats with its snout, and then it turned and gazed down through the newly made hole in the floor, its blazing yellow eyes fixing on Somar's lifeless form.

"Yes," Cassian whispered, "he is dead."

The dragon's lips curled back, revealing curved teeth. If Titus thought of Cassian as its father, then Somar was something of an uncle. The old man had walked with the dragon in the gardens some days, and he had spoken to Titus like a child, telling it about the world and even reading to it in the evenings.

"We are going to destroy this place," Cassian whispered, putting a hand on the back of his companion's neck. "We shall leave a gaping scar in the world as has never been created by man." Titus emitted a metallic growl of anger and a nod. It continued to stare at Somar's body as Cassian climbed onto its scaly back.

He grabbed hold of the bone-spikes on the dragon's head he had used so many times before as handles. Seated, Cassian made a slow gesture toward the old man. His magic reached out and cradled Somar's limp form, raising him up carefully through the hole in the floor.

"Soulic," Cassian said, sensing the eyes of the Sansrit warrior behind him, "take Somar's body outside. He needs to be at least fifty paces back from the temple walls. Make sure the protestors are likewise drawn back from the parameter."

"Understood," Soulic said as he stepped around Titus. He held up his arms and accepted the corpse, and then looked up at Cassian and said: "What are you going to do?"

"I am not entirely certain. Just go."

Soulic nodded and hurried away, carrying the old man's body with an acceptable degree of respect.

Cassian reached then into the ether, his mind shifting back to the construction of the catlike creature Dimitris had unleashed upon him years ago in their duel. As with the Drathnakal, he had not learned the names of the spectral entities that went into this spell, yet they came anyhow. *Never had he felt so connected to his sorcery.*

Cassian shut his eyes and poured his anger into his magic, and it took shape into three massive, wolf-like creatures of shimmering blackness. He stared at them only for an instant before issuing a simple telepathic command: *<Rip everything here to shreds!>* The apparitions lurched into violent attacks upon the walls, the pews, the doors, and the stained glass windows that depicted horrible images suffering in the name of divine justice. The beasts were extensions of Cassian's will, yet they were alive and capable of acting on their own. The thrill of their wild frenzy filled him with a sense of omnipotence.

He rose with Titus, dragon and master as one, high above the chaos. The vaulted ceiling above them shattered with a thought. Cassian's power seemed to know no limits. Below, he sensed Soulic make it to the street. The Sansrit warrior began to shout at the enormous crowd, and they slowly drew back from the temple, which was now in flames. As Cassian rose higher into the sky, he felt their eyes upon him. He would give them a show that would be spoken of for centuries to come.

The air grew wet and icy as Titus carried him up into the clouds. When the height and angle felt right, the dragon spread its wings wide and called upon its wild, primal magic. They floated in stillness in the sky mist. Cassian shut his eyes and raised his hands out in front of himself, beginning to concentrate. His mind plunged further out into the ether of the universe than it ever had before. He was acting on mad instinct, reaching tendrils of his consciousness fully into other dimensions—places he would never have dared to go before. Rage pushed him through all hesitation. *The Nemesai had taken everything from him! His mother! His father! And now... the one he had allowed to step into their place!*

When Cassian opened his eyes, he saw an enormous mirror-like orb floating in the air before him. The shimmering surface, which was larger than he and Titus combined, seemed to swirl slowly around like liquid, giving the impression of calm, yet the mass emitted an impossibly deep hum that made Cassian's bones tingle within his flesh. He stared at it in wonder, seeing his image upon his dragon distorted and reflected back.

This was something the world had never seen. What was it? His creation pulsed in the air, and suddenly a cascade of lightning flashed at it from the clouds all around in a near blinding cascade. Cassian watched the spell drink in the electricity and grow larger.

"More," he whispered.

The dragon did not need to be given further explanation. It drew in a deep breath and then sent a stream of white fire into the mirror-orb's center. The hum of the spell grew louder as it consumed the primal magic, and when the torrent finally ended, it was the size of a house.

Cassian gazed down through the clouds to the temple below, and then he willed his spell at it. A thrill coursed through him as he observed the rapid descent, for he did not entirely know what was about to happen. The silver orb struck the roof of the church and splashed apart in a thousand different directions like water, and each glob of its strange, viscous mass somehow consumed whatever it touched. He watched in fascination as stone, wood, and metal disappeared in bursts of steam. Cassian could feel what was happing: the temple was being disintegrated in some fierce reaction of magic that tore it into countless trillions of pieces, each far smaller than a speck of dust. *This was complete destruction—a return of all matter to its base elements.*

The maelstrom continued to splash and spread, but Cassian still had enough control over his spell to keep it from spilling over and killing the people in the streets. Instead, he willed the silver substance into a spinning vortex and drilled downward, obliterating every stone. The church seemed to melt in on itself, and within perhaps twenty heartbeats, it was completely gone, *yet the spell was not finished.* It tore into the dirt below, into the underlying bedrock, and still further. A vast hole formed in the holy ground deeper than any well. The magic tore further and further until the silvery vortex was a distant light in the murky shadows of the tunnel, and still it went on. Then there came a deep rumble from the bowels of the world as the spell finally seemed to hit something it could not consume. The construction of magic shattered, but in its wake, something fierce rose up, and Cassian stared into the hole he had made in the world and saw the distant orange glow of magma.

"So ends the Nemesai Order," he whispered, his words coming out as steam in the icy air.

He and Titus glided slowly down toward the burning mass, which seemed to stare up at them like an eye from hell. *Had he just created a spell that surpassed those of the first starborn?* How was that even possible?

<Now you have done it, my boy,> the Emperor's voice rang in his mind.

Cassian gazed down, instinctively pinpointing the source. Tacitus stood below with several hundred craith at his back and a small retinue that included his one-armed son.

<Hello, my Emperor,> Cassian answered in kind.

<Come down here. *Now.*>

Cassian hesitated, then replied <Of course.> He glided with Titus to the street, feeling the eyes of hundreds upon him. Like his fight with Dimitris, this would be spoken of all over the empire and remembered centuries after his death.

Titus landed perhaps thirty paces or so in front of the Emperor and his army, and Cassian quickly dismounted. He took a brief moment to scratch the dragon in the tender spot just behind his left ear and whispered: "You should go. I believe I am about to die."

Titus glared at him, snorting in defiance. It could not yet form words with its mind, but it understood much of what was happening. Cassian gazed into the dragon's heart and saw it would not leave his side for anything in the world.

"I love you too," he whispered, scratching again. "Let us go and face him together then."

He turned then and locked eyes with the most powerful mortal in the world. Tacitus's magic burned and crackled around him. It was so grand and impossible in its scope. Cassian might have attempted to form his silvery spell a second time in the air and hurl it down at his Emperor, but even if that would have worked against such a powerful elder starborn, it would only amount to murder. What he had done had been done in honor, at least as he saw matters, and the only way to hold true to that was to face Tacitus Adronicus openly.

<Come here> the Emperor telepathically commanded.

Cassian took a deep breath and walked forward. As he did, he whispered quietly into the air: "I have avenged you, Mother. You as well, old man." He felt remarkably at peace as he stepped before his ruler, dropped to one knee, and said: "I submit myself to your justice, Great Tacitus."

"Hmm," the Emperor grunted.

Cassian remained still as ten craith stepped forward and encircled him. He knew he must face what was about to come with all the dignity of a prince.

"You have made some regrettable decisions this night," Tacitus said quietly so that only the two of them could hear. "You realize, of course, that your actions tonight warrant your execution."

"As I said, I submit myself to your justice."

The Emperor projected his voice then so that all in the city could hear him: "Cassian Asango, Starborn of the nineteenth generation, I place you under arrest for the crime-"

<CASSIAN ASANGO HAS COMMITTED NO CRIME!> A female voice thundered, cutting the air with a volume even greater than that of Tacitus's. *Cassian knew the speaker.* He turned, as did his Emperor. Only a few steps away was the Norn, standing taller than any figure present, her lanky body shrouded in black cloth just as it had been years ago when he had first met her.

She walked, or rather glided forward, and the craith parted to let her through. Cassian rose and turned to her, but the shrouded face was not angled at him. Her attention seemed focused upon the Emperor.

"I beg your pardon, Ancient One, but the young man's actions are not in question," Tacitus said, his tone laced with irritation rather than reverence for the immortal creature. *This was not the first time they had met,* Cassian sensed. The Emperor sighed and went on: "Asango killed a *bishop* of the church."

<He did not,> the Norn answered in her soft, telepathic voice. <He merely destroyed a building.>

"A holy temple to the gods!" Tacitus said, raising his voice. "There can be no greater crime!"

<There is no crime at all,> the Norn said. <I would remind you that Avinos Valenka, *First* Emperor of Denigoth, established the law of theocratic autonomy. Among the articles of this law resides the dictate that all matters of theological

disagreement, including even conflicts between the different embodiments of the church, must be held as matters of theocratic law, and not the laws of the empire.>

Tacitus frowned, weighing these words for a moment. Then he said in a loud voice: "You are calling this a *religious matter?*" The Emperor chuckled and made a sweeping gesture toward Cassian with his right hand, saying: "This is no priest or bishop. Cassian is a *heretic!* He professes it himself!"

<That does not make him one,> the Norn answered, her tone calm.

Tacitus shook his head, emitting an impatient chuckle. "Forgive me, but I have no idea what you are saying, and I fail to see how this vague and rather circular argument has any bearing at all on the matter before us."

<Then I shall enlighten you,> the Norn said, and she placed a hand on Cassian's shoulder. He felt no sense of mass at her touch, nor did his magical senses register much of anything, yet he felt a deep sense of calming warmth pervade his body. <Cassian Asango, whether he knows it or not, *is* a religious figure—one of *enormous* importance.>

"What?" Tacitus grunted. "How can that possibly be?"

<Cassian Asango is the chosen acolyte of the gods. He is the one the Enumis refers to in its prophecies as *The Messiah.*>

There was a bewildered silence that passed between Cassian, the Emperor, and the many craith that surrounded them both. Of all the outcomes Cassian had prepared himself for as he took his revenge, this was not one. He stared at The Norn, whose shimmering cloak billowed independently of any worldly wind. *Could this possibly be true*? The very idea collided with every thought in his mind.

"*I am the Messiah,*" Cassian said, breaking the silence. He blinked and then blinked again. Was this a joke? No, the Norn was incapable of lying. Cassian's thoughts began to race. He, who had spent most of his life denouncing the gods, was their chosen acolyte? The absurdity of it struck him so hard that he lost control and erupted into a fierce burst of laughter. He cackled so hard his knees wobbled beneath him, and he stumbled onto the stones beneath him.

"This—this *cannot* be true!" Tacitus said. His voice was utterly bewildered. Cassian gazed at the Emperor, and for the first time, the great man's face seemed to be without its cunning, or its superiority.

"I... am... the Messiah," Cassian said again, exhaling each word.

<You have always been thus,> the Norn said. <You stand as the highest religious figure in the whole of the world.> Cassian thought he sensed a flicker of amusement slip out through her psychic walls. The Ancient One's shrouded face fixed on his for a brief moment, and then she suddenly grew taller and spoke with all the power of her mind not only to him, or even merely to Tacitus and those within the capital, but somehow, Cassian sensed, to every sentient being in the world: <Let it be known that I, Norn, oracle of the gods, name Cassian Asango as *Messiah*! All actions he has taken against the Nemesai are deemed the holy will of the Gods, and thus above reproach!>

Cassian stared at her. The moment was surreal. He questioned whether all of this was merely a fantastical construction of his mind, and he was still in the Nemesai dungeon being tortured. Yet the bitter pain of the old man's death was too visceral in his soul to have been imagined. This was real, impossible as it was.

The Emperor turned to him, his wizened face pale as he whispered: "This is insanity."

"It certainly is," Cassian said, finding his voice. For the first time perhaps since his mother died so many years ago, he was too overwhelmed to think. *What in the hell did any of this mean?*

<I believe Lord Asango and I have matters to discuss now,> the Norn said, her shrouded visage aimed at the Emperor. <Unless you still wish to arrest him of course.>

Tacitus stared at Cassian for a long moment, breathing very deeply. Whatever thoughts were racing through his mind were well beyond Cassian's ability to see, yet still, the man seemed almost... *frightened.* Finally, he murmured: "No, I will not trample upon the laws laid down by our first emperor. You are free to go, Cassian."

The Emperor started to turn around, but Cassian said: "Hold on." Tacitus glanced back. With a still swimming head, Cassian said: "Bring my conflict with the Nemesai to a close without killing the Bishop. I believe that was your condition for naming me crown prince." It seemed practically absurd to bring up such a matter when issues of divinity surrounded him, and yet he could not help himself. "I believe I have met your requirements."

The Emperor swallowed, his face growing still a little paler. He still seemed unable to speak.

The Norn broke the silence: <Will you keep your word, Mighty Tacitus?>

Tacitus took a slow breath, then looked at Cassian and said in a voice that was surprisingly cold and distant: "The title... *is yours.*"

"I am profoundly grateful," Cassian said, though he was unsure at the moment of how he felt at all.

Tacitus swallowed and said in a low tone: "I will bid you good evening then, *Messiah.*" He made a sweeping gesture with his hand and muttered: "My craith will see you home if you wish. From this moment forward, they will know you as my second in command, and obey your orders." He turned then and ambled through the army.

Cassian spun to face the Norn, who was standing silently to the side after her world-altering proclamation. "What game are you and your gods playing with me?"

A soft, telepathic laugh whispered out from her, and she replied: <Is that a question of your future? You had your opportunity to hear your destiny when you were sixteen, and you refused. I cannot give it to you now.>

Cassian felt uncertain as to what to say next. Was she an ally? What did it mean that he was Messiah? How could such an absurd proclamation be true? His thoughts swam in a wild frenzy, and he gazed into the eons-old eyes of the Norn and said: "Why did they choose me, or are you allowed to tell me even that?"

<Not directly,> she answered.

Cassian exhaled a laugh, shaking his head. "Do you take pleasure in being confounding?"

<Do you imagine you could understand what *pleasure* is to one such as I?>

He stared at the ancient figure. How many thousands or even *millions* of years old was she? Perhaps she was correct that he could not conceive what a sentient mind would think and feel after such an eternity. All the same, *why not try?*

"I imagine that *we* are the only things that can give you pleasure now," he said.

<Interesting,> the Norn whispered. <Tell me, Asango, why do *you* believe you were chosen as the Messiah?>

"To right the horrendous perversions that have taken place in the church," Cassian said, not bothering to hesitate now.

<Ah,> the Norn moaned in seeming amusement, <I suppose any who know you well would not be surprised by such an assumption.>

"Are you saying the assumption is wrong?"

<As I indicated, I cannot answer such questions directly now.>

"What an irritating set of rules," Cassian sighed. "Why the hell do they exist?"

<To balance the contest.>

"What *contest*?" he said, seizing immediately on the word.

The Norn replied in a quiet whisper that echoed in his mind: <That is the great question with which you, above all others, shall soon come to grapple.>

"A fragment of an answer," Cassian said, frowning. "You told me years ago, when I refused your prophecy, that you would appear to help me three times. I can assume this is the first, which means I will see you twice more. The last time, if I remember correctly, I will ask you to come, and shortly thereafter I will die."

The Norn only stared at him through the blackness under her hood, as if to communicate that she would not expand upon this point. He might have grown infuriated, but as he continued to roll their first meeting in his mind, a new question emerged. "You told me that refusing to hear you would cost me dearly. If I had not, would Somar be alive now?"

<I can provide you no answer. What is done is done.>

Cassian clenched his jaw. Dozens of questions flooded his mind. Would he have had to fight Dimitris to the death if he had listened to the Norn years ago? How many mistakes and how much pain in his life might be traced back to that single moment of stubbornness? At the same time, he remembered *why* he had refused. What were the gods to him when his mother's and father's throats had been slit in their name?

"What do they expect of me?"

The Norn evidently did not need to be told who 'they' were in his question, for she answered: <To be Cassian Asango.>

He blinked, staring up at the cloaked figure. "Is that some *indirect* answer to my earlier inquiries, or should I allow you to give me several dozen more ridiculously cryptic answers before trying to piece things together?"

<You are not ready yet to *piece things together,*> she answered in a serene, patient tone. <I can tell you this much though, Starborn: you should *not* lower your guard. You are in more danger now than you were within that cell.> She leaned in toward him and whispered: <But you knew that, deep down, did you not? All the while when the Nemesai and the Emperor were speaking of your death, you remembered that I would appear to you three times before the end of your mortal life, and all their threats of execution rang hollow. Do you deny it?"

Cassian hesitated for a long moment, searching deep within himself before he answered: "No."

<It is good that you can be honest with yourself. That single quality may be your only hope in days to come.>

"More cryptic words," Cassian said, though inwardly he suspected that this might be the most important thing she had said to him. "Tell me, are you capable at all of speaking plainly with me on any subject?"

<Yes, in fact. I will share with you a destiny I have revealed to no other: *my own.*> The Norn leaned down so that their heads were level and whispered: <My time in this world will come to an end the moment your human heart ceases to beat.>

She faded then, her form shifting to translucence and then vanishing entirely from his sight. Cassian sensed no lingering presence of her mind either. The Ancient One was gone as if she had slipped from the universe. He stood there, looking at the still and silent army of craith who were now bound to follow his commands. Around the edges of this small force, many from the city had gathered to catch a glimpse of their newly discovered messiah, or far worse: *to fall on their knees.* His stomach twisted at the idea of being worshipped with the very blind faith that ran directly opposite to his most profound beliefs, and he wondered if the gods were possessed of a terribly poetic sense of justice.

CHAPTER 38: INVOKING HIS NAME

Livia sat in quiet stillness on her bed as the morning sunlight flowed in through her room's tiny window. She had not slept the night before—not since the searing telepathic proclamation that *Cassian Asango* was the Messiah prophesized in the Enumis. The world-altering message had come to her the same way as the telepathic vision of Asango speaking with the dragon years ago, *with tremendous pain*. She could still see Hervin stumbling into her room in his night clothes shortly after her agony reached its end, muttering: "Did you hear?" Apparently, from the whispers in the early morning outside her window, *everyone* had heard, but only *she* had felt hot irons being hammered into her skull.

"Livia?" Hervin's yawning voice came through the thin wood of her door. "Are you up, my dear?"

She reached over to the table by her bed and rapped her knuckles down in a double knock—their long-established answer of 'yes' to questions from across the house.

"Is it my turn to make breakfast today?" Hervin said, still yawning his words.

Livia knocked once: the signal for *'no.'* In truth, it was his turn, but she felt like cooking. *Anything to distract her mind.*

"Splendid!" Hervin bellowed, and she heard the creaking sound of him sitting back down in his bed.

Livia sighed and rose. She had already dressed for the day hours ago when it had become apparent she would not be able to return to sleep. Her head still ached slightly from the psychic onslaught, and she might be bitter over that fact if the news were not what it was. *Cassian Asango was not going to be executed!* That was an enormous relief for many, many reasons, not the least of which being that the continuation of Livia's own life was more assured. Would all Cassianites be pardoned of their crimes now? That seemed extremely likely given that the majority of their activities did not involve breaking imperial laws but only spreading sedition against the Nemesai. There were, of course, more zealous individuals who had freed slaves from their bondage, sometimes even using violence, but they were only a small minority.

Livia meandered to the wood stove in the left corner of the house. She had cleaned out the old ashes the other day, which made cooking easier to begin. Even so, as she reached to the wood collection on the left and drew dried sticks and spread them out into the bottom of the stove, the result was a tangled, poorly distributed mess that would burn unevenly. *Iona was so much better at cooking...* That thought tugged at her heart, biting into the joy of the morning. Even if Asango would become Emperor in a few decades, Iona was still gone.

A knock came at the door rather abruptly, and Livia jumped. She turned toward the entryway to her home, wondering who might be calling so early. She glanced back at the stove, feeling irritated that her work was being interrupted, and then walked forward and lifted the latch to her home's front door.

"Hello," Simius said. The young sorcerer had a cordial smile on his face, which Livia immediately sensed was a mask. His eyes held frustration. She frowned at the young noble. Only a few days ago he had been courting her, and then he had flipped in an instant to threatening her with death. What did he want now?

"May I come in?" he said. There was an edge to his tone which hinted that refusing would not be advisable. Still, Livia blocked the door with her foot and stared at him, giving no indication. She was feeling just a little empowered after learning that Cassian Asango was sacrosanct in the eyes of the church. Could she be arrested for associating with the Messiah?

"I'm coming in," Simius said in a sharp voice, and just as the other time, Livia felt the sudden push on her stomach and chest of some invisible force. She was shoved backward and lost her grip on the door, stumbling as Simius stepped inside her home, uninvited.

Hervin came wandering into the kitchen just then. He had just started to mutter something about helping Livia start the stove fire when he noticed Simius and exclaimed: "Goodness! Hello."

"Hello," Simius said, flashing a far friendlier grin than he had given Livia. He thought Hervin an oblivious fool, and so he poured on the charm. "My father is extremely pleased with your recent wine delivery."

"Oh?" Hervin muttered, standing stupefied at the presence of his lord's son in his home. "Well, uh, t-that is very good."

"Of course it is," Simius said. He stepped toward Hervin and drew out a silver coin from a pocket in his elegant, silken tunic and said: "I'm afraid my father and I must borrow your daughter for a short meeting. I know she was making you breakfast. Please allow me to purchase you a meal at the tavern." He flipped the coin with his thumb. <*Don't give him any indication that there is trouble if you want him to live,*> his telepathic voice rang in Livia's skull.

Hervin fumbled for the silver piece in the air and dropped it onto the floor. When he rose back up, he had a confused look on his face. "Uh... may I ask what you wish to speak to Livia about?"

"A small matter," Simius said with a dismissive wave. "I'm sure she'll write you an explanation later."

"Well..." Hervin muttered, and he turned to look at Livia.

<Don't make him suspicious,> Simius hissed in her mind.

She smiled and gave a nonchalant shrug and a forced smile. Hervin stared at her for a moment, then said with a confused sigh: "A-alright then."

"Let's go, my dear," Simius said, offering his arm.

The thought of touching the young man made Livia's skin crawl, yet she sidled up to him and slid her wrist through. They walked outside, where she saw a resplendent carriage with windows veiled in blue silk curtains waiting in the street. The side of one of those curtains drew back, and Simius's father, Lord Baradon, stared out at her. He bore a contemptuous look that made her blood run cold.

"We need to talk," Simius said, all pretense of kindness gone from him now.

Livia froze. *What was this?* She cast a look around and saw armed city guards standing in the streets. Each one was blocking off a route of escape and staring directly at her.

<It would be better if you did not cause a commotion,> Simius's voice whispered in her mind. <If you do that, your chances of making it through this alive will drop considerably.>

Livia felt herself begin to tremble. Her head was swimming, but she forced herself to give Simius a nod. An image flashed briefly through her mind of the thin dagger concealed in a pocket under her skirt. It was the only defense she had at the moment, and nowhere near enough to overcome the enemies surrounding her. The only thing to do was to move forward and try very hard to keep her wits.

"This way," Simius said. He made a quick gesture with his right hand, and a carriage door swung open. Livia allowed him to walk her up to the cart and help her up inside of it. She took a seat on a velvet cushion across from Lord Baradon, who continued to glare at her. *There was murder in his eyes.*

Simius moved into the cart and took a seat next to his father, and then swung the door shut. "Ho!" he grunted, reaching a hand up and out through the window to slap on the roof twice. The driver in front responded by snapping the reins, and the horses lurched forward.

"Did you sleep well, *Livia*?" Lord Baradon said, narrowing his eyes at her.

She swallowed, shrinking in her chair under the harsh stare as she shook her head.

"Neither did I," the old aristocrat said. He thumbed at his peppercorn beard nervously. "I doubt any lord in the empire caught much sleep last night—not with that radical starborn being deemed a *Holy Figure!*" Baradon narrowed his eyes at her and said: "I am certain you have read many of the things he has written about men of my stature—the *'ruling class'* as he calls us—not to mention the things put out in his name. You've written quite a bit yourself, have you not, *Slave of the West?"*

Livia felt a cold shiver rise from the pit of her stomach. She drew in a breath, meeting the man's stare. *Did he know for certain?* She tried not to appear nervous—not to give anything away.

"She's very good," Simius said. He was staring at her with eyebrows knitted together. "In truth, I've never seen *anyone* with this level of talent for occlusion. I can't even catch the vaguest trace of emotion."

"Where does a *slave* learn such skills?" Lord Baradon growled.

Livia gazed from one man to another, studying them. Beneath their anger was a deep fear, and that made them dangerous. She hesitated, not sure what to do, and then she looked nervously at Simius and made a writing gesture, scribbling with an imaginary pen onto a pantomimed paper in her hand.

"You may write," he said in a cold voice. "Do you need paper?"

Livia shook her head and drew out her paper. She tried not to let her hands shake as she pressed it against the wall of the cart while angling her charcoal pencil. The ride was already bumpy over the uneven road, and so her words came out somewhat squiggled:

Why do you believe I am the slave of the west?

She was careful not to actually deny the accusation, as that might lead to consequences if they had proof. When she held up the note, Simius read it and then breathed in very slowly through his nose. After a small bit of hesitation, he answered: "Because I had a more *aggressive* conversation with your dwarf friend." The young sorcerer's face became grim. "You might as well know he tried like hell not to give you away—even when he realized I was going to kill him."

Livia gasped aloud. *Domor was dead? Because of her!*

"Mhh," Lord Baradon grunted, leaning forward. Livia could feel the blood draining from her face. "Did you think your seditious writings would not carry consequence? You poor little fool, this is the *Denigoth Empire*, and you have been inciting rebellion!" He reached out a veiny hand and gripped her right arm while drawing back his other appendage to slap her.

"Father!" Simius said. The Lord turned to see his son staring at him. The young noble's blue eyes were filled with an intensity that gave the old lord pause. "There's no need to be brutish. I'll get what we need out of her. I already told you that."

Baradon glared at his offspring for a moment, and then relaxed, sinking back into his seat. He looked at Livia and made a grunting chuckle. "My son does not wish me to markup that lovely face of yours."

<I don't want to kill you,> Simius whispered into her mind. <Cooperate with me, *please*!>

"Stupid child," Lord Baradon muttered, oblivious to his son's psychic words. He stared at her. "You think the peasant class is fit to rule *itself*? Your kind has neither the wisdom nor the *wit* to govern! It is the nobility of this empire that keeps the peace! We are educated and bred to the role. If that power were given over to ignorant *peasants*, there would be chaos in the streets! Do you even know what anarchy looks like?" He leaned forward, his face reddening. "Rape! Murder! Buildings burning to the ground! I swear by the gods—"

"We want to know how many Cassianites are in this territory," Simius cut in, speaking in a markedly more composed voice than his father. "We need to know who they are, what resources they possess, and what their immediate plans are, now that their leader has been... *sanctified.*"

Livia stared at the two nobles. *Did they think there was some carefully orchestrated rebellion about to be executed?* She blinked. The attack on the Nemesai temple—these men had no idea who had carried it out. In their minds, she could have been a key figure in the operation. They were desperate to cling to their power, and she was the closest thing they had to a leader in *Cassian Asango's secret army.*

The cart slowed to a stop, and Livia heard a man climb down in front. The door swung open, and a soldier in ring mail stood outside, a large sword at his belt. She looked past him and saw a dozen more armed men, and suddenly it was sickeningly clear that there was no clever escape to any of this.

"Get out," Lord Baradon snarled at her.

Shaking, Livia moved to the door of the carriage. The soldier in front of her grabbed her forearm and pulled her roughly out onto the paver stones below. Her feet hit with a slap, and as soon as they did, her eyes raised to the wall of Lord Baradon's keep. She had seen it many times from a distance but never gotten close. The building looked like a fortress, with thick stones and heavy wooden doors preventing any unlawful entry or exit.

"Take her to the dungeon," Baradon's voice boomed from behind.

Two additional armored figures moved to grab hold of Livia, but both of them were abruptly jerked back in different directions. Both stumbled to the ground, wide-eyed.

"I'll walk her down," Simius said, casting a sharp look at the soldiers and then back at his father. He offered his arm once more to Livia, and, trembling even harder now, she took it. As they began to move, he said in a psychic whisper: <Just cooperate. I do not wish this to grow even uglier than it already has. My father is right. This empire needs the noble class in power. Just give us what we want so that we can keep order.>

Livia swallowed. *She did not have what they wanted.* Other than Domor, she had only communicated with other Cassianites through codenames. They had never communicated about any militant contingent within her city, or anywhere else really. Livia still had no idea who attacked the Nemesai, or what 'Elyria' meant. Her entire involvement with the organization had been limited to writing essays and drawing cartoons. She *could* tell them the locations she sent her documents, but that would be a shameful betrayal and probably not enough to satisfy them.

Simius led her in through a large hall with large tapestries and elegantly carved and varnished tables. This opulent entryway was quickly contrasted as the young sorcerer waved his hand and a steel door on the left swung open, revealing a dark, winding stairway from which the scent of sweat and death rose up.

Livia heard her own breathing, rapid and frantic as the sorcerer led her down. It all seemed like a horrible dream from which she needed to awaken. As they descended the dark corridor, every step took her farther and farther away from saving Iona, from her freedom, *from safety*.

The bottom floor was lit by wall torches that burned a soft orange in the shadowy room. The dungeon was much smaller than Livia might have imagined – basically a hallway of stone with two tiny cells on the side. A table sat in the center, with several rusted iron tools that could only have one purpose.

<Just tell us what we want,> Simius whispered in her mind. He brought her to the closer of the two cells and said aloud: "On your knees, please."

The world was spinning as Livia walked to the center of the cell. She turned to face the young sorcerer and went down on her knees. *What was he going to do?*

Lord Baradon and six of the armed guards crammed into the dungeon behind, each positioning himself to look at her. "Take it *all* out of her brain," Lord Baradon hissed at his son.

"I will," Simius said, and he raised his right hand, fingers extended toward Livia's forehead. "Drop your psychic walls," he said in a soft voice as he stepped forward.

Livia's eyes widened. Simius was going to try to force his way through the barriers in her mind. She remembered in visceral detail what had happened the last time a sorcerer had tried to do that, and somehow, she knew with terrifying certainty it would happen again now. The curse—or whatever it was that resided within her—would eviscerate the young aristocrat's mind, and he would draw back screaming. She eyed the six armed men before her. The instant something happened to their lord's son, they would plunge their blades into her body. She had no defense... If she did not think of something—*anything*—she would die in the next moment.

"Don't resist," Simius whispered. His voice was almost gentle, though it had a coldness just beneath. *He had killed Domor only a few hours before!* His outstretched hand moved closer, and closer, and closer, and panic began to boil up through Livia's body. She searched as she had many times before for the power that had shown itself once in her life, but nothing came.

Livia lurched to her feet, her right hand rising with the forefinger extended, indicating for Simius to wait a moment. The guards drew their weapons at the sudden movement, and the sorcerer paused, a startled look coming over his face. She stared at him and made her writing gesture in the air, trying not to let her hands shake. She did not wait for his permission then but drew out her paper and slapped it against the floor with her left hand while yanking out her pencil in her right. With a ferocity that nearly tore the sheet, she wrote two words:

I confess.

When she held up the paper to Simius, he stared at it in the dim light and then gave her a quizzical look. "What do you confess?"

Once again Livia held up her finger and put her paper on the floor. She moved her pencil over the parchment sheet, writing things that terrified her nearly to death. This was insanity, but she could think of nothing else that would save her life. Her soul contracted with each word. She had thought that working with the Cassianites was the most dangerous gamble she would ever take, but this was worse. Finally, she finished and held up the sheet, which read:

I am the one who obliterated the memories of the Nemesai sorcerer two years ago. The reason my mind cannot be read is that Cassian Asango himself constructed the barriers within it and laid traps for anyone who would look inside. I am his agent, and if you kill me, he will know.

Perhaps halfway through the reading, Simius snatched the paper out of her hand. He glared at it, and then at her, and then back as he continued to read.

"W-what did that little slave write?" Baradon hissed, gripping the bars of the cell. Simius handed his father the note, keeping his eyes on Livia. She stared back at him, forcing herself to display confidence she did not at all feel. These men were terrified of Cassian Asango. That was her only power over them. *Could it possibly be enough to save her life?*

"The Nemesai..." Baradon muttered, staring at the paper. "You're the one who—" He glanced at her, a look of disbelief on his face. "Simius, is that possible?"

"I don't know... perhaps it is," Simius muttered. He continued to stare at Livia, but he took a somewhat nervous step back from her. "I suppose... if anyone could lay a mental curse that powerful, it would be a starborn." He edged still further away.

"Is she a sorceress?" Baradon said, looking frightened himself.

"No," Simius whispered. "I've scanned her thoroughly. If she had magic, I'd know."

"Then what the hell is she?" Baradon growled.

Livia stared at the two noblemen. If they saw how frightened she was, they would see through her deception, so she made her hands stop shaking and forced the closest thing she could come to confidence into her features. She had no clear plan—no thought out path of leaving the dungeon alive—but her death had been halted a few moments at least, and that was a start.

"What do you mean he'll know if we kill you?" Baradon said in a low voice, staring at Livia. She gave no answer. *Keeping them guessing was keeping them off balance.*

"A trigger spell," Simius muttered, gazing at the floor with a look of consternation. "It's something small I'm not seeing—so fine and subtle that only a starborn could create it."

"What the hell is a trigger spell?" Baradon snapped.

"It's magic that only activates under a specific condition," the young noble said, and his eyes traveled to Livia, "like death."

Lord Baradon drew in a very slow, deep breath through his nose as he continued to glare at Livia. "Asango really might be able to tell if we killed her? Would he be able to tell we did it?"

"I don't know, but plenty of people saw her get into our cart, Father," Simius said. "It won't be difficult for him to figure out if he comes looking."

"If he... *c-comes looking?"* Baradon whispered, his face going pale. He gazed down at the floor for a long moment, saying nothing.

"Father," Simius said in a calm voice, "I think I know what to do."

Baradon let out an angry laugh. "That is quite good, because I sure as hell do not." The Lord went still suddenly, and Livia noticed that Simius had the look on his face he had gotten before when telepathically communicating. An eerie silence lingered for some time, and then Baradon muttered: "I see your point. Yes, you have my approval." The old nobleman straightened up, cast Livia a hateful look, and then turned and walked from the dungeon.

Simius swallowed, then whispered: "It seems you get to survive the night, my dear." He made a gesture toward the stairway leading up to the inner keep and said: "Come with me, please."

Unsure what to think, Livia stepped toward the young sorcerer. She forced her face to into something at least resembling a calm expression as he led her out of the gloomy dungeon and managed to hold it even as she heard the enormous soldiers moving close behind. *An agent of Cassian Asango would not be afraid.*

When they emerged from the stairway, Livia glanced at the door leading out, but Simius put his hand on her back and gently nudged her in the opposite direction, muttering: "I'll have a nice room made up for you—better than anything you're used to in that peasant hovel, I'm sure." There was a smoothness to the young man's tone that almost hid the dark, quaking nerves underneath. "You're going to be our... *guest.*" He sounded uncertain.

Livia clenched her jaw and made her writing gesture in the air.

Simius pursed his lips, then muttered impatiently: "I'm sure I can guess what your questions are. Yes, you are a prisoner. You cannot leave. You should have anticipated at least that much the second you decided to confess to attacking a man of the church in our territory." He sighed. "You'll be well fed at least. We don't really want to hurt you—*at least I don't.* Still, you'll need to cooperate. I'm happy to have you simply write out the names of the Cassianites. If you do, that sweet old man who adopted you can remain healthy."

Livia tensed and gave Simius as much of a glare as she dared.

He stared back, and his telepathic voice permeated her skull: <You might as well understand your position. I am not going to start a war with the Starborn Messiah, but there may well be a war coming nonetheless. I won't watch my birthright be stolen away in the name of *social progress,* and I'm quite sure I am not alone among my peers in this view. I *will* be ready for what comes, and so you're going to give me the

names and locations I want.> His eyes narrowed into a predatory glare as he added: <We are not negotiating. That is what you are going to do, or else if Cassian Asango does come here, he'll find a very pretty dead mute girl right next to the tortured corpse of her father.>

Livia stared at him, holding back tears. The only thing she had—her only hope in the world, was to keep her head.

"I'll give you one day to put your hesitations to rest and do as I say," Simius said, returning to speaking with his mouth. "After that, my patience will diminish significantly."

Livia stifled all emotion and lowered her gaze to the stone floor. She could not actually give this horrible aristocrat what he was asking, and that was a deathly serious problem, but at least there was time to think now.

Simius brought a hand up to her cheek and cupped it gently, running his thumb over her cheek in a manner that made her nerves twist. "Asango was very wise to choose you. You're smarter than anyone realizes, resourceful as hell, and probably the most beautiful girl I've ever seen." He leaned in very close to her face and whispered: "I *really* do not want to hurt you, but I will." The nobleman turned then and strode quickly out of the room, shutting the door and locking Livia inside.

CHAPTER 39: DREAM STATE

Kota was running on the wet sand, his powerful strides launching him forward as the salty mist splashed up against his face. He was the beast, ancient and primal. His massive, four-legged form tore craters in the ground as he bounded. Now he was the shamalak, running on two feet, all that vast power focused into a far smaller body. He was both of them, switching back and forth in vibrant flashes of thought and feeling. Every sense told him this was real, and he wanted so desperately to believe it.

<Bring me wax and a seal,> Tacitus's voice came from all around. The words jostled Kota's concentration, and his mental world faltered. He could feel his real body responding to the order in the opulent room that was his master's study.

Kota considered slipping back into reality. There might be something important to read within the letter. His life as a craith, cold and empty as it was, provided a great deal of valuable sensory input. He had witnessed his old friend, Cassian, hurl down an impossible spell that had utterly obliterated the last Nemesai Temple in the world, and he had heard the Norn's impossible proclamation that Asango was the Messiah. For many hours after, Kota had stood near Tacitus, listening to the man shout at his scholars for answers on *'what the hell'* this meant. There had been dozens of interpretations of the Holy Enumis's scant passages on the coming Messiah, and what his role would be. The learned men had failed to reach any meaningful consensus, much to the irritation of their Emperor.

Kota felt his hands close around a neatly rolled scroll, and he decided there was no reason to abandon his dream. He could not command his fingers to unroll the letter, which meant he would not be reading anything. Thus, he drew in a breath of the imaginary, salt-misted air, and tore forward.

For a long time, Kota ran between the tree line and the ocean. The beach upon which he ran was small, and yet, in a way, it went on forever as a landscape he and the beast created together moment-to-moment. At some point in his bounding, Kota felt eyes upon him, and his ethereal body experienced a shiver. More than once, he had sensed the presence of another gazing upon him but had never seen anyone. This mental world did not have other creatures - not even insects or small animals. Kota's refuge was a solitary island in some endless, foggy ocean, and yet... *there was something here.*

<In the morning, Asango will address the Senate,> the Emperor's voice rippled through the world. <You will take your standard positions throughout the city. Be ready to keep the peasants from swarming their *messiah,* but unless he is in immediate danger or you receive a direct order from him or myself, do not act.>

This was an order to all craith, Kota knew. His own 'standard position' was at Tacitus's side at all times, with one notable exception: The Emperor kept him away from Cassian and the other starborn. Kota wondered at times if that was because they might sense whom he was—that they might even be able to save him. Perhaps that was wishful thinking though. Perhaps he was desperate to believe that all of his training—*and Gretis's death*—had to lead to something more than slavery to a murderer.

A howl came from behind, and Kota whirled as the beast to see a wolf-like creature crouched at the edge of the trees, staring at him. As Kota the shamalak, he blinked his eyes in disbelief, a thrill running through his heart, yet in that instant, the creature vanished. He lunged forward as the beast, covering the hundred or so human paces in three quick bounds to the place where the creature had been standing. There was nothing there—no prints in the sand nor even a scent. Kota, the shamalak, swallowed, a cold feeling of hopelessness seeping through him. *Was he going mad?*

There was a growl from behind. He whirled around as the beast and saw the wolf baring its teeth at him. He was so overwhelmed by the presence that he failed to act when the thing's jaws opened and darted in at his foreleg. The bite was quick, and the wolf sprang back, bouncing on its paws in the sand. Kota the shamalak held up his arm and gazed at a series of tiny pinpricks in his bronze skin. *Had it even been trying to hurt him?* He stared at the wolf unafraid. As the beast, he could rip it to shreds, but this visitor did not seem to fear that.

The wolf was gone rather abruptly, and Kota sensed motion behind him. He gripped the haft of his sword—which seemed to exist in this world though he could not remember if it had a moment ago—and whirled around to block a strike aimed at his neck.

"Don't lose focus!" Gretis said with a wry grin. She slashed at his side, and he blocked again, his arm moving automatically despite the bewilderment he felt at seeing her here, uninjured and attacking him.

He was the beast again, staring down at the feisty wolf below. It snapped at him once more, but this time his great head came down, jaws open. The wolf leaped backward, and Gretis landed on the sand, the same smirk on her face.

"How are you here?" Kota shouted, realizing that he was himself again.

"I'm not entirely sure," Gretis chuckled. She reached to her belt and drew a dagger. Then her hand moved in a blur, sending the blade flying at his face.

Kota's right arm snapped up instinctively, and he caught the weapon by the handle. "Is this a dream?" he said. He felt his body start to shift to the beast, but he fought against it, wanting an answer.

"Whose dream?" Gretis laughed. "Mine, or yours?" He felt somehow that he was holding her in human form as well.

"I saw you impaled through the stomach by a demon blade," he said.

"Ah," Gretis muttered, frowning, "I think... I think I remember that." She blinked, lowering her sword a little. "Yes." She stared into Kota's eyes. "Is this death?" She looked around, wide-eyed.

"Gretis," he whispered. It hurt to see her, and yet it was wonderful. He moved toward her, but she dodged back, suddenly the wolf again. She snarled at him, and suddenly *she seemed afraid.*

"I'm not dead?" Gretis's voice said. She had vanished and reappeared behind him. He whirled to see her staring down at her own hands, turning them in the air. "Not... not yet," she whispered, "but I can feel myself... *slipping away.*"

"No!" Kota grunted, and he reached out and gripped her hand in his.

Gretis let out a gasp at his touch, and her eyes went very, very wide. "Kota!" she exclaimed as if suddenly remembering who he was. She stared at him, breathing rapidly, and her voice rose: "Gods, what's happening?"

"Don't be afraid," he said, releasing her hand. "I'm not going to hurt you."

"No..." she whispered, clutching her fist to her chest, "you would never hurt me. I... I made certain of who you were before I trained you."

Kota hesitated, then asked: "What do you remember?"

Gretis blinked and whispered: "Pieces..." She took a deep breath and then muttered: "I think... it's all here, but I can't... sort through it."

"How can you be with me in this place?" he said.

"You drew me here," she answered in a quiet voice, gazing down at the sand, "I was... with Glavius I think."

"Glavius?" Kota said, feeling confused.

"Yes... he keeps talking to me. Sometimes I can focus on it." Another of wave of awareness seemed to flash in Gretis's eyes as she looked up at him and said: "Gods, Kota, what did the Emperor do to you?"

He clenched his jaw. "Tacitus used magic to enslave me. I am a craith, except that I am not. I still have my soul—my mind, though it doesn't seem to do me any good. All I can do is run around in this dream world while my body carries out his will."

"I see," Gretis whispered. She gazed about again and said: "This is all from you? All of this place?"

Kota shrugged. "I don't know." He shook his head and laughed. "It doesn't matter. You're alive! I can't believe it! Are you in the Onkai Temple?"

"I don't think so," Gretis said, and some of the confusion seemed to be setting back in. "I feel bounces sometimes, like I'm in... a cart. I think Glavius has been talking to me about elves, but I don't know." She glared suddenly. "You're a craith? How? How can that be true? I've read the prophecy about you *hundreds* of times! I know every word by heart!"

Kota swallowed. "I think the prophecy was wrong. After all, whatever you were trying to tell me about Cassian Asango was wrong. He's just been named as the Messiah!"

"Messiah?" Gretis exhaled, her eyes going wide once again. "Then... then it's true—it's all coming true!"

"What?" Kota said, feeling extremely confused. "You said he could become the greatest evil the world has ever seen."

"He can!" Gretis exclaimed, looking deathly afraid. She shook her head. "Oh Gods, it's happening too quickly! I can't stop any of it, and neither can you!" She put a hand over her mouth.

"Gretis!" Kota shouted, "What do you mean? Cassian is the chosen one of the Gods."

"You don't understand," she almost sobbed. "He is the thrice-blessed one—*All Sides* have chosen him! First the dragon, now the gods..." She winced as she added: "That means the forces of hell will not be far behind. They will make their play for him soon *if they have not already*."

As Kota stared at Gretis, he knew her mind was not whole, but she was still the wisest person he knew, and so he put his hands on her shoulders and said: "Please, what are you talking about?"

The woman went still and stared at him with an expression bursting at the seams with fear. "Your friend, Cassian," she whispered, "He is very special. He has something—some strength or quality—that all three sides want." She shut her eyes and whispered: "We're all just pieces on the cornerstone board—me, you, Iona..." Gretis's face constricted at speaking the last name, and Kota remembered the Nathret hissing it back in the forest. "The other side has its pieces as well," Gretis went on. "It is a game that has been building up for thousands of years, and it is about to reach a final conclusion." She swallowed. "But Asango... he's different from any other figure on the board. He is going to stand in the middle, as the fulcrum of *everything.*"

"What does that mean?" Kota said, gritting his teeth.

"I... I don't know," Gretis whispered. She opened her eyes and gave him a desperate look. "I do know that the prophecy speaks of a young man driven by deep anger. The forces of hell can prey upon such things."

"They won't succeed," Kota said.

"They've been *succeeding* for millennia!" the woman said with a shaky laugh. "All those demons you killed—they were *men* once! That is how the game is played, you see. Neither Heaven nor Hell can act on its own in this world. They require mortals who choose to embrace what they offer." She grimaced. "For most of his life, your friend Cassian has been pushed to despise his own society. I have studied him for years, and I know he tries hard to channel it into noble ideals, but the fuel burning within him is *rage.*"

"We—we should postpone this talk," Kota said. "I want to know where you are. If Glavius is taking you to the elves, then surely, they can heal you. Then you can—"

"Kota," Gretis whispered, reaching up and gripping his forearms, "there may well be nothing left of me by the time I reach the elves. We must prepare for that eventuality."

He felt himself tremble. "No, I just found out you're still alive! I cannot accept losing you again!"

"That is neither my decision nor yours," Gretis whispered, and her image seemed to fade a little as she spoke the words. Her gaze became translucent. "You must be ready to face what comes, Kota. Your fate is tied to Cassian Asango's, and his to yours." Her image faded still further.

"Wait!" Kota shouted. "Don't go!" He tried to grab onto her, but his fingers passed through as if she had no substance at all.

"The darkness is coming for him," Gretis said, her voice a distant whisper in the wind. "As long as he lives, he will never be free of it—of the temptation." Her form vanished completely, but her voice continued on a few heartbeats longer: "It is too much responsibility for any mortal to bear. You must be ready to stop him, Kota... *if you can.*"

"Gretis!" Kota shouted, though he knew she was gone. He was alone again and more confused than ever. *What did it all mean?* How could he stop Cassian? He was a craith, enslaved to the Emperor and unable to so much as blink his eyes of his own volition. Even if he gained control again and possessed all the powers of his animus, could he really hope to prevail against Cassian? He had watched his old friend hurl down a spell that had obliterated stone and earth and torn into the heart of the world...

Kota swallowed and gazed around at the oasis his mind had created. It was only a fantasy. Gretis was on the verge of death, and he could do nothing to help her. That hurt more than anything else. Perhaps Glavius and the elves could save her, but all Kota could do was hope. Here and now, he was powerless and alone, and the solitude had never felt more crushing.

CHAPTER 40: CONVERGENCE

Cassian sat at the desk next to his palace bed, finishing his second read-through of the eulogy he had prepared for the old man. He was fully dressed in the regal attire picked for him by imperial attendants. An arm's length away on his nightstand rested the golden laurel that Tacitus had sent him to signify his ascension to the rank of crown prince. Cassian wondered vaguely as he reached out and brushed his fingers over the surface of it if any of the Bishops of the church would be sending him additional icons. Was there any sort of protocol for a Messiah?

"And he shall be the righteous sufferer," Soulic quoted the Enumis as he walked into the room. Cassian cast a quick scowl back over at his servant, which of course only encouraged him. Soulic had taken to memorizing every passage he could find that pertained to the Messiah.

"Does it say anything about him murdering his impudent servant?"

Soulic's grin widened, and with a sweep of his hand he said: "His *purity* shall be tested many times, for his is the burden of all mankind."

Cassian rolled his eyes and returned to his document. Evidently, though, the Sansrit warrior was in an especially talkative mood this morning and would not be deterred by something so simple as being ignored. He moved to Cassian's side and stared down at the words.

"I've never seen you actually *write* a speech before," the Soulic said, leaning over his shoulder. "You just sort of start talking and something that's at least passably eloquent comes out. It's one of the few things I genuinely admire about you.

What's wrong? Has the pressure of becoming the most important religious figure in history unnerved you?"

Cassian smiled. At least Soulic was still an ass. After the ordeal they had been through together, that was somehow very comforting. "How many people have come to see me?"

"Last I checked, there were about eighteen-hundred petitioners outside the palace gates, but that was at sunrise. After glancing out the window a moment ago, I would guess that number has possibly doubled."

"Wonderful," Cassian said with a sigh of profound annoyance. He rose and wrapped his speech around its wooden roller, tied it with a leather band, and placed it in the corner of his desk. Then he picked up the golden laurel and put it on his head. He turned and gazed at his reflection in the mirror on his dresser and found that the ensemble made him appear exactly as he might imagine a crown prince should look. Strangely, there was no elation in seeing this image.

There were certainly advantages to the new title. Cassian had a yearly discretionary fund of fifteen *million* desseks – more than enough to begin implementing his plans for public education. He also had veto power over all bills in the Senate, he could sit in as judge on any criminal or civil trial in the Empire and could pardon individuals of their crimes, and he was now essentially the second highest ranking military official in the world, beholden only to Emperor Tacitus himself. Expensive gifts were already starting to pour in from the nobles of the capital and the surrounding great cities, and more were sure to follow from every corner of the empire. All these things should have filled him with... *something*—a feeling of accomplishment, but they did not. The laurel on his head had been paid for with the life of his mentor and best friend.

Cassian reached toward the top right cubby hole across from his desk, and the piece of legislation he had written with the old man shot from its resting place and into his hand. He knew the document perfectly, but he unraveled the vellum sheet and did so anyhow, his mind flashing through the hours of debate that had gone into every word. He could actually pass this law on freedom of religion now. As both crown prince and 'messiah," his point of view on freedom of religion would be extremely difficult to refute now. The bill he had written with Dojinko on slavery would be a different matter. The old man had proposed beginning by following the kingdom of Aloria's example and dictating that slaves could not remain in bondage for more than five years. This would allow a transitional period for slave-driven sections of the empire's economy such as food production to adjust. The wealthy senators and their families—who owned more than two-thirds of the Empire's slaves—would not *want* to adjust of course, but there were numerous ways to deal with their intransigence.

Cassian turned and headed toward the mahogany door to his room, willing it to swing open before him. Still in a somber mood, he walked down the winding spiral stairway to the lower level, and as he did, he reached in and clutched his Elokien. With a simple mental command, an illusion was cast around him, and he was no longer the messiah but a simple, middle-aged and very plain looking soldier of the Imperium. His illusionary chainmail even made chinking and scraping sounds as he moved. In this guise, he passed through the front gates and past his own soldiers into the crowd of worshippers. The instant he did, a rather large peasant man with a gray mane of hair around the lower half of a bald head clutched his arm exclaimed: "Did you see him? Did you lay eyes on the Messiah? Please tell us!" A handful of accompanying faces turned in anticipation of the answer.

"Yes, and he was irritable with me," Cassian said in a voice that came out a little deeper than his own. He pulled free of the man's grip and hurried on through the capital streets, trying to enjoy the few moments he had without the burden of his new titles. Most of the shops were empty, as so much of the city's population was clamoring to see *him,* but here and there he saw men and women going about their regular business. *At least some people had sense.*

Cassian felt somewhat refreshed when he came to the massive cylinder-shaped structure of pillar and stone that was the imperial senate-house. A small contingent of guards stood outside brandishing spears and swords. They eyed him suspiciously, but he simply unfurled the illusion around his body, and, with astonished looks, they saluted him and made room, the largest of them muttering: "Greetings, Messiah." Every soldier immediately dropped into a kneel.

"T-thank you," Cassian said, hoping exasperation did not leak into his voice as he brushed passed the men. *The senators ahead were far less likely to hold him in adulation.* As he mentally prepared for the arguments that surely lay ahead, his senses focused suddenly on a strange, unnatural convergence of magic just ahead, and then every muscle in his body constricted in anger and disbelief. *Would the little bastard dare show his face now?*

Cassian moved up the polished granite steps and onto the famous senate floor, distantly hearing his name announced ahead of him. Senators rose from their curving bench seats and applauded his entrance, but he paid them no attention whatsoever. His eyes were fixed down the long purple carpet to the iron chair where the newly appointed senatorial consul was seated. Pale-faced and nervous as ever, Arkas Adronicus occupied the seat.

<My father says we are to make peace,> Arkas said in a desperate telepathic whisper.

<*Peace?!*> Cassian answered. The image of Somar Dojinko's dead body flashed in his mind, and a flare of anger passed through him so intense that waves of his magic rippled out and cracked the beautiful stone beneath his feet. The applause from all the wealthy men in their rich silks came to a fairly abrupt stop.

<Cassian,> Arkas almost shrieked across the psychic plane as he trembled in his chair, <we have both lost a great deal.> He made a fidgeting gesture with his good hand to the empty

sleeve where his right should be. <My brother, the time has come now—>

<I am not *your brother!*> Cassian hissed. He could feel desperation coming off the horrid son of the Emperor in waves. Arkas had not wanted to be here of course, but it was not difficult to guess why he was: *his father had forced him.* Nearly everyone in the capital knew by now that *the 'claw-hand-prince'* had worked directly with the Nemesai to apprehend Cassian. The fact that Arkas had been away during the now infamous prison break and destruction of the Nemesai temple was already drawing whispers from the people that he was a coward. Tacitus would bear no such disgrace from his offspring, and so he had given the little son of a bitch a seat directly next to Cassian's in the Senate. *They were to work side by side!*

"Crown Prince Asango!" the speaker of the senate rasped. Cassian's eyes shifted to an exceptionally old man in white robes he knew to be Senator Baelen Makah. The poor, decrepit creature was oozing anxiety at the destruction of the floor, but at least he had the courage to try to bring the situation under control. "T-there is an inaugural ceremony which we need to—"

"Prince Arkas, Stand Up!" Cassian snapped, and his tone silenced every whisper in the room.

Arkas began to visibly shake in his chair. He rasped: "Prince C-Cassian, we are in the Senate and this—"

"STAND UP!" Cassian shouted, this time letting his power amplify his voice to inhuman volume.

Arkas flinched so hard he nearly toppled backward in his chair. As this happened, Cassian suddenly heard the telepathic voice of the Emperor in his mind from off at the palace: <Asango, whatever you are doing, cease it immediately. You will not threaten my son.>

"Arkas Adronicus, I challenge you to a duel," Cassian said.

Arkas's face went several shades whiter. Again, the Emperor's telepathic voice tore into Cassian's mind: <You will take back those words! I command it!>

Cassian took several steps toward the sniveling prince and said: "Stand up, or I will kill you where you sit."

Arkas somehow rose to his feet, though his body was shaking so violently that he could barely keep his balance. His breathing became a series of high-pitched whimpers as his mind shrieked: <You cannot do this! My father will not allow it!>

"This venue is as good as any," Cassian said. He looked around at the senators in their high seats and their many wide eyes and raised his voice to them: "I give you my word that none of you are in danger. This *duel* will be over in seconds."

<ASANGO, YOU WILL STAND DOWN!> Tacitus's psychic voice came like thunder in his skull.

"On the count of ten, Arkas," Cassian said, glaring at the terrified prince.

A pair of tears appeared in Arkas's eyes, and he dropped to his knees. "I yield!" he whimpered.

"I do not accept your yield. Stand up or die on your knees."

"Please!" Arkas shrieked, and he bowed his head to the floor before Cassian's feet. "I beg for mercy!"

Whispers began to echo through the Senate chamber. This groveling was beyond disgraceful. If Arkas lived, he would never again be able to command respect in Imperial society. It was a kind of victory, but it was not enough to pay the debt for the old man's life.

"Ten." Cassian counted.

<STOP THIS, OR YOU WILL DIE!> Tacitus snarled.

"Nine."

"Gods!" Arkas whimpered, and he crawled forward and began to openly sob at Cassian's feet, shrieking: "Please!" over and over again.

"Eight."

<Cassian, stop!> Telemachus's psychic voice screamed. <Are you out of your mind?>

"Seven. Six. Five."

Suddenly Arkas jerked upward and moved his left hand toward Cassian's stomach. The prince had not summoned a spell but simply willed all the raw magic he had into a quick, focused burst. Cassian had been expecting exactly this. If Arkas were going to muster the courage to attack, of course it would not be honorable. *He would move like the little snake he was.*

Cassian's own hand shot out, and it was power against power, only his magic was so vastly superior to Arkas's that he completely enveloped and contained the attack. There was nothing more than a white flash, and then the prince jerked his hand back in a scream.

"Mercy!" the Prince sobbed.

Cassian reached out to Arkas's forehead and gripped. The battle – *if it could even be called a battle* – was over. His telepathic might overwhelmed the fractured psyche of the little coward's mind and assumed control.

The prince went rigid as he lost the ability to control his own muscles, and he had just enough control to manage a psychic whimper: <Don't kill me! Oh Gods! Please don't kill me!>

'If you kill in hatred, it mutilates your soul,' the old man had said. The memory flashed with sudden and overwhelming vividness. Somar had taken Cromlic's life to save Cassian from his "darkest sin." It had been his dear friend's dying act, and it gave him pause. *Killing Arkas now would be self-indulgent betrayal of that sacrifice.*

<I am not going to take your life,> Cassian said in a telepathic voice as he stared down at the trembling prince, <But no longer will I allow the lie to go on that *you* are a starborn!>

Cassian plunged deeper into the mind of his victim—into the core of Arkas's magical aura. He could see it suddenly in his mind's eye: the brilliant golden energy meant for the true fifth starborn was held by unnatural tethers of dark and terrible power. These, Cassian knew, had been constructed by Tacitus himself years ago. They were incredibly concentrated threads of magic, but Cassian was more than happy to test the limits of his abilities against those of a younger Tacitus. He focused his own magic into a fine blade within Arkas's brain and slashed at the first of these threads, severing it.

<NO!> Arkas cried out within his own mind. <DON'T TAKE MY POWER!>

<It was *never yours*!> Cassian snapped back as he held Arkas still and cut the second thread, and then the third, and the fourth. The prince continued to beg and shriek within his own mind until Cassian severed the final tether, and he let out a horrified scream and dropped to the floor, a sweating and limp mass.

The starborn aura rose out of its unnatural host, and Cassian watched it float in front of him in a brilliant flare of sparkling energy. He stared at it—a disembodied power just like his own. The rest of the world seemed to fade away as it glided toward him. He sensed it touch his own aura and felt the essence of the abounding love that he and the other starborn instinctively felt for one another.

Suddenly Cassian was rising, yet when he looked down, his body was standing below him on the floor. He held up his hands and saw that they were translucent—almost invisible. This was mental projection, but on a level he had never before achieved. His conscious was wholly separated from his body yet still in the physical world, gliding up with the swell of starborn magic. As disorienting as the situation was, he did not feel afraid. The aura did not want to hurt him, he was certain. It seemed to be seeking his help for some yet unknown purpose, and he felt inclined to cooperate.

They rose together over the heads of the gawking senators and passed through the stone ceiling of the Senate building. The aura carried Cassian through the air over the townspeople in the capital and all the myriad buildings strewn about the bustling streets. Gradually, they gained speed together and soared past the borders of the great city into the vast expanses of forests, mountains, and valleys. The movement was without physical sensation save the inner thrill at moving more swiftly even than Titus could fly. In the span of a moment or two, they seemed to cross half the empire—dozens of mountains, lakes, villages, and forests—and then the pace slowed as they came to a city near the lower western coast, where the aura took them down.

Cassian observed in wonder as his massless form passed through the wooden roof of a small keep in the center of this city and then whisked downward into what appeared to be a small chamber lit only by a few candles. Against the wall of this room, a very pretty girl around Cassian's age with straw-like blond hair looked up, casting her blue eyes around suspiciously, yet she could not seem to decipher either his existence or the aura's. At that moment though, Cassian saw the thin slave mark on her cheek that was crossed to indicate she had been freed. This former slave had a remarkably powerful veil around her mind—the strongest he had ever seen—but he pressed his mental strength against it and forced a psychic tendril inside, desperate to know who she was. The girl gave a gasp at the invasion just as a tumult of information flashed from her consciousness to Cassian: she was wrongfully imprisoned, she was the true fifth starborn—*his lost sister*—and her name was *Livia.*

It was in that instant that Cassian felt a defensive mechanism trigger within this Livia's brain—a curse. It attacked him viciously, trying to rip his psyche apart, but he focused his will and knocked it back. Livia shrieked in pain, clutching at her head. The dark spell was rebounding on her, and this infuriated Cassian. He forced his way still further into her mind, and when he did, he perceived not only the curse that had tried to block him out but others as well. Tacitus had laid spells to block the poor girl from using her voice so that she might never attempt a spell and draw upon the fraction of magic left behind when he had stolen her power. There was a curse to block her telepathy, though he sensed Livia's mind was so strong that she had broken through it to a degree. The most virulent spell of all was a wall around her brain, blocking the reentrance of the aura that had brought Cassian to her—closing her off from everything she was meant to be.

<Help me,> Cassian whispered, and instantly Livia's aura responded, lending its power to his mind. He used it and slashed at the curses inside his sister. They were fiercely resilient, but Cassian used every shred of his strength and tore them away one after another, and then all the power of the aura rushed into Livia in a brilliant, almost blinding flash.

"AHHH!" she cried in a hoarse rasp. The sound of her own voice seemed to frighten her nearly as much as the awesome energy that was welling up inside her. Cassian watched in wonder as his lost sibling's mind awakened to powers she never dreamed of and could not possibly understand within the span of a few seconds. The poor girl was terrified, and she let out several more rasping shrieks, gripping at her throat with her hand. Then her eyes fixed suddenly on Cassian. Already, her psychic senses had taken root, and she could perceive him.

<Hello, sister,> he said.

Livia gasped again and flattened against the wall.

<You have no reason to fear me at all,> Cassian said, casting his warmest and friendliest smile through the translucent projection of his face. <In truth, there is little in this world you need ever fear again.>

Livia panted and then coughed. Cassian sensed that her throat hurt from only the few sounds it had made. *Her vocal chords must have atrophied.* He could feel the confusion in her racing mind. Amidst that chaos of thought, a small table to Livia's right lifted up off the stone floor and then fell back down, which in turn caused her to flinch away from it and raise her hands in a defensive gesture. The magic inside Livia reacted to her fear, and a tendril of it shot out and attacked the offending desk, ripping it into a dozen pieces that went flying at the walls of the room.

<Calm down,> Cassian laughed. Despite how terrified Livia was at that moment, he was elated beyond measure at this situation. For years he had bitterly stomached Arkas walking around with power stolen from his true starborn sibling because Tacitus had taken the laws of magic into his own hands, but *no more!* The wrong was righted, and whatever consequences might come, this was a beautiful moment. *He had finally found her.*

<It is your own magic you are feeling,> Cassian whispered, willing his translucent form down to the floor and coming as close as he could in his intangible state to kneeling next to her. <Do not fear it. Embrace it! I will help you! I will do anything in the world for you!>

Livia swallowed and looked at him. She was so confused, but he sensed within her the desire to trust him. She reached a trembling hand into a pocket in her skirt and drew out a pencil and paper. Glancing nervously at him, she flattened the sheet against the wall of her room and scribbled with quaking fingers. When she finished, she held up the note, which read:

Who are you?

Cassian blinked at the scrap of paper, and he felt a swell of anger. *This was how his sister had been forced to communicate!* Still, there was no time to dwell on such things. He looked her in the eyes and said: <My name is Cassian Asango, and I am your brother.>

Livia's eyes went so wide that they looked as though they would burst from her skull. He gave her a moment to imbibe this information before continuing in a gentle voice: <I do not know how long I can remain here. I can feel this projection—> he held up his translucent hands, <being drawn back to my body, which is all the way off in the Capital of Denigoth. There are so many things I want to tell you, and so many things I want to know about you.> He leaned in closer to her and said: <But at the moment, all I can do is try to help you understand

what has happened. I know this may seem impossible to believe, but you, Livia, are Starborn.>

She just gaped at him, her shoulders rising and falling as she drew in deep breaths of shock. Cassian felt the long tether from his body to his projection pull harder, and he strained against it. <You were always the true fifth starborn,> he said, speaking quickly now, <but your power was ripped away from you when you were too young to remember, and you were...> he grimaced, <evidently sold into slavery. I am so horribly sorry for that. If I had known you were still alive—if *any of us* had known—we would have sought you out years ago!>

Livia stared at him. He perceived that she was still too overwhelmed to wrap her mind around this revelation, but some part of her was following his words, and so he went on: <Your magical aura was grafted unnaturally to the son of the Emperor, Arkas Adronicus.>

She jolted at the name, and her eyebrows knitted together. *Arkas already had significance to her.* This was a mystery Cassian would have liked to unravel, but his time with Livia was growing shorter and shorter, so he rushed forward with his words: <I fought Arkas a few moments ago and cut the bonds that held your power to him. I had no idea what would happen when I did, but your aura reached out to me. It brought me here, to you. It is yours now, as it was always meant to be.>

His sister blinked at him several times. He could only imagine what she was thinking—what she was *feeling* as the tremendous magic of a starborn crackled inside her. Very timidly, Livia raised her hand at the cot that whoever had imprisoned her had furnished. She made a nervous flick of her wrist, and her magic flared out. The small bed rose up instantly, launched forward, and crashed into the wall.

"HEY!" a gruff, male voice shouted from outside, "KEEP QUIET IN THERE!"

Cassian turned and glared at the wooden door to the room, instantly sensing the fairly simple mind of a guard walking the hall outside. He did not know the specific circumstances of

Livia's imprisonment but had at least caught that she was being wrongfully held. He wanted to break her free, but... *there was no need now.*

The tether of Cassian's physical body became too difficult to fight, and he began to be pulled up and away from his sister. Her face filled with worry at his departure, but he smiled at her. <You do not need me. Your magic is your ally now, and it is more powerful than you can yet imagine. You will be far stronger than Arkas ever was.> He began to pass up toward the ceiling as he said: <I know you have never spoken, but it is possible now. More than that though, you need to find your psychic voice. Telepathy is a skill, and once you build it up enough, we can communicate even over vast distances.>

Livia stood and reached out to him as if begging him to stay. He cast her the same fierce grin he had used to inspire his soldiers to fight many times before and said: <Master your power and free yourself from this place, and once you do, come to me. I should be quite easy to find. I reside in the Imperial Palace.>

His will gave out then, and he reeled backward and up through the stone ceiling. His psychic projection traveled back even faster it had come, whipping over hundreds of miles of towns and cities and wilderness. He soared to the capital and was yanked into the senate building where he crashed into his body in a violent, yet surprisingly painless collision.

Cassian found himself standing over Arkas, who was lying on the floor, hissing and drooling. All magic was gone from the cruel young man, and, it seemed, his mind had been somewhat shattered by the amputation. Cassian turned to the nearest of the senate guard, a broad-shouldered red-head in bronze armor whose face had gone quite pale, and said: "Prince Arkas will need to be taken to the palace infirmary. Go and fetch a gurney." The large man swallowed, then turned and stepped nervously away with several of his compatriots.

Cassian turned around and saw a room full of senators still gaping at him. "My apologies to you all for that ugly business," he said aloud, turning and meeting many of their eyes, letting them see he felt no shame at all for what he had done. Most glanced down or away. "Still, we have important work to do, gentlemen. Shall we begin the day's agenda? I do not mind dispensing with my inaugural ceremony, as I have already consumed several minutes of the senate's time in my little duel."

<Cassian, you will excuse yourself and come to my throne room immediately!> Emperor Tacitus's telepathic voice snapped in his skull.

<Not now,> he responded, <I am addressing the senate.>

Cassian felt rage emanate from his ruler, but no further words came. There would be hell to pay, surely, but he knew he would make the same decision again a thousand times over, so it did not matter. He stepped over Arkas's still twitching body, moved in front of his princely seat, and then whirled on the crowd. *Livia had put him in an excellent mood!*

"Now then," he said aloud, "let us discuss freedom of religion in the Empire."

CHAPTER 41: THE END OF SUBMISSION

Livia expected that at any moment she would wake up and find this had all been a dream. As she wiggled her fingers, invisible tendrils of power whipped pieces of wood through the air from the table she had broken earlier. *She was a starborn!* It seemed far too impossible to believe—nothing so fantastic could ever happen to *her*. And yet... she could feel the strange energy in every part of her body. It was intoxicating. *She was powerful!*

Livia could still recall the glowing face of Cassian Asango with perfect clarity. The fact that it had been *him* surely meant this was a fantasy. There had been such sincerity in his translucent expression, in his fiercely honest eyes. '*I will do anything in the world for you,*' he had said. Her heart gave a little flutter at the memory, which must have caused her concentration to lapse, for the pieces of wood dropped to the floor.

Livia sensed something outside her wall then, though she could not immediately understand the impression. It was not sound but more the sort of sense she sometimes received when looking into someone's eyes—only far stronger. Her mind seemed to flash to a different pair of eyes and... *a different body*. For an instant, she was a large man walking along the hall to bring breakfast to the lovely prisoner. The food smelled good. She, or *he*, had not yet eaten this day. He was excited to open the cell door. Maybe he could catch the girl changing... that would be a delightful accident!

Livia was back within herself again, staring at the door to her room as the bar slid across, and then a man in ring mail armor poked his head in and looked at her. He had a grin on his face, which faltered and then shifted to a frown as he looked around.

"What happened to the table?" the soldier grunted, staring at the broken mass of wood on the floor.

Livia's magic whirred within her like a tempest. It seemed almost to *want* to fight. She hesitated though, feeling uncertain at her control.

"Bah!" the man grunted. "Can't talk, can ya?" He shook his head, and an impression leaped to Livia's mind that the soldier was planning to tell Lord Simius just before he said: "I'm gonna tell Lord Simius. He can decide if you need to be punished or not." The gruff man shut her in once more.

Livia remained still for a long moment, staring at the wooden door to her cell. Kamis—the soldier's name came to her without conscious thought—would tell Simius, and of course, Simius would come. Her time was probably up anyhow to produce a list of names of Cassianites, which she had not done. *He had said he would hurt Hervin...* Livia had almost forgotten that looming threat. As it returned to the forefront of her thoughts, she felt a ripple of anger, and, to her shock, there was a loud crack in the floor beneath her. She looked down and saw a deep fissure between her feet. *Had she just split solid stone?*

"Where is Lord Simius?" Livia said in the deep, almost guttural voice of Kamis. *Speaking...* for a split second it registered perfectly in her mind—the movement of the lips and tongue in effortless synergy with audible rumbles from the throat. The revelation was cut short when a soldier in front of Kamis stood up and said: "He's in the east tower."

Livia shook her head and was suddenly herself again in the cell. *Was this telepathy*? Whatever it was, the urgency of the situation left little time to question the flash. Simius would be alerted soon. *Could she fight him?* She had possessed magic for a few hours while Simius had wielded his for decades. Sorcery required tremendous practice to master, did it not?

Livia swallowed and gazed again at the wooden door that blocked her escape route. It would be best to abscond before Simius came and avoid the confrontation altogether. There might be guards blocking her way at the keep's exit—that thought troubled her—but it seemed better not to allow herself to be cornered in her cell if at all possible. Yes, it was better to act...

Livia raised a trembling hand in the direction of the door. It was solid wood and held shut with a thick crossbar. She could not imagine producing the kind of physical force necessary to break through such a barrier with her body, but perhaps the power of a starborn could do such a thing. She drew her hand back, doing her best to focus the magic she barely understood, and then thrust her hand forward.

The entire wall ripped free of the floor and ceiling in a sudden cacophony of shattering thunder, and the debris exploded outward, crashing into the opposite wall and breaking through it in dozens of places. Livia flinched back in terror as her newly returned voice let out a shriek. She fell back onto her hands, gaping at what she had just done. There was a thick cloud of gray dust in the air, but she could see well into the room opposite her own—a small bedroom newly destroyed from the spray of rock-chunks. The ceiling above her was creaking. As she gazed up at the wooden rafters and heard them squeal, the realization came that she had destabilized the building.

"What the hell's going on?!" a voice Livia was sure belonged to Simius came from far to the left. She turned her head and found that, with the wall removed, she could see down the hall to where he emerged red-faced from a doorway with ten or eleven armed guards at his sides. Simius's eyes went wide as he surveyed the destruction, and then he spotted her through the dust.

"What the hell happened?" he screamed, the veins standing up around his eyes.

Livia felt afraid. She had never been in any real fight save a brief skirmish with the cow. Simius and his armed men were not something she felt ready to face, starborn or not.

"ANSWER ME!" he shouted with such ferocity that she flinched. The nobleman glared around as if searching for others. She could sense his fear—his uncertainty—*They were as clear to her as the color of his hair*. Simius had no idea what had happened, and his confusion was leading to rage. He charged toward her suddenly, shouting: "You're going to gods-damned answer me, you—" He froze suddenly, and an expression of complete shock came over his face. "Y-you—" he rasped, and Livia sensed a jolt of pure terror in him. "H-how did you get all that power?" He took several fear-stricken breaths, and then turned to his soldiers and hissed: "Fill her full of arrows! NOW!"

Four of the guards had crossbows, and, bewildered though they were, they scarcely gave a heartbeat's hesitation before raising their weapons. Again, Livia heard the shriek of her own voice as she shut her eyes and brought her hands up in an instinctive cringe. She then heard the mechanisms of the weapons snapping forth their bolts in quick succession, but... *there was no accompanying sensation of arrowheads piercing her flesh*. Instead, there was the sound of gasps.

Heart pounding in her chest, Livia dared to open one eye and gaze through the mesh of her fingers. Four arrows hung frozen in the air between herself and her attackers. They simply floated in place until she lowered her hands, and then they dropped and clattered on the stone debris below.

"How the hell can you do this?" Simius rasped, his face pale now.

Some part of Livia's mind experienced a tiny thrill of confidence. Four armed men had tried to kill her *and failed.* Still, there was more confusion about her power than anything else. Nervously, she rose to her feet and looked at Simius. He was hesitating, unsure what to do. She turned in the opposite direction and saw an open door down the hallway leading to a set of stairs going down. Livia swallowed and then broke into a sprint toward the escape route, darting around chunks of stone and wood.

"STOP!" Simius's voice shouted from behind. Livia ignored him and charged for the doorway, making it to the steps. Her fingers scraped over the rough stone banister as she ran down to the floor below. The patter of boots clamored from above her as she stumbled down the last step into the keep's entry hall. There were eight hulking men in ring mail with swords and shields in their hands standing shoulder to shoulder waiting for her, blocking the path to the outside world.

<Don't let her through!> Simius's voice snapped in the psychic reverberation Livia had learned to recognize, but she sensed the words were not for her. He was communicating with his soldiers and had not meant her to perceive the command, *but she had.*

Livia stared at the guards and then glanced back to see Simius coming down the steps behind her. He met her eyes, and his pace slowed as he hissed: "Don't try to run! I'm going to figure out what the HELL you're doing!"

Livia edged back from him, yet she was keenly aware of the soldiers moving in on her from behind. One of them dashed ahead of his comrades. She could see into his thoughts: he had not seen her use magic and still thought of her as a slender, defenseless girl. Thus, he tossed away his shield, slid his sword back into its scabbard, and moved to grab her.

Livia glanced back at the soldier, and something invisible lashed out from her mind. His outstretched forearm snapped and bent unnaturally, and he let loose a scream. As the man stumbled back and clutched at his broken appendage, the men behind him seemed to lose some of their confidence, for they ceased advancing, and Livia felt waves of fear come off them.

"Did you take a potion, slave girl?" Simius shouted, glaring at her. He had stopped just short of the foot of the stairs. " Maybe some kind of elven charm? Whatever it is, there's no way in the world someone like you can hold on to *that* much power for long!"

More guards poured in behind Simius from the stairway, and even Lord Baradon appeared at the back. His eyes immediately fixed on Livia, and he shouted: "What in the name of the GODS is going on here?"

"She's throwing around magic!" Simius said without turning to face his father. "It's insane how much—like she's a damned starborn!"

Baradon narrowed his eyes. "The little slave has to die!" he snapped. "If she makes it back to Asango, she could bring him here!"

"I know," Simius said in a grim voice. He held out his right hand and began to whisper words.

Livia perceived something extraordinary begin to happen. It was as if doorways to *other worlds* opened around the young man. Two invisible creatures—if they were even alive—emerged from these small holes in the fabric of the universe and congealed together, taking some of Simius's magical energy with them. Despite the danger she was in, a small part of Livia's mind was locked in fascination at the way these unseen forces manipulated the world. One created a sphere the size of a human head that she somehow understood would filter the gasses in the air, drawing in only the elements of it that were most flammable. Another of the creatures heated and ignited within the sphere. The result was a crackling orb of flame that Simius held above his palm. He drew his arm back, seeming to take aim at her, and then flung it.

Livia should have been terrified, but... *the spell was so weak.* Her new array of senses analyzed the attack almost faster than she could think. The magical construct was simple, the energy within it minuscule, and the mental will behind it inferior to her own. Almost by instinct, she raised her hand and sent tendrils of her power out. They whipped instantly to the orb and brought it to a halt in the air, just like the arrows.

"What?!" Simius screamed, and he lurched forward, sending a new wave of focused will into his spell, which Livia found to be... *pathetic.* He was straining desperately, his face red. She could almost see the tenuous strands of his mental will focused on the spell. *Hers were stronger.*

Experimentally, Livia wrapped her own power around the fireball, severing Simius's connection to it yet holding its construction together.

"Gods!" he shrieked, stumbling back.

Livia felt unseen entities that made up its construction begin reaching out to her for energy. *They belonged to her now.* She fed them a fraction of her power, and the flaming orb tripled in size in the blink of an eye, expanding into a crackling inferno that caused everyone in the room to draw back. *This was spellcraft,* and already, without any training at all, her starborn talent was making itself known.

'There is little in this world you need ever fear again,' Cassian Asango had said to her.

Another arrow flew at her from a frightened soldier who was shaking too hard to aim accurately. Its trajectory was to the left of Livia's shoulder, yet her aura still stopped the projectile in the air. *Was this a reflex?* Was she doing this, or was her aura acting on its own? There was so much she did not know, yet it was evident as her eyes swept the room and watched the armored men drawing back from her in fear, that she was more powerful than the people who wanted to hurt her.

"W-we have men outside!" Simius shouted. "I can send them to cut Hervin's throat with a thought, so don't even think of—"

Words formed in Livia's mind and leaped forth with deafening volume: <YOU WILL NOT *TOUCH* MY FATHER!> She heard what seemed to be *her own voice* thunder across the psychic plane, and as this happened, the flaming orb under her control grew still larger. It was the size of a carriage now, and the flames churned and spun like the currents of a powerful river, responding to her fury.

Simius's face went pale, and he shrank back. Everyone in the room, in fact, drew away, for the spell she controlled was now radiating heat in every direction.

Sweat dripped down Livia cheeks. It was intoxicating to control such terrible power, and yet... what was she going to do with it? Would she burn everyone around her to death? *Was that who she was?*

Livia cut off the flow of energy to the spell and it fizzled into nothingness. A swell of relief emanated from all around her, but of course, the danger was not over. She walked toward Simius and his father, staring the two nobles in the eyes with an open contempt she would never have dared before. Both of them were utterly terrified.

A soldier nervously moved to block her path. Livia flicked her wrist, willing her magic into what she hoped would be a gentle push. The man's body was whipped to the right, and he went skidding along the stone floor, his armor sending up sparks. She felt a small twinge of guilt at this. The man was only trying to protect his lord, and he was braver than his comrades. All the same, she needed to make this show of force. Hervin's life might depend upon it. The display seemed to be working, for none of the other guards moved to intercept her.

Simius cringed as Livia stepped up to him, his hands shaking at his sides. She leaned into his face and watched him flinch. This dashing young son of a lord had murdered her dwarven friend to ensure his own power. He would have killed her too, she knew. At these thoughts, her anger rose. The stone tiles beneath both of their feet cracked, and Simius shrank further away from her, letting out a high pitched whimper.

Livia tried to form words again with her mind but found she could not. That power—whatever it was—had come by reflex rather than conscious thought, and it seemed she could not yet use it at will.

"I—I won't hurt your f-father!" the young nobleman shrieked, his bottom lip trembling as he spoke. "I s-swear by the gods, I'll never touch him!"

Livia narrowed her eyes. *Was that a lie?* Her powers of perception had vastly increased, and yet many of the nuances of telepathy were incredibly new to her, and Simius was guarding his thoughts. That alone told her not to trust him.

She leaned in still closer to the man's face, and he flattened against the wall, trembling. She drew out her paper and pencil, put it against the stone next to him and began writing a message. There was no fear at all of attack as she composed her words. Never had Livia felt so powerful—so invincible. She breathed softly as she finished her simple note, which read:

If your house troubles Hervin or anyone else I love,
I will come for you, and I will bring Cassian
Asango with me.

She flung the paper in Simius's face and turned toward the keep's exit, not bothering to watch him read it. This place irritated her. She would have died here or spent the rest of her life as a prisoner and... *whatever else* Simius had in mind for her. Now she was beyond the grotesque power of aristocratic lords—a notion that would have seemed madness only a few hours ago.

The guards near the exit parted as Livia approached, none of them meeting her eyes. She walked between them and stepped up to the door. It was barred shut, just like the one that had held her a few minutes ago, but this time the crossbar was on the inside. Livia made a quick gesture with her right hand. A thin tendril of power whipped out from the tip of her index finger and shifted the mass of wood to the left, sending it skittering along the floor to the left. A second gesture pushed the door open—a little harder than she had intended—making the hinges squeal and bend. *At least she had not knocked the wall out this time.*

As Livia stepped out into the sunlight, it dawned on her that a different person was emerging than the one who had been taken prisoner. She walked without fear along the stone path into the city where she had spent nearly all of her life. Gods but it seemed different now—smaller, less imposing. She was beyond the power of the aristocrats behind her. The magic that whirred inside made her feel that perhaps anything was possible now.

Livia strolled back to her home, basking in the elation that *she was a starborn!* She felt the eyes of others on her—the judgmental thoughts of some of the townswomen, and the lustful notions of several men. There were other impressions besides the negatives. Children were at play, having fun. Men and women were concentrating on work. Livia felt the joy of a man inside a tavern savoring the delicious stew he had been anticipating all morning, and so many other impressions. This was the mosaic of humanity, and she could see it now in all its chaos, its ugliness, and its profound beauty.

Livia was in a beautiful haze when she came upon the Sondal home. Hervin was inside. She recognized his mind immediately. He was pacing back and forth in the house, thinking about what he would say when he begged to see her. The poor little man was so filled with worry. This touched Livia's heart. She was a starborn, and that would almost certainly lead to wealth, fame, and importance, yet only two people in her entire life had loved her as the mute slave she had been, and here was one of them.

She pushed open the door and stepped inside to find Hervin turn in mid-pace and gape at her. "Livia!" he exclaimed. She felt his mind fill with excitement. "A-are you free?"

She smiled at him, and then her eyes flicked to the desk where her extra paper rested. She considered willing one of the drawers open with her mind but thought better of it for worry both of frightening Hervin and ripping the desk to splinters. There was no need anyhow. The luxury of time existed for her. She could search for Iona now. Perhaps Cassian and even the other starborn might help. For the moment though, she could spare some time to share this wonderful revelation with her father. Thus, she moved to the desk, drew out a fresh piece of paper and placed it down, and then retrieved the pencil from her pocket and wrote:

I have so much to tell you.

CHAPTER 42: THE IMMORTAL PEOPLE

"Remember that time you made me try to snatch the pebble out of your hand?" Glavius said as he carefully poured a single drop of the elf-blood concoction into Gretis's open mouth. "I think you were just taunting me, watching me leap for it, knowing I could never match your damned Sansrit reflexes. You never made Kota do that crap. I asked." He stared at Gretis's throat, watching for any constriction of the muscles. If she were swallowing the potion at all, he never saw it, but then she had always been a tricky one.

He glanced at the black sword that was still through her gut and wondered for perhaps the three-hundredth time if she were secretly in pain. The cart was rickety, especially on the back roads of uneven dirt and stone Darius had ordered him to take. The blade must have jostled over and over inside of her, yet no fresh blood dripped out. That was a good sign, *wasn't it?*

They were near a stream, and Glavius had disconnected the horses to let them have a drink and rest. The steeds were lapping up the water a dozen paces away while Glavius stood at the back of the cart. He was bare-chested, enjoying the hot sun on his tattooed back. The ride had been long and uneventful, and he had not been sleeping at night. Anxiety over Gretis's condition made drifting off virtually impossible. He kept suspecting that if he closed his eyes, he would wake up to find her entirely dead.

"Is Kota still alive?" he whispered, gazing into the woman's olive-skinned face. If he could have her only answer one question, that would be it, but she never responded no matter how many times he asked. "Gods," he muttered, shutting his eyes, "sometimes I wish I were just a farmer like my father was. Have I told you about him yet?" He chuckled aloud. "He was the son of a lord if you can believe it, but the *seventh* son. No chance of inheriting title or lands, of course."

Glavius walked over to the horses and removed their hobbles, and then led them back to the cart where he hitched them. As he worked the straps, a sigh escaped his throat. "When my parents died, my grandfather paid my tuition at the Onkai Academy and *sent me away.* I'd never even met him before. I don't think he gave a shite about me or even my father. Ah well..." Glavius climbed up onto the driver's seat and gave the reigns a gentle snap, and the horses jolted into a trot. "I had a little sister," he muttered distantly. "Her name was Annalique. The flood got her too. I was off, messing around with my friends." He shook his head. "I don't think I can picture her face anymore—not exactly—but... I remember I loved her a lot."

Glavius was silent for a long time after that. He knew it was silly to pick at old wounds, but he was bored and nervous and trying to distract himself. Over the next few hours, he spoke quietly to Gretis about dozens of things. He told her about the fight with the kobold demon down in the caves of Narethor Mountain. A spinning counter she had taught him had saved his life then. He told her about the girl he had rescued from a handful of wild ogres. She had been very pretty and... *very grateful.*

Throughout the day, Glavius carefully studied Darius's map. Some of the landmarks did not align precisely, but he felt reasonably confident they were on the right track. The mountains at least were easy to recognize. The last human-made road ended by midday, and he had to take the cart over grass and brush, which made the going slower. The horses did not seem to like the trudging from the way they snorted and came to abrupt stops every so often. Glavius wondered if they were afraid. Being so far from human civilization was dangerous. Some of the older creatures of the world were said to roam these forests—wild beasts whose blood still burned with primal magic. Glavius found himself gazing into the trees as the sun began to set, searching for the scaly coils of a basilisk, and he even scanned the evening sky every so often to make certain that a manticore did not drop in silence from above and sink its teeth into him.

Twilight had set in when he came upon the mountainside that matched what Darius had described in his notes. It was a rock face of sorts, constructed of dozens upon dozens of jagged spires twisting and curling up into sharp ends high in the sky. The stone was dark and gloomy, with numerous crevices large enough to hold dangerous creatures. Glavius noticed paw prints on the ground, catlike and greater in diameter than his head. Black wasps the size of pigeons buzzed about through sharp spires, some of them darting down very close to the cart.

It was all an illusion. Glavius forced himself to believe this as a wasp buzzed near to his face, baring a black, finger-length stinger. He couldn't help imagining being swarmed by these hideous insects. *Wouldn't that be a cruel twist?* He would fail to save Gretis and die screaming on the ground because of a misinterpretation of a map. But then his eyes fell upon a single gray patch of stone roughly the size and shape of a handprint in the middle of one of the black rocks. He ambled toward it and put his right palm against the rough surface, just as Darius had instructed.

"Kaontis Massal," he said, hoping that his pronunciation of the elven words was at least somewhat accurate.

"Raise your hands very slowly and turn around, human," a sharply accented voice said from behind with a strange, electric cadence. "Any sudden moves, and you die."

Glavius lifted his hands. As he did, he noticed he was no longer staring at jagged rock but what looked like a solid wall of polished white marble. He had not seen any change take place. It was if it had happened as he blinked, though he could not remember shutting his eyes. He turned around very slowly and saw, to his great surprise, at least twenty elves surrounding him. There were both males and females, some holding silver bows with what appeared to be crystal-tipped arrows aimed at his chest, while others held ornate shields studded with jewels and swords that glowed a brilliant yellow that lit up the evening. They were clad in sleek golden armor with incredibly fine chain mail draped over intricately complicated hinges at the joints. All of them had either blond or red hair and turquoise eyes that visibly glowed, and every set of those eyes were locked on him.

"You are not supposed to be here, Onkai," a slender male with auburn hair running out the back of his helmet said. Glavius could not decipher his age. All of them appeared to be in their twenties in human terms, though any or all could be centuries old.

"We have a unique situation," Glavius said, finding his voice and meeting the gaze of the one who appeared to be the leader.

"The terms of our treaty are quite clear," the elf answered in a cold voice. "You are not to visit our cities unless invited. By all rights, we should kill you for this intrusion."

"I have a dying Sansrit master with a demon's sword through her stomach in my cart," he said.

"We saw her," the leader said, his expression not changing. "The treaty makes no special allowances, even for followers of the Sansrit. Her wounds are a human matter, for humans to contend with."

Glavius twitched in irritation. The elf speaking so dispassionately about Gretis's life was shorter and considerably thinner than he was—*they were all smaller*. He briefly imagined ramming his fist into the flawless face. What the hell kind of people could look at a dying woman and not give help? He recalled one of Master Bendick's lectures on the 'fair folk.' They were a once great but now diminished people guided by self-preservation, and their emotions were much, *much* further beneath the surface than humans. *Did that mean they possessed no compassion?*

"We will allow you to take the woman away if you leave immediately," the leader said, his glowing eyes unblinking.

Glavius drew in a breath, stifling his frustration as best he could as he said: "That is Lady Gretis in the cart. She was invited here by one of your people—a girl named Thalice of... I think it was house Corostine."

The elf gave no visible reaction to this other than a slight narrowing of his eyes. His soldiers behind him did not seem to be moving at all—not even breathing. They stood statue-still in battle poses, and Glavius briefly wondered at how much strength and speed lay in their slender forms. They were said to be incredibly formidable, though no one had reportedly seen an elf in battle in hundreds of years.

"I have notified Lady Thalice," the leader said, still staring at Glavius.

“Really?” Glavius muttered. *Telepathy was such a strange thing.*

“She is on her way here,” said the elf. “I hope for your sake, human, that you are telling the truth. It would bring me no pleasure to remove the head of an Onkai."

"Your concern for me is moving," Glavius muttered, keeping his hands raised. He and the elves waited in perfect silence for several long, icy moments. Eventually, he heard the sound of exceptionally light footsteps behind, and then a feminine form in a blue dress glided into his view.

"Where is Lady Gretis?" Thalice said, turning to Glavius. Unlike the other elves, her face and voice gave evidence of emotion, and she seemed quite alarmed.

"In the wagon," he said.

"Nocass vien clen Onkai," Thalice snapped as she rushed past the elven soldiers. Glavius had no idea what the first three words meant, but most of the soldiers lowered their weapons, blinking at him.

The leader frowned, then said: "It seems your life will be spared for the moment." He held out his hand, palm up. "Please surrender your weapons."

Glavius looked past him to Thalice, who had climbed up into the cart and was kneeling down over Gretis. Absently, he pulled his sword free of its scabbard, placed the hilt into the elf commander's palm, and then stepped around him, but a thin hand snapped up with remarkable speed to Glavius's chest, bringing his momentum to an abrupt halt.

"*All* of your weapons," the elf said.

Glavius gritted his teeth and drew the dagger from his belt, and then bent down and took his spare knife from inside his boot and handed both to the commander. "Good enough?" he said through his teeth.

"No," the elf said. "You will need to be searched."

"Nee kay ondus!" Thalice snapped, turning and glaring at the commander.

The elf hesitated for a brief moment, then gestured toward the cart and said: "You are free to move, but be warned that—"

"Uh huh," Glavius grunted and brushed past him. He rushed through the soldiers and climbed up onto the cart next to Thalice. In a voice filled with nerves, he said: "C-can you save her?"

"I do not know," she whispered. Her slender fingers were on Gretis's stomach where the blade was protruding. "You were intelligent to leave the weapon in its place."

"What do we do?" Glavius said.

Thalice's glowing eyes blinked down at Gretis's still form. "Her honnis—what perhaps you call her *animus*—has been working very hard to keep her body in a suspended state." She turned and looked at him. "A demon did this? What kind?"

"We found the body of an oily, bat-like creature about the size of a man next to her, but no one saw what happened."

"What of her pupil, Kota?" Thalice said.

"We don't know what happened to him," Glavius muttered, his nerves afire. "I hope he's not dead, but the only one who might know one way or another is *her*," he waved his hand at Gretis.

"I see," Thalice whispered, her exquisite features contorting into worry. She glanced up at the soldiers and issued what sounded like a command in her people's sharp language. Four of the elves nodded and disappeared inside what Glavius now saw was an enormous palace of white stone. The spires of jagged rock had become towers with domed tops ending in fiercely glowing blue crystals the size of watermelons. Many other details might have fascinated him about the structure's exterior, but he scarcely registered them. Instead, his eyes fixed upon four new elves in white robes who came out of the arched doorway carrying what appeared to be a silver-framed gurney. It had smooth white cloth lain upon it rather than the rough fabrics his order used.

Glavius hopped down off the cart and reached to scoop up Gretis in his arms, but Thalice stayed his hands with a soft touch. "They can move her far more gently than you can," she said. Her tone was kind and gentle. He found it reassuring and stepped back, lowering his arms. She climbed down next to him and said: "Please come. We must talk."

He looked with uncertainty back at Gretis and said: "We can talk later. Right now—"

"Right now, you must let our healers do their work," Thalice said in the same soothing, patient voice. "I assure you, from this moment forward she will receive the most excellent possible care. Our physicians have centuries upon centuries of study."

Glavius breathed slowly as he watched the white-robed elves move to Gretis. Their icy faces offered no assurance that they cared at all whether she lived or died, yet he supposed that did not mean they would not do their jobs well. In the end, he decided it was better to be gracious, and so he muttered: "Thank you for helping us."

Thalice cast him an absurdly gorgeous smile that might have set his heart racing at another time. "I am worried for Kota, as perhaps you are. What is your name, Onkai?"

"Glavius," he said.

She frowned for a moment. "My Cassian did not know you when he and I had our exchange."

"What?" he murmured, confused by the sentence.

"It does not matter," Thalice whispered. Unlike the other elves, she spoke with a perfect Denigoth accent. "Do you know Cassian Asango now?"

"I know *of* the... I guess he is the *Messiah* now, but I've never had the pleasure of meeting him." Glavius glanced back at the elven healers. They had Gretis up on the gurney and were carrying her with a gliding speed toward the large doors from whence they came. "Where will they take her?"

"To their laboratory," Thalice whispered. "It is important to act quickly."

"I see," he sighed.

"You must stay inside our palace," Thalice said. "Our veil cannot remain down. Already my people are irritated that it has been disturbed for this long."

Glavius eyed the soldiers who remained outside the palace walls, staring at him. They were no longer pointing their weapons at his chest, but nor had they put their swords and bows away. "I wouldn't want to make them uncomfortable," he muttered.

"Your horses shall be seen to," Thalice said, and she offered her arm, "Come." Glavius slid his much thicker limb through and around hers. Thalice's body, he noticed immediately, gave off a subtle warmth even through both her clothing and his.

He stepped with her inside to a large hallway of polished white stone and exact angles. The entryway was large, pristinely clean, and... *barren*. Glavius noticed immediately that there was no coat of arms nor any tapestries, or indeed ornamentation of any kind. The room seemed beautiful yet cold—*much like most of the elves he had just met.* Thalice led him through this room to a door and then into a vast, round courtyard with a circular opening in the roof at least several thousand paces wide. The sun shone down onto a carefully organized jungle inside. Trees of many different varieties had been planted into raised garden beds along with bushes and vines that produced exotic pink and gold flowers. There were what appeared to be hawks the size of dogs, whose feathers were a silver-gray rimmed with blue. Monkeys with golden fur and inky black faces leaped from branch to branch while butterfly-like creatures flitted about, leaving a soft trail of green energy in their wake that flared for half a heartbeat before vanishing.

To Glavius's greatest shock, there was an entire pack of manticores lying atop an artificially constructed hill of grass. The lone male was silver furred, with a black mane of hair. He had the appearance of a lion with reptilian wings at his sides and an arching scorpion tail, just as the stories told, but his body... *he was the size of an elephant!* A half dozen females, perhaps two-thirds the size of the male, were lying about the hill while cubs with underdeveloped wings frolicked on the ground and battled one another. Glavius was in awe of the lot of them. If the elves could tame and control such creatures, then they were even more formidable than some of the legends told.

Within this carefully walled paradise, the immortal people sat on benches reading books or writing on paper placed upon small desks in front of them. They hardly seemed to notice when he entered, though a few cast him what appeared to be disapproving glances before returning to their studies.

"My people—*at least collectively*—do not agree with bringing you inside," Thalice said.

Glavius blinked at this. He had only arrived at the palace moments ago. How had the elves 'collectively' formed any opinion of him at all? Then he remembered that, unlike humans, *all elves* possessed telepathy, and Master Bendick had said that their thoughts were interconnected on a continuous basis. Glavius found such a concept to be unnerving, and thus he stayed away from the subject and said: "We have reason to suspect the demons are coming again. Whether your people appreciate my company or not, they would be wise to at least listen to what I have to say." He swallowed and glanced back in the direction they had come, wondering where his old teacher had been taken. "Lady Gretis will have far more information than I if your healers can revive her."

"For now, I will listen to you," Thalice said in a troubled voice, and then her turquoise eyes shifted to the floor as she added: "Even if the demons are returning though, I do not know if my people will come to the aid of yours."

Glavius drew in a breath, forcing back all the invectives welling up in his throat. *Had he expected a different response?* The elves had hidden all throughout the second demon war even as entire human cities were being butchered. After a moment, he managed to reduce his frustration down to a whisper of: "Your people do not think much of the lives of mine, do they?"

Thalice pulled him by the arm toward a corridor to the left, and he was surprised at the force her slender, feminine body could produce. "There are many things you do not understand," she whispered.

I understand cowardice, Glavius thought but did not say. He only made a vague grunt and allowed the elf girl to lead him into a very long hallway with dozens of gray doors that were pristinely carved from what appeared to be light gray stone so that each one was an exact match for every other. There were at least thirty such doors, and Glavius, of course, could not decipher the black markings on a single one.

"This way," she said, and she took him to perhaps the ninth door on the right and brought him inside. Here, he found what appeared to be an office with a finely carved black desk and a stack of the whitest paper he had ever seen, along with a golden quill and ink. Thalice led him to a pair of chairs in front of the desk that faced each other and gestured for him to take one while she sat in the other. Glavius seated himself and started to speak, but the elf blinked and held up a finger. She stared intensely at the wall past him for several seconds and then said: "The sword has been removed from Lady Gretis's stomach. Death did not take her, and our physicians are at least somewhat optimistic she can be revived."

Glavius sat up in his chair, forgetting all his irritation. "They did it that quickly? How long until she will awaken?"

Thalice breathed in through her thin nose, then said: "The best estimation would be ten to fifteen days. However," she paused, again going still, then said: "The damage to her organs was quite extensive and several days old. Much of the tissue has necrotized. Even if she can be restored to consciousness, Lady Gretis will never be the warrior she was."

Glavius stiffened, then muttered: "Well, we'll take what we can get. Please express my gratitude to your healers."

"Of course," she said, and then suddenly she paused a third time. "Lady Gretis was just given a small infusion of elf blood mixed with medicinal herbs, and it seems she became animated for several seconds. Before collapsing back into her coma, she rasped out three names: Kota, Livia, and Iona."

Again, Glavius tensed in his chair. The blade-witch had spoken Kota's name. *Did that mean that he was alive?* No, not for certain... 'Livia' was the name of the girl who had been writing letters to Gretis at the temple. What of this 'Iona?' He had no idea who that was. It sounded like the name of a commoner.

"Do you know who Iona might be?" he said.

"No," Thalice whispered, "but I do know of a human named Livia. She is one of your starborn."

"What?" Glavius exclaimed, a wave of confusion washing over him. "What are you talking about?" *There were only five starborn in the world, and everyone knew who they were.*

"Oh," Thalice exclaimed, her right hand going over her mouth, "I am not certain I should have said that." She cast Glavius a nervous look and said: "A recent... *action* taken by my Cassian has not been explained to your people as yet. The truth could put him in enormous danger."

"What... the hell are you talking about?" Glavius said, scratching his head. *A new starborn?* How was that even possible? And what in the world could put Cassian Asango in danger? *Was he not supposed to be the Messiah?* Had the crazy son of a bitch not recently taken on the entire Nemesai Order and won?

Thalice frowned. "I will speak no more on the subject. It does not matter anyhow—not for our purposes. What matters is any information you have that might stir my people to action."

"Why?" Glavius said with a shrug. "You said the elves probably wouldn't help mine even if the demons return."

"Not for your sake, no," she said, and there was a note of frustration in her voice. "My people were once the most powerful of any race, yet now our numbers are but a fraction of what they once were. We lack the ability to reproduce quickly as your people can. Another great battle with the demons could exterminate us." She gazed down at the floor. "And I shall be honest with you, human: elf-kind has long-held resentment for your race. You stole the world from us."

Glavius frowned. "And you would like to see us dead, eh?"

"No, but the elves will not sacrifice their immortal lives for your sake, not unless..." She drew in another deep breath, suddenly appearing quite nervous, "Kota—he may be the key to everything."

"What do you mean?" Glavius said.

Thalice's face contorted in frustration, and she stared at the desk for several seconds. "My elders do not wish me to say more. I will respect their authority... *for now.*" She shook her head. "You will have to trust me, Onkai. The future of your entire race may rest upon your shamalak friend's shoulders. I need you to tell me all you know—not only about his disappearance, but of his training, and his power." The glow in her turquoise eyes seemed to flare brighter as she said: "You must tell me *everything.*"

Glavius swallowed. He did not know how well he could trust this elf, or what Kota or Gretis might want him to keep secret. Neither could be asked now though, and so all he had to rely upon were his instincts.

"Alright," he said.

CHAPTER 43: CASSIAN'S CHOICE

Cassian stared up the marble steps into the dark, furious eyes of Tacitus. The emperor was sitting upon his legendary throne glaring down. They were alone except for perhaps a hundred craith who stood along the walls like deathly statues. Cassian had finally answered his Emperor's summons after concluding his business with the senate and delivering his speech at Somar Dojinko's funeral. It was all a show of disrespect he never would have dared before, but things had changed between himself and Tacitus in recent days.

"You seem to believe yourself beyond my command now that you have become *the Messiah*," the Emperor said. His rumbling voice was ice-cold.

"I suspect it complicates the matter of executing me," Cassian answered evenly. "All the same, you summoned me here, and I stand before you, awaiting any consequences you deem fit for my having chosen to ignore your commands."

"*Ignore—my—commands,*" Tacitus said slowly. His voice contained an undercurrent of anger, and yet he sounded like the words fascinated him—as if he could not believe they had been spoken.

"Yes," Cassian said, staring directly into the Emperor's eyes. This confrontation was crucial. It would set the tone for the rest of their time together.

"I must assume from your cavalier response that you believe this decision was justified."

"It *was* justified," Cassian replied. "Allowing the power you granted Arkas to continue within him was not in the best interest of our people. He was bumbling around with the power of a starborn but none of the natural control. He was also a twisted monster who inflicted suffering and committed numerous murders. I wonder if you allowed that to go on out of love for your son, or else to protect the secret of your sin."

"*My sin*?" Tacitus said, glaring with a look of murder.

"Did you kill Livia's parents?" Cassian said, not blinking. "I assume you would not leave such loose ends untied. Who were they?"

Tacitus stared at Cassian for a long moment, and then said: "Do you believe I would explain myself to *you*?"

"No, but I will find out who they were. She is my sister after all—the one all of us have wondered about for years. You never told us she was alive. Why *did* you spare her anyhow? Was it because you were worried that ending her life might disrupt the tenuous grip your son had on her power, or was it out of guilt?"

The Emperor's lips curled up, revealing his teeth, and Cassian sensed a hundred craith reaching for their swords around him. "Careful, boy," Tacitus said in his low, oaky voice. "I kept you from death in that dungeon because I believe, under all that brazen insanity, you have the capacity to be a great man. You seem to be working very hard right now to convince me you are too reckless to bother with."

Cassian took a step toward the elder starborn and sensed a twitching of undead muscles all around him. "Arkas was a petty murderer of your creation - your sin - and I refused to abide the evil that he was. As Crown Prince, I am not an obedient dog eager to carry out your will. I am a servant of the people, and I did what was best for them."

Tacitus leaned forward on his throne, seeming almost darkly amused. "Tell me, young man, do you believe your head cannot be cut from your body just as any other man's"

Cassian took another step forward and craned his neck, making a little slicing gesture across his throat. "Do as you like, my Emperor. I would do *exactly* as I have done if given the chance again."

Tacitus's eyes narrowed, and a long silence passed between them as he quietly drummed his fingers upon the arm of his great golden throne. "At times, I cannot decide if the Great Dragon did you a favor or not by burning away your fear. Perhaps it has left you ill-suited to rule." He rose from his throne, drawing in a slow breath. "You purport to understand the burden of an emperor: the task of carefully weighing many different pieces of information and then doing what is ultimately correct. We will come back to that in a moment." Tacitus stepped down from his throne and muttered: "Yes, my son was a vicious beast, and you put him down, *and* you managed to do it without killing him. At the same time though, you have introduced a new starborn into the world without much thought of the consequence."

"I have given a great deal of thought to the consequences, actually," Cassian said. "You, my Emperor, delivered the human race from the Demon War, and for this alone you are possibly the most beloved ruler in history. To reveal that you violated the sanctity of Promethiock's gift and produced a false 'living miracle' would have tremendous ramifications to our government and the people. It could tear the Empire apart."

"Indeed," Tacitus sighed, and he reached up and ran his fingers through his black and gray hair. "I assume that you believe I created Arkas out of my own vanity. I was willing to cheat a chosen one out of her destiny simply to have a starborn son."

"I do not claim to know your mind," Cassian said, feeling slightly off-put by the implication that there was a greater purpose to what the Emperor had done. "Of course, I did not know Livia was even alive. I attacked Arkas out of personal vendetta."

"Yes," Tacitus said, "but you *did* save her, which of course you believe to be *right*."

Cassian stared at the emperor, unsure where this line of reasoning was moving. "I do, yes."

Tacitus let out a soft chuckle. "But what *is* right? You may find that this question becomes superbly complicated in the scope of an empire the size of Denigoth. It may, at times, even involve allowing things that seem *evil* on their surface to go on."

"I understand this concept," Cassian said. "I stomached the existence of the Nemesai for over ten years after my mother's death." He stared into the wizened face of the elder starborn as he added: "For all that time, I let them continue to take actions that I found deplorable, just as I let your vicious son walk out of my village the first time he tried to attack me."

"Yes, and you also killed your brother, Dimitris," Tacitus said, his thick eyebrows knitting together. Cassian started to speak, but the Emperor held up a hand and said: "I know that he challenged you, and that I indirectly instigated the duel, but you chose to face him and to end his life when the time came."

Cassian said nothing. Was Tacitus making some kind of moral equivocation between the killing of Dimitris and what he had done to Livia? There would have to have been a greater good served in stealing the power of a starborn and grafting it on to another—perhaps some aspect of self-preservation. *Could there be?* In truth, Cassian *had* simply assumed the act was one of vanity, and he had tolerated it only out of respect for the Emperor who had defeated the Demon King and saved the human race from extinction.

"I did not tell the senate what Arkas was," Cassian finally said.

"Of course, you did not," Tacitus said with a soft chuckle, "because you are not an idiot. All the same, we will eventually have to deal with the existence of this *Livia*, and all it implies."

"Are you going to kill her?"

"That is certainly one option," Tacitus replied.

"You will have to kill me first," Cassian said, glaring.

"Oh, I know that," Tacitus said with a casual shrug. "I know you quite well, Cassian, and I can guess what this girl has come to represent in your mind. You took the life of a starborn, and now you have essentially given one back to the world. I am certain that penance is quite important to you, given your intense if somewhat *unique* sense of justice. That is why I hope you and I can come to an understanding that will keep her alive."

Again, Cassian said nothing, though his stomach twisted at the naked threat. He could not warn Livia of the danger looming over her. His sister's telepathic mind was not developed enough for such long distance communication, and there was no telling how long it would take her to build it up. She was entirely untrained in magic and could not likely defend herself from imperial assassins.

"I have no wish at all to harm the girl," Tacitus said, his tone quiet and serious. "All the same, her life is not worth plunging this empire into civil war. Neither, even, is yours."

"What is this *understanding* at which you wish us to arrive?" Cassian said. He felt caged, and it angered him. Gambling with his own life was one thing, but doing so with his sister, who had been robbed of her birthright and forced into a life of slavery, was quite another.

"Tell me, my boy," the Emperor said, taking a slow step toward him, "did you warn that girl not to tell the world what she was?"

Cassian hesitated for a long moment, then said: "No."

Tacitus let out a sarcastic chuckle and said: "I see. Well, presumably she will be coming here to the capital to meet her savior."

"Presumably," Cassian said, but he knew the assumption was incorrect. In the few moments he had been in Livia's mind, he had caught many impressions that had slowly unraveled in the hours since. One was of a missing little sister who had been wrongfully taken. He had caught a sense of Livia's character and did not believe she would embark on a glamorous visit to the capital when someone she loved was in peril. Tacitus did not seem to know this, nor did he appear to know about the secret help Cassian had sent her.

"We have some time to prepare then," the Emperor sighed, seeming to relax—even smiling. "It will matter little if some mute girl makes claims of being a starborn in a few inns on the road. Still, she will have to be dealt with once she reaches this city."

"Dealt with how?"

"However best serves this empire," Tacitus replied, gazing into Cassian's eyes. "You and I are long overdue for a talk, my boy. There are decisions of grave importance to be made."

Cassian drew in a breath, calming himself as best he could, then said: "I am listening."

"Good," Tacitus said with a nod, "for there is much I need to tell you." He steepled his fingers in front of his chest. "We must begin when I became emperor. You may know I was scarcely older than you are now. At that time, our people were a straggling pack of dogs in the wilderness. We did not have great cities as we now do, but really *memories* of cities." The Emperor's eyes lifted to the ceiling. "Can you even imagine it? Cracked and burned walls, long dried aqueducts, forgotten libraries full of inaccessible knowledge. All the problems you cast your disapproving eyes upon today would have been *luxuries* to our people then. I faced children starving in the streets – not simply poor children, because the distinction of wealth had ceased to have much meaning. The famine was a *tactic*. Daibok and his demonic army had salted the earth and killed the wildlife so that humanity had no choice but to turn to him. *Many did*, and this in and of itself became a dire problem."

Tacitus cast Cassian a level look. "You took several walled cities in your brief military career that were thought to be all but impenetrable. Tell me, did you have agents inside?"

"I did," Cassian said, swallowing as he thought of one soldier in particular he had turned. The man had been in charge of the city gates, and he had quietly allowed virtually Cassian's entire army inside over several weeks. When the time came, the organized troops had taken the city almost before the ruler knew they were there. This had spared a great deal of bloodshed of course, but Cassian could only imagine what a similarly turned individual might do for invading hordes of demons who had no desire for bloodless victory.

“Many think of Daibok and his legions as crude, unthinking monsters,” Tacitus sighed, “but they were every bit as clever as we were, and far, far more ruthless.” The Emperor exhaled slowly through his nose. “You would scarcely believe it today from the way the Nemesai have marched about, torturing sinners, but they were incredibly *useful* to me back when I was trying to save the human race from obliteration. They could sniff out the dissenters – the ones who had pledged themselves to Daibok. The harsh policies Bishop Cromlic implemented ultimately saved thousands upon thousands of lives and very possibly helped turn the tide of the war."

Tacitus moved closer and put a hand on Cassian’s shoulder. "You were not alive back then. You grew up in the world that I created." His fingers tightened as he added: "I am sorry – truly sorry – for what happened to your mother. Every Gods-damned thing you create manages to find a way to become corrupt as long as there are humans making the decisions. You may find that out one day if you don't have your head so deep into your own ideals to realize it. Still, the actions I took were necessary. You have no idea what an unthinkable paradise it was fifty years ago to have a world where a newborn had greater than one-in-ten odds of surviving. You never witnessed *any* of the horrors of that primitive age because *I solved them."*

Cassian swallowed before saying: "I have never held you or your accomplishments in anything less than the full extent of my esteem." Then he straightened as he added: "Yet progress *must* continue. I only seek to build upon the great work that you once took up and advance our people."

"Yes-s-s-s," the Emperor said with a sigh as if Cassian were speaking of something childish. "What you need to understand for this conversation to progress is that *our people* would have more or less ceased to exist if not for certain key decisions." Tacitus stepped back, releasing Cassian’s shoulder. "I am going to tell you how I saved our people. I only ask that you set aside your moral certitude and preconceptions and listen to me with a truly open mind for a few moments. Can you do that?"

"Yes," Cassian said, swallowing. His attention was utterly rapt.

The Emperor stroked his brow and exhaled: "I would like you to picture pious men and women kneeling in temples, praying to the Gods for help. All over the empire, countless millions reacted to the encroachment of the demons in this manner. So many ran to the church for help that the temples could not contain them, and priests had to hold sermons in the streets." The muscles around Tacitus's eyes tightened as he said: "Tell me, Cassian, for you are an excellent student of history, what did their prayers avail them?"

"Nothing," Cassian said.

"*Nothing at all,*" Tacitus muttered through his teeth. "The entire eastern border of Denigoth fell within a few weeks. Here in the west, the damage is not so obvious, but on the other end of this continent, there are *still* ruins of cities. Hundreds of thousands were slaughtered. We believed it was the end of the world..." his voice broke off, and he shut his eyes. "Sometimes the dark army would give their victims a choice: either consume demon blood and become one of the immortal damned or be put to a horrible death. Would you believe that most chose the latter? Even as they watched their families die, they clung to their *faith.*"

Cassian frowned. *What was the purpose of this speech?* It sounded almost like an indictment of religion.

"I prayed as well," the Emperor whispered. "As I am sure you know, I was not the intended heir to the throne. I abdicated, just as your brother Telemachus did." Tacitus let out a soft chuckle. "I wanted a *simpler* life—to be among the people. I was on a pilgrimage in the west when the attacks began. By the time I even knew what was happening, three of my starborn siblings were dead, and two elders from the previous generation as well. They had been much closer to the threat and, of course, had tried to *act.*" The Emperor swallowed. "No one living at that time had seen the Demon King—no one realized how horribly powerful he had grown. He cut my brethren down like they were *nothing.*"

With his heart racing, Cassian asked his Emperor the question he had longed to for most of his life: "How did you defeat him?"

"*With a sacrifice,*" Tacitus said in a grave whisper. He gazed at Cassian, his face filled with pain. "An Emperor is sometimes forced to make very *hard* decisions, my boy, and none in history so much so as myself. Can you even imagine my position? Thousands dying every day... all looking to *me* to save them from something I could not begin to overcome. Tell me, Cassian, what would you have done in my place?"

"I... do not know."

"Neither did I," Tacitus said in an icy whisper. "I spent countless hours begging the Gods for help, but they did not answer, and, *privately,* I began to hate the celestial beings to whom the human race had built countless temples. They offered me *nothing,* but..." The Emperor locked eyes with Cassian as he said: "I was a starborn, capable of extending my consciousness outward in search of... *other* help."

"What did you do?" Cassian said, barely able to find his voice.

"I saved our people," Tacitus said, and he gazed down at the floor for a moment, seeming to consider his words. "I am about to reveal to you the deepest secrets of this empire, Crown Prince, and then I shall present you with a choice. If you do not choose correctly, *you will die.*"

Cassian's muscles tightened. He looked around at the craith, remembering how relentless their attack had been on him weeks before. They were not the real danger though.

"Your power," Cassian whispered, "it is greater than anything I ever dreamed a starborn could achieve. It is not natural, is it?"

"No," Tacitus sighed.

Cassian thought he felt his heart sink into his stomach as he rasped: "You are *a demon*."

Tacitus's face did not change except that something in his cold, intelligent eyes confirmed the suspicion. He gave no hint that he was either ashamed or proud, but rather he seemed to be studying Cassian. After a moment, he said: "I made a bargain. It is because of that bargain that you, Telemachus, Keska, and more or less our entire race now draw breath."

Cassian felt numb. The enormity of this revelation was too great to process.

"Tell me, boy," Tacitus said, his thick eyebrows knitted together, "what would you do to keep your people alive? Consider all the horrible sins you have committed in the name of this Empire. Would you go further if it meant you could save the human race from annihilation? I chose to do so, knowing what it would cost me. Would you call that courage or cowardice?"

"I... I do not know," Cassian said in a very dry voice, and this was the truth. He stared at the Emperor. If what Tacitus was saying were true, then the man was damned - *truly and horribly damned*. After a long moment, Cassian swallowed and said: "Let me see it."

Tacitus did not need to know what Cassian meant. He gave a nod and lowered the veil he had somehow constructed around his own power. As soon as it was done, Cassian physically staggered and nearly fell to his knees. The Emperor's aura was sickening. The only word that came to Cassian's mind was *'evil.'* The scope of power coursing through the elder starborn overwhelmed his senses. The only thing in the world that compared to it was Promethiock himself.

"Yes," Tacitus said softly. "Only another starborn could ever truly understand what I had to sacrifice, and what I gained." He raised the barrier around his power, and Cassian could breathe again. "I have held this secret for nearly fifty years."

"I am deeply sorry, my Emperor." Cassian reached up and wiped a heavy layer of sweat from his forehead. Merely perceiving the darkness in Tacitus had been physically taxing. He could only imagine what the man felt with it coursing through him.

"I have no need of your pity, my boy. I simply wish you to understand. This was the cost of our people's existence. Since the gods could not or *would not* help us, I turned to another source. A demon was watching from the cosmos—one older and stronger than the *deities* who claim dominion over the human souls of this world. His name... is *Bacchid."*

The word seemed to conjure a ripple in the universe, and Cassian jolted back, panting. *This was true darkness...* For a long moment, he did not speak but only rolled all of this strange and terrible information around in his mind, considering Tacitus's every word. All the while, he was conscious of the Emperor watching him.

"You said I must make a choice in this chamber," Cassian finally said. "I imagine this cosmic demon desires another starborn in his retinue."

"Yes-s-s," Tacitus said, "and you are his chosen one. He is deeply impressed by your strength of will, as am I."

"Why do either of you need me?" Cassian hissed, suddenly glaring. "Our people are already protected. I imagine all that demonic power could provide you with many thousands of years of unnatural life. Why do you need an *heir* at all?"

"You are not to be my heir, Cassian," the Emperor said, a strange excitement beginning to grow in his eyes. "You are to be my *partner* in the great task that lies ahead. You and I will bring order to the human race as it has never known." The sides of Tacitus's mouth curled up. "We will drive the Gods you hate so much from this world. If you have the courage now to do what is required, you will be able to create every aspect of the perfect and equal society you imagine. End slavery, end intolerance, educate the masses, and usher in an entirely new code of ethics that does not rely on the vague and ambiguous will of abstract and unknowable deities. You will possess eternal life and near godlike power so that you may ensure your creation is never corrupted."

Cassian stared down at the stone floor beneath him. He could feel his hands trembling. *Could he actually consider such a thing—to become a demon?*

"You are the Messiah, Cassian," Tacitus continued. "The gods who allowed your own mother to be executed in their name have the arrogance to presume you their servant. *Refuse them*! They would not help our people in their darkest hour any more than they helped you. Spit in their faces! You have the free will. *That* is what it is to be *human*!"

"How does one accomplish such a thing?" Cassian said in a soft whisper. The clarity and decisiveness with which he lived his life had never been further from him.

"With *sin,* I am afraid," Tacitus said in a somber voice. "Come." The Emperor walked to the wall to the left of his throne and waved his hand. One of the stone blocks dislodged itself from the wall and floated down to the floor. Behind where it had rested, unearthly green light radiated, bathing Tacitus's face. He reached into a hidden chamber and retrieved a blazing green orb roughly the size of a skull. Inside what appeared to be a spherical barrier of crystal, a glowing storm of emerald whirled in silent fury.

"What is that?" Cassian said, feeling a chill pass through him. His senses were somehow unable to penetrate the outer shell, but some part of him knew the object to be malevolent.

"This is a plague," Tacitus said. "It is perhaps the most terrible pestilence this world has ever seen, and *you* will release it." He held the orb out to Cassian.

With trembling hesitation, Cassian took the unholy object in his hands and was surprised to find it had virtually no weight. It was only tangentially physical matter from what he could tell, existing in a state of almost pure and unnatural energy.

"Wonderful, is it not?" Tacitus whispered. "It was forged in the deepest pits of hell *just for you."*

Cassian stared into the sphere. It seemed to gaze into his soul as if alive. "Will this kill people?"

"Not *our* people, Cassian. It is a mystical pestilence that is deadly only to one race – the only one that might actually pose a threat to us – *the elves."*

Cassian's heart began to slam in his chest. Immediately he thought of Thalice. This sin was designed perfectly for him—the ultimate betrayal of the only girl with whom he had ever shared his heart. He could scarcely begin to imagine the scope of dark magic reeling in his hands. How many thousands of years might it have taken to create? All of it must have been in anticipation for this moment—*for his choice.*

"I must murder the one I love most," Cassian rasped. He understood the sacrifice. The sin would destroy his soul. He would no longer be human, but a hollow shell in which the powers of an ancient demon could reside.

Tacitus patted him on the arm and whispered: "The sacrifice is terrible, I know. It will be the hardest thing you ever do, but once you release this darkness into the world, your heart will harden. In a way you cannot yet imagine, you will be free, and you will wield power of a magnitude no mortal but I has ever known."

Cassian let his mind touch the orb's energy. The demonic magic filled his psyche with images of death. The plague would spread out into the world the instant he willed it, and in every corner of every continent, elves would sicken and perish. None would escape the horrible wave. Such was the power of the cosmic demon Tacitus served, yet all of it was dependent upon a single mortal. This, Cassian understood in a moment of clarity, was the strange balance between humans and the Gods and Demons. Their vast, other-dimensional power could only come into the world through the free will of a mortal. It all came down to his decision, and, if done, the sin would be entirely his.

"Make your choice, Asango," Tacitus said. "Join me, or I will be forced to kill you here and now."

Cassian's heart burning, he made his decision. Sweat dripped down his face as he willed the membrane that housed the terrible plague to vanish back into the ether from whence it had come. The swirling green magic floated between his hands, subject entirely to his will. The godlike power was unbelievable— *control over the life of an entire race*. He knew in that moment the deepest truth in his own heart.

"Goodbye, my love," he whispered. Then he willed all the power in his starborn body at once and destroyed the demonic plague.

"NO!" Tacitus screamed as the dark spell vanished in a brilliant emerald flare. "DAMN YOU!" Cassian felt the tremendous power of the Emperor wrap around him and squeeze. "YOU LITTLE FOOL!"

"HUAH!" Cassian cried out as he felt his left arm snap in two places along with several of his ribs. Force beyond comprehension crushed in on his skin, in his throat and even in his eyes.

"You pathetic little COWARD!" Tacitus made a sharp gesture, and Cassian was brought down to his knees. He could no more resist the power than a human child might resist the strength of an ogre.

Death was about to come. Cassian willed all of his memories of this incident to Telemachus along with the command: <Get out of the city right now!>

"Hah!" Tacitus grunted. "You think he can run from *Me*?" Cassian felt the dark magic around him squeeze tighter around his neck. It restricted both the flow of blood and air to the degree that his vision began to go black.

"You will not be buried, *Messiah*," Tacitus said in a hateful snarl. "There will be nothing left of you but ash that my slaves will sweep up and toss away with the rest of the day's rubbish."

The force crushing Cassian's body abated but was immediately replaced by a yellow flame that burst up around him. He felt his skin begin to burn, and he let out a scream. The pain was unbelievable, yet the instinct to preserve himself from death was still greater. Cassian forced himself to call upon the Dakshai barrier spell—the most efficient shield against heat he knew. It was nearly impossible amidst his agony to summon spectrals from the ether and focus power into them, but he did it anyway. The protective cocoon formed, and for an instant, the fire was not eating his flesh, but then his spell collapsed under the weight of Tacitus's awesome power, as Cassian had known it would. The second shield was already going up around him, and he was casting a third, then a fourth, a fifth, a sixth, a seventh—*a spell within a spell within a spell.* His mind worked faster than it ever had, yet even as he threw up barrier after barrier, he could feel the hellfire slipping through cracks in his defense and searing strips of his flesh. The pain threatened to shatter his mind, but Cassian fought through it and focused his protection most intensely around his head, for if his brain were damaged, *all was lost!*

The heat was beyond that of even the white fire that Titus breathed. Cassian could see the stone tiles beneath him begin to melt into a glowing orange liquid, and his feet sank into them, only barely protected by his magic. The inferno went on and on, and somewhere beyond its terrible hiss, he heard the Emperor say: "Goodbye, Cassian Asango, *Messiah*."

Finally, the conflagration began to dissipate. Cassian's body screamed in agony all over, yet somehow, he was still standing. He looked at Tacitus through the vanishing yellow flame and saw the demon stare back at him with an expression of shock. The soldier in Cassian took over. *The Emperor's surprise would only last an instant!*

Cassian sprang forward, slashing his right hand as if the tips of his fingers were a blade. In a way, they were, for he willed every shred of power he had left within into a thin scythe of white magic. It was the same technique he had used to kill Dimitris years ago, only he was stronger now, and his ability to focus his energy had expanded.

Tacitus let out the beginning of a cry before the gleaming blade cut into his neck. It tore into the trachea, the muscles, and all the veins and arteries. Cassian watched chunks of tissue fly away in a spray of red, and the Emperor stumbled back, clutching at his neck as blood spilled rapidly out between his fingers.

"DIE!" Cassian shouted. The pain in his body seemed to be growing. Would his wounds kill him before he could heal them? It did not matter at that moment. He needed to see the life of this monster end.

Cassian sensed the elder starborn's mind begin to sink into oblivion. The blood drained away, and all the reactions of death started to occur in the brain. Cassian knew them well. And yet... the process seemed to stop abruptly. The horrible demonic energy whirled up in a red blaze around the Emperor's throat. *It was conscious*, Cassian suddenly realized, and was capable of acting independently of its host. In a moment of horror, he watched the dark power began to repair Tacitus's neck, stitching the sinew back together even as he gurgled blood.

The patter of steps began then. Cassian turned and saw the craith in the room moving toward him. He glanced back at the Emperor, whose wounds were closing before his eyes. There was too much of a disadvantage.

Cassian looked up at the ceiling and cried: "VASHDAK!" Spectrals shot into the world and combined at the speed of thought, consuming the tiny flickers of magic left in his flesh and combining into a blazing conflagration of yellow energy that blasted a hole in the stone above his head. He willed himself upward. The craith were rushing at him, and they could leap, but Cassian's will was stronger than it had ever been. He soared up into the cool, evening sky.

<TITUS, I NEED YOU NOW!> his mind shouted.

The dragon, who had been resting in the courtyard outside Tacitus's throne room, rose up instantly and took to the sky, spreading his great wings and moving like an arrow from a crossbow. They met in the air, and Cassian dropped onto Titus's back and grabbed hold of one of the horns. <FLY! FLY AS FAST AS YOU CAN OR WE BOTH DIE!> his mind screamed.

The dragon flapped its great wings, and Cassian telepathically commanded his men below to leave all their possessions and flee the city. The Denigoth Empire was no longer safe—*not for anyone...*

CHAPTER 44: STARBORN

"Bwah," Livia managed to rasp as she stepped out of her room. She sounded ridiculous—like an infant with the voice of a young woman. Her throat ached from engaging her long neglected vocal cords. The pain of her curse did not come though, *and it never would again.* This was only one of the gifts Cassian Asango had given her. The power of a starborn flowed through her every minute of the day, which more than made up for difficulties of learning to speak for the first time at twenty-two years old. It was, after all, a necessary component of casting spells, *or at least she thought so.*

Livia sat down at the table across from Hervin. He had volunteered to cook, but she had insisted on doing it herself. It felt right to do him at least that kindness before setting out. The poor, sweet little man was poking at his eggs, seeming lost in thought. She could still see the expression on his face when she had willed a spoon to rise up off the table. *He had nearly fainted!*

In the many hours since Livia had returned home, Hervin had slowly wrapped around her being a starborn. He was proud of course, as any father would be, yet the limited explanation she had provided for becoming a living miracle left him quite bewildered. Livia could sense dozens of questions swimming around in his thoughts about who she really was, and how or why such power could have been stolen from her. She had not dared tell him about Arkas. It was, after all, entirely unclear what the consequences from the Emperor might be for reclaiming her power.

There were things Livia could reveal now, such as that she knew where Iona was. The fact that there was reportedly an enormous ogre-like creature who had murdered dozens of people did not need to be mentioned though. Why worry Hervin? She was frightened enough all on her own. Moving spoons around with magic was quite a different matter than facing a hardened killer with supernatural strength, *but one thing at a time.*

"Did you finish the accounting?" Hervin whispered after swallowing a mouthful of food.

Livia nodded. The shop was in excellent condition and would fetch a high price. Hervin had agreed to sell whilst she went to rescue Iona. They would soon leave this simple town and start their new life together.

"Thank you," he sighed. The poor man was glad to be getting rid of his shop. Livia could see more clearly into his nature than ever before. He had never had a keen talent for business. Always, his mind was on other things. *Her father wanted to write plays!* That revelation had made her smile, just as her heart had throbbed when the memory of purchasing her many years ago had flashed through his thoughts. The cow had demanded a girl to cook and clean, and Hervin had gone to the slavers, already innately uncomfortable at the idea of *owning* another human being. There had been dozens of young females for purchase, but he had seen Livia standing off to the side. She had been sullen and quiet, and the slave master had explained that she was a cripple, unable to speak, but Hervin had seen something in her eyes—a depth and intelligence, and he had wanted to save her from whatever hardships might lay ahead. Thus, bringing years of anger from his horrid wife upon himself, he brought home a mute girl that no one else wanted.

"What?" Hervin muttered, glancing up at her. "Are you alright?"

Livia smiled at him, clandestinely wiping away the moisture in her eyes. She would be able to repay his kindness to her soon. Starborn were given positions of power and prestige and showered with gifts from all over the empire. Hervin would have a beautiful home, close to her own—*wherever she ended up residing*—and he could have all the books he desired and servants to see to his comfort. There would be no slaves of course. *Not ever!* If there were one direction to which Livia might wish to focus her newly acquired status, it would be to help Cassian Asango rid the Empire of the practice of slavery once and for all.

"If only Iona could see you now," Hervin whispered, and she turned to see him staring at her. "I... uh... I hope you have no trouble finding her."

<Nothing will stop me,> her mind said, forming what seemed like audible words. She had not meant to do this. It simply happened, much to her own shock.

Hervin was bewildered as well, for he fidgeted in his seat. "Did you just... *speak*?"

Livia nodded, a burst of excitement coursing through her. She tried to focus her mind on forming words again, *but nothing happened.* She swallowed and pushed harder, closing her eyes. The chair next to her slid a few paces to the left as a tendril of her magic swept out, but no words. *Control...* she did not seem to have it yet, but that did not mean it was beyond her reach.

"Amazing," Hervin whispered, staring at the chair as if it were a holy object. "I'm so proud of you!"

Livia reached out and took his hand, and as she did, she noted that the telepathic connection to him intensified. There was a network of thought interconnected to memory, desire, logic, and emotion, and Livia could see all of it. With this revelation came a troubling understanding: she the power to alter these things—to bend Hervin's mind to her will. This frightened her, and she drew her hand away.

"What's wrong?" Hervin said. His thoughts were distant again, but concern still flowed out from his mind as plain to Livia's perceptions as the scent of a pungent stew.

She shook her head and cast him a grin once again, and her vocal chords inadvertently engaged, emitting an: "eh-h-h."

"Hah!" Hervin laughed. "Your voice!" A wide grin coming across his face that showed most of the crooked upper teeth.

"My Livia's voice!" He lowered his head, and she sensed a deflation of his excitement as he whispered: "You're not really *my* Livia though. Gods know you must have come from stock far greater than mine." He grinned at her, and a mixture of pain and delight radiated from him as he said: "You were always better than any of us. I knew that immediately. I don't have any right to call myself your father."

<You *ARE my father!*> her psychic mind almost shouted, and as it did, she began to understand something about its nature: *It was tied to her heart.* Her telepathic voice had come out fierce and electric, and entirely *honest.* Livia had the sense that she could not transmit something her heart did not wholly accept. Was this true for all starborn? Was telepathy the pristine language of the soul, or was she simply inexperienced and romanticizing? Whatever the case, Livia found her hands moving to the paper still clutched in Hervin's hands. She took it and wrote with her pencil:

You are the only father I have ever known.
My life would have been hell if not for your
compassion, and I shall never forget that.

She passed him the note, and just as he started to read it, there was a sharp and rapid knock at the door. Livia whirled around, nerves rising in the pit of her stomach as instinct told her that something was wrong, though it took her a few heartbeats to register precisely why: *she could not sense a mind outside.*

"Hello?" a male voice said.

"Y-yes?" Hervin said aloud. He stood, but Livia held up a hand, motioning him not to move.

"I'm looking for a *Livia,*" the voice said. "I was told she lives here.

Livia crept toward her home's entryway. The voice did not seem particularly hostile, but nor did it seem friendly, and there seemed to be... *power* of some kind just on the other side of the door. It was not like the magic of a sorcerer, but something else. Taking an uneasy step forward, she readied her own energy to fight, her heart thumping in her chest.

"Oh Gods," the voice grunted, "stop tiptoeing around! I'm not here to attack you. Cassian sent me, so will you please open the gods-damned door?"

Cassian Asango had sent this visitor? Livia blinked. Could it be a trick? She still could not catch a shred of thought from this visitor, and yet the irritation in his voice had sounded so unabashedly genuine that it somehow removed most of her suspicion. With a mostly steady hand, Livia opened the door. On the other side was a tall, broad-shouldered man with tanned skin and dark brown hair. He was dressed in well-crafted leather and bronze linen, and she noted immediately that he had two swords on his belt and an array of knives sheathed about his waist and vest.

The man's deep brown eyes fixed on her and looked her up and down unabashedly. "Yeah, that's definitely starborn power," he said. "It's about time!" Without asking permission, he brushed past her into the house. "Do you have water?" he grunted, his eyes fixing on Hervin.

"Uh-h-h," Hervin murmured, and he made a nervous gesture to the clay urn on the table.

"Many thanks," the stranger exhaled, and he darted over and snatched up the urn and tilted it to his lips. Without another word, he proceeded to gulp down the contents at a furious pace while both Livia and Hervin stared at him. It seemed the man had consumed the entire container by the time he set it down and let out a hissing sigh. Then he tilted his neck to one side and then the other, eliciting a series of loud pops from his spine, and walked over to the table, dropping down into the chair opposite Hervin.

"Sorry," he muttered, leaning forward and running his fingers over his brow. "*Do not rest until you find her*—those were his gods-damned words! I don't know if he *forgot* that I am compelled to follow his instructions exactly, or if he was just being an ass. Probably the latter."

"Um," Hervin whispered, blinking, "m-may I ask who you are?"

"My name is Soulic," the stranger said, leaning back in the chair. He jerked his chin to the side, somehow drawing out yet another loud pop from his neck before exhaling: "Again, sorry for my *brisk* behavior. I have been riding well over thirty straight hours to find—" he turned his head and looked Livia in the eyes, "*you.*" Soulic sank a little deeper into his chair and muttered: "Had to change horses six gods-damned times. Paid a fortune to the last stable master." With a shrug, he added: "Ah well, my employer can afford it."

Livia stared at the peculiar man. Cassian Asango's name had gotten him in the door unchallenged, but he was still a heavily armed stranger with power burning inside his flesh that she did not understand. Feeling it prudent, Livia willed out a psychic tendril and tried hard to penetrate into the nothingness that seemed to be his mind.

Soulic immediately stiffened in his chair and turned to her. This time she did not merely perceive nothing, but sensed... *a wall* perhaps? He looked her in the eyes and said: "You need a bit more skill than that to get in here," touching his index finger to the side of his head. Then he smiled and said: "Relax. I'm actually here to keep you safe and give you a hand with your current set of concerns." The man opened his vest and drew out a slightly crumpled scroll with a red seal and tossed it to her. As Livia caught it, he added in a vaguely sardonic tone: "This is from *the Messiah.*"

Livia's heart accelerated as she saw a beautiful insignia of a griffon's head burned into the wax, along with the word: *Asango.* She carried the scroll over to her desk with reverence, her head swimming as she very carefully thumbed the edge of the seal up, breaking and yet preserving it as much as possible. She unrolled the document and saw the crisp, elegant writing that somehow did not seem to be from ink:

Dear Sister,
I hope that your newfound power allowed you to escape your unjust imprisonment. If not, I have sent my servant, Soulic, to provide you with any help you might require. He is one of the few Sansrit masters left in the world and the best warrior I have at my disposal. I shall feel better knowing he is with you until we meet.
You cannot imagine how thrilled the other starborn and I are to know that you are alive and finally whole. We all wish to meet you. Our sister Keska invites you to be her honored guest in the kingdom of Aloria, but I selfishly hope you will come to the capital first to spend some time with Telemachus and me.
I caught only a glimpse of your mind, but I sensed you have a sibling in some kind of trouble. As I told you, there is very little you need to fear from now on, but you have yet to receive training in the use of your power. Thus, Soulic may be very useful to you. He will follow your orders as if they were from me. His manners and crude sense of humor leave something to be desired at times, but he will fight, kill, and even die for you without hesitation. I have sent him with ten thousand desseks to cover any expenses you might have at this time. Please feel free to use it any way you see fit. It is a gift without condition. Please also be safe. None of us wish to lose you now that you are finally returned to us.
I wish you luck in settling your family business and hope to see you soon after its conclusion.

Your Brother,
Cassian Asango

Livia traced his signature with her fingers. *He had written so affectionately.* It seemed impossible that so many wonderful things in her life were happening. She sighed as she began to read the note again, and it was then that she noticed, in the last bit of curl of the paper at the bottom, a postscript message, which read:

> *I advise you not to spread the knowledge that you are a starborn any more than you find absolutely necessary for the moment. Your existence is something of a political problem for the empire at the moment. Do not worry too much on the issue though. I am meeting with Emperor Tacitus later today to discuss how we shall proceed on the matter.*

A 'political problem for the empire...' Yes, the fact that her power had been stolen and somehow grafted onto the son of the Emperor was certainly a problem. This continued to loom in the back of her mind. She still did not know how her magic had been taken from her, or why. Had Tacitus Adronicus himself performed the spell, and would he then be angry that his work was undone? Would he come after her? That thought sent a shiver through her. Still, Asango was speaking on her behalf, and there was no indication he was afraid so much as being cautious.

Livia's mind drifted back to the moment, years ago, when she had encountered Prince Arkas. He had attacked her with the very power she now possessed, but the instant it had come into contact with her, there had been a furious reaction. The magic had recoiled back at him and shattered his hand. *It must have been trying to return to its true host.* Livia could not help but smile as she considered this, yet the memory led to other far more troubling places.

Arkas had believed Iona to be a 'weapon.' How absurd a coincidence had it been that, of all people in the vast Denigoth Empire, Livia was the one he found standing next to Iona? *Had he been tricked?* Had the stolen magic inside him somehow manipulated him into coming into contact with Livia to get back to her? Perhaps, and yet Arkas had been confident enough of what Iona was to abscond with her. What did all of it mean? Even as a full starborn, Livia could not see the answer. There were forces at play that she did not yet understand.

"Are we going somewhere?" Soulic yawned. "If you wouldn't mind, I would prefer to travel by wagon for the first leg of our journey. I can sleep in the back."

Livia thought for a brief moment, and then took out a new piece of paper from her desk, flattened it next to the note from her brother, and wrote for several minutes. She decided that if Cassian trusted this man, then she should share the details of Iona's capture and who was holding her—*things she had not even shared with Hervin.* Her note touched carefully on her encounter with Arkas and then moved to the stories gleaned from the Cassianites over the months. She included the murderous ogre-like creature that was most likely Iona's guard and all she knew about the mountain range where they both allegedly were. There was a strange relief in writing it all out to share with someone else after keeping it to herself for so long.

Livia eventually handed the paper to this Soulic, and he took it in a smooth gesture and held it up in front of his face, muttering: "Cassian said you would be *talking* like this." She watched his eyes move and was fascinated by the way that, unlike seemingly everyone else in the city, she could still decipher nothing in his thoughts. Yet she did sense something when his eyes narrowed on a certain section of the page – *anger.* The emotion rippled his mental barrier, and as it did, his power flared. It was so sudden and so fierce that Livia flinched. *He had magic*, but not like her own—so much more... *wild.* For a brief second, she saw a fierce orange silhouette of a forest cat in her mind's eye. It enveloped Soulic's body. It *was* him!

The Sansrit warrior's dark eyes shifted to hers, and they seemed to hold awareness of what she perceived. As if to give an answer to it, he said: "I have a particular... *intolerance* for men who mistreat women. I confess I would not at all mind opening this creature's neck for you."

"Creature?" Hervin said, and Livia felt a swell of confusion in her poor father. She had almost forgotten he was there.

"You don't know?" Soulic said, and before she could do anything to stop him, he sighed: "Some ogre-like-thing has your Iona."

Livia's irritation erupted, and without consciously meaning to she sent an invisible tendril of magic outward to the chair upon which Soulic sat. The legs ripped to splinters in an instant, and the seat clattered down to the floor, *but Soulic did not.* He reacted instantly, his legs shifting to accommodate the loss of his support so smoothly that his upper half scarcely seemed to move.

"Quick temper, eh?" he chuckled, staring at her. "He had a right to know. It's his daughter."

<It was not your place to decide that!> Her telepathic mind snapped before she even realized it was speaking.

"Ah," Soulic grunted with a nod, "now you're starting to sound like a starborn." He turned to Hervin and said: "Don't worry about it too much. Your daughter is powerful as hell, and as for me," his hand dropped to the hilt of his sword. The blade snapped out of its scabbard and extended forward in a blur of motion faster than Livia would have believed anything in the world could move. In the same instant, there was a sharp '*THK'* sound from behind, and she turned reflexively to see a dagger buried up to the handle in one of the beams to her house. *Soulic had thrown it without her even seeing*! With a smirk, the Sansrit warrior said: "I'm not entirely useless in a fight myself."

"I... s-see," Hervin muttered.

Soulic turned to Livia. "We could hire mercenaries, or maybe even conscript soldiers from the Imperium, but if we go in loud, it may get your sister killed," his brow furrowed, "or we could end up with a damn hostage standoff."

"Hostage standoff?" Hervin whispered, his face going pale.

Soulic went on as if the conversation were entirely casual: "If it's just one or two people holding her—even if one of those people is a monster—I think you and I should go in alone. Actually, maybe just me with you in reserve. Stealth is one of my specialties." He moved to the wall and pulled his dagger from the wood and placed it neatly back into the sheath at his belt.

Livia frowned at the man. She was intensely irritated he was upsetting Hervin, yet it was somewhat relieving to hear him speak competently about Iona's rescue. For all her power, Livia had no combat experience whatsoever. It was good to have someone who did, and she could imagine the skills he had just displayed being quite useful.

"I... I prefer you go in ahead as well," Hervin said.

"There," Soulic said with an exaggerated gesture toward Hervin, "your father has *spoken*." A wry grin touched his face as he added: "You wrote this in the Vengal region, no? We'll free your sister inside of a week, I'm sure of it!"

Livia's frustration involuntarily softened. There was something vaguely charming about Soulic, vexing as he was. Still, these were her last moments with Hervin before she set out, so she decided to put her temporary new servant to work if only to get him out of the house. She walked back to her desk and retrieved yet another piece of paper, then wrote:

A cart will be fine. Please go and purchase one for the journey. Do not spend more than one hundred desseks.

Livia walked the note over to Soulic, and he took it and began to read. After a few heartbeats, he looked up and shrugged. "Alright. A hundred desseks. Bet I can do it for fifty." He rose from his chair and turned to Hervin. "It was a pleasure... uh... your name is Hervy Sondal, no?"

"Hervin," said Hervin, swallowing.

"Of course," Soulic sighed, and he turned toward the door. When his hand touched the latch though, he glanced back over his shoulder at Livia. "I really have to say, I envy your position. All of a sudden, you find out that you're a *starborn* of all things, and your brother is the Crown Prince of Denigoth. I mean, I know we have to go to some trouble to help your little sister, but, other than that, your life is going quite well, no?"

Livia's mouth twitched into an uncontrolled smile. *Yes, things were going well.* Surely Cassian could talk the emperor out of doing her harm.

After Soulic left, Livia walked over to the wall panel where she kept her secret desseks hidden away. A memory flashed of Lady Gretis holding out the bag of golden coins. That kind woman told her she could rise above her slave status. *If only she could see Livia now.* Perhaps there would be time to seek out this Gretis. She was a Sansrit master, like Soulic. Maybe they even knew one another.

Livia opened the concealed panel and drew out the clinking sack inside, which she carried over to the breakfast table. Hervin was still sitting there, running all the bewildering information he had just acquired through his mind, she sensed.

"You'll be careful, won't you?" he said, and then he fidgeted in his seat and muttered: "Perhaps I should go with you. Iona is my daughter, after all."

Livia smiled at him and shook her head. Then she set the purse down on the table, untied it, and retrieved a handful of the silver and gold coins and held them out to Hervin.

"What?" he said, looking confused.

Livia nodded and held the coins still closer. Hervin hesitantly held out his hands, and she dropped the money into them. Doing a quick count, Livia estimated the amount to be roughly four hundred and fifty desseks. This was a more than adequate amount. She tightened the pouch back up and then took the paper Soulic had left on the table, snatched her pencil from her pocket once more, and wrote on the back:

Buy yourself a handsome new cloak and suit and boots, as well as the best horse you can find. Do this before you put the shop up for sale.

When she handed him the note, he looked over it, then said: "A-alright... if you insist." He eyed the coin purse and said: "Wherever did you get all that money, if I may ask." There was no accusation in his voice, only bewilderment.

Livia shrugged and winked at him, and then tapped the note she had written, emphasizing what she wished him to do. An expensive set of new clothes and a beautiful horse would subtly convey that Hervin was not desperate to sell the shop but was comfortable and had no need to accept the first offer. Moreover, she simply wanted to give him something.

Livia rose then, tucking away her money and writing implements in the pockets of her dress. She would also need new clothing. The thought of donning a beautiful dress excited her. *What was Cassian Asango's favorite color?* Livia chuckled to herself at her girlish thoughts. There was an exhilarating excitement to all that lay ahead. Her life would soon be filled with riches and adventure. Only five points of the star were chosen in all the world when the comet came, *and she was one of them!* That had to mean that her life was worth something—that she was of value to the human race and to history. Such a notion would have seemed impossible only a short time ago, but already those days were beginning to feel like another life. Aside from the hopefully brief predicament of Iona's imprisonment, what in the world could go wrong for her now?

CHAPTER 45: THE PSYCHIC PLANE

Tacitus lay back upon the silk sheets of his supple feather mattress, still fully clothed in his imperial robes. It was late into the night, and most of the palace was asleep. The metal-masked faces of his craith reflected the soft candlelight in the room as they stood like statues around the bed. Tacitus shut his eyes and sank into concentration, letting his hands fall down to his sides. He was still feeling tense. The psychic plane abhorred inner turmoil, but then he was the oldest and strongest human telepath in the world, and the way was well known to him. Within a few moments, his consciousness was gliding through the dark and beautiful ether of the mental universe.

There were hundreds of thousands of minds around him. They shined and flickered in brilliant white like stars. Some were larger and brighter than others. The mental sphere of Cassian Asango, he knew, burned more fiercely than any other mortal's save his own. Because of this, the boy's was the easiest to find in the psychic plane. He could feel it always—the one with the greatest potential. It was surprisingly close. *Asango had not fled Denigoth then...* Tacitus had expected to traverse the psychic plane for hours to find his defiant little opponent, but it took less than thirty minutes of whisking through the lesser telepaths of Denigoth before he came to the crackling orb that was Cassian's mind. It floated in the darkness, a sphere the size of a castle.

<Asango?> Tacitus said in his mental voice. <Can you hear me?>

<I can,> the boy's mind answered immediately in a cold whisper. Perhaps he had been anticipating this meeting, *not that it mattered*. The young prince was no match for him.

Tacitus put his hands against the side of the tremendous orb and felt himself vanish and reappear inside at the speed of thought. He was shocked at what a simple matter it was—*no defense at all*—but then Cassian had been severely injured in their battle. This would, of course, impair his ability to concentrate.

Inside the sphere were dark, curving, reflective walls and a smooth floor that appeared to be a giant cornerstone board. There was nothing else—no abhorrent memories or stray whispers of thought. The boy's inner psychic world was clean and ordered, except... Tacitus gazed around and suddenly saw Cassian crouched down in the darkness, shirtless and trembling. There were streaks of horribly burned skin on his shoulders, arms, and chest. The boy's face seemed to have survived the ordeal save that his scalp was now shaven to stubble—likely it had been cut because so much of his sandy blond hair had been burned in the fight.

<You are quite foolish for coming here,> Cassian hissed, his deep green eyes glaring up.

<You silly little child,> Tacitus chuckled. <Do you believe the defenses of your twenty-two-year-old mind could somehow threaten *me*?> He glided to Cassian and dropped to his feet on the checkered floor. <Your wounds must be unimaginably painful for them to transfer so vividly onto the mental plane. It troubles me to see you like this. You were meant for greatness.> He knelt down closer and whispered: <I offered you a chance to become a *God!*>

A vicious smile crossed the boy's face. <A *God*? Is that what you think you are?> He let out a hissing, full-throated laugh.

The Emperor bristled, glaring down, and Cassian stared back, cackling even harder. *The little bastard!* A rage came over Tacitus. There was no magic on the mental plane, yet he had learned over the years to bend and manipulate many of its aspects to his will. He held out his hand and pooled a portion of the mental ether into a long, smooth staff, which congealed and solidified between his fingers. Then Tacitus swung the weapon with all his might and struck Cassian across his impudent face. <You arrogant little fool!> he cried as the boy's head snapped back. Cassian hissed in pain, but somehow, he continued to grin. <Do not smirk! You are but an *insect* to me!> The Emperor swung the staff again and struck the boy in the back and then kicked him over and rammed the pole into his stomach.

<HAHAHA!!> Cassian rasped. *His smile was maddening!*

Tacitus bashed the little fool in the face, screaming in rage, and then lifted his weapon and brought it down again, over and over until all life seemed to have gone out of the defiant green eyes, and he stood glaring over a bloody corpse.

<Well *that* was interesting,> Cassian's voice came from behind. Tacitus whirled to see the young man standing calmly behind him, wearing his princely clothing with not a single burn-mark visible. <I expected more composure from *the greatest man* in history.>

The Emperor turned to the disfigured creature he had been beating, but there was nothing there. He noticed as well that the weapon had vanished from his hands. When he turned back to Cassian, the boy was holding the staff in front of him, seeming to inspect it.

Tacitus forced himself not to show irritation. This *younger* starborn would not take control of this encounter. <Your resilience is quite impressive, but for all your clever tricks, we both know you are lying somewhere covered in mortal wounds.>

<Sitting actually,> Cassian said, rolling Tacitus's staff between his fingers. <You are correct of course that my body was burned significantly, but my brain is entirely intact. I can rebuild everything else, and I have Telemachus with me, who is a strong contender for the greatest healer in history.>

<I scarcely know why you would bother. You must know you will not live much longer. I can find you anywhere.>

<*Can you*?> Cassian said, his eyes shifted up from the staff, full of challenge. <I wonder at the limits of your omniscience.>

The Emperor smirked. <I have twenty-*thousand* men scouring the countryside in every direction, and there will be fifty thousand more within a day. Standing against me is standing against the full might of Denigoth.> He took a step toward the boy. <More than that though, you now know *what* I am. You live only because of a very slight underestimation on my part. I shall make no such mistake again.> He took another step. <For all your magic, you are nothing but a frail mortal before my power, Cassian. If you had any sense at all, you would beg my forgiveness, and if you are too proud to do that, then you should kill yourself, for when I capture you again, I will inflict horrors upon you beyond imagination.>

The boy stared into his eyes for a long moment, seeming to study him, and then said: <Why did you come here, my Emperor?>

<Because I *can!*> Tacitus said, returning the boy's hateful gaze. <And because I wish to ask what you possibly hope to accomplish out here. I have spent so many years observing your life. You are an investment of mine—perhaps one that might be salvageable even now. Do you really wish to throw your magnificent life away for the gods you hate so much?>

Cassian gazed down at the reflective floor beneath him and said softly: <I will answer your question if you will first answer one of mine.> He lifted his gaze and said: <How did the starborn of your generation truly die?> Tacitus felt a chill pass through him. The boy's eyes narrowed, and he spoke in a scathing tone: <There is something that has been bothering me for years about the history of my brethren. You see, I like to look where my siblings are afraid to set their mind's eyes, and I have focused perceptions upon the Demon King many times. Daibok is tremendously powerful – certainly too much for any starborn to defeat alone. However, he is not *all powerful* by any means. If Telemachus, Keska, and I faced him together right now, perhaps we would die, but I am confident we could rid the world of him in the process, which begs the question: how did he manage to kill *Seven* starborn in the Demon War?>

Cassian gave a mocking shrug and said: <Did they each independently decide to face him one at a time, *like idiots*? Did he manage to outmaneuver beings who could track his movements and telepathically communicate with one another from around the world?> Cassian's image vanished, and a fraction of a second later he reappeared close in front of Tacitus, hissing: <That was your sin to open yourself to Bacchid, was it not? You *Murdered* your own siblings, and the elders as well.>

Hatred rose in Tacitus's stomach. This child was daring to judge him—he who had saved the world!

Cassian's image vanished once more, but his voice continued from seemingly every direction: <Your story always impressed me. The historical texts say you abdicated your claim to the throne and only reluctantly took up power when the others had died. *How noble.*> The vast echoing suddenly ended, and a sharp voice came from behind: <You told me that you renounced the throne to be closer to the people, but I think you did it because you were not the strongest of your generation, *and you knew it.*>

Tacitus whirled to see Cassian, glaring at him, and he reached out to grab the little bastard by his throat, but the boy vanished yet again.

<Tell me, Mighty Emperor, did you kill the first several of them through cunning—using the love and trust they must have had for you to trick them? I do not imagine you were brave enough to face any of them openly until Bacchid had fed you several meals of power from the deepest pits of hell. No, you must have plotted from the shadows like your *craven little son*!"

<ENOUGH!> Tacitus screamed, glaring around. <Stop hiding! Face me!>

<Certainly,> Cassian said, and he appeared just a few steps away.

Tacitus lurched for the boy, focusing his full psychic might, yet his outstretched arms stopped short, halted suddenly by the presence of restraints. He cocked his head and saw that shackles had formed on both of his wrists and, as he glanced down, his ankles as well. They were fastened to chains that reached out into the blackness behind, seeming to disappear into it, yet they held firm as if bound to iron.

<What is this?> Tacitus roared. <You think you can restrain me?!>

<I do,> Cassian said, his eyes burning with a terrible confidence. <Show me I am wrong. Show me your strength, *Elder Starborn*!>

Tacitus drew in a slow, furious breath. This was the realm of the mind, and the chains were only a construct of Cassian's will, just as Tacitus's form in this place was a projection of his psyche. He focused all the powers of his mind into tearing the metal cuffs on his wrists. There was a brilliant flare of crackling psychic energy that ripped out like lightning, yet when the flash subsided, the shackles remained, completely unharmed.

<It is true then,> Cassian whispered.

<WHAT?!> The Emperor screamed, <What the HELL is true, you little son of a bitch? You have managed some clever trick here, but—>

<Trick?> Cassian's voice hissed from every direction. <Can you really not decipher the truth? Do you not even see what you have become?>

<What are you talking about!> Tacitus snarled.

Cassian vanished and reappeared immediately in front of Tacitus and said: <Your demon, Mighty Tacitus—I did not allow *it* into my mind, just you.> The boy pointed up and to the left, and Tacitus turned and let out a gasp. He saw a tremendous face much like his own but composed of blazing red flame. He knew with sudden and sickening certainty that he was looking at the malevolent force that granted him all his dark strength.

<NO!> Tacitus roared. *There was no way this boy could strip him of what he was!* He reached out to the demonic essence. It was *his*, and once he had it back, he would shatter Asango's

mind. His psychic tendrils leaped out, but the wall around Cassian's psyche shimmered a brilliant white, and the power recoiled back. His demonic half raged and battered against the barrier in response but could not seem to break through.

<You did not even notice when you were separated, did you?> Cassian whispered.

<Separated!> Tacitus practically screamed. <You stupid little bastard! You think you have the power to stand against the might of a *Cosmic Demon?*>

<Of course not,> Cassian hissed, the vaguest hint of a smirk coming across his face, <But you see, I have an ally on the psychic plane as well.> Above the boy's head, a pair of tremendous, burning yellow eyes appeared from the blackness, illuminating a reptilian face the size of a castle wall.

<GUH!> Tacitus screamed, shrinking back. *The Great Dragon!* The Emperor could not believe he was finally staring into the legendary golden eyes. For as long as he could remember, the ancient titan had lain at the edges of the psychic realm, never acting, yet it seemed he could be summoned by Cassian Asango.

<Promethiock is not afraid of your Bacchid,> the boy said, standing calmly beneath the dragon's titanic jaws. <He has agreed to keep your demon busy so that you and I can have this confrontation, *man to man.*> A rumble of thunderous laughter erupted from the Great Dragon, and then he vanished and reappeared an instant later outside Cassian's mental sphere—a vast and brilliant golden form that began to clash against the red inferno that was Tacitus's demonic half.

The Emperor stared at the incomprehensible psychic battle going on between the two tremendous forces for several heartbeats and then turned back to the boy, who was studying him with an infuriatingly confident expression.

<Do you think I require help to defeat you, boy?> Tacitus said through gritted teeth. <I had nearly five decades to hone my strength before you were even born!>

<You are a *pathetic shell!*> Cassian snapped back. <You gave over too much of your will to the demon inside you, while I have faced every challenge in front of me with my *own strength*, persevering and growing stronger.> Cassian vanished again, but Tacitus immediately heard his voice in a soft whisper behind him say: <*It seems I have surpassed you.*> The chains tightened suddenly, and Tacitus felt such visceral pain that a scream escaped him. He writhed and twisted against the bonds, but Cassian's will was beyond anything he had ever imagined.

<I am going to kill you, my Emperor,> the young man said, appearing again in front of Tacitus and locking eyes.

<*Kill me?*> The Emperor snarled. Never had he been so furious in his life. <You do not have the *Power* to kill me! I am Tacitus! I will murder everyone who ever loved you, including your little elf whore! I will burn her to death in front of you! You DARE to threaten me?! I have hundreds of thousands of soldiers under my command, and, in the real world, I can kill you for all your *strength* with but a thought!>

As Tacitus had been speaking, a faint smile had begun to form on Cassian's face, and by the time he was finished, it had grown into a fierce grin. <You think you can frighten me, *Demon*? All these years I thought you understood me. But you know nothing of strength or courage because in your heart *you are a coward!*> An even greater wave of fury moved through Tacitus, and he harnessed it to wrestle free of his bonds, but the chains simply tightened.

<Even if you had every soldier in the world against me, I would still fight you! That is who I am—who the dragon helped me become!> Cassian let out a soft chuckle. <But you do *not* have the whole of the world under your command, do you, Mighty Tacitus? That is the real reason you have come here, is it not? *You are afraid.*>

<Afraid of *you*?> The Emperor growled with a chuckle. <How long can you hold me here, perhaps an hour or two? Then I will return to myself and regain the full scope of my

power—something which you do not begin to understand. I defeated Daibok in *seconds!* I am the real Demon King! Nothing and no one can stand against me! I am the most powerful being in all of history!"

Cassian met his eyes with a maddeningly cold stare and said: <Then I have a question, Demon King: why have you not conquered the whole of the world?> He leaned into Tacitus's face, his voice rising: <With all your power, you should have been able to bring every kingdom on the globe to its knees long ago! Why did you not ride at the head of your armies? Why do you even *NEED* armies?> The boy leaned in still closer, his eyes filled with wild fury. <You *hid* in your palace for over two decades. Why? If nothing can stand against you, then what held you back?> Cassian's lips curled up slightly as he whispered: <And why do you need *me?*>

The Emperor glared at the young man, dreaming of the revenge he would take for all of this, but then Asango said something that sent a chill of terror through him: <I think there is something in this world that can *kill you*. That is why you are here. You are terrified I will discover what it is.>

For a long moment, neither of them spoke. Tacitus saw the certitude in the young man's expression and knew there was no point in trying to persuade him he was wrong. Instead, the Emperor said through gritted teeth: <But you do not know, do you, *Messiah*? Perhaps the Norn might have given some clue when she came to speak to you years ago, but you were too *arrogant* to hear anything she had to say.>

Cassian lowered his eyes and let out a very soft, troubled laugh as he shook his head. <Yes, I was too arrogant, and that was probably a terrible decision.> He shrugged and added: <So I shall just have to work very, *very* hard to make up for it now.> The young man's face rose, suddenly filled with grim determination. <That is why I allowed you to enter my mind. I have no idea whatsoever how to kill you, but *you* know something!> Cassian's hands moved to the sides of Tacitus's head, and fierce psychic tendrils leaped out.

<STOP!> the Emperor cried as the assault began. <DO NOT DARE!> The boy had no fear of him but pried with a psychic strength that was incomprehensible. The barriers Tacitus had spent decades constructing around his memories began to tear like sheets of paper, and all the horrible secrets began to spill out. <YOU WILL DIE SCREAMING! STOP! STOP!> And then he lost the power to speak.

For a time – *he knew not how long* – Tacitus became lost in a dream where his sins were plucked out in bits and pieces to form a mosaic of evil. He saw his fellow starborn, Valeena, die screaming on the ground in their garden at his hands, and he remembered that only moments before she had been speaking to him of their upcoming wedding. He saw himself drawing upon the powers of damnation to force the shamalak, Kota, to his will. He saw himself ripping the beautiful starborn aura away from a crying baby girl and bestowing it upon his son. He heard the terrible voice of his demon master warning him of a mortal child who might destroy him. One memory among all the others seemed of particular significance: Tacitus was standing in a Nemesai church speaking to Bishop Cromlic about the upcoming inquisition of the Asango family. He gave the command: "You must not stand for such heresy from the nobility. Kill both the parents, even if they confess, but do not touch the boy."

The Emperor awoke hours later soaked in his own sweat and panting. His craith stood impassively around his bed, and the palace was quiet save for the soft chirping sounds of birds in the distance. His window was beginning to glow with faint morning light, and this sight filled him with a sickly terror. *Cassian had held him in the mental plane for six—perhaps even seven hours!* How many secrets might the young prodigy have been able to rip from him in that time? The Emperor did not know. He could not remember.

The tremendous power of Bacchid crackled inside of his flesh, burning to be unleashed. Cassian Asango was his most dangerous enemy in the world now. *He had to be killed!* The young man would know, as the world would soon know, the terrible demon Tacitus had become.

CHAPTER 46: THE RACE

Telemachus stared at his brother, watching the eyes of the chosen *Messiah of the Gods* slowly began to blink open. The two of them were in a clearing in a forest some day and a half's ride northeast from the capital. Cassian had been sitting atop a blanket for the past ten hours with his legs crossed and his chest and back bare so that Telemachus could work on the ugly, streaking scars that crisscrossed his skin. They were surrounded by a perimeter of Cassian's personal guard soldiers. These men had had to flee the capital on incredibly short notice, and many of them had no armor, but they still stood tall, ready to fight and die at their beloved commander's order.

Telemachus had ordered these tattooed killers to give him a wide berth. They had obeyed him not because he was starborn, but because he was Cassian's brother. The dragon was another matter though. Titus showed a very slight deference to Telemachus, refusing to stray too far from its wounded master for anything. Telemachus had felt the creature's blazing golden eyes upon him all through the night as he did what he could for his brother's mutilated skin. It had been almost as imposing a distraction as the fact that Cassian was engaging possibly the most powerful being in the world in psychic combat.

Evidently, the Messiah had come through his battle unscathed, for when he was fully returned to himself, he drew in a deep breath and rose to his feet. There was a wave of relief from all around the make-shift encampment at the sight of him standing, and even a few cheers started to rumble from the men, but Cassian raised a hand in the air and closed his fist, and instantaneously his soldiers went silent.

"How did it go?" Telemachus murmured, his stomach full of nerves. It had been less than a day since he had learned that the Denigoth Empire was ruled by a demon—the most powerful nathret in history in fact. He had not fully wrapped his mind around all that that meant.

"I learned... quite a bit," Cassian said in a grim voice, gazing up at the sky. Ashen storm clouds were slowly seeping over the sky as if to reverse the dawn.

Telemachus swallowed. His brother's thoughts were impossible to read, so all he could do was whisper: "Can Tacitus be stopped?"

Cassian met his eyes and said: "Yes, but not by us. There is..." he frowned, seeming to consider his words, "an... opposite force in this world to what our Emperor has become. It lies within a mortal vessel. Tacitus does not know who it is."

"You *took* this from his mind by force?" Telemachus asked, feeling a little incredulous.

"I did," Cassian said, once again staring down, a somber look on his face.

Telemachus swallowed. "When I was working on your wounds, I... felt something enormously powerful move through you."

"That was Promethiock," Cassian muttered, not looking up. Telemachus sensed a flicker of pain leak through the wall around his brother's mind. Something in the psychic confrontation with the Emperor had shaken him. Sweat dripped off his skin as he asked: "Have there been any soldiers poking around for us?"

"No," Telemachus replied, "nothing has been organized this far from the capital... *yet.* Quite a few members of the Obsidian Guild have been taken for questioning by the craith though."

"Are you in psychic contact with them?" Cassian said, raising an eyebrow.

"No. Last night I sensed the Emperor looking for me—*me specifically*. I made certain not to leave any open pathways to my mind."

"Good," Cassian said with a nod, and then he muttered: "I would give it half a day at most before imperial soldiers are combing this area. Tacitus will be ready to do virtually anything to kill me at this point."

"Because you know about the *mortal vessel*?"

"Because I know *everything*," Cassian said, the veins standing up around his temples, "everything he knows at least." He brought his gaze back up to Telemachus. "I trust you have contacted Keska."

"Of course," Telemachus sighed, briefly recalling the intense telepathic conversation in which he had shared the revelations of the last day with the princess of Aloria. "As you might imagine, she is coming."

"You warned her not to use any standard ports, correct?"

"No official ports and no official Alorian ship. She's posing as a fishing girl on a small sailing vessel, though she told her subjects she was traveling to the Kunsar port, and even sent a close look alike to herself bestowed with several expensive dresses and an array of jewels."

"Sensible enough," Cassian said. "I will try to get her an Elokien from the elves. We should each have one if possible."

"Mhh," Telemachus grunted as he eyed the amulet of gold and crystal that hung from Cassian's neck. "What about this Livia? Where is she?"

"Looking for her abducted sister," Cassian said, frowning. "I sent Soulic to help her."

Telemachus stiffened. "You sent that half-insane murderer to look after her? What the hell is wrong with you?"

"Soulic and I have been through a great deal together, and I trust him," Cassian said, meeting Telemachus's gaze. "You will perhaps recall the Nemesai torture cells? They are where you sent my favorite tutor to die."

Telemachus flinched at these words. The death of Somar Dojinko weighed on him continually. "Cassian, I—"

"Relax," his brother said, gazing down and shaking his head. "I am responsible for the old man's death; not you. I am the one that continuously provoked the Nemesai. I am the one who walked into a room full of craith just to show Bishop Cromlic I was not afraid. Most of all though," Cassian's face twitched, "I refused to listen when the Norn came to warn me about my destiny. She said it would *cost me dearly.*" He shut his eyes and balled his fists at his sides. "Would you believe, my dear brother, that all that hatred I felt for her and the Gods was a manipulation of our Emperor and his demon master?"

"What?" Telemachus said.

"Tacitus goaded Cromlic into executing my parents," Cassian whispered. "A young man alienated by divinity and religion would be far more likely to accept allying with a cosmic demon—that was his logic, and that is why my parents' throats were slit."

"Gods," Telemachus said, swallowing. "All this time... everything you built your life around—"

"Was a lie," Cassian hissed. "Even my imprisonment in that Nemesai cell was just an attempt to push me to desperation. Tacitus would have made his offer of dark power a moment before my supposed execution if the old man had not done what he did." Cassian's face contorted in pain. "I would have had leeches on my skin, and thus would not be able to defend myself. I would have died."

"Then Somar *did* save your life," Telemachus exclaimed. The notion brought him a small sense of relief. It would have been terrible to know that the wonderful old man had sacrificed himself for no reason.

"Yes," Cassian said, and he was silent for a moment.

"I'm so sorry," Telemachus said.

Cassian nodded and then drew in a deep breath and straightened, his face suddenly becoming more focused. Telemachus' could see that the moment of quiet reflection was gone, and the Cassian Asango most of the world knew had re-emerged. He said in a suddenly sharper voice: "We will need to get Livia's father out of his home immediately. Your parents too. I can send men to get them. You should write a letter explaining... *circumstances* to them."

"Neither of my parents can read," Telemachus said in a dry voice, his hands trembling slightly at the thought of Imperial soldiers taking his family hostage. "They're peasants, remember? They never learned." He stared at Cassian as a swell of nerves rose up from his stomach. "Do you really think my mother and father are in danger?"

"Tacitus will definitely go after our loved ones to get to us if we let him," Cassian said. "He needs a second starborn to enact all of Bacchid's plans for this world." His eyes narrowed. "You have a sister, correct?"

"Yeah," Telemachus muttered, staring at the bark on a tree across from him as beads of sweat dripped down his forehead. "She's fourteen..."

Cassian put a hand on his shoulder and squeezed. "We will move quickly. I searched every corner of the Emperor's mind. He has not yet ordered his men to go after your family. There is still time."

His mind spinning, Telemachus said: "I'll get them myself."

"No," Cassian said, his voice hard. "I need you with me."

Telemachus shrugged free of his brother's hand and glared. "Why?"

"Because this is a *race*," Cassian snapped. "There is a mortal somewhere in the world that has the power to kill Tacitus. We have to find that person before he does."

"How?!" Telemachus exclaimed with an exasperated shrug. "You said Tacitus himself does not know where to find this individual. *Do you*?"

"No," Cassian replied.

Telemachus gestured around the camp to the contingent of perhaps a few hundred soldiers and the dragon. "This is all we have at our disposal! Tacitus Adronicus has the largest army in *history* under his command. How in the hell are we supposed to find someone he could not in over twenty years with all the resources of Denigoth to wield?"

"You and I are more capable than any of his servants," Cassian said. "That is the advantage we have. We will work together – you, me, Keska, and even Livia now. We are the starborn of this generation, and, unlike him, we can approach this vessel without fear of instantaneous obliteration." Cassian drew in a deep breath and said: "That is why our Emperor has remained in his palace for over two decades. He has no idea from what direction death might come for him, and he is terrified."

Telemachus blinked. "So... this *mortal vessel*—with power on par to Tacitus—is not dangerous to ordinary people?"

"No. Only to demons."

He raised an eyebrow at Cassian. "And this person isn't you? You're the *Messiah*, aren't you?"

"I do not know the significance of my being anointed by the Gods," Cassian said, biting his lip. "I *do* know that when I slashed open Tacitus's throat with my magic, the wound just started closing up. I cannot kill him, but there is a person in the world who can. We *must* find him... or her."

"Then what?" Telemachus exhaled, stroking his forehead. "When we find this remarkable mortal, what do we do? Are we going to attack the palace – kill our way through the city and the whole Imperial Guard?" He shut his eyes, feeling completely overwhelmed. "What about the craith? What about the hundreds of *thousands* of soldiers Tacitus can summon from every corner of this world? Gods, Cassian, is it even possible to fight him?"

"The task before us is extremely difficult," Cassian said, his green eyes burning with intensity. "Unfortunately, we do not have the luxury of being able to turn away from it. We are the points of the star. This burden falls to us because no one else can take it up. Do you not understand that?"

"Of course I do," Telemachus whispered. "All the same, I was hoping your plunge into Tacitus's mind might yield some sort of stratagem that did not lead to mass slaughter."

"So was I," Cassian said with a tense shake of his head, "but I discovered no simple tricks to defeating the Emperor. In fact, doing so seems nigh impossible at the present moment, but if we cannot find a way, then this world will be plunged into countless millennia of darkness. The demons will rise again. All that is good will be corrupted or destroyed, the Gods will be driven away, and a vile religion of greed and lust and hatred will rise and be forced upon the poor, damned souls who remain."

"*Why?*" Telemachus said in a dry voice. "Why is Tacitus doing this?"

"He was tricked," Cassian sighed, gazing down at the ground, "at least that is one way to put it... not that it matters. Understanding why does not help us, I promise you, and we have far more pressing issues."

Telemachus clenched his jaw, weighing Cassian's words. All of this was moving terrifyingly fast. In the span of a few moments, his entire world had been upended, and now he had to fight alongside his half-mad brother against a demon-starborn with not only the resources of the Denigoth Empire, but possibly even the unknowable multitude of demons that hid on the edges of the world. It all felt like a surreal nightmare.

"We need to contact the Onkai," Telemachus finally said.

"Do you think they would believe us?" Cassian said with a shrug. "Tacitus has been touted as the savior of the human race for a generation."

"But you are the Messiah," Telemachus said, "proclaimed to all by the Norn herself."

"Yes," Cassian whispered, pursing his lips. "It is a card I am hesitant to play. Once I do, I will be plunging the empire into civil war."

"Is there any other way?"

Cassian grimaced. "The truth is... I do not know. I hope some answer will come to me, but none has." He cast Telemachus an uneasy smile as he said: "I cannot do this alone. You, Keska, and I should be making decisions together—even Livia when we find her."

A nervous chuckle burst from Telemachus's throat as he said: "You mean you're actually willing to listen to us for once?"

Cassian reached out a scarred arm and gripped Telemachus's shoulder once more. "We are in this fight together, and I doubt we shall all live to see its end." He swallowed, hesitating, and then whispered: "You have long been a better brother to me than I to you. I am sorry for that, and... I am sorry for killing Dimitris."

Telemachus blinked. They had never spoken of the death of their brother. There had been complete telepathic silence between them for over a year after it happened, and they had only resumed conversing by degrees, never mentioning the terrible subject.

"I am sorry for so many things," Cassian went on. "I have been an arrogant, self-righteous ass for most of my life, and now I know that it was all predicated on the manipulations of Tacitus and his demon master." His eyes moistened, but no tears rolled out as he added: "I cannot take *any* of it back, but I can stand with my brother and sisters against the doom of our world. Will you accept that?" His fingers tightened on Telemachus's shoulder as he rasped: "Please?"

Telemachus bit his lip, then murmured: "Yes."

"Thank you," Cassian said with a nod, and then he released his grip and walked over to his dragon. Titus, who had been curled up as an enormous ball of scales, claws, and horns, lifted his blazing golden eyes and made something like a reptilian smile as Cassian patted his head.

Telemachus remained still, watching them. He knew Cassian had meant every word from the bottom of his heart, yet, at the same time, he could not be trusted. Telemachus had not shared with his brother the prophecy the Norn had spoken to him when she appeared shortly after he had given Somar Dojinko the deathly pill and sent him to the Nemesai dungeon. The words echoed in his mind now with sickening clarity:

<You have set the final battle into motion, Telemachus Vale. Cassian Asango will escape his bonds now, and I will reveal to this world what he truly is. Do not bask in the revelation. The darkness will come to seduce him, and even if he rises above the first temptation, there will be others. Hell wants your brother as it has never wanted any mortal. You would do well to watch over him. He is this world's greatest hope, but also its most significant threat. Be prepared.>

Telemachus's heart rumbled in his chest as he watched Cassian scratch the dragon's throat and grin. For all of the brash arrogance, and even after the death of Dimitris, Telemachus loved his brother. Was he supposed to somehow kill Cassian if matters went awry? Even if he could bring himself to take such an action, he had primarily dedicated his studies to healing magic and spells to help rather than harm, while his war-minded-sibling had somehow constructed a spell in a matter of minutes that had ripped a hole in the world down to the molten liquid below. Telemachus also knew in his heart that if it ever came down to a fight to the death, both he and Keska would hesitate to deliver the final blow, where Cassian would not.

"Gods..." he whispered, gazing up at the darkening sky.

EPILOGUE:

The Emperor gazed down at the twitching face of his son. Arkas's pale skin was covered in a sheen of sweat that glistened in the soft glow of the candlelight. The two of them were alone in Arkas's chambers save the dozen craith that stood against the walls. It was best if no one saw what was about to happen.

Tacitus put a hand on his son's damp hair and ran his thumb gently over the boy's temple. He had loved this child once. *At least he thought so.* His heart had become something distant to him, though it was still there—the part that brought him failure. Arkas was the first of those failures. Tacitus could recall the decision, two decades before, when Bacchid had revealed to him that a second starborn would be needed. He had believed until then that he alone had been chosen for immortality and ultimate power. The proclamation had stung.

"C-Cassian," Arkas rasped, his pallid lips trembling at the name.

"Sh-h-h," Tacitus whispered, patting his son's head. "There is no need to fear him now."

"Father?" the boy panted.

"Yes, I am here."

"You... you h-hate me," Arkas panted, and his breathing accelerated to a frenzied pace for a few seconds, then broke into a series of moans.

"Nothing is your fault," the Emperor said, his voice soft. The words were only a partial truth. Everything Arkas had done wrong had, by definition, been the result of his 'faults,' but Tacitus was responsible for those deficiencies. He had made alterations to Arkas's mind, eviscerating the capacity for such troublesome aspects as compassion. It had all been part of a careful series of calculations that had failed miserably. No starborn other than himself had ever turned to the forces of hell, but Tacitus had wanted to create one that would have very little trouble with the concept. It all might have worked if he had possessed the competence to bind a starborn aura to a child without any gift whatsoever for magic, but the task had proven far too complicated for his human intellect to carry out. Arkas had become a pale imitation of a starborn, filled with all the ruthless ambition Bacchid might have desired but none of the mental talents innate in those chosen by the comet.

The Emperor let out a low sigh. He should have killed the baby girl—the one who was now calling herself 'Livia.' But murdering a beautiful infant... The demon inside him had urged the action, but Tacitus had not wanted to admit to himself that he had become so vile a creature. *What threat could she ever pose with the minuscule fraction of power left to her?* He had wrapped her in a blanket and left her in the center of a nearby village in the early morning to be found. A baby who could not cry... He had not known what would happen to her, but the sin was washed from his hands. That had been his thinking.

Always, it was the man inside of him that made such errors. The demon was untroubled by mercy or the pride of a human heart. It would have killed Cassian Asango in an instant rather than draw the moment out in order *to show* the boy how foolish he was. But then... *had it wanted Asango to survive?* Tacitus had never fully understood the way the darkness guided his actions. It seemed to know things he did not. There was a lingering sense in the back of his mind that it still had plans for the young Messiah.

"The N-Norn... Cassian will kill me, father," Arkas rasped.

"No," the Emperor whispered, and then he took a breath and added the lie: "You are safe."

"I w-want you to... choose me.".

"I did," Tacitus sighed, and he thought but did not say: *But Bacchid chose differently.*

"Thank you!" his son exclaimed, a wide grin playing across his thin face.

"You are welcome, now rest." Perhaps Arkas's soul would ascend to some distant heaven. After all, his sins derived from alterations Tacitus had made to his brain. Could the boy truly be to blame for anything he had ever done?

The Emperor had asked a similar question about himself many times over the years. The Cosmic Demon had shattered his happiness with nine words whispered in a dream. Cassian Asango must have seen that moment just before the second demon war had begun. Bacchid's burning face, vast and terrible, had come to him in the midst of sleep, eclipsing all thought as it hissed: <Your soul will burn in hell for all eternity!> Tacitus could remember jolting up in his bed, his heart pounding so hard it had seemed ready to break free of his chest. *Burn in hell? Why?* He had thought of himself as a good person then. Never had he taken a life nor stolen what was not his.

Tacitus had stood before the Norn five days later, stumbling in as a disheveled wreck of the rising starborn he had been. Every waking moment since the dream had been pervaded by the sickening fear of eternal torment. With tears running down his face, he had begged the Norn to tell him the demon had lied.

<You shall forever belong to hell,> she had answered in her cold, psychic voice. It had been the most horrible moment of Tacitus's life. When Bacchid had appeared to him again a week later—after he had become too paranoid to sleep for fear of slipping into death—the terrible bargain the demon offered had seemed acceptable. Tacitus had been ready to do absolutely anything, *and he had.* So many deaths... He could recall in superlative detail the final moments of his fellow starborn, whom he had loved with all his heart. His dear Valeena had stared at him with such shock as his magic had ripped into her chest. Her soul had surely ascended to paradise, for it had been unbelievably beautiful. Tacitus had at least spared her from seeing the horrors of the Demon War. As for the others, they would have died anyhow trying to kill the Demon King and might or might not have succeeded before Daibok wiped humanity from the face of the world.

There were arguments to be made that Tacitus's choice was ultimately noble. Though the Demon War had claimed hundreds of thousands of lives, it could have been *millions* if the conflict had not been brought to such an abrupt halt. Daibok's forces had descended upon nigh every corner of the world, and this had left many small kingdoms and tribes weak. After the conflict's end, the Denigoth army had been able to move in and expand the territory of the empire as never before. Tacitus had been able to create order on a scale humanity had never known, for there had been no one and nothing that could oppose him. His acts of supposed evil had resulted in unparalleled peace and order for the human race.

The Emperor shut his eyes and rested his palm against the side of his son's head. A quick, infinitesimal burst of power would put an end to Arkas's pathetic life. Tacitus felt himself tremble. *Love was a weakness.* He was a demon still trying to convince himself he was a man, and he could no longer afford such delusion. A *man* could not live forever, after all. The wrinkles in his skin and gray in his hair were an illusion. His true form had not aged in nearly fifty years, and it never would. He would be locked in his body a thousand years from now—ten-thousand years from now—*a million*... No mortal mind had the stamina for such an existence, but the darkness inside him could endure on through eternity. It was better simply to surrender to it, and perhaps with this final sacrifice, he could cleanse himself of all human weakness.

"F-father," Arkas whispered.

"Just rest, my son."

The boy's pale lips rasped out: "I... I need to tell you... I h-have the weapon."

"What?" The Emperor said, frowning, staying the burst of energy a moment longer.

Arkas wheezed: "The Norn... she told me h-how to kill you, but n-now that you've c-chosen me... I don't need to d-do it."

Every muscle in Tacitus's body coiled in shock, and he felt the evil aura inside him leap to attention as well. "Arkas," he hissed, his limbs shaking, "what did the Norn tell you?"

"W-where to... f-find her, father." His son looked up and smiled. "Y-you never thought I could do anything right, b-but I found her—the girl that can... d-destroy you."

Tacitus began to tremble. Without even realizing what he was doing, he dug his fingers into his son's scalp and reached in with the psychic strength of a cosmic demon. As the boy shrieked in pain, Tacitus saw the moment, years ago, when Arkas had asked his three questions of the oracle, and he saw the answers she had given. His son had waited for years to find the promised 'weapon' that could kill him, and then a *slave* of all people had fallen into his lap. Tacitus saw the girl. IONA! *His destroyer!* The boy had hidden her away with his grotesque, half-ogre comrade, but Tacitus could see where she was clearly in the boy's memories. *She was there now!*

The Emperor ripped his hand away, laughing aloud as Arkas began to thrash on the bed from the psychic damage Bacchid's power had inflicted. Tacitus could not believe the gift his pathetic offspring had given him. A quick slice to this Iona's throat and all his fears would be forever ended. Cassian would have no way to stop him. *His soul would never know the fires of damnation!*

There was no time to hesitate. Tacitus stood and whirled around to the strongest of all his craith, his blood pumping like liquid fire in his veins as he grinned and snarled: "Kota, there is someone I want you to kill!"

END OF BOOK II

DEDICATION:

Though this book is dedicated to all my children, I feel like all of this was most guided by my little girl, Lilly. I didn't know I was going to write a young adult book series until I watched my tiny baby start to become a person. It was then that I knew what I wanted to say, and how I wanted to say it.
I love you, Lilly, and I'm so proud of who you are,

--Papa

ACKNOWLEDGMENTS

Editor – Angelique Russell
Editor – Stephen Parolini
Proof Reader – Kristina H Russell

Wattpad Proof Readers who have provided me with invaluable help, mentioned here as I have known them, in their usernames:

"Ectheldir"
"DragonKingCole"
"Writing-new-worlds"
"Finish-your-book"
"SkyAngel_"
"TheGybberishGod"
"Alainson8"
"Disneymedley"
"Joshua _Timi"
"Jhatka"
"Steenee"
"Jaderock101"
"WillPische"
"Ame84"
"Darthschrik"
"JimmyRichardson9"
"ArtemisDa1"

Thank you so much for your feedback and encouragement. This has been a wild ride, and it was good to have all of you with me on the way.

AUTHOR'S SOCIAL MEDIA

Website: www.dragontoothpress.com/Authors

Twitter: @AuthorRussell

Facebook: Search "Age of Asango" to join the fan group

Made in the USA
San Bernardino, CA
05 March 2019